OPTICAL ~~IL~~DELUSIONS IN DEADWOOD

What Authors and Reviewers are saying about
Ann Charles' first book

~~D~~NEARLY DEPARTED IN DEADWOOD

"Full of thrills and chills, a fun rollercoaster ride of a book!"
~Susan Andersen, New York Times Bestselling author of
Burning Up

"Smooth, solid and very entertaining, *Nearly Departed in Deadwood* smartly blends all the elements of a great read and guarantees to be a page-turner!"
~Jane Porter, award-winning author of *She's Gone Country* and *Flirting with Forty*

"*Nearly Departed in Deadwood* is a delightful mix of on the edge suspense and laugh-out-loud humor. An impressive debut. Ann Charles is a star in the making!"
~Gerri Russell, award-winning author of *Seducing the Knight*

"Ann Charles has written an intriguing mystery laced with a wicked sense of humor. Her dialogue sparkles, her characters are quirky fun, and the storyline keeps you turning the page to see what is going to happen next. Watch out Stephanie Plum, because Violet Parker is coming your way."
~Deborah Schneider, author of *Promise Me* and RWA Librarian of the Year 2009

"Both barrels loaded with offbeat charm, *Nearly Departed in Deadwood* aims to entertain and never misses the funny bone."
~Terry McLaughlin, author of Built to Last series

"*Nearly Departed in Deadwood* is an exciting, fast-moving story with fantastic characters and a riveting plot. This is Ann Charles' debut novel and she couldn't have started it off better. This is a must read that I highly recommend."
~John Foxjohn, bestselling author of *Tattered Justice*

"Vicariously living Violet Parker's escapades through Deadwood feels like being with a best friend. You fret, you nod, you laugh out loud, and the secrets you find out might put you in the grave, too! Yep. I'm completely addicted."
~Amber Scott, bestselling author of *Fierce Dawn*

"Ann Charles has truly done it. She plunges you into the story from the very beginning and keeps you there every page. Even at the end you're begging for more! It's no wonder *Nearly Departed in Deadwood* was chosen as best overall for the 2010 Daphne Award!"
~Susan Schreyer, author *Death By A Dark Horse* and *Levels of Deception*

"Mystery, humor, and romance—a fabulous book from a talented author that you'll be hearing about for a long time!"
~Jacquie Rogers, award-winning author of *Much Ado About Marshals*

"If you like boring mysteries, then you won't like *Nearly Departed in Deadwood.*"
~Elena Gray, Author

"Violet Parker follows a path blazed by Stephanie Plum (the heroine in Janet Evanovich's best-selling series), but she is no copycat. Violet is sexy and smart. Charles' mystery *Nearly Departed in Deadwood* is out of this world."
~Sarah M. Anderson, Reviewer for Romance Novel News

to be a wonderful book to read. It sucked me in and kept me on the edge of my seat and left me excited to read more when I finally reached the end."
~Angela Spencer, Reviewer for Rise Reviews

"Fast paced, from the very first sentence I was hooked on this book. Charles is a phenomenal writer! I loved the sexual tension that Charles portrayed and built along with a phenomenal plot. It was all amazing and I cannot, absolutely cannot wait for the next installment in this series."
~Immortality and Beyond Book Reviews

" ... the author captured the true essence of small town living and its quirky people within the pages. The characters were well defined, credible, and easy to relate to. I thought the overall plot was simplistic in nature, provocative in intrigue, and written in style. *Nearly Departed In Deadwood* was a contemporary mystery romance with a touch of paranormal that kept me enthralled with goosebump-creepiness and belly aching laughter." ***** FIVE STARS!
~Escape Between the Pages Book Reviews

"If you like mystery, then you will love *Nearly Departed in Deadwood* by Ann Charles. With colorful characters and witty dialogue, this is a book sure to please all fans of mystery, romance and the paranormal."
~The Pen & Muse Book Reviews

"Violet is a fantastic character, and I loved her sassy attitude, as well as her protective mother instincts, and her quest to sell a house to keep her job. Throw in the mystery of missing children that she finds herself embroiled in, and

Nearly Departed in Deadwood has a little bit of something for everyone, while still delivering a satisfyingly good plot that doesn't meander or lose its readers."
~Read My Mind Book Reviews

"An exciting romping ride into Deadwood. This book makes me think of ghost towns from years past. I enjoyed this story from the start, Ann reeling me in like a big fish gasping for air. I would recommend this book for people who like everyday people thrust into mystery. It has enough of a paranormal twist for those seeking thrills with moments of wit and humor."
~Earth's Book Nook Reviews

"If you like romantic mysteries with a tinge of paranormal creepiness, this one is well worth your time."
~To Publish or Not to Publish Book Reviews

Dear Reader,

I have an itchy case of gold fever. I came down with it decades ago when I first traveled through the Deadwood area. I'm not talking about a hunger for shiny treasures, rather a need to know all about the people and places from which the shiny pieces are unearthed.

When it comes to the Black Hills, one town reaches out to scratch my gold-fever itch—the city of Lead (pronounced *Leed*). While Deadwood was busy leaving its mark on the history books with tales of Wild Bill Hickok and Seth Bullock, Lead was busy staking its claim on the land. The Open Cut mine in the middle of Lead brings its industrious past front and center.

The Open Cut has always fascinated me. I have studied "before" and "after" pictures, read all about its creation (at the Black Hills Mining Museum), and stared at the geological timeline in its walls through the Homestake Visitor Center's chain-link fence. Why am I so fascinated with a big hole in the ground? Because it reveals a history full of hard work, spent lives, and change. It intrigues me how people adapt to these changes.

Over the years, I've met several Homestake miners. I've listened to their stories of what it was like to work deep inside the Earth. At the butcher in King's Grocery, I stood in line with their wives and kids. These days, Homestake is no longer an operating gold mine; most of the drifts and shafts below the town are filled with water rather than men. But Lead's industrious spirit is still alive, its down-to-earth hardiness still apparent.

I'd always planned to incorporate Lead into the Deadwood Mystery series. The two towns are like sisters, each enchanting with separate but entangled histories. Before I began writing this second book, I cruised the back streets of Lead, along Sunnyhill Road, from East Summit

Street to West, and down Gold Street, searching to see how life off the main drag had changed since Homestake stopped digging for gold. I took my kids to the little park on Miners Avenue and the big park next to the Open Cut. I climbed the steep hill on Mill Street, retracing the going-to-work route of many miners. I located the exact piece of land next to the Open Cut where I'd place the house that would play center stage in the story—the Carhart house.

I hope you get a kick out of reading *Optical Delusions in Deadwood*. While I enjoyed introducing Violet and her friends in the first book of the series, *Nearly Departed in Deadwood*, this second book allowed me to shed light on the kaleidoscope of colorful characters and historical settings.

Most of you reading this have already dipped a toe into Violet's world. Thank you for returning for more Deadwood fun.

Grab your boots, because the water is getting deeper.

Welcome back to Deadwood ... and Lead.

Ann Charles

www.anncharles.com/deadwood

Optical **DE**Llusions in Deadwood

Ann Charles (signature)

Ann Charles

Illustrated by C.S. Kunkle

Corvallis Press

OPTICAL DELUSIONS IN DEADWOOD

Cover Art by C.S. Kunkle
Cover Design by Mona Weiss
Line Editing by Christy Karras and Mimi Munk

Printed in the United States of America

First Edition
First Printing, 2011

ISBN: 978-0-9832568-3-0

Corvallis Press, Publisher
630 NW Hickory Str., Ste. 120
Albany, OR 97321
www.corvallispress.com

Dedication

This book is for my parents—all of you.

I've been blessed with twice as many parents as most, and due to that fact I've been on the receiving end of a lot of love, encouragement, and guidance over the years.

Without all of you, I would not be where I am today. Thank you for everything. I love you.

(*Now* can I have something other than chunks of coal in my stocking at Christmas? Ha ha!)

Acknowledgments

It is amazing how many people it takes to get a book from a blank page with a blinking cursor to a published book. For me, it's a small village-worth of helpers. It takes another group of folks to help take that published book and make it fly. I'm going to try to thank some of the brilliant people involved in both parts of this book business.

To start, thank you to my husband for your help with brainstorming and critiquing. Without you, not only would the story not be as entertaining, but I'd starve and have twigs and leaves in my matted hair after just a week, and the kids would wear burlap bags for clothes and carry their homework to school in Crown Royal liquor bottle bags.

Thanks to Corvallis Press for allowing me to try this publishing venture yet again.

Thank you to my agent, Mary Louise Schwartz of the Belfrey Literary Agency. You have stuck by me for years during highs and lows. Here is to many more highs!

Thanks to my brother, Charles Kunkle, for allowing me the opportunity to see some of my crazy ideas on paper. Your artwork never ceases to amaze me and I love having it on my book's cover and inside its pages.

Thank you to Mona Weiss for your talented graphic artist help with making the cover really "pop" and for all of your ideas about promotion.

Once again, I have to bow to Margo Taylor for all of your help in spreading word about this second book, and to Dave Taylor for making sure Margo stayed in one piece during her trips to and fro during the process. I also have to thank Judy and Frank Routt (and Jessica and James) for sharing the book in Northwest Ohio.

Now, for the readers and critiquers. Thank you to the following for reading this book time and again and giving me the feedback I needed to make it shine: Wendy Delaney, Beth Harris, Marcia Britton, Mary Ida Kunkle, Amber Scott, Paul Franklin (for edits and research help), Jody Sherin, Renelle Wilson, Robin Weaver, Marguerite Phipps, Denise Garlington, Stephanie Kunkle, Thea Taylor, Sharon Benton, Heidi Mott, Susan Schreyer, Margo Taylor, Nancy Goebel-Fehr, Kim Rupp, Carol Cabrian, Gigi Murfitt, Cammie Hall, and my husband.

Thanks to Nancy Goebel-Fehr and Justin Harvey for not stoning me when I forgot to include your names in the Acknowledgements for *Nearly Departed in Deadwood*. Also, for all of the coffees and laughs that kept me awake at work after late nights of writing.

Thanks to Christy Karras of Proof Positive for your thorough, yet entertaining edits.

Thanks to Mimi "The Grammar Chick" for your final editing polish and always making me laugh.

Thanks to Stephen Harris for your wonderful talent with your camera and actually making me look ten pounds lighter on film just as I'd requested.

Thanks to the magnificent reviewers who offered your time to read and comment about this book; and to the amazing authors who gave me incredible cover quotes.

Thanks to the Deranged crew: Jacquie Rogers, Wendy Delaney, and Sherry Walker for years of friendship and patience with me. Thanks to the columnists and crew at 1st Turning Point for years of teaching and generosity. Thanks to Gerri Russell, Joleen James, and Wendy Delaney for keeping me neck deep in weekly goals. Thanks to the AuthorUp crew (Amber Scott, Susan Schreyer, and Deena Remiel) for not allowing me to be a slacker.

Thanks to Amber Scott for your never-ending support and ingenious ideas. You and me, woman, poolside with margaritas!

Thanks to my friends and fans for your continual support and tireless help in spreading word about Violet and her friends. You all make my day every day!

Thank you to my coworkers for the continual cheers and excitement every time I share more news with you.

Thanks to Bill Durning for making my Kindle dreams come true and to Vickie Haskell for the tons of shipping help and laughs while doing it.

Thanks to Neil McNeill for your excellent classes on paranormal investigation.

Thanks to my siblings and step-siblings, and your fantastic spouses, for talking me up around town.

And finally, thanks to Clint Taylor, for hanging out with me day-after-day in the Black Hills when we were kids. I'm sorry I tried to strangle you way back then. I was doing it out of love. Ha!

From Deadwood and Lead, I'd like to thank the following for all of the help in spreading word about the Deadwood Mystery Series:

Kim Rupp from Executive Lodging of the Black Hills, the Adams Bros. Bookstore, the Homestake Visitor Center, the Lead Chamber of Commerce, the Deadwood Chamber of Commerce, the Lead-Deadwood Arts Council, the Pack Horse Liquor & Convenience Store and crew, the congregation of the Nemo Church, Janelle Andis from Custer Crossing Store and Campground, and Mary Abell.

Thank you to the people of Lead and Deadwood for your wonderful support.

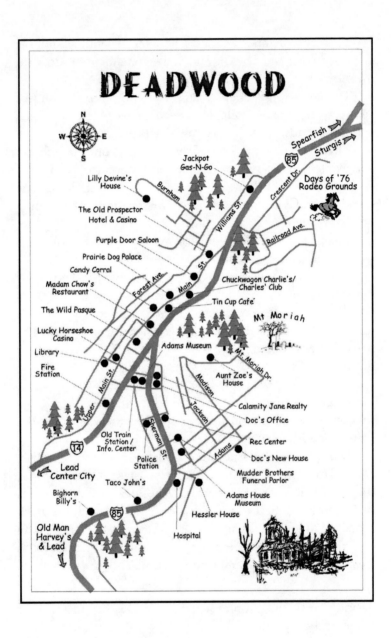

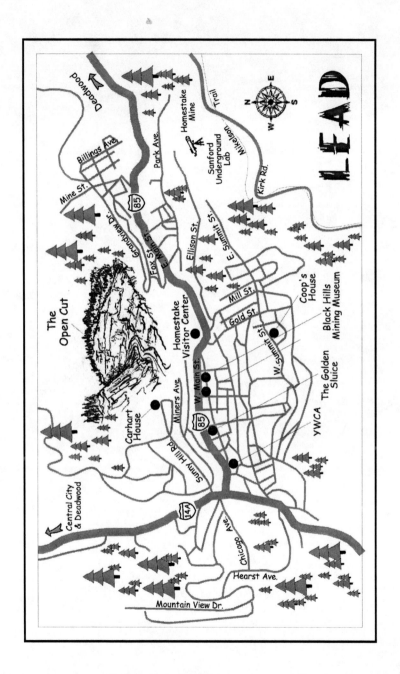

OPTICAL DELUSIONS
IN DEADWOOD

Chapter One

Some jackass was spreading rumors around Deadwood about me chatting with dead folks.

I didn't believe in ghosts, or hadn't since I started wearing a training bra. But a couple of weeks ago, a psychotic serial killer tricked me into being the guest of honor at a macabre tea party with his sister's ghost and three of his decomposing victims. Since then, my reputation had suffered.

Normally, I'd just shrug off the stares, whispers, and snickers of sidewalk onlookers and fellow Piggly Wiggly shoppers, but I was relatively new in town—and even newer at this real estate agent venture. With two young kids to support and raise on my own, big smiles and friendly service were my bread and butter.

Lucky for me, my fellow diners this morning at Bighorn Billy's restaurant were mainly tourists, who'd been too busy chattering away about what was on their agenda to rubberneck when I'd passed by on my way to a cleared booth. The din of their excited conversations drowned out all of Bighorn Billy's usual sounds except for the occasional "order up!" shout from the kitchen window.

With the infamous Sturgis Motorcycle Rally right around the corner, the Black Hills were crawling with chromed-out bikes. I stirred cream and sugar into my steaming coffee, happy as hell to be upstaged by the leather-clad crew for now. My stomach growled, antsy from the bacon-and-egg aroma that wafted thick in the air. A glance at the chrome hands on the orange and black Harley-Davidson clock above the saloon-style doors leading into the kitchen reminded me how long it had been since my last meal. My stomach growled again.

My breakfast date was fifteen minutes late, and if Old Man Harvey didn't get his ornery butt here soon, I was going to order without him.

I'd already caught a glare from my waitress when I'd asked to wait a little longer before deciding on what I wanted. With the lineup for a free table now extending into the parking lot, booth squatting wasn't winning me any new fans.

A shadow fell over my table. "Excuse me, are you Violet Parker?" a squeaky, female voice asked.

I looked up into a pair of owl-eye glasses. The silver-blue eyes on the other side were magnified by lenses thick enough to read *War and Peace* etched on a grain of rice. The woman's hair was a helmet of brown, frizzy curls that made my crazy, spiraling blonde locks look tame. My gaze lowered to the thick gray turtleneck sweater and long wool skirt. Somebody should tell her it was August outside.

I smiled extra wide, always the saleswoman. "That's me. What can I do for you?"

She seemed harmless enough, but I'd recently found out the hard way that looks could be deceiving. My eyebrows were just beginning to fill back in after learning that traumatic lesson firsthand from a previous client.

She pushed her glasses higher up on her nose. "A gentleman from your office told me we could find you here."

Gentleman? My smile almost slipped. I had only one male coworker at Calamity Jane Realty. He hated my guts for stealing this Realtor job from his nephew and had made it his personal mission to destroy my career before it could even get one wheel off the ground. We'd hit it off like a sledgehammer and old TNT right from the start.

"I'm Millie Carhart," the woman said. "My mother would like to hire you to sell her house."

I peeked at the woman cowering behind Millie. With her white hair twirled up into a bun on top of her head and her ample bosom restrained in a faded red gingham dress, she looked straight out of *Little House on the Prairie*.

My eyes returned to Millie's magnified irises. "Is your mother's place in Deadwood?" I assumed they were local, but with all the tourists around, it didn't hurt to double-check.

"No. We live up the hill in Lead."

Lead was Deadwood's golden-veined twin. Its history books were filled with mining tales rather than gambling legends.

I had no issues with selling a house in either city. Money was money, and it was something I had very little of at the moment. I needed every opportunity to hold onto my job I could find these days, and another house on my plate would be great, but I wasn't agreeing to anything until I saw the place. I'd learned my lesson last time. "When's a good time for me to come take a look at your house?"

"As soon as you can."

Nice, a motivated seller. Now if I could only find a buyer half as eager. Heck, just find a buyer—period. "How about this afternoon at two?"

"Good." Millie pulled a piece of paper from one of the folds in her sweater and placed it next to my coffee cup. "Here's our address. We'll be waiting for you."

Before I had a chance to fish one of my cards from my purse, she left, her mother trailing after her. They passed my tardy breakfast date on their way to the door.

"Sorry I'm late." Old Man Harvey slid onto the seat across from me, his grizzled beard in desperate need of a trim. "I was putting out a fire all night."

Another fire? I frowned. "At your ranch?"

His grin was broad, his gold tooth gleaming. "Nah. In an old flame's bed. I left her smoldering."

I choked on an involuntary chuckle and sipped my sweetened coffee to wash it down.

I'd met Harvey and his 12-gauge shotgun up-close and personal about a month ago. After we'd straightened out that I was a Realtor interested in helping him sell his ranch and not a banker bent on taking it, we'd tossed back some hard liquor over a listing agreement. He'd confessed he was lonely and then proved it by insisting I include a once-a-week-meal-on-me clause. Desperate, I'd made him promise there would be no funny business between us since he was almost twice as old as my thirty-five years, and then I'd agreed.

"What's for breakfast?" Harvey opened his menu. "After all of that bumping and grinding last night, I could eat a herd of elk."

Grimacing, I set my cup on the table. "Stop. You're going to kill my appetite."

He snorted, then buried his nose in the plastic pages. "What did the Carharts want?"

"You know them?" I shouldn't have been surprised. Harvey had grown up in the Hills. The dirty bird liked to brag about all the cousins he'd kissed.

"Wanda was a few grades ahead of me in school," he said.

"They want me to sell their house."

Harvey squinted at me over the menu. "And?"

"And what? I'm paying them a visit this afternoon."

He leaned across the table, his forehead puckered. "What are you thinking?"

I blinked. Had I missed the memo? "What do you mean?"

"Are you really going to take them on as clients?"

"Sure." If their place wasn't a pit. "Why not?"

He tossed his menu on the table. "Maybe because six months ago in that very house, Millie's brother bashed her father's head in with a rolling pin and then blew his own brains out."

I swallowed wrong, hot coffee seared the back of my tongue. "You're kidding me."

"I wish I was." He crossed his arms. "If you take this job, you might as well plug your nose and hold your breath, because your career is gonna go swirling down the crapper."

Chapter Two

With my reputation already smudged, Harvey was probably right about not signing a sales contract with Millie and her mom. He and I parted ways under the hot August sunshine—he antsy to return to stoke his old flame; I anxious to check in at my office where I'd be roasted over the fire, as usual.

Calamity Jane Realty employed two other Realtors besides me, and both of their newer SUVs were parked behind the building, sparkling in the sunshine. I parked between them, my clean but sun-faded Bronco in desperate need of more paint. At the moment, however, feeding and clothing my kids meant more to me than looking good on the road.

I slipped inside the back door, my mule sandals clomping on the wood plank floor as I passed my boss' darkened office on the way to my desk. The smell of stale varnish gave way to the sweet scent of jasmine mixed with the sharp tones of leather cleaner as I stepped into the front room where my coworkers sat at their desks under the buzzing fluorescent lights.

"Morning, Vi." Mona Hollister, my mentor and number one fan in the realty business, smiled. Her dark red-orange hair wisped around her face and rhinestone-rimmed reading glasses, emphasizing her strong cheekbones. Her crimson lipstick matched her fingernails, which clacked away on her keyboard. "How was breakfast?"

"Ummm, interesting." I detoured to the coffee pot. I

needed a hit of liquid gumption before engaging my other coworker, Ray Underhill, owl-eyed Millie's so-called *gentleman*. The jerk was busy polishing his cowboy boots while he schmoozed a client on the phone.

"Doc Nyce called." Mona told me as I headed for my desk, coffee in hand. "He said he had something come up and couldn't make it to the inspection today. He'll give you a call later."

"Thanks." *Dang it!* I wanted to kick something, but I'd just painted my toenails this morning.

I dug my new cell phone out of my purse. No private voicemails or texts from Doc. Not even a single missed call from him. I dropped into my chair, the weight of rejection shoving me down. Doc's repeated absenteeism was an obvious sign that I needed to heed, no matter how much it stung.

A short time ago, I'd broken one of my personal career rules and shared some good vibrations with Mr. Dane "Doc" Nyce, my sexy-as-hell friend and sole buying client, after he'd risked his life to save mine in a burning house. Just the memory of being with Doc in the back room of his office, his muscles straining under my fingers, made me hot and shivery all over. But reality kept dousing me with a bucket of ice water. One trip to the moon had apparently been enough for Doc, whereas I was all suited up and ready to rocket out of my boots again.

As much as I wanted to stomp next door to his office, slam things around, and threaten bodily harm if he didn't ravish me all over again, my self-respect barred the way, doing its job of keeping my dignity intact.

"Nice of you to show up for work, Blondie," Ray said. I'd been so distracted fuming about Doc, I hadn't heard him hang up the phone. "Did you enjoy the pair of nut-jobs I sent your way this morning?"

I didn't waste a glance on him, logging on to my

computer instead. "If you're referring to Millie and Wanda Carhart—two very nice ladies—then yes, I met them."

Okay, I didn't really know for a fact whether Millie and Wanda were nice. But in the face of Ray's snide smirk, they could be professional puppy spankers and I'd still speak well of them. Any other reaction would let Ray think he put one over on me.

"*Nice*, right," Ray said. "Nice and fruity, maybe. Homely as a pair of inbred hillbillies, definitely. It's a wonder Junior didn't get busy on them with that rolling pin."

"*What?*" My jaw agape, I glared at the scumbag. He'd hit an all-time low. I was used to him taking shots at me, but not at innocent bystanders.

"If I'd had to go home to those two women every night, I probably would have—"

"Ray!" Mona's brown eyes flashed, her fingers frozen above the keyboard.

"I'm just saying what everyone else is thinking."

"Not everyone," Mona said, her tone clipped.

I crossed my arms over my chest. "Just certain assholes."

"Oh, Christ. Don't tell me you guys actually feel sorry for those two losers."

"Sunshine," Mona used the nickname she often employed when trying to out-condescend Ray. "Just because they don't wear designer cowboy boots and visit Gilda's Golden Glow for a spray tan three times a week doesn't make them losers."

"Really, Red? Tell me, then, what do they offer to society besides a drain on its resources via that Social Security check they're now squandering every month?" His chair squeaked as he leaned forward, his nostrils flaring as he huffed his point. "That Millie could work if she wanted to—not in the public eye, mind you, not with those glasses. Unless the goal is to scare away customers. But she could make an honest living just like the rest of us taxpayers instead of leeching off the system. She's not even fifty yet."

"You call what you do honest?" I faked a laugh. Ray was the King of Schmooze. He had a Ph.D. in exaggeration with a master's degree in bullshit.

"At least I'm making this place money, Blondie. How many sales do you have on the Sales Pending board?" He pointed at the white board that Jane, our left-brained, list-happy boss, used to keep track of upcoming sales.

I lifted my chin. "One." It was my first and only, and I was damned proud of it.

"Oh, is that an actual mark? I thought Jane just slipped with the marker when adding my eleventh sale last month."

"You can shove your eleven sales up your—"

"What's your point with all of this, Ray?" Mona's crimson lips were pressed thin, her cheeks a shade pinker than usual. "Or are you just being rude to pass time?"

Ray leaned back in his chair, clasping his hands behind his head, kicking his Tony Lama boots up onto his desktop. His icy blue eyes locked onto mine. "I don't want a Calamity Jane Realty sign sitting in Wanda Carhart's front yard. It would be a black mark on the reputation that I've worked damned hard to build for this office."

My neck bristled. Of all the elitist, arrogant, pompous—

"That's a legitimate point." Mona interrupted my mental rant, surprising me by siding with Ray.

My tattered eyebrows shot to the top of my forehead. "What?"

Ray's gloating grin made me want to grab my stapler and play whack-a-mole on his pearly whites.

"I'm not saying I agree completely with him, but as agents of Calamity Jane Realty, we need to appear as professional and trustworthy as possible. The locations we choose to represent reflect on our character. Our feelings for the client can't cloud our judgment."

I opened my mouth to object, but then thought of my handful of clients and how fuzzy the dividing line was between my personal and professional relationships.

Old Man Harvey now came for dinner a couple of nights a week. Jeff Wymonds and I took turns babysitting each other's kids. Wolfgang Hessler had wined and dined me before trying to sacrifice me to appease his dead sister's ghost. Doc and I had knocked boots once already, and given the opportunity, I'd most likely do it again. That left Detective Cooper, Harvey's favorite nephew, who was on my calendar for a business lunch tomorrow. Lord only knew what was going to come of that.

I snapped my jaw closed, a guilty blush heating my neck. A glance at Mona's half-smile confirmed that she and I were in sync on her unspoken meaning.

"I didn't agree to sell the Carhart house," I told both of them. No need to explain that Harvey had already talked me out of taking on the Carharts as clients because of the family's recent tragedy. "I just said I'd go up to Lead and look at it."

Ray snorted. "That's a waste of time."

"What Violet chooses to do with her time is her business, Ray."

"Thank you, Mona."

"You're welcome." She pushed her glasses up her nose and returned to clacking away on her keyboard. "But you might want to take a look at the clock. You're running late."

"Crap!" The home inspector was probably at Doc's house already, waiting to be let inside. I grabbed my keys.

"Try not to burn the house down this time, Blondie."

"You should take something for that impulsive oral discharge, Ray." I slung my purse over my shoulder, giving him my sweetest smile. "Before someone plugs your pie hole with her size eights."

* * *

I cruised along back streets to Doc's new place, during which I tried not to think about the Carhart women and their sad state of affairs. A small part of me felt akin to them on the social pariah front.

The home inspector waited for me in the shade on the gabled porch of what would soon be Doc's Queen-Anne-style beauty. The guy's gray polo shirt stuck to his super-sized belly in several dark spots.

I scurried up the porch steps, trying to smile away my tardiness. "Sorry I'm late."

He grunted, his red face rigid. Sweat ran down the side of his double chin.

So much for small talk during the inspection. I unlocked the front door and pushed it wide; the air rushing out to greet us was stale, but cool. I followed him inside, my nose wrinkling. God, I should have brought a can of air freshener along. He must have rooted in a plate of red onions for lunch.

Leaving the inspector to work his magic, I detoured to the kitchen, thirsty from the heat. A small stack of disposable cups sat next to the sink.

I stared out into the backyard as I drank the lukewarm water, watching a dragonfly flicker around the birdbath, wondering what the Carhart house looked like. The way Ray had protested, I imagined another redneck kegger-mess like Jeff Wymonds' place, with junk cars overflowing the driveway and coffee cans full of used oil sitting about like yard lights. With Jeff's project house already on my plate, I didn't need a second.

Something thumped under my feet. The inspector must have found the door to the crawlspace on his own.

Would any agent want to represent the Carhart house after the horror that had occurred within its walls? There was no way Millie and Wanda could pull off a For-Sale-By-Owner. They were way too timid, especially Wanda. Not to mention the amount of energy and stress that came with FSBO's. They really needed a professional to guide them through all the paperwork.

What would drive someone to bludgeon his own father with a rolling pin? It must have been marble; a wood one probably wouldn't have been hard enough. Or would it? I recoiled at the direction of my thoughts and dumped the last swallow of water down the sink.

"Hello, Violet."

Jerking in surprise, I dropped the cup and whirled around. "What are *you* doing here?"

Doc leaned against the counter, his usual lazy grin on his lips, dark hair ruffled, hands in his pockets. Wearing a pair of blue cargo shorts and a white T-shirt that emphasized his broad shoulders, he looked tanner than he had the last time I'd ogled him. "Awaiting the inspector's report," he answered.

"I thought you couldn't make it."

"Something changed my priorities."

"What?"

His dark brown eyes held mine. "You."

"I haven't even talked to you." Not that I hadn't tried—*for almost two damned weeks now!* "Only your voicemail." I couldn't resist that little dig.

"Frustrated?" He prodded back.

Hell, yes! "A little. But only as your Realtor, of course."

His smile widened. "Of course."

More muffled thumps below reminded me that we weren't the only two people on Earth. "The inspector is under the house," I said. Pride held a tight rein on my tongue, keeping me from asking why Doc hadn't bothered to call me back.

"So I hear." His gaze made a leisurely crawl down to my

painted toes and back up. "Great dress. It matches your eyes."

"Thanks." I straightened my green wrap dress; a blush heated my cheeks and spread south. I fanned myself with my hand. Dang it! How was it he could make me feel naked when I was fully clothed?

"I like those shoes."

"They were a Christmas present." My mother fed my shoe addiction annually—not that Doc cared about my gifts from Santa.

"But I prefer your purple boots."

I shivered at the memory of digging my boot heels into his bare flesh and then fanned harder, my internal temperature spiraling out of control. "Doc, what are you doing?"

"Making small talk while we wait for the inspector to finish."

"Right." Bullshit. "What are you really doing here?"

"Harvey called me."

I groaned. I should have known.

"He said you were on the verge of signing a listing agreement to sell another albatross."

My blush roasted even hotter, fueled by exasperation. "Harvey has a bucket mouth."

"So you've mentioned before. Do you think this is a good idea after what happened last time?"

I aimed my index finger at Doc. "Let's get something straight here. It's nobody's business but mine which houses I contract to sell."

Having sex with me didn't give Doc the right to question my actions, especially if sex wasn't going to become a hobby for us.

He raised a brow. "Maybe so, but you do tend to have a nose for trouble."

"Leave my nose out of this."

"But it's a cute nose."

My libido sat up and panted for more. "Quit trying to distract me with your flirting."

"Is it working?"

"No." I glanced away from his dark chocolate eyes before my underwear caught fire.

"Then why is your cute little nose twitching?"

We both knew why, for the same reason I was rotten at playing poker.

I heard footfalls going up the stairs. The inspector was heading north, probably into the attic.

Sighing, I rubbed my forehead. There were so many questions I wanted to ask Doc, so many answers I needed to know about us—if there even was an "us." But baring my soul like that, risking the ultimate rejection, scared the living daylights out of me. "So, let me guess. You think my selling the Carhart place is a bad idea?"

"If that's the albatross, then yes."

"Because it will add further damage to my already tarnished reputation?"

"Partly."

I stared at him, waiting to hear what the other part was to his reasoning. When he didn't elaborate, I nodded about nothing. "Okay, then. Your opinion has been heard. Shall we head upstairs to see how Mr. Inspector is doing?"

I didn't wait for an answer, moving past Doc toward the main stairs.

"Violet." He caught my arm, stopping me.

I looked over my shoulder at him. The grin was gone from his face, a furrowed brow in its place. "What?"

"This could be dangerous."

"Are we still talking about the Carhart house?"

"Yes." His frown deepened. "And no."

I glared. I couldn't help it. It was that or pinch him. "Have I ever told you how much I adore the way you speak in riddles?" I tugged my arm free and tightened the belt to my dress. "I mean, really, is this some kind of special torture you save just for me? Because I certainly don't see you spinning Harvey in circles."

"I spin you in circles?"

A fresh dew of anger coated my skin. I dropped the professional veneer. "Yes, damn it. You do. With this whole hot-for-me one moment and then cold-as-a-glacier the next. I'm beginning to think I'm just some kind of plaything for you. A little toy to keep you from getting bored."

A muscle ticked in his jaw, but still nothing from him but a scowl.

I threw my hands in the air. "This is exactly what I'm talking about! You can obviously see how twisted up I am about you, about us—about what happened back in your office. Yet you just stand there, cool as an emperor penguin in the middle of an Antarctic winter." I huffed, which did little to calm me. I needed some space—and to stop letting my son talk me into watching the National Geographic Channel so often. "I'm going upstairs."

"No!" He moved so fast that my back was up against the kitchen wall before I realized he'd moved. He loomed over me, the woodsy scent of his cologne cranking up my senses. "You think you're the only one messed up inside? The only one confused as hell?"

"Yes ... I did, anyway. But with that crazed look in your eyes right now, I'm starting to have some doubts."

"Why do you think I left town for a while and didn't return your calls?"

That was the million dollar question. "You wanted to see more of America?"

The intensity lining his face softened. "Not quite."

"Inquiring minds would like to know."

"I can't stop thinking about you." His gaze fell on my mouth. "Or your boots."

"So you left town? Sheesh, you're hard on a girl's self-esteem."

"This thing between you and me—" He loosened his grip on my shoulders, trailing his fingers down my arms, his eyes climbing back to mine. "It's a little unnerving."

"Unnerving?" I laughed. I couldn't help it. "Spoken by a man who claims to be able to sniff out ghosts and frolic with the spirit world."

During the long days and nights since our last encounter, I hadn't forgotten about Doc's so-called ability to interact with the dead. As a matter of fact, I'd gone so far as to check out a couple of books at the Deadwood library about some of history's most famous psychics, mediums, and clairvoyants—which probably hadn't helped my newfound reputation for ghost-loving, judging from the raised eyebrow I caught from the starchy librarian.

"Shhh." Doc pointed at the ceiling, his voice low. "That's different. I can control that a little." He paused before adding, "Well, sometimes."

Ah, there it was, the heart of our problem. "You don't like to be out of control."

"You do?"

"Doc, I have two kids—twins, with no father on the scene since their conception. My life's been twirling out of control since the day they popped into this world."

His frown returned. "I like to at least *think* I have some control."

"I'm more interested in what you're going to do about this."

"I'm still working on that. There's a lot at stake here."

"Yes, there is." As in me and my feelings.

"I don't want to hurt you, Violet."

This was getting way too serious for a Wednesday. All I wanted was Doc to return my phone calls for a change. Everything else could just wait. I tried to lighten things up with a fake smile. "Don't worry. My skin is tough. Rhinos have nothing on me."

Doc's fingers skimmed back up to my shoulders, then slid around and cupped the back of my neck. "Don't take on the Carhart house."

"I probably won't."

His chuckle came from deep in his chest. "Is that as far as you're going to bend?"

"On this subject, yes. But I'm willing to bend a lot more for other purposes."

He leaned toward me, his eyes focusing on my lips. "If that's a come-on, it's working."

"It's not a come-on." I rose up on my tiptoes, closing the distance, clutching his T-shirt. "It's a shut-up-and-kiss-me."

"Uhhh-hmmmm." Someone cleared his throat.

The inspector. *Crud!* Where'd he come from? I hadn't heard his footfalls.

Doc groaned and pulled free of my grip, bee-lining out of the kitchen before I could catch my breath.

Every cell blushing, I stepped away from the wall and tried to act as if I hadn't been about to play tongue twister with the home's future owner.

The inspector avoided my gaze. "I need to check out your plumbing."

Doc's bark of laughter coming from the other room made my skin tinge even redder. The inspector's jowls darkened.

"I mean the plumbing," he said, staring at the clipboard in his hands. "Here. In the kitchen."

"Yeah, sure. Have at it." I couldn't escape the room fast enough.

I found Doc sitting on a stair step, staring at the closed front door. Dropping onto the step next to him, I clasped my hands so they wouldn't wander his way. My mind fumbled for a safe subject. "Have you been in the Carhart house?"

"Nope. Where is it?"

"Lead." I dropped my voice to a whisper. "You think there's a ghost in it?"

Doc looked at me for a long pause, his eyes narrowed. "You don't believe in ghosts, remember?"

"Maybe I've changed my mind about that."

"Have you?"

"Not really." I didn't think so, anyway. "I need some proof."

"If it were only that easy." Doc turned back to the front door. "I don't know if there's a ghost or not. I haven't been in the place."

"You interested in finding out?"

"Violet, stop right there."

"What? I'm just saying you could come with me this afternoon when I go."

"Why are you even going?"

"I told them I'd come."

"You could just call them."

"We have an appointment. You're a businessman. You know what that means."

He nudged my knee with his. "You just want to see the house where the murders occurred."

"Maybe." A dark curiosity had been growing inside of me since Harvey had mentioned the chilling event.

"I can't join you. I also have an appointment."

With whom? When Doc wasn't sniffing out ghosts, he was running his own financial planning business. I looked forward to the day when I could talk money with Doc. But until I had more than a pocketful of finances that wasn't already earmarked for my kids, I could only stand on the sidelines and watch.

"But you're not going to sell that house, right?"

"Probably not."

"Violet."

"What?"

His cell phone chirped. He kept his focus on me as he dug it from his pocket. "Promise me."

"Come on. What are we? Ten?"

"I know you, Violet. You don't have to seek out trouble. It finds you." Whatever was on his phone's screen made him grimace.

"Then what's the use of me making a promise?"

"Humor me." He stood, pocketing his phone. "I have to go."

"Where?"

The inspector chose that moment to interrupt again. "I need the key to the detached garage."

Doc opened the front door. "Promise me, Violet."

"Doc—" I stood.

"If you could just give me the key, I can wrap this up." *And get the hell out of here*, the look on the inspector's face finished his sentence.

"Just a second. It's in my purse in the kitchen."

"Violet." Doc pressed, straddling the threshold.

"Doc, I ..." I didn't know why I was hesitating.

"Lady, the key."

"Just say it, Violet."

"Fine!" I yelled. "I promise. Happy now?" I glared at both men in turn.

"I will be, lady," the inspector said, "as soon as you give me the damned key."

Doc shut the door behind him, the sound of his laughter seeping through the seams.

Chapter Three

The inspector didn't stick around long after Doc left. Either the house and garage were in tip-top shape, or I unknowingly had leprosy. I hoped it was the former as I watched him lumber down the sidewalk to his pickup and disappear in a belch of stinky black exhaust.

With an hour to spare before I had to show up on the Carharts' welcome mat, I headed home for lunch. Call it mother's intuition, but something told me that I needed to check on my kids to make sure they weren't dissecting road kill on the front porch or creating *awesome* fireballs with the microwave again.

I rolled to a stop in the drive of my Aunt Zoe's house, a spruced-up, no-fuss Victorian that my aunt was sharing with my kids and me. The sun cooked my roots as my sandals flopped and crunched along the gravel. A lawnmower growled from somewhere nearby.

On the porch, a couple of yellow jackets harassed each other, but that was it for beings—alive or dead. The sharp scent of citrus tickled my nose when I stepped inside the front door.

"Addy? Layne?" I called out.

"They're out back." Aunt Zoe's voice came from the kitchen.

I found her standing at the sink, squeezing lemons into a glass pitcher. With her long, silver-streaked hair secured in a braid, the scene looked the same as it had twenty-five-plus years ago when I used to visit for a month each summer.

The same sunshine-yellow kitchen, the same Aunt Zoe in blue jeans and a faded cotton shirt, the same warm and fuzzy feeling in my stomach.

"Good, I'm glad I caught you alone." I opened the cupboard next to her, thirsty as all get out suddenly. "I need to talk to you."

"If it's about that foot Layne found, Harvey already called and told me the newsflash."

I stopped mid-reach, the warm and fuzzy feeling gone. "What newsflash?"

A little over a week ago, the same day I'd played doctor with Doc in his office, Layne had found a human foot dangling from a red satin ribbon in a tree up the hillside behind Aunt Zoe's house. The ribbon had been threaded through the Achilles heel and a sprig of mistletoe stapled to the big toe—one of only three toes still attached. Detective Cooper and his motley crew had yet to find the rest of the owner ... unless something had changed.

Aunt Zoe's forehead creased. "Coop told Harvey someone found a hand up on Mount Roosevelt, near the monument. He thinks it goes with the foot."

I wasn't sure I wanted to know more, but I asked anyway. "What makes Detective Cooper think they're both part of the same ..." I paused. It was easier to think of these parts as individual pieces rather than a whole person. "Same body?"

"More red satin ribbon."

"Oh."

"And mistletoe."

I grimaced.

"And a little silver bell tied to the thumb."

"Jesus!" I grabbed a glass from the cupboard and closed the door. "This is kind of scary."

"Tell me about it." Aunt Zoe tossed the squeezed lemon onto the pile of rinds in the sink. "We just got rid of one monster, thanks to you."

Thanks to me? Right. That made me sound heroic. My memories of the whole Hessler Haunt climax involved a lot of shrill screaming and tail-between-my-legs scampering.

"It'd be nice to have a little break before the next one shows up to terrorize the town," Aunt Zoe said, moving over so I could get some water from the tap.

"Or a big break." I could feel her eyes on me as I filled my glass. "Like lifetime big."

"How are the nightmares?"

I turned off the faucet. I wanted to deny that I was still having them, but the dark circles under my eyes most mornings undoubtedly gave me away. "Still coming."

"How often?"

"Every now and then." They showed nightly on the big screen in my brain, sometimes in 3-D—a special feature. But Aunt Zoe didn't need to hear that. She had enough on her plate with creating all the spun glass pieces required to fill an order from a fancy gallery in Denver. She needed to focus, not have her creativity sapped from worrying about me. I gulped several swallows of cold tap water, quenching my thirst, wishing I could quench the nightmares with it.

"You sure you don't want to pay a visit to that therapist the Emergency doctor recommended?"

Glass in hand, I moved to the back door and looked out at my kids, who were filling one of Aunt Zoe's big plastic storage tubs with water from the garden hose. "I'm fine. It's just some residual stuff still bouncing around in my head, that's all."

"Violet Lynn."

The sound of my middle name made me turn her way. "What?" That came out sounding more defensive than I'd have liked.

"You experienced a very traumatic event. While most of the physical evidence has disappeared—"

I pointed at my eyebrows, or rather the patches of them.

"I said 'most.'" She lifted the pitcher from the sink and placed it on the counter. "The mental bruises will take longer to fade." She grabbed the sugar canister and dumped a heap into the lemon juice. "You should think about calling that therapist and setting up an appointment with her."

Absolutely not. I couldn't afford to pay a therapist right now, unless she accepted Monopoly money as currency. "I'll consider it."

I could tell by the set of her mouth as she stirred the juice that she didn't believe me. Aunt Zoe had been able to read me like a Wall Drug billboard since I stopped wearing diapers.

"If anything, she could give you a prescription for something to help you sleep better."

Sleep? Bah. Who needed it?

Movement out the back door caught my attention. I grinned at the sight of Layne squatting in the plastic tub, his head the only thing above water, his teeth visibly chattering. Meanwhile, Addy chased her chicken, Elvis, around the swing set and then around Layne. Addy's red checkered one-piece bathing suit reminded me of Wanda Carhart's red gingham dress, which in turn jogged my memory about what I'd wanted to talk to Aunt Zoe about when I walked into the kitchen.

"Aunt Zoe?"

She looked up from filling the pitcher.

"Do you know Millie and Wanda Carhart?"

The slight narrowing of her eyes spoke volumes. "A little. Why?"

"I'm going to go walk through their place up in Lead this afternoon. They want me to sell it for them."

"That was an ugly scene." She shook her head as she

dumped a tray of ice cubes into the lemonade.

"Do you remember the details?"

"Well enough." She grabbed the towel, wiping her hands. "Are you going to sell it?"

"I don't know. What do you think?" I might as well solicit her opinion. Everyone else had already thrown their two cents at me.

"I think you're going to do what you believe is the right thing." She held out her hand for my glass. I gulped the last bit of water and obliged. "Which might not be the best thing," she continued, "but if there is one thing I've learned about you in the last thirty-five years, it's that there's no stopping you once you get up a head of steam."

She handed me back my glass. Ice cubes clinked and swirled in the murky lemonade. I raised it to my lips as the back door crashed open and two dripping kids slid inside with a chicken pecking at their heels.

"Hi, Mom!" Layne wrapped two wet arms around my hips and hugged my stomach. "Did you bring the glue?"

My son went through Elmer's glue faster than a scrapbooking convention. I kissed the top of his head, the only dry spot on him. "I forgot."

"Awww, Mom ..." He pulled away.

"You can finish gluing your Zeppelin after supper."

"Can Kelly come over tonight?" Addy asked me as I air-dried the damp spots Layne had left on my dress.

The chicken clucked toward the living room.

"Addy, what did I tell you about that chicken?"

"But Elvis is housebroken now."

"I'm tired of picking chicken feathers off my pillow. Elvis stays outside or in her cage in the basement, and that's final." Addy was lucky Aunt Zoe even allowed the damned bird in her house.

"Fine." Addy grabbed Elvis and tucked her under her arm. "But can Kelly come over, please?"

Kelly was Addy's best friend. She also happened to be the daughter of Jeff Wymonds, whose place I was knee-deep in cleaning up so I could put it on the market as soon as possible. Jeff's soon-to-be ex-wife wanted her half of the house's value immediately. She had big plans for herself and her new girlfriend.

"I don't know," I told Addy. "Let me ask her dad."

"Okay." Addy shifted the chicken to her other arm. "Umm, Mom?"

"What?" I took a drink of my lemonade, savoring the sweet and sour flavors that reminded me of childhood. Aunt Zoe's fresh lemonade came in second only to her legendary Christmas Whiskey Slush.

"Do you want to kiss Kelly's dad?"

I nearly choked on my mouthful of lemonade. Gulping it all down at once, I coughed, cleared my throat, and then gaped at my daughter. "What?"

"Do. You. Want. To. Kiss. Kel—"

"I heard you the first time, Adelynn Renee."

Aunt Zoe snickered and poured lemonade into two smaller cups.

"Well, do you?"

"Yeah," Layne chimed in, his arms crossed. "Do you?"

Kiss Jeff Wymonds? "No." The only lips I was interested in sampling were Doc's. But nobody knew that except me, especially since my best friend, Natalie, believed herself to be in love with Doc, which was a problem I was doing my best to skirt.

"Good." Layne's smile returned, widening further when Aunt Zoe handed him the cup of lemonade.

Addy wasn't smiling. "Why not?"

"Because I just don't."

"Not even a little? Not even like as a friend? Like how Harvey and Ms. Geary are kissing friends?"

Ms. Geary was Aunt Zoe's sixty-ish next-door neighbor

who preferred to weed her flower beds in rhinestone-hemmed short shorts and fish-net stockings—usually when she knew Harvey was watching. He "watered her flowers" a few times a week.

"No, not even a little, Addy. So don't even think about playing matchmaker with Mr. Wymonds and me."

Addy made Cupid look like a fumbling fledgling.

"But Mom, if you and Mr. Wymonds got married, Kelly would be my sister."

Ohhhh. Now I understood what was going on. Addy's mission in life this last year had been to marry me off to the most qualified candidate. "Qualified" by her standards usually meant a love for all animals—especially chickens—and a deep wallet, since she was often concerned about my lack of cash.

"No, Addy. I'm not marrying Kelly's dad. Get that through your head right now."

"She's never marrying anyone." Layne faced down his sister with me, standing shoulder to my ribcage. "Right, Mom?"

Well, I wouldn't go that far.

"But I need stuff." Addy's whine made my lower back tighten.

"Like what?"

"Candy."

"You have plenty of candy." I didn't even know where she found half of it. I swore there was a candy fairy who stopped by Addy's pillow nightly.

"School clothes."

"Your stuff from last year still fits fine."

"A new bicycle."

"Your bike has a couple of broken spokes; that's no big deal."

"Some glasses."

"Your gl—what?" *Glasses?* "What makes you think you

need glasses?"

"The eye chart back by the pharmacy at Piggly Wiggly. When I stand behind the red line like the instructions say, I can't read the bottom three lines."

"Really?" At her nod, I sighed. This wasn't going to be cheap. With no vision insurance to help me cover costs, I was probably looking at shelling out close to five hundred bucks.

"If you had a husband, you could afford me better," Addy explained.

That stung clear down to my toes. "Sweetheart, I can afford you just fine without a husband," I lied.

If only I had some kind of child support coming in from the kids' father. But as soon as he'd heard I was pregnant, he'd hightailed it out of town never to be heard from again. Such was my luck with men since I started stuffing my bra and wearing lipstick back in eleventh grade.

I could borrow money from my parents or Aunt Zoe— again—to pay for the glasses, but I was tired of mooching off family.

As soon as my commission from Doc's house purchase came in, I'd have a bit of cash to refill my bank account's sparse coffers, but I had other bills to pay, too. Plus, Layne's toes were beginning to push out through both pairs of his tennis shoes. I couldn't expect him to wear his big snow boots to school every day. He'd be the laughing stock of the school.

Sheesh! I had to get some fresh air before I cowered in the corner, hyperventilating. I gulped down the rest of my lemonade and set the glass on the counter.

"Don't worry, honey." I squeezed Addy's chin as I passed. "I'll take care of everything. See you guys tonight."

Ignoring the concern creasing Aunt Zoe's mouth, I kissed her cheek and practically ran out the front door.

I needed to find where money was growing on trees

around here, and fast.

But with my luck, I'd discover a foot or hand hanging on the tree with it.

* * *

I found the money tree.

It was sitting next to the Carhart house, which shined with Gothic-Revival-style finery, from its steeply pitched roof and even steeper cross gables and point-arched windows. While it could use a coat of paint, if the inside was in as good a shape as the outside, this place would have buyers reaching for their checkbooks.

There was just one tiny problem.

Well, maybe not so tiny.

The house overlooked one of Lead's current claims to fame—the remnants of Homestake Mining Company's vast open-cut gold mine.

The huge hole in the ground had always struck me as odd, not due to its manmade immensity but rather the way it seemed plunked in the middle of the small town, located at the corner of Main Street and Gold as if that were perfectly normal.

The Open Cut's edge was not a hundred feet from the Carharts' side porch. An eight-foot chain-link fence topped with razor wire acted as the dividing line between land and no man's land. A buffer strip of tall, scraggly weeds bunched up along the fence's base.

I tested the fence to make sure it wasn't electrified, then clasped my fingers around the wire and peered down, down, down. I couldn't see the bottom.

How could I sell this?

The answer popped in my head—*territorial view*.

I grinned against the wire. Perfect!

Then I remembered all of the warnings I'd been

battered with this morning. I pushed away from the fence, back-peddling to the drive, hesitating in front of my Bronco.

Okay, so Addy needed glasses and Layne needed shoes. Maybe I could find a part-time job in the evenings to help pay the bills until my clientele grew and regular commission checks started pouring in.

A sheer white curtain twitched inside one of the downstairs windows, just enough to make me wonder if I'd really seen it move. I stared. It twitched again.

Someone was watching me. I might as well make my appearance, see the inside of the place, and then say my goodbyes.

I was not going to offer to list the Carharts' house, I reminded myself on the way up the steps of the wide, one-story porch. No way, not even if their home's interior glimmered with as much potential as the exterior. I'd catch way too much crap for even considering it.

The porch floorboards didn't creak under my feet. I added a little extra bounce with each step. Still nothing. Hmmm. Maybe it was newly rebuilt. I could add that as a selling point ... if I were going to list their house, which I wasn't, of course.

The front door opened before I had a chance to knock.

Millie's owl eyes met mine through the screen door. "Come in, Miss Parker." She opened the screen just enough to hurry me through it.

I'd anticipated a musty smell for some reason, probably because Millie and Wanda had a musty look about them. I'd also envisioned long shadows and dark wood accents—a structural version of Millie herself.

Apparently, my inner prophet needed glasses, too.

Myriad Tiffany-style stained glass lights filled the foyer and adjacent formal sitting room. From table lamps to floor lamps to wall sconces to chandeliers, stained glass tints filled the rooms with pastel shades of red, blue, green, and yellow happiness.

Light caramel stain added warm charm. In the sitting room, islands of thick cream-colored shag rugs floated on long, narrow slabs of birch flooring. A burgundy leather sofa pinned down one rug; a matching chair and ottoman occupied the other. Millie ushered me toward the chair. Its ultra-soft leather caressed the backs of my bare legs as I settled in.

"I'll go get Mother." Millie spoke so quietly that I had to lean forward to hear her. "Would you like something to drink?"

"A glass of water would be great, thank you."

Millie's long wool skirt swished away, leaving me alone to absorb more of my surroundings. Off-white silk wallpaper dotted with flowers covered the walls. The high ceiling gleamed with a pearlescent shade of pink paint on pressed tin squares, each trimmed with decorative swirls.

The scent of vanilla filled the rooms, so rich I could almost taste it on the back of my tongue. The faint sound of a Flamenco guitar filtered down a wide stairwell trimmed with an elaborately carved banister ending in pineapple-shaped newel posts.

I settled into the soft cushions, imagining the bidding war this place could spur. If the rest of the house was as polished and enchanting, the online pictures alone would sell the property.

I wondered in which room the murder took place. It certainly couldn't have been this one. It was too calming, too pretty for such a gruesome scene. Maybe it was in the kitchen, where the rolling pin resided close and handy.

A portrait of a couple sat on a sideboard across the room, luring me. I picked up the brass frame, recoiling as I focused on the man's harsh features: eyes too far apart, nose bent in two places, teeth crooked and stained a gray-beige, blond hair cowlicky over each temple. The raven-haired beauty cozied up next to him made me blink, the contrast stark, mesmerizing. With her ivory skin and amethyst eyes, she would have piled up traffic on Interstate 90 during biker week.

"What are you doing?"

I tensed at the sound of Millie's voice. She stood rigid, watching, expressionless.

"I'm, uh," I showed her the picture, "just looking at—"

She rushed up to me, yanked the frame from my hands. "Sit down!"

I stood rooted, shocked immobile by her sudden ferocity.

She hugged the frame against her chest, and then stepped back, her face visibly softening behind the thick circles of glass. Her hand trembled when she tucked a strand of hair behind her ear. "I'm sorry, I ... please, would you sit?"

"Sure." Feeling a bit wobbly myself, I followed her back toward the chair and obeyed. She handed me a glass of warm water and joined Wanda, who had sneaked in during Millie's schizophrenic episode and planted herself on the sofa.

I gave Wanda a mega-watt smile, wanting to connect, to offer her some friendly compassion after the horrific distress she'd undoubtedly experienced during the last year. The corners of her lips creased, barely. She held eye contact for all of half a heartbeat. Then her gaze darted about, not remaining on anything for any length of time, and certainly not on me.

The chair I sat in didn't feel so comfy anymore.

I cleared my throat. "Thank you for the drink." I sipped the warm water and winced inwardly at the acrid taste of it. Setting my glass on the side table next to me, I addressed both of my hostesses. "I'd also like to thank you for opening your home to me and offering the first opportunity at selling it for you. However, I can't—"

"You're not the first," Millie interrupted me.

"I'm not?"

Wanda shook her head.

"We tried four other realty offices." Millie fiddled with a loose piece of yarn unraveling from her sweater. "None of them would even drive by, let alone come take a look inside. It's because of what happened, I just know it."

"Well..." She was undoubtedly right. Ray and Mona weren't the only ones in the area concerned about a reputation.

It was my turn to fiddle. Discussing the brutal murder and violent suicide of Millie's father and brother was a bit of a delicate, complicated matter.

"The last real estate agent mentioned your name," Millie said. "After we heard about you, we knew you were the one for us."

Alarms whooped in my head. "What did you hear?"

"That you dealt with ..." Millie's eyes darted to her mother, a worried look on her face. "With houses that were rumored to have ghosts."

"An agent told you that?" It was this kind of comment being tossed around town that was causing all of the stares and whispers ... and my heartburn.

Millie nodded. "So, do you think you could sell Mother's house?"

Maybe to an out-of-towner, and only because I'd want to stick the sale up the other agent's nose. Well, and I needed the money—bad. "Possibly."

"How long do you think it would take?"

"If the rest of the house has been taken care of as well as this room, maybe a month. Two at the most." Optimism was one of my strengths, along with following through on retribution. I'd bet my mother's fine China it was Ray who'd told them the rumor about me.

"Really?" Millie leaned forward, her hands no longer fidgeting, but rather clutched so tight her knuckles were turning white. "That soon?"

"Most likely, yes." I glanced at Wanda, who was frowning at something over by the stairwell. I looked to see what had her attention. The large Corn Plant? The brass umbrella holder? What?

Millie stood. "Would you like to see the rest of the house?"

"Yes." Curiosity had me hooked. I rose, still a bit distracted by Wanda's odd behavior. "Will your mother be joining us?" If not, I planned to ask about the state of her mental well-being. Wanda needed to be coherent enough to claim ownership, or Millie was going to need a power of attorney before we could put the house on the market.

I meant, *IF* I were even going to consider taking the listing. Which I wasn't.

"Yes, of course. Mother, come on."

Wanda smiled shyly again at me and followed us up the carpet-lined stair steps.

Fifteen minutes later, we stood in the kitchen, which oozed old-style charm with an apple theme and was trimmed with white modern appliances, and a shiny green porcelain sink. I didn't see a single drop of blood or any other evidence of the gruesome events that might have taken place within these walls.

I was in love. And I knew in my heart that while none of the locals wanted anything to do with this gem, some out-of-towners, like the hundreds of thousands passing through over the next couple of weeks, would jump at the chance to call it their own. Especially if it was priced low enough.

"So, Miss Parker," Millie was back to fidgeting with that same thread. "Will you help us sell it?"

"Well..." There was that sticky bit about me telling Doc I probably wouldn't list their house—not to mention Ray's bellows, Mona's reprimands, and Harvey's snorts of disgust. I hadn't even mentioned anything about it to my boss, Jane, yet.

"We'd be willing to give you three percent more than your normal rate."

On the other hand, Layne's feet were growing faster than I could keep them contained in expensive canvas, and Addy needed to be able to read the board in school without squinting all day.

"You'd need to have someone paint the outside this weekend," I told them both, making sure Wanda was focusing on me, not something behind me. She'd been touch-and-go upstairs, skittish almost, jumping when one of the curtains swayed in a breeze.

Wanda's nod of acceptance was slight, but her gaze stayed on my chin. Progress.

"The paint is in the garage," Millie said. "It just needs to be stirred."

Millie gave new meaning to "motivated seller."

"What color?" I wasn't going to get burned at the last minute with purple and pink Barbie townhouse colors.

"Butter cream. Chocolate brown for the trim."

"Wonderful."

"Does that mean you'll help us, Miss Parker?" Millie asked.

I hesitated, considering telling Millie I'd think about it and get back to her. The Carhart ladies' well-being wasn't my responsibility. I had enough trouble already just caring for the two little people under Aunt Zoe's roof.

Wanda lifted her milky gaze to mine. Tears rimmed her lower eyelids. "Please, help us," she whispered.

Oh, hell. Not tears. Anything but tears.

Sighing, I held out my hand. "I'll bring the necessary

paperwork by tomorrow."

Millie's handshake felt like squeezing a damp Kleenex.

I turned to Wanda, my smile softening, my hand extended. "I look forward to doing business with you, Mrs. Carhart."

Wanda's focus shot upward, above my head, her watery eyes wide, round, and bulging. She opened her mouth and made a jarring screech. Then she keeled over backward onto the wood floor.

Chapter Four

Hours later, long after Wanda Carhart awoke and made a quiet recovery from her temporary bout of insanity, I stood in front of Mudder Brothers Funeral Parlor.

Why was it that in nine out of ten small towns in America, funeral homes were the most posh buildings? So much finery and fancy dress on the outside, all for guests of honor on the inside who would never be able to appreciate the big event.

Mudder Brothers, a century-old two-story house decked out in white paint, was one of the nine. The warm early evening sunlight spotlighted its impressive architecture: four neoclassical columns decorated the front porch, a massive front gable bracketed a fanlight, and black shutters framed the windows.

The place reminded me of a stately old gent clad in a white tuxedo with black lapels and a bowtie; the flower-filled window boxes his pink carnation.

"All right, Vi," said Natalie, my best friend since Barbie-doll-hood, as she crutched across the parking lot toward me, her lower right leg cast almost hidden by her swishy long black skirt. "Explain to me why I'm meeting you at Mudder Brothers this evening when you didn't even know the late, great Mr. Haskell."

I tugged at the collar of my dark blue silk shirt, trying to get more air. The heat rolling off the parking lot combined with my jitters and produced a sheen of sweat all over my skin. I waited for Natalie to reach my side before whispering, "I was hoping you could get me in."

"Get you in?" Her loud laugh snared the attention of two pale-faced, lanky white-haired men standing near the far left column. Their cigarette smoke swirled around them in a slow vortex. With their bulbous eyes and puffing lips, they were grizzled versions of Donald Duck's nephews, Huey and Dewey. Where was Louie?

"It's not the Rainbow Room, girlfriend," Natalie said.

"Shhh." I kept my voice low. "You know I'm still a stranger around here." One with a tarnished reputation, besides. "You were born and raised in this town. Nobody will look twice if you walk into the room."

"You mean hobble."

A few weeks ago, Natalie had tried walking across a wet tin roof in a pair of cowboy boots. A clever Puss in Boots she was not. The fractured fibula barely slowed her down.

I led the way up a short ramp onto the wide porch and held open one of the two double doors for her. Huey and Dewey eyeballed us from their leaning posts ... well, mainly they eyeballed Natalie. With a siren's lips, striking cheekbones, and a body that inspired lovesick poetry, Natalie transformed men into Pepé Le Pew clones. Unfortunately, many of them changed back into assholes and cheaters when the instant lust wore off.

"So," Natalie paused just inside the door, "is there a reason for dragging me to this particular funeral, or did you just circle the first one on the obituary page that sounded fun?"

I closed the door. Soft murmurs of grief flowed around us. "I'm not here for the funeral."

Natalie grinned. "Please tell me you're not here to pick up men."

I scoffed and grabbed one of the programs from the sign-in podium. "I don't need a man." But that didn't keep me from wanting one in particular. Unfortunately, Doc was the exact same man Natalie wanted ... as in, waiting for her with a wedding band at the preacher end of an aisle. "Neither do you."

"*Au contraire*, my dear. And I'm determined to get him." She nudged her head toward an open set of French doors on our left and angled her crutches in that direction. "Doc is the *one*, you know."

"Yeah." Guilt made me sweat more. I fanned myself with Mr. Haskell's program. "I remember." I also remembered that a couple of weeks ago she'd *staked a claim* on Doc, which was supposed to mean that he was off limits to me—something I kept forgetting every time he was near. If Natalie found out I'd had sex with Doc, she'd probably dye all my lingerie puke green and cut my hair with dull pruning shears. If she knew I wanted to do it again and again and again, she'd stop talking to me. Forever. After two-plus-decades of friendship, I didn't want to live my life without her in it.

We rounded the open French doors and slid into an empty row of chairs in the back of an expansive parlor half-full of mourners, who were taking turns parading past the open casket at the front. Intermittent sniffles blended with the murmurs. The length of the left wall was covered with paintings of clouds, sunsets, and sunrises; the right wall was lined with mirrored windows that ended at a closed door in the front corner. Up by the casket, wreaths and sprays of white lilies, yellow gladiolas, purple mums, and red carnations added bright color to an otherwise neutral décor. Their subtle fragrance filled the room, blanketing death with sweet freshness.

"So," Natalie whispered in my ear. "Why are we here?"

"I want a closer look at George Mudder."

"No, you don't. He looks much better from a distance."

That made me smile—which I hid behind my hand. Smiles at a funeral would draw attention, and my goal was to blend in with the wallpaper.

"Why do you want to see George?" Natalie asked.

"Ray and he are up to something."

A few weeks ago, I'd seen Ray and George hauling a huge crate out of the back of the funeral parlor and loading it into Ray's SUV. There were no markings on the crate, at least none visible from across the big parking lot between Calamity Jane Realty and Mudder Brothers. Whatever was in the crate had made the springs on Ray's SUV bounce under its weight.

Later, when I poked Ray about what he and George were up to, he'd nearly bitten off my finger. It didn't take me long to conclude that these two boys had their dirty hands in the cookie jar. Tonight, I hoped to catch a glimpse of what they were up.

Natalie scooted closer, her cast bumping my foot. "If it involves Ray, it can't be good. You better be careful. Word on the street is his bite *is* actually worse than his bark. "

"He does tend to foam at the mouth a lot." And I had the teeth marks on my butt to prove her warning was on the mark.

Natalie nudged me with her cast. "Are you really going to sell the Carhart place?"

I nodded. I had called Natalie as I was backing out of the Carharts' drive earlier to tell her this new secret of mine and ask her to meet me at Mudder Brothers tonight.

Natalie waved discreetly at a middle-aged woman passing by on her way out the French doors as she leaned closer and whispered, "That's pretty ballsy with you still being new on the job. You have heard about that house, right?"

"Yes, but I need the money. My kids need stuff," I whispered back.

"We all need stuff. Is it worth risking your career? I have money you can borrow."

"I don't want your damned money." At the hurt look she shot me, I added, "I mean that in the nicest way possible, of course." I'd leaned on Natalie too often over the past few years. This time, I wanted to stand on my own.

"Fine," she grinned. "It's your funeral."

I chuckled at her double entendre. Natalie was the sister I wished my sister had grown up to be—rather than a two-bit whore who liked to sleep with my boyfriends when I wasn't watching. I lingered on that thought for a few seconds, my smile sliding south as I absorbed the irony that now Natalie did want to sleep with my sort-of boyfriend. Unlike my sister, Natalie wouldn't do it just to lash out at me. At least I hoped not. Then again, I was now the evil "sister" who'd had sex with the man Natalie wanted. Criminy! My life was morphing into a daytime soap opera. If I played my cards right, I just might win an Emmy.

The front-corner door opened, and the short beefy guy with a white buzz cut I had seen helping Ray load the crate into the SUV entered the room.

"There's George," Natalie confirmed.

Dapper in a charcoal gray suit with a pale pink tie, George rubbed the arm of an older woman who hunched over the casket, as if to comfort her. Then he moved a tripod holding a wreath of white gerbera daisies and red roses a couple of feet to the right and went back through the doorway. He returned carrying another basket bursting with blue delphiniums and lavender asters.

"Come on," Natalie pushed to her feet, grabbing her crutches. "Let's go pay our respects."

"What? Wait!" I scrambled after her. When I caught up, I whispered in her ear, "I don't want anyone to see me."

"Violet." Her crutches creaked as we approached the casket. "With your hair loose, you're not exactly a wallflower."

I tried to squish down my curls. "My clip broke."

"Next time bring a black veil."

George Mudder stood to the right as Natalie and I viewed Mr. Haskell, who looked pretty good for a dead man. I wondered if George did the makeup, or if he hired someone else to spruce up the corpse.

"By the way," Natalie said as she picked lint off the main attraction's suit jacket, "you have a date Saturday night."

I yanked Natalie's hand out of the casket. "No, I don't."

"Yes, you do. You owe me, remember?"

Crap. She meant the blind date with some comic-book geek I'd agreed to go on in exchange for her help on the Hessler Haunt weeks ago. I'd hoped she'd forgotten about that when the house burned down. I'd certainly tried to forget.

"Fine. When and where?"

"Seven o'clock at The Buffalo Corral."

The Buffalo Corral meant jeans, boots, old-time twangy music, and lots of red meat. My kind of place. I could suffer through a couple of hours of blind-date hell with a big old T-bone to keep me company.

"Natalie," George Mudder had crept up when I wasn't watching. "I haven't seen you since Mrs. Winkle's wake."

Natalie didn't miss a beat, her smile all warm and chummy. "George, you've done a lovely job today."

"Thanks." He ushered us toward the foot of the casket, near the open door he'd entered moments before. When we'd joined him, he asked, "How's your Aunt Beatrix? As charming as ever?"

Something in George's tone made me think this was more than just pleasantries. Natalie mirrored many of her Aunt Beatrix's striking features; unfortunately, they also shared bad luck when it came to philandering bedfellows. Was George part of Beatrix's past or just a wannabe?

I glanced behind him through the open doorway and

nearly fell over, not hearing Natalie's answer. In the semi-shadows, not just one but two big crates exactly like the one I'd watched George and Ray load were stacked against the far wall. I leaned toward the doorway. What else was stored in that room?

"Right, Violet?" Natalie's voice snapped me back.

"Uhhhh," I stammered, looking to her for help.

Natalie's brow wrinkled for just a second. Then she said, "I'm sorry, George. How rude of me. You probably haven't met my friend Violet. She's new to town. She's a Realtor over at Calamity Jane's."

"My pleasure," George said, his pale blue eyes kind, his palm silky soft and warm. I squirmed when I clasped it.

I pulled my hand free as fast as I politely could. "Thanks for having me." What a stupid thing to say to the owner of a funeral parlor. I added, "Your gable is impressive." Which landed me on a corner stool with a dunce cap.

Natalie coughed on her laugh.

"Nobody has ever complimented me on my gable before." George grinned at me, his tiny yellow teeth almost swallowed by his oversized gums.

I winced at his features' unsightly transformation, then tried to cover my reaction with a fake shoulder twitch.

"You'll have to excuse Violet," Natalie said, reaching behind me and poking my back hard enough that I flinched. *Ouch!* I elbowed her hand away.

"She's high-strung and twitchy tonight. Feeling a little antsy about a potential sale."

George's bushy silver eyebrows raised. "Whose house?"

"Wanda Carhart's place up in Lead." Natalie spilled it before I could duct tape her mouth shut.

That was still top-secret information. I tried to shrivel her head with my superhero laser vision.

She ignored me.

"The Carharts, huh?" George leaned in close, his voice for our ears only, his aftershave citrus-scented, subtle. "I had a packed house for their double funeral, had to turn people away. We debated clearing out the other viewing room to allow more folks inside." He pointed his thumb toward the open door. "But the Carhart boy's fiancée insisted that she didn't want to hide behind the one-way glass."

I stared at my reflection in the windows lining the wall. One-way glass. Was something moving behind them? I squinted, getting nowhere, feeling a bit creeped out. Someone could be back there right now, watching.

Were more crates back there, too? Filled?

"Why so many people? Was it because of the—" Natalie mouthed *murder*?

"Possibly. But the Carhart boy was pretty popular back in school, in spite of that nasty temper of his." George smirked. "You should have seen the waterworks show that fiancée of his put on."

The image of the happy couple in the photo flashed in my head.

I huddled closer, matching his voice level. I wanted to know if he'd handled the Carhart bodies when they'd come in, but I thought that might earn me another poke from Natalie. Instead, I asked, "How long had Millie's brother been engaged?"

George shrugged. "I didn't even know he was until the fiancée showed up with Millie and Wanda to make arrangements. Quite a looker she is, too. Wonder what she saw in that boy."

I'd wondered the same thing just hours prior. "I'll have to show you a picture of her sometime," I told Natalie.

"Maybe you can sneak a peek at the video," George said.

"Video?" Natalie and I jinxed.

"The fiancée requested we tape the funeral service. She wanted it as a keepsake to remember him by."

My jaw slackened. "Is that normal?"

"As requests go, that's pretty mild." George nodded at someone over my shoulder. "I need to go. Nice to meet you, Violet." He squeezed Natalie's shoulder. "Tell your Aunt Beatrix I said hello."

George detoured to lock the crate room's door before heading off across the parlor.

As soon as he was out of earshot, Natalie asked, "Well, what do you think? Is George up to no good with Ray?"

"I don't know. He seemed nice enough." Surprisingly so, considering he consorted with Ray. "But we're coming back here again."

"We are? Why?"

"I'm going to check out that storage room. And you're going to help me."

* * *

Thursday, August 2ⁿᵈ

The noon-time biker crowd at Bighorn Billy's had a cow fetish. I hadn't seen so much leather under one roof since my sixth-grade class toured the stockyards and an adjacent meat packing plant in Rapid City. But today's visit wouldn't end with me puking my guts out onto my Buster Browns.

I glanced over my shoulder at the door, checking for Detective Cooper, my lunch date, who should be walking through it any minute now. I figured he'd be punctual, being a member of the Deadwood city police force and all.

Then again, what did I really know about the guy? The few phone calls we'd shared had been either to talk about a dead man or to reschedule this very appointment due to other dead men. Besides knowing his uncle a little too intimately thanks to Harvey's lack of a filter most days,

Detective "Coop" Cooper could be Jack the Ripper's law-upholding cousin.

I checked my cell phone. No calls, no messages. Doc was still playing hard to get. Over the last twelve hours, I'd picked up my phone to call him a humiliating number of times. But the nervous sweat of rejection kept me from dialing. Just once, I wished Doc would call me, show some interest instead of making me work for it.

"What's for lunch?" Harvey's gruff voice stopped my woe-is-me bender before it could get rolling.

"What are you doing here?" I asked as he slid onto the bench seat opposite me.

"Getting some grub."

"Our weekly dinner deal was yesterday."

"That didn't count. It was breakfast, not dinner." He snickered at my glare. "Okay, I'll let you off easy this time."

"That's big of you." At my sarcasm, he grinned, his gold tooth glinting. "So what are you doing here?"

"Waiting for Coop with you."

"Wait no more, old man." Detective Cooper, dressed in jeans and a navy blue T-shirt, nudged his uncle over and scooted in next to him. He flashed me a quick, no frills smile. "Good afternoon, Ms. Parker."

"You can call her Violet." Harvey handed his nephew a menu.

With sandy blond hair, a craggy face, and a day's worth of scruff, Detective Cooper looked like James Bond—the Daniel Craig version. Only his eyes were olive-colored rather than blue. And Mr. Bond smiled at least once in awhile.

"Violet it is." The detective flipped his coffee mug right-side up and waggled his finger at a passing waitress. "I apologize for my tardiness. Something came up."

I imagined something "came up" a lot for the detective. I hoped it wasn't another body part somewhere. "No apology necessary, Detective Cooper."

"And you can call him Coop." Harvey butted in again. "Now stop running your yap-trap and let's get something to eat."

The waitress stopped by with coffee and took our orders. After she was out of earshot, Harvey asked Coop, "Did those lab rats send anything back yet on that ear?"

I grimaced. Last month, Harvey had complained to me about something making "funny" noises behind his barn at night—*funny* as in made my skin crawl at the mere thought and sent Harvey reaching for his shotgun. So Harvey, being the crazy old bugger that he was, set a trap. A big trap, squirrel bait included, fluffy tail and all.

Instead of catching a varmint, he'd caught an ear. A human ear. Plus a flap of skull skin. All licked clean of blood. Last I'd heard, Cooper and the Lawrence County sheriff were still baffled by it. To date, nobody has shown up at the Northern Hills Hospital crying about a torn-off ear.

Cooper fiddled with his coffee spoon, his olive eyes on mine. "You've heard about the ear, I take it?"

"I've told her everything," Harvey spoke in my place. "She's my Realtor."

I squirmed, uncomfortable under the serious weight of the detective's gaze. "Harvey and I have an open relationship," I explained. *Eye-opening* most of the time.

Cooper set his spoon down. "Nothing's come in from the lab yet. It can take weeks to get results, especially since it's not a life-or-death priority."

Grunting, Harvey muttered, "I bet it's one of those damned Slagton whangdoodles."

Slagton was the name of a *nearly* ghost town just a few as-the-crow-flies miles from Harvey's ranch. A big mining accident shut down the place decades ago. But there were stragglers—Harvey liked to call them "whangdoodles," his synonym for loony kooks—holding out, still living up in the hills.

I hadn't made it to Slagton. I'd watched *The Hills Have Eyes* too many times to stroll into that place without the National Guard on my heels.

"Whangdoodles or not," Cooper said, "we haven't seen any sign of activity since we cleaned out the nest."

The nest. I shuddered. Scouring the hillside behind Harvey's barn, Cooper and the sheriff's deputies found a burrow of sorts in an old mine, containing a pair of broken glasses, an old boot, dirty underwear, a half-eaten possum, and human teeth.

"Have you heard any sounds coming from behind your barn this last week?" Cooper asked Harvey.

"Nope. But something was horsin' around in that old cemetery back there again. The ground is all torn up."

"Are any of the graves disturbed?" I asked in a low voice.

"Not that I could tell, but I didn't get off my Gator to take a closer look." He nudged Cooper's arm. "You remember what happened in that cemetery in Slagton a few years back?"

Cooper nodded. "More like twenty years ago, old man."

"That's right. You were still wet behind the ears and working for the sheriff's department when you helped on that one."

Cooper had worked for the sheriff's department? I guess I'd pictured him in Deadwood since high school graduation. "So when did you make the switch to being a detective for Deadwood?"

"He switched teams about eight years ago, wasn't it, Coop?" Harvey spoke for his nephew and didn't wait for confirmation before adding, "He still helps out that no-good, double-crossing, lousy excuse for a sheriff whenever he's asked, though."

Cooper raised his eyebrows. "Which is coming in awful handy with the ruckus you've been causing lately."

"What's your beef with the sheriff, Harvey?"

"He's a cheatin' thief."

Cooper's mouth slipped into a smirk. "You still got your tail feathers all ruffled up about him stealing Edwina out from under you? They've been married for almost fifteen years now."

"You don't understand," Harvey said. "She was flexible."

Oh, Lord. "So what happened back in Slagton?" I asked, elbows on the table, goosebumps at the ready.

Harvey looked at his nephew. "Can I tell her?"

"Why not? You've told her everything else."

"A bunch of the graves were dug up, coffins opened, the remains all chewed up," Harvey said.

I cringed. "What do you mean 'chewed up'?"

"Skulls smashed," Cooper supplied. "Bones shredded like they'd gone through a wood chipper. Teeth marks were the only evidence left behind."

I sat back, mouth open, goosebumps forgotten. "What would do something like that?" And why?

"Some old timers said it was the white grizzly," Cooper said with a slight eye-roll. "Personally, I think it was some kids screwing around back there, trying to stir up some entertainment. The Black Hills' equivalent of crop circles."

"What's the white grizzly?" I was going to have to stop over at the library and read up on Slagton's history.

Stirring sugar into his coffee, Cooper answered, "It's a legend passed down from the Lakota Indians, who considered the Black Hills sacred ground."

Harvey leaned toward me and whispered, "Some people say it's not a bear at all but a demon with milky eyes, spiked teeth, claws like scythes, and a coat made up of its victims' scalps—their hair scared white before it killed 'em."

Here came the goosebumps. My chances of selling Harvey's place were sliding downhill, avalanche style. "So you think all this has something to do with what was going on in that mine up behind your barn?"

"Yes," Harvey said, drowning out Cooper's "No."

I held my breath while the waitress placed Harvey's Coke and my diet down in front of us, along with a side salad for Cooper.

After she left I asked the detective, "What are you going to do about Harvey's cemetery?" My interest was part curiosity, part need-to-know as Harvey's Realtor.

Cooper looked up at me, a forkful of salad halfway to his mouth, his forehead creased. "Aren't we here to discuss selling *my* place?"

"Oh, right." My cheeks heated. "Of course."

Harvey elbowed his nephew hard enough to send pieces of lettuce flying from Cooper's fork. "You didn't answer her question, Coop. That was rude. You need to apologize to Violet, or I'll tell your ma you were being disrespectful to a lady."

My face burned even hotter. Cooper was a cop. He didn't need to apologize. "That's okay, Harvey. It's no big deal. It's really not my business."

"Shut up, Violet," Harvey said.

I blinked. "Talk about rude."

"Fine." Cooper picked up the bits of lettuce from the table and dropped them on his plate. "I'm sorry, Violet."

"That's better. Now answer her question about your plans for my cemetery problem."

Cooper nailed Harvey with a glare but obliged his uncle. "I'll probably head out there and take a look around again, see if we missed any evidence."

"You want to use Bessie?" Harvey had named his favorite 12-gauge shotgun after a cow.

Cooper closed his eyes in a silent sigh. "I'll be packing my own firearm, thank you very much. And I'd prefer you kept Bessie in the closet a little more often."

"What good will she do in there? You're not keeping score very well, son. The boogeyman isn't hiding in the closet any more. He's out behind the barn."

Scooping up another forkful of salad, Cooper eyed me, his nostrils flared. "Can we talk about my house now, please?"

"Not until you tell Violet what you told me about that hand you found up on Mount Roosevelt."

Cooper cursed under his breath and lowered his fork.

"You probably told her everything already."

"Not her. Not everything."

"I heard about the hand," I confirmed. "But only that you found one. I hadn't heard anything more about the foot."

"We're still waiting for lab results on the foot."

Harvey snorted. "You need to find another lab. The guy at this one is sleeping on the job."

Chewing on that, along with his salad, Cooper waited until he swallowed to speak. "We think the hand and foot belong to the same guy, but we have to wait until the lab confirms it."

"Is there another serial killer at large?" I asked.

Cooper met my eyes. "I'm sorry you had to go through what you did, Violet. And that I didn't figure out Hessler was behind those missing girls sooner, before you were compromised."

Compromised? That must be the polite cop term for sautéed in lighter fluid and fricasseed.

His apology caught me by surprise. I sat back, stricken shy. "That's uh ... okay. I mean, it's no big ... it's fine. Thanks. What doesn't kill you makes you stronger, right?" Or maybe that was *who* doesn't kill you. I grabbed my Diet Coke and sucked down a few mouthfuls, wanting to drown my tongue before it said something else incredibly obtuse.

"I told you she was no shrinking Violet."

Maybe not shrinking, but definitely shrieking. Especially when I was staring death in the face, as I was last night in my dreams during yet another 3-D rehash of the whole horrific circus.

Cooper's eyes were beginning to burn holes in my head. "I meant to tell you that we figured out Hessler was calling you from Spearfish when he said he was in San Francisco."

So Wolfgang had lied about that, too. No surprise there.

Cooper continued, "I don't know if what we're dealing

with here is another serial killer, Violet. Or if it's just a plain old murderer suffering from a lack of attention from his mommy."

"Or *her* mommy," I added, equal rights and all.

"Or *her*." Cooper sat back to let the waitress slide a plate full of French fries and a grilled cheese sandwich in front of Harvey. My stomach growled at the bouquet of fried butter and cheese.

After the waitress unloaded Cooper's and my plates and left us again, the detective picked up a fry and bit it in half. "Now, can we please talk about my goddamned house?"

"No," Harvey said through a mouth full of grilled cheese. "I want to hear about Violet's date yesterday with the Carharts." His pale blue eyes locked onto mine.

"There's nothing to tell." I stuffed a handful of fries in my mouth.

"Which Carharts are we talking about?" Cooper asked.

"Wanda Carhart." Harvey stopped chewing, his eyes narrowed on me. "Your nose is twitchin'."

"So what?" I rubbed it. "It itches."

"You're hiding something." He pointed his fork at me. "What happened at the Carharts' place?"

"Nothing happened."

"Bullshit."

"We had a nice chat."

"Hogwash."

"What? They showed me their house."

"And?"

"And it's a beautiful house."

Cooper watched us as if this was match point in a ping-pong game. "Wanda Carhart's house?"

"Damn it, woman!"

"What?"

"You're gonna sell it, aren't you?"

I gulped more Diet Coke, avoiding Harvey's squint.

"What's wrong with her selling the Carhart house?" Cooper asked.

"Did you get kicked in the head by a mule, son?"

"It's a beautiful house," I repeated.

"With blood all over it."

"The blood has been cleaned up," Cooper said.

I could confirm that. "The place will sell within a month," I told Harvey. "The Carharts are motivated sellers. *Very* motivated."

Harvey grunted and took a huge bite from his sandwich, grumbling as he chewed.

Cooper on the other hand was watching me with his head cocked to the side. "I didn't realize Wanda was so gung-ho to get out of town."

"Not so much Wanda." She hadn't said more than five words to me yet. "But Millie seems very excited about selling."

"Hmmm." Cooper picked up his pickle, his face still thoughtful. Something in the crook of his lips made me rush to the Carharts' defense.

"Can you blame them for wanting to leave?"

He shrugged and crunched on the pickle.

"That house has bad juju," Harvey mumbled through his cheese.

"Jeez, Harvey." I rolled my eyes. "Next you're going to tell me it's haunted."

"Damned tootin'," Harvey said.

"Not exactly," Cooper corrected. "Although there are rumors."

Rumors, shmoomers. This town overflowed with all varieties of tall tales. "What, then?" I wiped my mouth, ready to be done talking about the Carharts. "Possessed?"

"It's got bad luck." Harvey shook his head. "You're gonna get yourself into trouble again. Doc's gonna be pissed."

"Leave him out of it, Harvey." I turned to his nephew. "Cooper, please explain to your crazy uncle that one incident in the house doesn't mean the place should be razed and bulldozed."

"That's not the only incident," Cooper said.

I blinked. "It's not? What are you saying?"

"That house has a history."

"A history of what?"

"Murder."

Chapter Five

The rest of lunch was filled with Realtor talk about Detective 007's selling and buying needs, interspersed with Harvey's growls and grumbles about my always going off half-cocked. I did my best to listen to one and ignore the other over the ebb and flow of leather-clad biker patrons.

When lunch ended, I had an appointment to keep, so I removed Harvey's rat-terrier teeth from my ass and made Cooper promise to call me and set up a time to pay his house a visit. As I scooted on up the road to Lead, I could see Harvey in my rearview mirror, sending me on my way with a pointed-finger warning.

The Carhart's house perched in all its lovely splendor on the edge of the man-made canyon. Two lanky boys on ladders scraped paint off the front of it. They stopped working to watch me approach the porch, their up-to-no-good grins wide. Had they heard the rumor about me? I couldn't be that notorious, could I?

"Hey, aren't you Spooky Parker, the ghost Realtor?" the ganglier of the two asked from the top of his ladder.

The other snickered and stared.

I guess they'd heard. I shoved them both off their ladders ... in my diabolical dreams. In reality, I ignored them and knocked on the front door. Millie answered before I finished with my fourth rap. Her frizzy hair framed her owl eyes; her black cardigan, matching her wool skirt.

Seriously, did this woman have any warm blood flowing through her veins? It hovered near ninety degrees today with blue skies and sunshine all around town. The top of my head had been baked twice already.

"Hi, Millie. I'm here to—"

"Hurry, before the flies get in." She grabbed my arm and yanked me over the threshold into the ten-degrees cooler house.

I was unaware that we had such a big fly problem in the Hills. She slammed the door behind me, throwing all three deadbolts. Wanda waited just inside the kitchen archway, her red gingham replaced with cornflower blue today. She shrank into the shadows when I smiled at her. All seemed par for the course here in Murderville, USA.

"Do you have the listing agreement?" Millie asked, ushering me into the sitting room. The thick velvet curtains were drawn, turning afternoon into early evening.

"It's in my bag." I took a seat on the soft leather sofa.

The house still smelled of vanilla, making me crave Aunt Zoe's homemade vanilla wafers. Spirited Mexican music trickled down the stairwell. One or both women seemed to have some kind of a hankering for a fiesta.

As I pulled the listing agreement and a pen from my tote, I glanced over at the sideboard, looking for the picture of the happy couple, and did a double-take. The picture frame remained, but half of the picture was missing—the Carhart oaf half. The raven-haired beauty still sat in the frame.

I turned away, peeking at Millie and Wanda under my lashes to see if they'd observed me gawking, but both seemed distracted. Millie watched the door, chewing on her nails; Wanda stared at something over in the corner, just as she had the last time I'd visited.

Smoothing out the listing agreement, I decided to hurry up and procure Wanda's signature and get the hell out of Dodge. There was something about those two women that made me feel like I was walking around in a tilted room with the furniture stuck to the ceiling.

"Okay, Wanda," I addressed the silent partner, since her name was on the deed. "Read through this while I'm here and let me know if you have any questions. I've included the increased percentage rate we agreed to during my last visit." I held out the listing agreement for Wanda, but Millie snatched it from my hand.

"I'll read it." Millie scanned the document. Wanda spared her daughter a glance, then focused back on the corner, her lips tight.

There was no easy way to do it, but I had to ask, "Millie, is your mother able to sign the listing agreement?"

Millie didn't look up. "What do you mean?"

"Is she of sound body and ..." I shifted, smoothed an invisible wrinkle on my pink paisley skirt, "mind?"

"Uh-huh."

Well, that had less impact than I'd figured. "So you don't have a power of attorney?"

Her owl glasses remained glued to the listing agreement. "She wouldn't sign one."

Hmm. Wanda wasn't quite as "gone" as she appeared. Interesting. Could have fooled me.

"This seems right to me." Millie placed the listing agreement on Wanda's lap. "Sign it, Mother."

The front doorknob rattled, then the deadbolts clicked, one by one.

"Lila," Millie whispered and jumped to her feet as the door swung wide.

Catcalls and whistles followed a dark-haired beauty in through the front door—the same beauty whose picture sat solo on the sideboard.

Smiling like the happiest girl in the whole USA, Junior Carhart's fiancée shut the door and leaned against it. Her smile clouded over and her eyes narrowed when she noticed me. "Who are you?"

I stood and faced the woman who'd wanted the Carhart funerals taped. My hackles rose right off. She was too damned gorgeous, without a single flaw. Call me a jealous bitch, but I wanted to rub poison ivy on her porcelain skin and bury wads of gum in those thick, wavy black locks. Those Liz Taylor eyes made my lip want to curl. "I'm the Carharts' Realtor."

Something brushed my arm. I looked over to find Wanda standing next to me, shoulder to shoulder, facing off against the fiancée.

"Oh, right." The beauty's smile returned, brighter now. Extra bright. I didn't trust it. She pushed away from the door, strolling toward me. "You're the one who specializes in selling haunted houses." Her belittling tone set me even more on edge.

"No." I almost lost the battle to retract my claws in a sudden surge of hostility. "I specialize in selling houses. Period."

She was too tall, towering a good six inches over me. Like a long-legged spider in a very mini light blue cheerleader-type skirt. Her red camisole hugged her small, super pert breasts. I wanted to hang Christmas tree ornaments from them.

"Millie," she said without breaking eye contact with me, "go get our little Realtor friend a drink, would you?"

Millie scurried off, as ordered.

"I'm Lila Beaumont, by the way." She didn't hold out her hand.

"Violet Parker." I didn't hold out mine, either.

"I know." She turned to Wanda, her gaze hardening. "Wanda, dear, go help Millie in the kitchen. I'd like a word with our new friend without you lurking about."

When Wanda didn't move, Lila snarled, "Now!"

With a squeak and a jump, Wanda hot-footed it out of there.

My dislike for Lila was growing at record speed. Somebody should've called Guinness; I was close to making the list.

I waited until Wanda was out of earshot. "What do you need to tell me that the owner of the house can't hear?"

"Bold. I like that in a woman." Lila crossed her arms, her teeth showing. They looked sharp. Seriously. I could have sworn her canines were extra pointed, like little daggers. Did she file them?

"What did you want to talk to me about?" I wanted to get this showdown over with and be on my merry way.

"It's imperative that you do your best to sell this house as soon as possible."

I wanted that as much as she did. But I didn't like being told what to do, especially by Miss Lila Beaumont.

I decided not to mince words, since she wasn't my client. "Exactly what business of yours is it if this house sells or not?"

"I have Millie and Wanda's best interests at heart, of course."

Right. Their best interests. Sure. I had to wonder if she would get a piece of the pie when the house sold. She had to have some other motivation. Why else would she still be sticking around half a year after her fiancé's death? It couldn't be Wanda and Millie's sparkling personalities.

I crossed my arms. "As I told Wanda and Millie yesterday when I agreed to sell the house, I will do my best to find them a buyer. But the market is slow, so there are no guarantees."

"Time is of the essence," Lila said.

So she had already insinuated. "For you or them?"

Her eyes turned frosty, her matching smile sending chills down my back. "Just do your job and sell the damned house."

Millie came from the kitchen holding a glass of water

and the signed listing agreement. Wanda followed, as usual.

"Never mind with that," Lila told Millie. "Miss Parker was just leaving, weren't you?"

I grabbed my tote. "Sure, but I want to talk to Wanda first." When nobody moved, I added, "Alone."

Millie turned to Lila, as if to get her approval. Lila continued to nail me with that maniacal smile, daggers showing. "Fine. Come, Millie." She headed toward the stairs, pausing on the first step to say, "Let yourself out when you're finished, Miss Parker. We'll be seeing you again soon, I hope."

Millie tramped up the stairs after her.

I moved to where Wanda stood next to the sofa. "Wanda?"

For a handful of seconds, I thought she wasn't going to acknowledge me. Then her eyes met mine.

"I need one more signature from you on this listing agreement." Which was true, luckily for me. Since I hadn't witnessed her signing it, I wanted to make sure Millie hadn't forged her signature. I fished a pen from my bag and held it toward her.

I heard rustling coming from the stairwell, so I lowered my voice. "Just sign right here on this line."

She took the pen, flattened the listing agreement on a side table, and signed without hesitation. The signature matched the other one. No foul play there.

Taking the pen and paper from her, I tri-folded the listing agreement. "Do you really want to sell your house, Wanda?"

She nodded once.

"Are you sure?"

Another nod.

"Why?"

She frowned and looked toward her favorite corner, but said nothing. I counted to ten, waiting, then stuffed the listing agreement in my tote. Officially, I had everything I needed for a legitimate deal. But something about this whole setup smelled sour.

Wanda wasn't going to answer. I hoisted my tote over my shoulder. "Thank you, Wanda, for choosing Calamity Jane to represent you in this business matter. I'll be in touch."

As I turned to leave, I heard a murmur come from her. I looked back at her. "What did you say?"

She mouthed something that I didn't catch. Miming was not my specialty. I always lost at charades.

I stepped closer. "Sorry, what?"

Her gaze locked onto mine, her eyes wide, frightened. My heart giddy-upped in response.

"This house," she whispered.

"What about it?"

"It's haunted."

* * *

The Deadwood library specialized in Black Hills legend and lore. It had a South Dakota room dedicated to that very subject, filled with all sorts of books, videos, and microfilm reels—which I was getting pretty handy at viewing in spite of my inability to speak *technologese*.

The room also had a computer with a list of links to some of the best historical websites on the World Wide Web. As I sat at this computer minding my own beeswax, searching for information on the Carhart house, Doc came ramming in. The door rattled in its frame when he closed it.

He stared me down, his jaw clenched along with the rest of his body. A five-o'clock shadow shaded the slight cleft in his chin and added a sexy flavor of ruggedness to his rigid demeanor. "You promised you wouldn't sell it."

"You didn't make me cross my heart." Harvey must

have been whispering sweet-and-sour nothings again, the big-mouth. "It's nice to see you, too, by the way."

It was, in spite of his nostril-flaring resemblance to a bull. A black T-shirt and blue jeans molded to his torso, making me want to do the same.

"Violet." His tone warned.

I didn't feel like being chewed on any more today, especially after Wanda's the-sky-is-falling disclosure. I turned my focus back to the website I'd been perusing before Doc's interruption. "I guess you should have sealed that promise with a kiss."

He moved like a hot breeze, stealthy, breathing in my ear before I even realized he'd left the doorway. "There's always that temptation with you."

The subtle scent of his woodsy cologne kicked my pulse into pitter-patter mode. "What are you doing here, Doc?"

If this were going to be another tease and leave session, I'd like to know before my engine really got to choo-chooing. I turned and faced him. "Are you here to dig through some more death registry names? Or were you just passing by, saw my Bronco, and decided to come in and start poking at me for some Thursday afternoon fun?"

He poked me, just above my left breast.

"Hey!" I rubbed the spot. "That's just a saying."

"You're tense."

"You're not supposed to really poke me."

"Why are you tense?" He looked at the computer screen. "And why are you reading about"—he leaned forward, his eyes scanning the screen, and read aloud my search criteria—"'murders in Lead, South Dakota'?"

"No reason." I avoided his prying eyes. "Just killing time before my next appointment." Which was twenty hours from now.

He growled deep in his throat. "You are such a lousy liar."

"I'll keep practicing."

"The Carhart murders were recent, but you're looking further back."

"Stop playing Sherlock."

"What happened today?"

How detailed a report did he want? "I woke up." And checked my cell phone to see if you'd called, but you hadn't.

"Then what?"

"Went to work." Checked my cell phone, still no call.

"Violet."

"What? Then I met Harvey and Cooper for lunch." *No call, no message, nada.*

"Harvey told me that part. What happened next?"

"I paid a visit to the Carharts and got Wanda's signature." Where I learned that Wanda Carhart thought she was being visited by Casper and his wispy pals. But I sure wasn't telling Doc the last bit.

"And then you came here?" Doc prodded, putting some space between us.

Not quite. First, I drove twenty-five miles to the Wyoming border where I cursed, spit, screamed and jumped up and down in the oven-hot air for ten minutes straight and scared a family of prairie dogs deep into their burrows. "Then I came here."

"So what aren't you telling me?"

Too much for one sitting. "It's a beautiful house." I still stood by that fact. "It'll sell quickly."

At least I hoped it would, because if word got out to the tourist crowd that it was supposedly haunted, I was going to have to turn in my Calamity Jane business cards and start participating in some of those paid medical research studies. I heard the malaria ones promised big bucks.

"Why are you being so evasive?" he asked.

"I've been taking notes from you."

His grin reached the corners of his eyes. "Touché."

"That was pretty good, huh?"

"Don't get cocky." He leaned against the long table holding down the center of the room. "What are you searching for?"

A long-term relationship with a nice, non-serial-killer man. Was that too much to ask? Probably. Playing another card from Doc's hand, I changed the subject. "Where did you run off to yesterday?"

"I had an appointment."

"I thought you cancelled the appointment you had in order to be at the house inspection with me."

"This was another appointment."

"Scheduled at the same time? Now who's the rotten liar?"

"I'll tell you my secret if you tell me yours."

I shook my head. "I prefer to take the 'dare' option."

"You really are getting good at this."

I was on a freaking roll. "What can I say? I'm taking lessons from a master."

One eyebrow lifted, his dark eyes challenging now. "Okay, dare it is."

I waited, my body tense for a whole different reason. Like a teenage girl, I wished and hoped for a dare involving my lips on his. I hadn't tasted the erotic blend of sugar and spice that was Doc for too long.

"I dare you to tell me the truth."

"Oh, come on." My balloon deflated. "That's cheating." I turned back to the computer and reached for the mouse. "And boring, too."

His hands gripped my shoulders, his palms warm through my thin cotton shirt. "Boring, huh?"

"What are you doing, Doc?"

"Not being boring." He leaned over and murmured, "Nice skirt. Shows off your knees."

I could hardly hear him. My shoulder muscles were

scrunched high and tight, blocking all blood flow to my ears.

"Relax, Violet." He squeezed and then released, massaging, turning me into Play-Doh. "You're so tight."

"Doc, stop." I couldn't handle casual caresses from him. It was either touch me all over or keep a six-foot field of play open between us.

"Just relax and enjoy it." He continued to work on my shoulders. My body clamored for so much more, starved for everything Doc. "I doubt you get this kind of attention very often."

Not without paying for it. I started sweating between my toes. "Doc." *Don't stop!* "Stop."

His hands moved to the outer edges of my shoulders, kneading my upper arms.

Oh, sweet Jesus! I let my head loll back, resting on the seatback, and peeked up at him. Much more of this and I'd risk having my library card permanently revoked for lewd behavior. "Doc, I can't handle this."

His eyes locked onto mine, his hands stopped. "Neither can I. Maybe it's for the best to end it now."

Wait. His tone was all wrong. "Are we talking about the same thing?"

"I think so."

"What are we going to do about it?"

"Stick to friendship."

I lunged forward, pulling free from his grip. "Hold on a second. I was talking about sex, right now." As in not having it in the library.

"So am I."

"No, you're talking about us and sex later."

"Or not."

Wow, if that wasn't just a cooler of ice-filled Gatorade poured down my underwear. "This is about that control issue of yours, isn't it?"

"Violet." He leaned on the edge of the table again and rubbed his jaw, the stubble rasping under his palm. "Whether or not *you* believe it, I have the ability to detect ghosts. And the reason I came to this town was to refine it. To control it, instead of it controlling me."

He looked at me as if that should explain everything.

It didn't. "What does that have to do with you and me?"

"You mess with my head."

"You say that as if I'm Pandora, box in hand."

"No, more like a Siren."

"I'm not trying to lure you anywhere." Except to bed. And maybe the back stairwell of his new house. Possibly the kitchen counter. Not that I'd put much thought into this.

"Probably not on purpose," he crossed his arms. "But you're a distraction."

"Damn." That one had a kick to it—to the gut. "You sure know how to sweet talk a girl."

His frown deepened, lining his cheeks now, too. "When you're around, I lose my focus. I can't concentrate on what I need to."

"Which is this elusive control you're so determined to gain?"

"Exactly. I used to deny this shit in my head, fight it. At my lowest point, I tried to hide from it inside a bottle of Jack Daniels." He shook his head. "That didn't work. I realized I had to learn to control it, before it killed me."

My stomach churned, stirring with frustration and anger. "And I represent what? Chaos?"

He nodded. "You like to leap without looking first, like with this latest house. Right now, it's just too much for me to handle."

Fire crawled up my throat, making me want to fry him with Godzilla-like, atomic heat-ray breath. Chaos? A distraction? Too much to handle? I didn't ask for this *thing* going on between us. I didn't enjoy the anxiety that came with it. And I sure as hell didn't like being made to feel like a high-maintenance hassle.

"Let me explain something to you, Mr. Nyce." I closed the distance between us, grabbed his hand, and placed it just above my left breast. "This is my heart. It's cast-iron tough. It doesn't fall in love on a whim—as a matter of fact, it's never even been in love—and it sure as hell doesn't need a man to make it feel whole. But it does beat loud and strong for my two children, for whom I am responsible both physically and financially."

"Violet, don't..." His brows drawn, he tried to pull his hand away, but I wouldn't let go.

"And while I made a promise to you that I would not sell the Carhart house, I broke that promise because those two children have needs, which are my job to fulfill. I don't expect you to understand my willingness to take this risk because you are only responsible for yourself, and as you just made crystal clear, that's all you can handle."

I let go of his hand, snatched up my purse, and backed toward the door. "Now, since you have explained how I am a burden to you—"

He reached toward me. "Violet, that's not what I said."

"—this is as much of the 'truth' about my reasons for being in this room today as you need to know."

Before I gave in to my rage and strung him up by his testicles, I hightailed my rejected ass out of the building.

Chapter Six

Friday, August 3rd

Bighorn Billy's really needed to change its breakfast menu. This morning, I started with black coffee and planned to order grapefruit. Both matched my mood—a little bitter and sour as hell.

Charlie Daniels and his crew blasted from the overhead speakers, singing about the devil heading down to Georgia. They were wrong. The devil was here in Deadwood, sniffing out ghosts, sexing me up, kicking me to the curb. And *now* he was calling me repeatedly without leaving any messages when I refused to answer.

"Are you okay, Vi?" Mona frowned at me across the table as she stirred sugar into her coffee. Her pink cashmere summer sweater matched her hair scarf. "You look a tad ..."

"Bitchy," Ray finished from his seat on the bench next to her, his icy blue eyes challenging me. He really shouldn't poke the bear today. He could lose a limb, most likely his third leg.

Mona aimed a glare at Ray before turning back to me, her smile soft on her cheeks. "I was going to say frazzled. Did you have a rough night?"

"Sort of." Sailing a skiff through a hurricane would have been less wearing. Between tossing and turning about today's weekly brunch with my boss and coworkers—during which I'd have to fess up about taking on the Carhart place—and grinding my molars over Doc's control issues, I'd counted enough sheep to cover the surface area of Montana.

"Prostituting yourself for sales is a tough marketing scheme, Blondie. You have to learn to *swallow* your pride."

I wasn't in the mood to trade insults this morning. "Fuck off, Ray."

He tsk-tsked me. "Such language in front of your boss."

Shit! I looked over my shoulder to find the owner of Calamity Jane Realty frowning, her eyes shifting between Ray and me. "Sorry, Jane. Ray and I are just exchanging some friendly banter."

She shrugged and dropped onto the bench seat next to me. The fruity floral and vanilla scent of her favorite perfume temporarily blanketed the smell of fried food. "A deaf and blind sloth could sense the tension between you two." She held up her coffee cup for the hovering waitress to fill. "Love or hate, I don't care, so long as you both make sales. Just keep it hidden from the customers. If I catch either of you badmouthing the other in public, you're out the door."

Ray and I exchanged lip curls while Jane unloaded her briefcase's contents and Mona shot flirty glances at the table full of burly bikers next to us.

"On that note," Jane flipped open her well-used day-planner, "Let's start today's meeting with some more unpleasant truths."

I gulped, worrying that Jane had caught wind of my secret. Of course, the waitress decided to step up and take orders at that moment, prolonging my torment. I should have asked for a side of Maalox.

Finally, Jane picked up where she'd left off. "Our pipeline is down to a trickle. Our buyer-to-seller ratio is one-to-four at the moment. The economy is still bleak as a nuclear winter. And to top it all off, the Deadwood Historical Society has come out with a new list of rules for real estate agents."

All three of us groaned. The society's goals were generally benevolent and geared to the town's welfare, but its red tape was sometimes like the rest of Deadwood's history—legendary.

"So, now that you know the score, tell me how you plan to turn this month's numbers into pluses and put your name on our 'Sold' white board."

Jane's lust for bulletin boards and dry-erase markers was surpassed only by her love for to-do lists and detailed marketing plans. She was so left-brained that her right brain had given up the battle for control and settled for an unpaid intern position.

"Mona." Jane held her pen over her notepad. "You go first."

As Mona spewed out an elaborate scheme to lure fat-walleted tourists, that involved open houses filled with biker memorabilia and hosted by local celebrities, my anxieties cranked up the heat and spun me slowly over open flames. I broke out in a dew that would make many a spring morning jealous. I had no elaborate plans, no brilliant designs, no customer-snaring schemes. I specialized in reactive scrambling and desperation-fueled clambering.

Ray went next, explaining the several high-priced luncheons he'd planned with some of the area's wealthiest citizens. He finished his pitch with a fastball straight up the middle that incorporated gold-plated buyer "rewards" for those who signed a contract.

That left me, sitting in a pool of my own sweat.

"What about you, Violet?" Jane asked as the waitress set my grapefruit in front of me. "You're fresh out of school. What tricks did you learn that you can share?"

The only trick I knew involved a fake flower that squirted water. "Well, uh ..." I inspected my spoon for smudges. "I have one idea."

"Yes?" Jane prompted.

If only I had the power to stop time long enough to come up with something brilliant. "I'm going to sell Wanda Carhart's house," I blurted, my heart break-dancing.

Mona groaned.

Ray cursed me under his breath.

Jane's smile flat-lined. "You do know it's haunted."

I almost fell out of the booth. "Excuse me?"

"It's haunted."

"You're messing with me, right?"

"Have you ever known me to joke?"

No. Jane was made up of equal parts salt and earth. I glanced at Mona and Ray; they wore matching grim expressions. My grip slackened, the spoon clattered onto the table. "Define what you mean by 'haunted'."

Jane shrugged. "Paranormal activity."

I gaped at Mona, seeking reality.

"Whispy beings," Mona added, then sipped her coffee.

"Dead folks, Blondie," Ray said. "Or rather all the crazy shit they leave behind."

I pinched myself. My eyes watered in pain, but the time continuum rolled on while I sat there catching flies in my open mouth. Had Doc been whispering in their ears? Did they all really believe in this? Was there a hidden video camera focused on me?

"I take it you already have a signed listing agreement," Jane said, scribbling something in her notebook.

I nodded. My tongue seemed to have fallen out of my yawning jaw and rolled under the table.

"So what's your plan on how to unload the Carhart place?" Jane asked.

"Wait a second. Back up. You guys believe in ghosts?"

Ray looked bored. "Yes, Blondie. Can we move on?"

Mona mimed a "shush" and nudged her head toward the biker table. "We talked about this last month, remember?"

"No. When?"

"When I told you about Lilly Devine's place. You know, the prostitute who was murdered in her own bedroom by her john."

"You said it was rumored to be haunted, not that you believe you can play patty-cake with her ghost."

"Oh. I thought you understood that I was serious."

"No. I didn't." Now that I remembered, Doc did get a bit agitated about the basement when I was touring him through that place, insisting I not go down there. "If you guys are serious, why am I the one with the notorious ghost-chatting reputation?"

"We keep pretty quiet about it," Mona said.

Ray snorted. "We don't go signing listing agreements for well-known haunted houses, either."

Chills peppered my arms. I looked back to Jane, my rock, my foundation. "Jane? You really think the Carhart place is haunted?"

"Yes."

She hadn't even hesitated.

"Why? How? By whom?"

Sighing, she placed her pen on her day-planner and pushed her reading glasses to the top of her head. "The house next to the Carhart place was one of my first listings back when I was still a greenhorn. But I can remember that sale clear as vodka. The couple had lived there for all six decades of their marriage. They'd seen a lot change in Lead in their time and had all kinds of photos to prove it. They also had photos of the house next door, both of the living and not-so-living owners."

"They had pictures?"

"Several."

"What did the ghost look like?" It was probably just a glare on the lens, a haloed sparkle from a reflection. I'd seen stills on television shows about ghost hunters. Most of the ghosts looked the same, like Tinker Bell's glow.

"She had on a pale, high-collared dress stained dark with blood from where her neck had been slit open." Jane lowered her glasses back in place and picked up her pen. "Now, what's your game plan?"

* * *

I couldn't return to the office when I left Bighorn Billy's. No way. For one thing, I was still trying to pick my jaw up off the ground after learning my seemingly normal coworkers and boss all believed in ghosts. For another, if I returned to my desk, I'd be too busy sneaking shell-shocked peeks at each of them to get any work done. Most importantly, though, was that Doc might be waiting for me to show up, and I wasn't ready to look him in the eyes and pretend I could handle just being his friend.

Instead, I decided to head over to Jeff Wymonds' place and get a head start on prepping it for sale. It needed a lot of work just to get it out of an "OMG, run!" state and into the "Needs TLC" category. A couple extra hours of work on my part would do some good.

Jeff's truck was not in the dirt drive when I rolled up in a cloud of dust. I had a key to get into the house, but I hesitated, my brain still stumbling over my lunchtime pseudo-séance. I needed to touch base with reality—realign my chakras, as Natalie would say. Or was it rebalance? Thinking of Natalie, I dug out my cell phone and pulled up her number.

She answered on the third ring. "Howdy, pilgrim."

I smiled. "Natalie, how many times do I have to tell you that your John Wayne impersonation sounds like Mae West? You really must stop this blasphemy of the Duke."

"John Wayne." She sighed like a teenage girl daydreaming about a first kiss. "Six foot, four inches of rugged, sexy male flesh. Reminds me of Doc Nyce."

Oh, Jeez! Not that again. I had no stomach for this subject, so I changed it. "Natalie, do you believe in ghosts?"

"Sure, why not?"

She said it as if we were talking about bubble gum. "Seriously?"

"Yeah, I guess."

I squeezed the bridge of my nose. "You guess? What the hell kind of an answer is that?"

"What's wrong with you? Did you see one or something?"

"No." Apparently I was the only one who hadn't. "Have you?"

"I don't know."

"How can you not know?"

"I've had some iffy moments."

Iffy moments with a ghost? "Explain, please."

"Well, there was that night back in high school when a bunch of us sneaked into an old abandoned mill back in Rochford to smoke some weed and something shattered one of the windows."

"It was probably just a bat."

"And then in my mid-twenties, I was re-roofing an old home back in Galena, and when I went into the attic to check on something, this creepy old baby stroller rolled across the floor toward me."

"How far?"

"I don't know. Two or three inches."

"You probably just bumped it on the way past and didn't realize it. Or you made the floorboard bend enough to cause it to roll."

There was silence from the other end. Then: "Are you going to explain away all of my near-experiences? I thought this was my opinion you were asking for."

"Sorry. But I struggle with believing ghosts exist."

"Who's asking you to?"

I couldn't mention Doc's name. Not to her, not to anyone. I'd promised. "Nobody. It just came up at work this morning and got me thinking." I covered my nose so she wouldn't see it twitching, then remembered I was on the phone.

"I wonder what sex would be like with a ghost," Natalie said.

"You've seen too many movies."

"Maybe, but if you had the opportunity, would you?"

"It's physically impossible, Nat."

"You don't know that. There may be some kind of energy flow that could go between you and the ghost."

No way were we really talking about this while I sat in Jeff's drive, perspiring under the late-morning sunshine.

"I would do it in a flash," she said.

"You're a sex addict, I swear."

"It's not my fault Doc is playing hard to get. Oh! Did I tell you we're going out this weekend? Wish me luck."

No! My heart seized up. "What? You're going on a date?" *That rotten bastard!*

"Well, not officially. He's going to go through my taxes and files for the last few years to help me get things straightened out. He suggested we meet at his office, but I insisted we go off-site."

Okay, maybe he's not much of a bastard, but still ... "Lovely. You two have fun."

"I have a surprise for him," she said in an excited tone, obviously missing the snarl in mine. "Do you know if he likes chocolate?"

"Nope." We hadn't reached the gift-of-foods level in our relationship before he'd terminated it.

"Because I found a pair of these naughty edible chocolate—"

"I gotta go, Nat." I cut her off before I had a coronary

from jealousy spasms. "I'll call you later."

"Okay. Don't forget about your blind date tomor—"

I hung up on her and practically fell out of the Bronco in my rush to escape the images she'd put in my head of her and Doc entwined, let alone the reminder that I had to spend tomorrow evening with a Captain Kirk wannabe. At least, I hoped for Kirk and not a night spent sitting across from a Klingon.

Deep breaths didn't calm me down, nor did kicks to my front tire, so I gave up, grabbed my tote, and headed for the house. I needed hard work to get my mind off the whole Doc debacle. An hour or two of pine-scented cleaner fumes should burn off all the rough edges and make that horse pill easier to swallow. I hoped.

A couple of hours later, Jeff showed up with his daughter, Kelly, in tow. He skidded to a stop just inside the front door. "Violet Parker, what are you doing to my kitchen floor?"

I didn't raise my head. "Your grout is dirty."

"Is that my toothbrush?"

"I'll buy you a new pack of them."

"You're early." Something thunked on the counter.

Sitting back on my heels, I swiped my sweaty brow with my forearm and glanced up at him, only to do a double-take. "Wow. You look ..." *different!* "Nice."

Jeff rubbed his hand over his jaw. "I need a shave."

I gaped at him. When I'd first met Jeff Wymonds more than a month ago, I'd pegged him for the one who'd been kidnapping little girls around town, especially after I'd caught him tossing girls' clothing in a Dumpster. I'd come within a phone call of turning him into the cops.

Smelling of beer, sporting a scraggly beard and hair, and wearing a stained T-shirt, Jeff had looked one notch above roadkill. Then I learned his wife was dumping him for another woman and taking their baby son with her, leaving him to care for their troubled daughter and pick up the pieces alone. On top of that, she wanted the house—or at least her half of the money for it—so Jeff was on the verge of being homeless, too. Given all that, his lack of hygiene and fondness for alcohol made a little more sense.

But this man, mostly clean-shaven and with freshly trimmed dark blond hair, looked nothing like the monster who'd leered at me through a screen door on our first meeting. Not even remotely. Now I could see why Natalie had once told me Jeff "cleaned up nicely" and why she'd bebopped naked with him in his back seat during high school.

"Your hair looks good," I said, unable to pull my eyes away, my brain stuck in a Before-and-After loop.

"It's a little short." He raked his fingers through his spiky groomed hair. "I stopped at the barber on the way home."

"I like it."

"Enough to go out to dinner with me?"

That broke my stare. I shook my head. "You know my rule."

"Yeah, that whole you-don't-date-your-clients crap."

"Exactly." Except for Wolfgang Hessler, who'd tried to turn me into a shish kabob; and Doc, who'd ditched me after rocketing me to the moon and back.

Jeff took a six-pack of Diet Coke out of the grocery bag and offered me a can. "Your preference, right?"

It was still cold from the store. "Thanks."

"You should wear jeans and a T-shirt more often." He winked at me, cracking open a can for himself. "We need to get this house sold and my divorce finalized. A single girl like you won't last long around these parts."

I looked away, gulping down some cool soda to keep from having to respond to his comment. While I was happy Jeff was on the road to recovery after having his heart tromped by a herd of rhinos—especially since his daughter and mine seemed to be attached at the hip these days—I wasn't exactly thrilled to be the focus of his rebound. Although his being easier on the eyes made the idea a bit more palatable.

He opened the fridge and I noticed a total lack of beer. Had he trimmed that along with his hair? I eyed him from head to toe as he put away the groceries. He seemed thinner in his clean white T-shirt and faded Levis. "Did you lose weight?"

He nodded. "I stopped drinking."

"Because of Kelly?"

"Partly." He folded the grocery bag and stuffed it under the sink. "With Donna gone, I don't need to escape anymore."

Who was this guy? Nobody turned a life corner this fast, did he? He must be catching *Dr. Phil* reruns late at night.

Jeff caught me staring. A smile crept onto his cheeks, making him look even more handsome, younger. I could easily picture him as the hot quarterback on the high school football team with those broad shoulders and muscled arms. Addy's whining this morning about me just giving Jeff a chance as a "future father" candidate echoed in my head.

"Jeff, do you believe in ghosts?"

His smile widened into a grin. "Is that a serious question?" At my nod, he continued. "Hell, no. That ghost shit is good for only one thing."

"What's that?"

"Scaring women into my arms."

It had had the opposite effect on me so far, but I didn't correct him. Finally, a fellow realist. Maybe Addy was onto something with Jeff and me, and I'd just been too blinded by Doc's dark appeal to see it all this time.

Grin still warming his face, he swayed toward me.

"Violet Parker." His voice sounded growly, husky. "You sure look good in my kitchen. I bet you'd look even better barefoot and pregnant."

Zap! I snapped out of my Prince Charming fantasy. I didn't do kitchens—cooking or baking. Only eating. And I sure as hell didn't need any more babies to raise and support.

I changed my mind. Jeff and I were not peas in a pod, no matter how many pennies and eyelashes Addy went through wishing for it. We had a few things in common, and he looked mighty fine in a pair of jeans. But that wouldn't get me through a first date, let alone a year.

Jeff apparently couldn't read my body language and didn't notice that I'd flipped my Open sign to Closed. "Are you sure about that rule of yours?" he asked, reaching for me.

"Positive." I shoved his toothbrush into his hand and dodged past him. "We have cleaning to do, Mr. Wymonds."

He groaned. "Damn, you're sexy when you play hard to get."

"Lots of cleaning!" I headed for the bucket of bleach water I'd left sitting on the bathroom floor.

One scrubbed and prepped-for-painting bathroom later, Harvey showed up with my two munchkins in tow, per my phoned request. Supper was on Jeff: pizza. Harvey supplied dessert in the form of Neapolitan ice cream.

After we'd filled our gullets, the kids went outside to play in the warm evening air. That left Jeff, Harvey, and me alone at the dining-room table, with strawberry, vanilla, and chocolate ice cream still coating the back of my tongue.

"Do you know who Lila Beaumont is?" I asked Jeff. The leggy broad had been on my mind as I cleaned and tried to figure out how to unload the Carhart house ASAP. With Jeff looking for love in all the wrong places, she'd be right up his alley.

"Never heard of her."

I turned to Harvey. "What about you?"

He shook his head. "Should I?"

Lila must not have been from this area, or one of these two guys would know her aunt or sister or second cousin. So, from under which rock had she emerged, and how had she gotten mixed up with Junior Carhart? "She was engaged to Millie Carhart's brother."

"Oh." Harvey smirked. "She's that dark-haired looker who was gushin' with fake tears and phony sobs at the funeral."

"Bingo."

"Why?" Harvey scooped up some more ice cream. "What about her?"

"I met her yesterday. She showed up at the Carhart house."

Jeff leaned forward. "What were you doing there?"

"She signed on to sell the place," Harvey explained, a definite grumble in his tone.

"No shit?" Jeff shook his head. "Violet Parker, you have an impressive set of balls on you."

"Because of the multiple murders there?" He couldn't mean because of its "haunted" reputation, since Jeff didn't believe in ghosts.

"Well, that, too." Jeff shut the pizza box and stacked it on top of the other one. "I was just thinking about the Open Cut next to it. Who'd want that just a spit in the wind away from their front door?"

"I sure wouldn't," mumbled Harvey through a mouthful of ice cream.

"It's a beautiful house."

"Yeah, but that's one big-ass hole." Jeff's cell phone rang. He looked at the display screen, his eyes narrowing. "Speaking of big assholes ..." He pushed to his feet, the phone held to his ear. "What do you want, Donna?"

Nonstop nattering came through the line loud enough for me to hear. Jeff's jaw tightened. He turned and stomped through the living room and down the hall, slamming his bedroom door behind him. Now what did she want? His other testicle?

"Jeff keeps staring at your butt," Harvey said, yanking my attention back to the dining room.

I stood and picked up the litter of paper plates. "Thanks for that inside information."

"I figured you should know."

"Now I do."

"Doc stares, too, but not at your butt as much. He's more of a breast man."

The lack of filter on Harvey's mouth never ceased to amaze me. "I don't want to talk about Doc," I said and left the room.

Harvey followed me into the kitchen. "He sure wants to talk about you lately. Or talk to you, anyway." He set the cups he'd carried into the sink. "He called me today, looking for you."

I shied away from eye contact, but I could feel Harvey watching me. "Did he?" I tried to sound nonchalant, as though my heart wasn't doing somersaults about Doc wanting me, even if it was just to talk.

"Yep. He says you're avoiding him."

"Really? I wonder where he got that idea." No sixth sense needed to pick up on the vibes I blasted his way.

"He said he left a message for you at work."

"I haven't been in the office all day."

"And on your cell phone."

"With all the cleaning I've been doing, I haven't had a chance to check my messages yet."

Harvey scoffed. "Bullshit. You're a Realtor and a mother. That cell phone is practically attached to you."

I cut Harvey off at the pass. "I said I don't want to talk

about Doc, Harvey."

"What happened between you two?"

"Did you hear what I just said?"

"Sure, I'm not deaf. What happened?"

"I'm beginning to understand why your harem is so big. You just don't give up, do you?"

"Nope. What happened?"

"We had a disagreement."

"A lovers' spat?"

I didn't dignify that with a response, mostly because I was afraid he'd see through me and know Doc and I had sex. Harvey's hearing may have been fading, but his bird-dog nose didn't miss a single scent. If he got hold of that juicy little tidbit, I'd be up shit creek during spring runoff when having a paddle didn't matter. I tried to distract the old buzzard. "Did Cooper find any more clues today about the *whangdoodle* problem back in your cemetery?"

"One of the shovels from my tool shed is missing." Harvey crossed his arms over his chest, his eyes unwavering. I felt like bacteria in a Petri dish. "Is that all you're going to tell me about Doc and you?"

"There is no 'Doc and me'." Not now, not ever, per Doc.

He snorted. "Somebody oughta tell him that."

My heart picked up speed. "Why? What else did he say?"

"Ha! I knew it. You can't hide things from this old man. Now tell me the truth. What happened?"

I sighed. "He said I'm too distracting."

"You are."

"Gee, thanks."

"But that's a good thing." Harvey grinned wide, his gold teeth gleaming under the kitchen lights. "Doc just doesn't realize it yet."

Harvey's pep talk wasn't cheering me up. "Yeah. Sure."

"Violet, nobody wants a boring woman. Where's the fun in that? Especially in the sack."

"Where do you want to go for dinner next week?" Maybe I could distract him with food.

"Hold the wagon!" He leaned in, his voice lowering. "Have you two already been in the sack?"

My cheeks warmed before I could stop them. Not that I could have. "What? I ... no ... that's none of your business."

"Well, I'll be a digger to China. You have."

Damn it! My lips pinched tight. "End of discussion. Subject closed. Forever!"

He followed me out onto the front porch. "Man, this is more fun than watching an *I Love Lucy* marathon."

God, I was so screwed. I sank down on the first step and buried my face in my palms. "Harvey, you have to promise me you won't say anything about this to anyone. I mean it. Got it? If you do, I'll—"

"Okay, okay. My lips are sealed." His knees creaked and popped as he sank down onto the step next to me. "So, how long have you two been playing hide the pepper?"

I groaned at all the entertainment at my expense that Harvey would probably extract from this. "I can't emphasize how much I *really* don't want to talk about this right now."

"Fine. What do you want to talk about, then?"

I searched for a safe subject. "Ghosts."

"What about them?"

"Do you believe in them?"

"Hell, yes."

What? I dropped my hands and frowned at him. Not Harvey, too. "What makes you so damned certain?"

This time, his shit-eating grin was absent. "I live with one."

Chapter Seven

Saturday, August 4th

Dawn awoke. Unfortunately, I didn't and overslept. I made a frenzied dash through the house but stopped when I realized it was silent, empty. Where was everyone? Had I slipped into a parallel dimension? Then I remembered Aunt Zoe's planned day trip to Custer State Park with the kids and zipped out the door with my mouth stuffed full of leftover pizza.

I called Natalie on the way to Calamity Jane's, rolling into the parking lot as her voicemail told me to leave a message.

"Hey, Nat, I need you to get a hold of my date tonight and cancel. I can't make it." I hung up quickly, guilt heavy in my gut as I parked in my spot between Mona's and Ray's SUVs and killed the engine. I hated to welch on Nat like this, but now was just not a good time for me to consume calories with a stranger. Not with Doc sharing the same longitude and latitude with me. The memories of his skin were too fresh.

Speaking of Doc, his black '69 Chevy Camaro was nowhere to be seen, thank God. I wasn't ready to face him yet. First of all, I had pepperoni breath; second, there was still the matter of that chip on my shoulder.

While my cell phone had remained stubbornly quiet last night no matter how many times I willed it to ring, I doubted he'd given up. At least I hoped not, dang it.

I popped a stick of mint gum into my mouth as I

crossed the hot parking lot. Mona's jasmine scent greeted me at the back door. The sound of strange voices lured me past the closed bathroom door and Jane's empty office and into the front room.

"Are you sure you wouldn't like some coffee while you wait?" Mona asked. As I entered, she added, "Here she is."

Smiling through my surprise at seeing a leather-clad biker couple waiting for me first thing today, I dropped my purse on my desk and held out a hand. "Hello, I'm Violet Parker. How can I help you?"

They stood and shook my hand in turn, introducing themselves as Zeke and Zelda Britton. Their black leather chaps and vests creaked as they sank back into the chairs opposite my desk.

I liked Zelda instantly because of the daisy-covered bandana wrapped around her auburn hair. Any woman who wore my favorite flowers with a pair of chaps won my vote. Her perky smile and friendly green eyes didn't hurt, either.

They both appeared to be in their mid-forties, Zeke maybe nearing his early fifties. Zelda couldn't weigh much more than my right leg and arm put together. Zeke, on the other hand, looked like a refrigerator draped with cowhide. The buzzing fluorescents overhead glared off his shaven head.

Zelda crossed her legs and said, "We're considering buying a house in the area. The owner of the glass gallery on Main Street overheard us talking about our plans and recommended you."

That would be Aunt Zoe, taking care of me yet again. Sweet! Walk-in buyers were as plentiful as Dodo-bird soup these days. "A place in town or a house with some acreage?"

"Something in town, definitely," Zelda answered. "Something old. Really old."

That was a bit of an odd request. Typically, I started by

focusing on bedrooms and baths, not the number of years sitting on a foundation. But if old is what they wanted, the Black Hills could provide. "Any particular town? Deadwood? Lead? Central City? Spearfish?"

"Spearfish is too far away." Zelda was still running the show. Zeke watched his wife, his expression adoring, as she said, "Deadwood or Lead, preferably."

That left Jeff Wymonds' place out, since it was only about fifty years old and in Central City. Harvey's ranch in the country was out, too, even if it fit the "old" bill. I hadn't seen Cooper's home yet, so that would be a no-go as well, at least for today. Precluding another agent's listing, that left the Carhart house. I wondered if Zeke or Zelda had an issue with ghost rumors.

"Were you interested in seeing something today?"

"Today, definitely. And tomorrow, too. After that, we'll have to play it by ear because of the rally."

This year's Sturgis Motorcycle Rally officially kicked off two days from now, on Monday. Festivities included a motorcycle challenge during the day and some yesteryear heavy metal band playing out at the Buffalo Chip campground in the evening. After that, according to Zoe, the shirtless shenanigans would really kick into high gear. I was expecting to have a birds-and-bees discussion with my kids by midweek.

"I have one house ready to show right now," I fingered through my purse, searching for my Day-Timer and the Carharts' phone number. I heard the front door open as I flipped open the planner. "I just need to make a phone—"

I looked up and locked eyes with Doc, who stood just inside the threshold, a gunslinger glare on his face. He pointed at me and crooked his finger. The set of his jaw left no room for argument.

"Call." My heart hopped into my ears and pounded out a wicked drum solo.

"That's no problem," Zelda's voice sounded tinny, far away. "We can wait. Right, Zeke?"

I stood, not waiting for Zeke's reply. "I'll be right back."

Grabbing my cell phone and the planner, I motioned for Doc to follow me outside.

The mid-morning heat filled the air with tar-scented waves. I stopped next door, in the shade of the awning in front of Doc's office, and braced myself mentally for battle.

"You need to talk to me?" I tried to sound professional. All business, no naked flesh.

He kept a respectable distance between us, but his dark stare had me pinned against his front window. "You're ignoring my calls."

"I've been busy."

"Not that busy."

"I had a house to clean."

"Jeff Wymonds?"

"Harvey told you."

"He mentioned it in passing."

The old buzzard had better not have mentioned anything else. I glanced into Doc's glass front door and did a double-take at the sight of a pair of suitcases sitting on the floor next to his desk. Was he leaving town again? "What's with the suitcases?"

"Nothing." He moved between me and the door, blocking my view.

He answered too quickly for it to be "nothing." I tried to see around him, but he dodged and weaved along with me. "Why are they sitting in your office?"

"Because they're a pair."

Okay, now he was just toying with me. I didn't have time for games. I leveled a glare at him. "I have customers waiting. What do you need to talk to me about?"

"I have something you want."

Boy, was that ever a loaded statement. "I'll be the judge of that."

The door to Calamity Jane's opened and Mona popped her head out. "Vi," she whispered loudly, "you'd better hurry up. Ray's out of the bathroom and schmoozing your potential clients."

I cursed Ray twelve ways from Sunday under my breath. He had a history of stealing my clients. "I gotta go," I told Doc and followed after Mona.

Doc caught my hand and held me. "Come see me when they're gone."

"Sure," I lied, straight-faced, knowing I would be gone for most of the day showing houses to Zeke and Zelda. I pulled free of his grip and scuttled inside Calamity Jane's.

The sight of Ray sitting behind my desk, all smarmy and full of gush, made me want to rip the stuffing out of a teddy bear and cram it down his throat. He grinned at me as I approached, his eyes challenging me.

"All right, are you two ready?" I asked the Brittons. "I have a place in Lead to show you."

"Yes!" Zelda practically leaped out of her seat, jittery with obvious excitement.

That gave me pause. Talk about a motivated buyer. Maybe I'd be able to buy Addy's glasses with cash instead of maxing out my credit card after all. "Great." I resisted the urge to thumb my nose at Ray. "I can drive us, or you two can follow me."

"We'll follow on the bike," Zeke said in a deep, gravelly voice that matched his bulk. "We're parked in back."

"Perfect." I'd call the Carharts on the way there and alert them of pending visitors. That'd give them a ten-minute window to prepare. "Follow me, then." I snatched up my notebook of recent MLS listings, grabbed my purse, and led the way out the back door.

Two shakes later, I pulled into the Carharts' drive, and

Zeke and Zelda rumbled to a stop behind me. My shoulders tense, I waited next to my Bronco for them to join me and comment on the huge chasm in the earth on the other side of the chain-link fence.

Zeke kept frowning toward the Open Cut as they approached, but the wide-eyed wonder in Zelda's expression appeared reserved solely for the house.

"That's a big hole," Zeke said when they reached me.

Here we go. I took a deep breath and focused on the power of positive thought. "It sure is. Wonderful view from here, don't you think?"

"Ummm," Zeke squinted at the abyss. "I guess."

Zelda was quicker to jump on my bandwagon. "How fun! Zeke, we could build a little viewing platform and have parties overlooking it."

Nodding slowly, he said, "It is pretty interesting. Do they still do blasting down there?"

"Oh no, not at all. The Open Cut is a Lead landmark now."

"I'd love to get some measurements of it."

Zelda turned back to me and explained, "Zeke is a surveyor. He has his own business."

"Really?" I looked him up and down. "You remind me a little of one of those professional wrestlers."

"Oh, he was, years ago," Zelda said. "His ring name was Jugular-Knot."

"You mean Juggernaut?" I asked.

"No." She spelled out the name for me. "The Jugular-Knot was a famous headlock move Zeke came up with where he'd knot his legs around his opponents' necks, cutting off the circulation from their jugular veins until they passed out." Zelda reached up and tweaked her husband's chin.

Zeke, pinker than usual, asked, "So, are the walls of the pit stable?"

"Yes, according to the paperwork. Several geotechs have tested the perimeter." I pointed at the house, having exhausted my knowledge of the Open Cut. "You two ready to take a look inside?"

At their mutual nod, I led them toward the front door, admiring the new paint job as I climbed the porch steps. I touched the wall next to the doorbell and confirmed it was dry even though it still smelled wet.

Millie answered the door before I could even knock.

"Hi, Millie." I cranked up the wattage of happiness in my voice, noticing her long gray skirt and matching cable sweater. Would a little color kill her? On second thought, gray was good. She'd blend into the shadows.

"I've brought some visitors," I told her, even though she already knew I was coming per my phone call.

As I'd instructed, she let us in and then disappeared into the kitchen while I started the tour of the house in the living room. Lucky for me, Lila was nowhere to be seen. Neither was Wanda, for that matter. I wasn't sure about the so-called ghost's attendance, not without Doc by my side to sniff and bristle; and I'd forgotten my travel-sized Ouija board, darn it. I grinned, enjoying my own little inner joke.

"What's that wonderful smell?" Zelda asked, skimming her fingers down the drapes. She didn't give me time to answer. "Oh Zeke, look at this beautiful hand-crafted molding."

The great thing about the Carhart place was that it basically sold itself. All that was required of me was to lead Zeke and Zelda from room to room, pointing out the highlights, and mentally ordering all of the ghost talkers to keep their big yaps shut.

My phone vibrated as we started climbing the stairs. I saw Natalie's number and told the Brittons to go on up without me; I'd join them in a minute.

"Did you get a hold of him?" I asked Nat, not wasting

time on formalities.

"He's not answering his phone."

"Did you leave him a message?"

"I couldn't. His voicemail was full. You're stuck."

"Crikey." I squeezed the back of my neck, trying to loosen the invisible winch that had just cinched it up.

"It'll be fine, Violet. He's a really good guy."

If he was that "good," Natalie would have staked a claim, so there must be something wrong with him. "Okay, I'll go." I didn't exactly have a choice, damn it. "But I want you to promise that if I call you mid-date, you'll rescue me."

"How?"

"I don't know … call back and pretend that there's an emergency with my kids?"

"Fine. But I'm telling you, you're going to like this one."

"You said that the last two times."

"Yeah, well, he has no visible rashes and isn't trying to become a famous ventriloquist."

God. I still shuddered at the memory of that freaky hand puppet trying to feel me up under the table.

"Besides, Vi, the third time is a charm, right?"

Grumbling under my breath, I hung up, realizing I didn't even know the guy's name. After several deep breaths, I went looking for Zeke and Zelda and found them upstairs in what Millie had previously informed me was Junior's old bedroom. Rich brown carpeting and masculine accents filled the space.

Zelda sniffed as I entered and said, "Hmm."

I looked at her with raised brows. Could she smell my desperation?

"This looks like a man's room but smells like a woman's."

I sniffed, picking up the hint of something spicy yet sweet.

"What have we here?" Zelda floated over to a bookcase

next to the queen-sized bed and scanned the spines. "I'm guessing we have a real pacifist here."

I thought of Junior, the rolling pin, and the shotgun. "Yes, the owners are very mild mannered." At least the ones left were.

"Zelda is a librarian," Zeke told me as he leaned against the door frame. "She likes to try to get a read on people based on their books."

A librarian and an ex-wrestler. Interesting. How had that happened?

"Is it okay if I check out the room next door? It's the perfect size for my office."

I nodded, happy that he was daydreaming about what could be. If they decided to put a bid on the place, I'd be able to do some daydreaming of my own.

After Zeke left, Zelda pulled out one of the books and opened it. Dried rose petals drifted to the carpet. "Oops." She squatted to pick them up.

I dropped onto one knee to help and noticed a book shoved under the bed. Millie must have missed it when she was prepping for our arrival. I pulled it out, noticing the texture on the tan-colored cover seemed more rough in some spots than usual for a book, and handed it to Zelda to stack it on the shelf with the others.

"What's this?" As Zelda flipped the book open, its spine creaked softly. "Look at the old-fashioned style of binding. And it's in Latin. This is old. I mean *really* old."

I leaned closer, inhaling a whiff of Zelda's leather, and perused the pages with her. "What? Like a hundred years old?"

Maybe it belonged to the original owner. Jane's words from yesterday replayed in my head ... *She had on a pale, high-collared dress stained dark with blood from where her neck had been slit open.* I shivered at the gruesome image that popped into my head, then cursed Jane mentally for planting that little seed.

"No, double that and then some."

"You're kidding me." What was it doing stuffed under a bed in Lead, South Dakota?

"I never lie about books. That's sacrilege."

I watched as she flipped through the pages, pausing at pictures with pentagrams and other wince-inspiring symbols and drawings. "What's it say?"

"I don't know," she whispered. "I can't read Latin."

"Zelda," Zeke interrupted from the doorway, making us both jerk. "Come here, you have to see this."

Frowning, she handed me the book. "Be careful with that. They should probably store it in a special air-tight container." She pushed to her feet and followed Zeke's footsteps.

I had every intention of putting the book away, but curiosity stalled me. Whose book was this and why had it been shoved under the bed? It was obviously about some kind of unusual religion. There was way too much symbolism scrawled on the pages for it to be otherwise. Had Junior been reading it before he killed his father? Had the words on the pages compelled him to commit murder?

I fished one of my business cards and a pen from my pocket and scrawled the Latin title on the back of my card.

A hissing sound behind me made me whirl in surprise just in time to see Lila rush me, claws extended, lips curled back from her dagger-like canines. With nowhere to go, I cringed, frozen, shielding my face with the book.

She ripped the book from my hands, my card drifting to the carpet between us. "How dare you!" She growled under her breath so only I could hear, clutching the book to her chest. "This is mine. Never touch it again." She shoved in close, nose-to-nose. Her pupils were dilated wide, big black holes, creepy as hell. "You have no idea what I can do to you."

I dislodged my heart from the top of my mouth and swallowed it back down to its rightful place. I scooped up my business card, stuffed it in my pocket, and backed out of the room, holding Lila's unnerving glare until I'd closed the door behind me.

Holy fuck! That woman needed to work on her anger management skills. As much as I wanted to pull on a pair of chain-mail gloves, throw open the door, and go slay that crazy bitch, I didn't dare. I had customers to impress—and not with my cat-fighting skills. But Lila and I weren't finished yet. I didn't like the way she'd treated Wanda, and I certainly didn't appreciate her hissing at me.

I found Zeke and Zelda cooing over the upstairs view of the gaping hole in the earth next door.

"Are you two ready to see the kitchen?"

"Definitely." Zelda's excitement made her whole face light up. Quite the opposite expression from what I'd just witnessed behind Door Number One. She walked over and squeezed my forearm. "Violet, this house is so beautiful."

I told everyone so! "Isn't it?"

She nodded. "And so vintage. I just wish it was haunted. I'd love to have my very own ghost."

After I picked my jaw up from the floor and hinged it back into place, I led them out of the room.

* * *

Later that evening, with minutes to spare before seven o'clock, I sat in the parking lot of The Buffalo Corral giving myself a get-back-in-the-dating-ring pep talk, Rocky Balboa style.

But in my hand, I clutched my cell phone—my white towel of surrender. Natalie's phone number was already queued up, just waiting for me to push the Call button and tell her I couldn't go through with it.

Labeling what I was about to go through as a "blind date" was a misnomer. A truly blind date would mean one—or both—of us was actually blind, or at least temporarily masked with a blindfold for the duration. So, at no point would we both be able to look into each other's eyes and experience that awkward, tongue-stumbling, heart pattering moment of *see*-sickness when one of us would itch to race off to her bedroom, alone with a tub of peanut butter fudge ice cream, to hide out from the male half of the world.

Doubt demons had my insides churning. I stuck my key back in the ignition.

On the other hand, I liked men. I liked to look at them and touch them. I liked being liked back by them. And if I didn't drag my sorry ass out of my Bronco and into that restaurant, I'd have to keep settling for fantasies instead of the real flesh-and-blood deal. I was tired of waking up in the morning with my arms wrapped around empty tubs of Ben & Jerry's and my cheek glued to the pillowcase with dried ice cream.

I grabbed my keys, shoved them and my phone into my purse, and climbed out into the warm evening air. After a quick straightening of my lucky green snap-up jean dress and a swab of gloss over my lips, I marched across the parking lot, chin held high, reminding myself that I was a successful Realtor and could smile and fib my way through just about anything.

Just as I had earlier today, when I'd told Zelda the Carhart house was haunted and made up a story surrounding the woman with the slit throat. The other house I'd shown them, the so-called haunted one belonging to long-dead Lilly Devine, had elicited even more excitement and interest. Shame on me for playing up the ghost angle, but I had a child who needed new glasses I couldn't afford.

I approached the hostess. The smell of barbecued meat saturated the lobby. I couldn't tell if the pang in my stomach was hunger or nerves. "I believe someone is waiting for me." I really should have found out my date's name.

"You must be Violet," said the petite hostess. Natalie must have told my date mine. "Follow me."

We weaved through tables, her leading, me searching table-by-table for a set of eyebrows and nose I'd spend the next hour or two staring at while pretending to make eye contact. Johnny Cash's "Burning Ring of Fire," audible under the low din of conversation, seemed fitting for a restaurant popular for its seared meat.

"Here we are. Enjoy your meal." The hostess stepped aside and I found myself looking into a pair of familiar blue eyes.

No. Fucking. Way. "Ben?" I blinked. Then blinked again. "You're my blind date?"

"Hi, Violet." Benjamin Underhill, Ray's nephew and the man who would be my replacement at Calamity Jane's should I not land another sale soon, rose from his seat and took my limp hand, raising it to his lips. "You look lovely, as always." He kissed my knuckles then pulled out the chair for me.

I fell into my seat, smashing my purse under my left hip. Something beeped as I yanked it out from under me and shoved it under the table. I frowned across at the man who'd sent me a slew of creepy "Roses are Red" anonymous poems and several bouquets of daisies a few weeks ago in hopes of winning my affection. "You're wearing your colored contact."

Ben's eyes were different colors—one icy blue, the other light green. Tonight he'd covered the green eye with a blue contact.

"I didn't want to make you uncomfortable."

Uncomfortable? Just the sight of Ben's face would have been enough normally to make me wring my hands and perspire. Not that Ben was unattractive. Quite the opposite, actually, even though he had a strong resemblance to his jerk of an uncle, minus the fake tan, jowls, and ugly sneer. Tonight, Ben's black hair was cut shorter than it'd been a few weeks ago when he'd lured me to The Wild Pasque, Deadwood's finest restaurant, with a cryptic poem in which he'd tossed around my daughter's name.

"How's work?" Ben asked.

I shot him a suspicious look, but his white-toothed smile seemed genuine.

"It's good," I lied. "Things are looking up." Might as well pile it on thick while I was at it. "So, how do you and Natalie know each other?" Next time, I'd ask Natalie this question *before* agreeing to a blind date. Wait! On second thought, there'd be no next time. Three strikes—she was out.

"I worked for her grandfather for awhile when I was younger."

Natalie's grandpa had owned a contracting business for decades. That was how Natalie got her start in the handy-woman business. She'd grown up working for him every summer out of Nemo.

"After I quit helping him," Ben continued, "I became a home inspector and sent work his way whenever possible. He in turn spread my name around the Hills. That was before he sold his business and moved south."

The grumpy old codger had fallen for the owner of some R.V. park in Arizona and left the Black Hills for good, taking Nat's cousin, Claire, with him.

"Are you still inspecting homes?"

"On the side, until I build up my real-estate business. How's working with my Uncle Ray going?"

"Great. Just wonderful." I'd rather spend each day

skimming the solid matter off the top of sewage ponds.

"He can be a little hard-headed at times, I'm sure."

"Oh, he's a real gem." More like a petrified turd.

The waiter stopped by and asked to take our drink orders. When he left, I said, "So, did you purposely arrange this so-called blind date with me?"

"No and yes. Initially, when Natalie offered to set me up with her best friend, I didn't know it was you. She didn't mention a name. It wasn't until last week that she told me it was you."

That took away a layer of creepiness, but I was still squirmy inside about Ben. Those poems of his had red-lined my wacko stalker meter. I tried to focus on something more comfortable. "Natalie tells me you are a Star Trek ..." *nut.* "Fan."

He grinned. "I'm not a Trekkie, if that's what you're thinking. I just enjoy science fiction books and movies."

Me, too. "Weren't you just at a comic book convention?"

"Is that what she told you?" He laughed outright. "No, I went to a conference in Sioux City for home inspectors, and while I was there, one of the museums was featuring a science-fiction exhibit, including some old comic books and a lot of Star Trek memorabilia."

"Why didn't you tell me about the home inspection business when we had dinner last month?"

He shrugged. "I was trying to impress you—agent to agent. Why didn't you tell me you pine for Captain Kirk?"

"Oh, God." My cheeks burned. "Natalie has a cavernous mouth."

His grin cooled the heat from my cheeks. "Okay, how about we stop trying to be something we're not and start over. No pressure, just friends."

"Just friends?" I squinted at him, not quite trusting yet. "You mean that?"

"Sure. And if something builds from that, so be it."

There'd be no building. Ben's method of wooing women was just too weird. Apparently, I preferred Doc's no-dating-allowed method. "Deal."

Thirty minutes later, we were neck deep in Tribbles and Captain Kirk imitations while waiting for our steaks when Natalie crutched and creaked up to the table.

"Violet! Imagine finding you here." She winked at me so broadly I'm sure the folks in the restaurant across the street witnessed it. "Oh, hi, Ben." Her wide-eyed, wide-mouthed expression was a sad, sad attempt at faking surprise. "That's right. Tonight was your date. I'd forgotten you were meeting here."

Wait a second! Tonight was her so-called date with Doc. My stomach queasy all of the sudden, I jumped out of my chair. "Ben," I said without looking at him, "Will you excuse us for a minute?"

Dragging Natalie and her crutches a few tables away, I whispered, "What are you doing here?"

"You called me."

"No, I didn't."

"Yes, you did."

"When?"

"About forty-five minutes ago. You didn't say anything, but I figured that was because you couldn't."

I remembered the beep when I'd sat on my purse upon arriving at the table. Crap, I must have butt-dialed her number. "That was an accident. Besides, you were supposed to call me back, not show up."

"Yeah, well, I came up with a better rescue plan. Something more fun."

That couldn't be good. "What do you mean 'more fun'? It's a rescue, not an adventure."

She smiled over my shoulder and waved. "A double date."

An anvil fell from the sky and landed smack-dab on my chest. "No."

"Come on, Vi. It'll be a blast. We haven't double-dated in years."

For good reason. The last time we had, my date ended up falling for Natalie during dinner and trying to grope her afterward in the darkened movie theater—while I was sitting between them. "Nat, please tell me you didn't bring Doc here."

"Shush. This will be great. Besides, Ben really likes you. You should have seen how excited he was when I showed him your picture." She squeezed my hand. "Trust me, the only boob that's going to be grabbed tonight is yours. Well, unless I can shake Doc out of this no-touching rule he's insisting upon."

No-touching rule? I knew that rule all too well. What had brought that on? Actual touching?

Natalie squeezed my arm and led me back to the table, where Ben stood shaking Doc's hand, the hostess weaving away. "Doc, look who's here."

When Doc saw me, thunder rumbled on his brow, and lightning clashed in his eyes.

"Hello, Doc."

"Violet wants us to join her and Ben for dinner."

"Really," Doc said. I was pretty sure I heard him growl.

"You don't mind sharing Violet tonight, do you, Ben?"

"Uh, no. I guess not." Ben glanced at me, his forehead slightly puckered, then turned back to our company with a big smile. "Pull up some chairs. I'll go find the waiter."

Doc towed two chairs over to our table. Natalie nudged me so that I was sitting next to Ben. She fell into the seat on my left, leaning her crutches against the empty table behind her. "This is going to be so much fun."

Doc's jaw ticked as he glared across the table at me.

I plopped into my chair before my knees gave out.

"Yeah, fun."

I could hardly wait for dessert.

Chapter Eight

Ben returned with our young waiter in tow. After we ordered our drinks and Doc and Natalie got menus, I sat back and waited for Natalie's "fun" to begin. I wasn't holding my breath.

Ben excused himself and headed toward the restroom.

"What are you having, Vi?" Natalie asked, perusing her menu.

A nightmare. "The garlic steak and red potatoes."

"Garlic?" Natalie lowered her menu, her face pinched with exasperation. "It's your first date and you're already trying to sabotage it."

Doc peered at me over the top of his menu. After a long, hard stare, he slipped behind it again.

"Blind date," I corrected just so *everyone* at the table would be clear why I was here tonight. Not that it was any of Doc's business, damn it. "And it's not our first date."

That won me double takes from both of them.

Natalie leaned toward me as if she hadn't heard me right. "It's not?"

I smiled, sweet and tight. "Nope."

When I didn't explain, Natalie grabbed my arm and squeezed. "Violet Lynn Parker, you'd better spill or I'll start bellowing 'Happy Birthday' to you in my Bobcat Goldthwait voice."

Blood rushed from my head. "Don't you dare." That scene still fell within the top ten of my most-embarrassing moments.

"Then start singing, my little canary."

"There's nothing much to tell. Last month, Ben sent me some flowers and a few poems and then asked me out to dinner, and I obliged." I left out the parts involving creepy shivers and night sweats.

Doc dropped his menu. "Ben was your secret admirer?"

I touched my nose, trying not to ogle him in front of Natalie. His fitted maroon button-up shirt creased in all the right places, allowing me to steal glimpses of his broad-shouldered torso.

"You told me that guy just went away," Natalie said.

"Well, he did. Kind of. Until tonight."

"How come you never told me you went out to dinner with him?" Natalie sat back in her chair, looking as if I'd stolen her Christmas present and opened it.

"It didn't seem like a big deal at the time."

Doc snorted. I shot him a glare.

Natalie studied the two of us in turn, those pouty lips of hers pursed. Natalie may be borderline sexually compulsive and look like a Playboy bunny, but she was no fluff-head. The only reason she hadn't caught on to my hot-to-trot vibes for Doc was that she trusted me—heart and soul. That, and she was temporarily insane due to this new obsession with everything Doc.

"If it were no big deal," Natalie said, "how come Doc knows about it?" *And I don't*, her frown finished.

This was becoming a bit of a sticky wicket. Natalie had good reason for her ruffled feathers. We'd been sharing secrets since our baby teeth started falling out. It wasn't until Doc came into my life that I'd started hiding truths from her.

"Doc was there when I got the dinner invite." There. An innocent fact. "Harvey was, too," I added to make her being left out less of a big deal.

"Oh, my God. Harvey knows, too? Who else? The rest

of Deadwood?"

Okay, that backfired.

Natalie crossed her arms over her chest. "What else haven't you told me?"

I had sex with Doc. "Nothing."

Had someone cranked up the heat in here? I grabbed the dessert menu from the center of the table and fanned myself. I couldn't look at Doc, afraid of what Natalie would read on my face, so I inspected the checkered tablecloth for BBQ stains until Ben returned.

He dropped into his seat. "What did I miss?"

"I was just telling Natalie about our previous date." I threw him under the bus. I couldn't help it. Desperation had me on the run.

Ben's lips formed an "Oh." He looked sheepishly at Natalie.

She pounced on him. "Why you didn't tell me you already knew Violet?"

"I wanted to surprise her. And, boy, did I." He patted my shoulder, winking at me. "You should have seen the look on her face."

I never had been able to make panic pretty. He should have seen me in the bathroom mirror about ten years ago when the pregnancy test showed positive.

With Natalie's focus on Ben, I risked a glance across the table and found Doc studying me, his hand rubbing his jaw. All traces of anger seemed gone, replaced by a mesmerizing dark heat that snaked out and wrapped itself around me. Something stirred deep in my belly, stealing my breath.

Holy crap! How did he do that with his eyes? I fanned harder, faster, tearing my gaze away, blinking away stars.

The young waiter stopped to drop off drinks and take the newcomers' orders. Natalie stuck with a light salad. It was the story of our lives—she nibbled on lettuce leaves and I gnawed on red meat, which explained the difference in our waist sizes.

"I'll have the garlic steak and red potatoes," Doc told the waiter, handing him the menu.

He seemed oblivious to Natalie's quick frown.

As Natalie added special requests to her dinner order, Ben tore into the basket of sourdough bread the kid had brought as an appetizer.

Doc drank from his glass of amber beer, his gaze sliding down to my chest. I peeked down to make sure I'd fastened enough snaps to hide my cleavage—woo-wee, just barely. When I looked up at him again, the obvious lust in his eyes twisted my bloomers into a pretzel knot. I squirmed, aching for something only he could ease.

I deliberately knocked my spoon off the table, bending over to grab it, staying down long enough to take several deep breaths. I needed a paper bag, an oxygen bar, a kick to the head. Closing my eyes, I tried to think about non-sexy things like greasy tractors, dung beetles, Darth Vader—hold up, Darth was kind of sexy with that long black cape and all of that heavy breathing.

I watched the waiter's shoes leave and popped up in time to hear Natalie ask Ben, "Did Vi tell you she has a soft spot for loonies?"

What? "Are you talking about Wolfgang?" I asked, wondering why she'd be bringing him up now. She knew I was still having nightmares. No, wait. I hadn't told her about those, either.

"No." Natalie looked at me as if I was mentally impaired—which I was at the moment. "But he fits, too, I guess."

"There is no way Violet could have known the truth about Hessler before that night," Doc said in my defense. "He even had the police fooled."

That wasn't true and we both knew it. Doc had warned me about Wolfgang's house and the danger within it; I just hadn't listened.

Ben turned to Doc, his head cocked to the side. "How exactly do you know Violet?"

Carnally, I thought, and almost laughed aloud before wrangling a little control over my inner smartass. "I'm his Realtor," I told Ben. *And his "distraction."* Remembering that sobered me right up.

"She's a good friend," Doc answered.

Excuse me? I blinked, momentarily stunned by his admission. Well, this was a fine and dandy little nugget to be shared over seared meat with friends.

"How do you know Natalie?" Doc asked Ben.

While Ben gave Doc the same explanation he'd given me earlier, and Natalie bantered with Ben about some playful flirting game they used to play when he worked for her grandfather, Doc watched me—the way he would if I was dancing half-naked wrapped around a fire pole.

I gulped.

He slowly ran his fingers down the sweating glass of beer. A simple act transformed into a slice of erotica.

I shivered. I was so out of my league here.

His lazy grin surfaced and he strummed his glass again.

I shivered again, damn it, and sent my libido to go sit in the corner. Nailing him with a knock-it-off glare, I kicked him under the table.

Ben grunted and jerked, spilling the soda pop he'd been drinking down his light blue pinstriped shirt.

"Oh, God! I'm sorry." I dabbed Ben's shirt with my napkin, mortification searing my cheeks. "I was crossing my leg."

Doc's grin widened at the angry squint I aimed his way between dabs.

"Here, use mine, too," Natalie said, handing me her napkin. "Anyway, I was actually talking about the Carharts, not Wolfgang," she explained to me, returning to her earlier comment on my loony state. "As in why you agreed to list their place."

Oh, silly me. I blamed Doc. His presence at the table caused a disturbance in the Force. I dropped back into my seat, grimacing at the soda stain on Ben's shirt, feeling foolish all over the place. Where was my dang steak? I needed something to chew on.

"Ben, didn't you used to hang out with Junior Carhart when you were younger?" Natalie asked.

"We frequented the same watering hole."

"Did he ever talk about his family?"

"Sure. When you add liquor, don't we all?"

I would have kissed Natalie for changing the subject—especially to one so near and dear to my curiosity. Feigning mild interest, I was all ears. Doc's attention had fallen in line, too, I noticed.

"What was Junior like?" I asked. What could possibly have drawn Lila to him?

"Mean as hell when he was sober. Just like his old man."

Nothing surprising there.

"But get him drunk and he morphed into your best friend."

"What do you mean?" I asked.

"He was an amiable drunk, buying drinks for all, adopting anyone within sight as his new pal. I'd usually avoid Junior until he was three sheets to the wind."

Lila must have met Junior at the bar. "Did you ever see Junior at the bar with a skinny, black-haired ..." *bitch* "woman who goes by the name Lila?"

Ben chewed on his bread for a few seconds. "No, I don't think so. But I hadn't been around as much since I was taking classes down in Rapid."

"Classes for what?" Doc asked.

"Real estate. I was getting my license."

Doc sized up Ben and me. "You're both agents."

"Ben's uncle works with me." I smiled for Ben's sake. He couldn't help that he shared DNA with Deadwood's number one asshole. "You remember Ray, don't you, Doc?"

"Sure." Doc kept a straight face, to his credit. Just the sound of Ray's name usually had me reaching for a blunt weapon.

Enough about Ben's violence-inspiring uncle. I wasn't done with the Carharts. "Did Junior ever show interest in the dark arts? Like say, I don't know, demonology?"

Ben slowly shook his head, his brow furrowed. "No, I don't think so."

"Did he have any creepy tattoos?" I thought about some of the pictures in that book I found in the Carhart house. "Like a pentagram or a three-headed snake or some weird Latin words?"

Doc cleared his throat, his brow furrowed as he reached for his beer. I avoided his eyes.

"Does this have anything to do with your ghost question yesterday?" Natalie asked me.

Doc froze, his glass midway to his lips. "What ghost question?"

"Utshay upway, Atnay," I whispered from the side of my mouth in the pig version of Latin.

She ignored my attempt to shush her and batted her eyelashes at Doc. "She wanted to know if I believed in ghosts."

Doc's glare drilled into me. I resisted the urge to slide down my chair and slink away.

"Do you?" Ben asked Natalie, grinning.

"Sure, why not?" Natalie said with the same flippancy she'd used when answering me yesterday.

"How about you, Doc?"

The ticking muscle was back in Doc's jaw.

Eek! I scrambled to change the subject. "Ben, did you go to Junior's funeral?"

"No, I was out of town that weekend."

That was too bad. I would've liked to hear his opinion of Lila.

"But you know what I never understood about the whole mess?" Ben wiped his hands on his napkin. "The newspaper claimed that Junior was in a drunken rage when he killed his father. They even mentioned empty whiskey bottles found in his bedroom."

"Yeah, I remember that bit," Natalie said.

"Well, had Junior been cold sober, I would buy that he killed his dad. That old geezer walked around screaming at little old ladies and ass-chewing Sunday school teachers at random. I'd never met a nastier drunk. But Junior turned into a regular Ghandi when you added liquor. I just can't see him smashing in anyone's brains with a rolling pin while he was wasted."

I leaned forward. "Are you saying you don't think Junior killed his father?"

Ben shrugged. "The police seem to believe he's guilty, so who am I to question their judgment?"

"But?" I pressed. I'd learned the hard way that the police weren't always right.

"But I have my doubts," He finished just as a tray of food arrived at our table, our waiter hidden behind it.

I jumped up. I needed a moment to digest what I'd just learned about Junior Carhart and didn't want to do that under a magnifying glass. "I need to use the ladies room."

The bathrooms were in the back of the restaurant, adjacent to a doorway leading into a darkened room. I peeked in between the accordion doors, curious, and saw a couple of long tables. The room must be reserved for group parties.

I pushed into the bathroom and locked myself in a stall,

leaning my back against the door.

So, if Junior didn't kill his father, who did? Lila? I so wanted it to be her, but while she was a long-taloned witch and an ace hisser, that didn't make her a killer. Why would she kill Junior's father? What did she have to gain? And what about Junior? He'd ended up on the morgue slab, too, after swallowing a cartridge of shotgun pellets. This didn't make sense.

I could see why the police would lean toward it being Junior. That made a nice, tightly wrapped little package to hand the curious public. *No panic necessary, folks, we have your killer and he's dead, too.* I should ask Cooper about this, but he wasn't exactly happy to share details about his uncle's place with me, let alone something that was really none of my business. Maybe if I used Harvey to help, have the questions come through his uncle, I could get some answers.

But why did I care? I thought about that while I stared up at some dead fly carcasses in the fluorescent light casing. All I could come up with was an image of Wanda's frightened face. Poor Wanda, stuck with a cruel son, an even crueler husband, a wallflower daughter, and a pushy potential daughter-in-law. She needed someone to watch out for her. Lord knew Millie didn't have the backbone to do the job.

Besides, what could a little digging into history hurt? And what if Lila *was* up to something, somehow intending to take the money from the house sale and disappear with it, leaving Wanda broke and homeless? That would make me a participant in Wanda's ruin. In that case, it was my responsibility to make sure Wanda, and nobody else, would benefit from a sale.

I flushed the toilet out of habit, unlocked the stall door, and stood at the sink, staring into the mirror above it. My cheeks were flushed light pink, and my lip gloss needed another coat. I washed my hands, swiped at a bit of mascara smudged on my eyelid, then pushed open the door.

Doc stood there, waiting. He grabbed my hand and dragged me into the shadow-filled party room, closing the accordion doors behind us.

"What in the hell are you doing?" I jammed my hands on my hips, ready for battle.

Doc ran his hand through his hair, his usual lazy grin missing. "We need to talk."

"You said plenty the other day. There's nothing else to talk about, unless it's about your house."

"You're right. Forget talking." He grabbed me by the shoulders and kissed me—hard, hungry.

It took a second or two of his lips working their magic for my head to catch up with current events. My body wasn't so slow on the uptake, shuddering to life under his hands as they skimmed, brushed, gripped, rubbed.

When his tongue touched mine, the old furnace kicked on, blasting heat out from my core. I closed my eyes, sliding down into the moment. He tasted of beer and sinful pleasures, and I ached to have my wicked way with him. My palms skated over his ribs, around his back, squeezing. His muscles tightened. I scraped my nails down his cotton shirt, digging. He groaned under my touch. Power rippled through me; a carnal high followed in its wake, floating me up to the ceiling.

He released my mouth and trailed his lips along my jaw, his hands buried in my hair, tugging my head back to expose my neck and collar bone to his kisses.

"You taste so sweet," he whispered.

"It's probably the caramel sauce."

"Caramel sauce?" He chuckled; the vibrations on his lips tickled my neck.

"I spilled my latte this afternoon." I hadn't showered before my blind date, not wanting to even consider the possibility that any clothing might come off. Had I known Doc would be ravishing me, I would have put more work into my presentation.

"That explains the hint of coffee."

"I shouldn't be letting you kiss me. I'm not done being pissed off."

His mouth trailed up my neck. "Let me help you blow off some steam."

Tempting. "That doesn't solve our problem."

His voice was husky in my ear. "I can't stop thinking about touching you. Everywhere. Does that make you feel better?"

Yes! Yes! Yes! I swatted the Doc-starved imp jumping up and down on my shoulder. "Maybe. Inflicting a little pain on you would help."

"Only a little? That's not your style."

"You're right." I yanked his shirt from his pants, wanting to refresh my memory of his contours, to feel his coarseness under my palms. "Where should I start?"

"You already have. What do you call tonight's date with Ben?"

"Blackmail, from my point of view." I ran my hands down his chest and abdomen, surveying his warm flesh inch by inch.

"The view was different from where I was sitting. What about your refusal to back down on the Carhart house no matter what I say?"

"Civic duty."

"How'd you come up with that?"

"I need to protect Wanda's ..." I gasped. "Interests. God, Doc! That whole bite-lick-suck thing you're doing ... ahhh."

"You like it?"

"More than peanut butter fudge ice cream."

He did it again, melting my toenail polish. "More than

Elvis?"

"The King?" I let my hands drift down over his front pockets, exploring the seams and the firm flesh underneath. "I'm not sure you have that in you."

"Is that a dare?"

"A double-dare."

"That reminds me." He cupped my head, turning it slightly to the side, and trailed butterfly kisses down from my temple. "I found what you were looking for."

Me, too. I began unbuttoning his clothes so I could have access to more of it.

"The murder took place in the early sixties."

My fingers paused. "Murder?"

"Uh, huh." Doc knocked aside my hands and yanked on the middle of my dress, several snaps popping apart. "Karen Snarky."

"Snarky?" Was that name for real?

"Stabbed to death by an ex-lover." He slipped his hands inside my dress.

My stomach tightened in a delicious little clench that spread south. His hands paused, resting on my ribcage. He stared down at me, eyebrows raised.

I wiggled against him. "You're not stopping there, are you?"

His lazy grin made an appearance. "Apparently not." His gaze traveled south.

My black satin bra covered with little daisies had been my quick pick for the night. The matching panties were in the wash, though. Again, had I known Doc and his hands would be part of the night's events, I'd have planned better.

"Was she killed in the house?" When he just stared at my chest, I added, "I'm talking about Karen Snarky."

"Oh. Right." His hands climbed my ribs. He ducked his head and caught my lower lip between his teeth. "Yeah. Sure."

Then he plunged his tongue in my mouth again while his fingers stole beneath my underwire. The double attack jarred me into sensory overload. I was inundated by the taste, scent, touch of Doc in one breath-taking sucker punch. My knees nearly buckled. I clung to his neck, sighing out an anthem of moans.

He broke his lock on my mouth, panting as hard as I was. "I can't do this."

I crashed back to Earth. "Don't start that shit again."

"I mean here, right now. With Ben and Natalie waiting for us in the other room."

"Oh." Hearing Natalie's name was like being dipped in a vat of cold petroleum jelly. If there was a sash for World's Worst Best Friend, I should be hanged with it in front of an angry mob. "Yeah. You're right. This is bad."

He pulled his hands out from the front of my dress and snapped it closed, but his palms lingered on my hips as if he wasn't sure this was the right course to take.

I wasn't either, but I was certain of one thing—I needed to come clean with Natalie about my feelings for Doc. The whole crazy-hot sex bit, on the other hand, could remain my fun little secret with Doc until Natalie moved on to her next *one*. "We have a problem," I told him, dragging him into my mess.

"Yeah, well, you tend to have this effect on me when you walk in a room. I'm going to need you to snap that dress up all the way to your chin for the rest of dinner, Boots, or I'll be stuck back here all night. Although now that I know about the daisies on your bra, I'm not sure even a nun's habit would help."

That made me grin. *Temptress* was a relatively new role for me, the potential that came with it heady as hell. I'd have to be careful or my skull could snap free and get caught in the jet stream.

"The problem I'm referring to is Natalie," I said. "And

you."

"There is no Natalie and me. Tonight was supposed to be a business meeting, but she called and said you needed help."

Damn. He'd come riding in to save me and found me with another man. No wonder he'd been all angry-eyed and clench-jawed upon arrival. I'd have planted a kiss on his lips, but then I'd want to follow it with popping the snaps on my dress again and we'd be back where we'd started. Instead, I touched his cheek and smiled like a helium-headed groupie.

"Stop looking at me like that, Violet."

I sighed and obliged. "Natalie has her sights set on you, you know."

"Yeah, well, I can't make it any clearer to her that I'm not interested in dating her. Why haven't you told her about us?"

"I haven't told anyone." Except Harvey. But officially, I didn't tell the old coot, he connived that fact out of me.

"Why not?"

As I closed the top two snaps of my dress, I tried to read in his eyes the real question he was asking. "It has nothing to do with your ghosts, if that's what you're wondering."

He nodded but said nothing, tucking his shirt back into his khaki pants.

"Speaking of dead people," I combed my hair with my fingers. "This Snarky lady who was killed way back when in the Carhart house, you said she was stabbed to death."

"That's what the article said."

"Did they specify where she was stabbed?"

"Yes." He adjusted the front of his pants, not quite hiding his predicament. Maybe just one touch ... I reached toward him but he grabbed my wrist. "Don't even think about it, Vixen."

Too late. Already thought about it and then some. I blew out a breath. Back to the Carharts. "Snarky was stabbed in the neck, right?" I asked.

"No. In the stomach, twice."

"Are you sure?"

"Positive. Why?"

Because Jane said the pictures of the ghost living in the Carhart house had a bloody neck, not gut. "No reason."

"Violet, what are you hiding?"

I wasn't ready to share this yet; it needed more sorting out. "Maybe I'll show you later." Tomorrow I was going to have a few questions for Detective Cooper that had nothing to do with listing his house. I pulled open the doors, leading the way. "Let's go."

He hesitated. "Together?"

"I have an idea."

Back at the table, Natalie and Ben were eating without us.

"Where in the hell did you two disappear to?" Natalie asked, not bothering with niceties.

"Sorry about that." I dropped into my chair, meeting her questioning gaze. "We got the inspector's report today. I needed to talk to my client." And stick my tongue in his mouth a few times.

I grimaced at my steak. There would be no easy way to deliver my Doc bomb to her. Maybe I should just break this thing with him off entirely.

I laughed aloud at that idea, then realized I'd goofed when three pairs of eyes looked my way. "Sorry." I picked up my fork and knife. "The voices were talking again."

Damn. It was going to be a longgggggg dinner.

Chapter Nine

Sunday, August 5ᵗʰ

The garlic worked its magic, keeping kissing at bay for one and all. After a dinner filled with shared tales of Natalie and Ben's past and stolen glances between Doc and me, we'd all parted ways in the parking lot. Well, Doc and Natalie had driven off together, neither to be heard from since, darn it. I did my best not to think about them during the long night. The nightmares helped, ironically.

I'd brushed the garlic off my tongue and teeth twice this morning since once proved not enough for Addy's sensitive nose. Later, when I picked Harvey up outside the Old Prospector Hotel and Casino for our appointment at Detective Cooper's place, his sniff and scowl had me digging in my purse for a stick of gum.

He grunted a hello, then asked, "You been ruttin' in a flower patch this morning?"

"It's air freshener," I said, through a mouthful of cinnamon, and rolled down the windows. Warm air whipped my curls.

"You don't have an air freshener."

"The bathroom at work does." My garlic-killing spritz wound up being a full-fledged dousing thanks to a faulty spray nozzle. Zeke and Zelda hadn't seemed to mind my Eau de "Toilet" when we walked through a few more homes this morning, but they'd followed me on their Harley from place to place. A couple of twitches of Zelda's nose had been her only reaction to me.

"Let's go. Coop's waiting." Harvey stuck his head out the window as I scooted down the road toward Lead. "Why are you coatin' yourself in air freshener, anyway?" he hollered at me.

I opted not to answer that. "Get your head back in here. I'm not that ripe." I grabbed his arm and tugged. "I need to talk to you."

"I can listen from out here."

"It's about sex," I lied.

That got him back in the cab, all ears.

"I need you to ask Cooper something for me."

"You want to have sex with Coop?" His bushy brows hit the roof. "Jesus, girl! How many men do you need?"

One repeat customer would be nice, thank you very much. "It's about the Carhart deaths."

"Turn here." Harvey pointed to a road that climbed a long, steep hill. "What about them?"

I waited a beat or two as my Bronco dropped a gear and clambered upward. How did I say what I was about to without sounding like some nutty conspiracy theorist? I decided to just spit it out. "I don't think Junior killed his dad."

Harvey snorted. "Here we go again."

"But I need proof." I glanced over, catching a frown in return. "Which is where you come in."

"Why do you care about those two assholes?"

That earned him a frown back. "You're supposed to have a little respect for the dead."

"You didn't know the Carhart boys. Removing them from the local population did us all a favor."

"Did you go to school with Junior's dad?"

"Nah. He was a good ten years older than me."

"But you knew him pretty well?"

"We didn't exchange Valentine's cards ever, if that's what ya mean, but I'd run into him around town."

"At the bar?"

"No. He wasn't much of a social drinker. Take a right up there by that old fillin' station."

"So he usually drank at home?" Maybe those empty whiskey bottles were his and not Junior's.

"Home, his pickup, a dirt road, his girlfriend's place, wherever he pleased, just like the rest of us."

"Girlfriend?"

"Did I stutter?"

"If he was such an asshole, how did he manage to find a wife *and* a girlfriend?"

"He knocked Wanda up while she was still in high school. And Claudette—well, women love bastards."

"Not all women." I preferred generous control freaks.

"The clingy ones do. It's no secret. Just read any of those women's magazines and you'll see."

"You read women's magazines?"

"Sure. They're chock full of bonanza. Read a couple of those rags, and luring a dame to bed is easier than shooting fish in a barrel."

Did Doc read women's magazines? How many guys were in on this secret? I glanced at Harvey a couple of times, unsure whether he was serious or not. He just grinned back, looking cocky as usual.

"Back to Junior's dad," I said, wanting to scrub all thoughts about Harvey and sex from my brain and get back to less nauseating stuff—like murder. "Someone told me drinking made him mean."

"Mean as a pissed-off hornet," Harvey said. He pointed out the front window. "It's up there on the left."

I stopped in front of a small pale-blue 1940-ish bungalow with a detached garage whose big barn-like doors were propped open. Cooper's unmarked patrol SUV was parked in the drive. Sitting in front of the SUV was a red motorcycle, a bucket of sudsy water on the ground next to it.

I turned to Harvey. "I need you to find out from Cooper if Junior was definitely drunk when the murder took place."

"The paper already said so."

"Yeah, well the paper might have been wrong. Ask Cooper if they tested Junior's blood and confirmed he was drunk."

Harvey sighed. "Okay. But I think this is a bad idea. You don't want to let Coop know you're sniffin' around one of his cases."

"His case?" I'd figured Cooper would know about the murder details due to police chatter. "I thought he was a detective for Deadwood, not Lead."

"Lead contracts with Deadwood for Coop's services to save money."

Swell. There was no escaping Cooper's all-seeing eye.

Harvey was still grumbling about helping me when we climbed out of the Bronco. Cooper came from behind the garage, wiping his hands on a blotchy white cloth. His black T-shirt sported several little round holes on the right side, leaking glimpses of bare flesh.

"Looks like a moth got in your closet," I said.

Cooper frowned, then glanced down when I pointed. "Oh. Bullet holes."

I winced. "You must leak when you drink now."

That earned me a hint of a smile. "I no longer trust old women toting shotguns."

Harvey snickered. "I still say you should have let me have a try at her. She just needed a little sweet talkin'."

"I took your advice once." He pointed at a small scar line on his left cheekbone. "Remember?"

"How was I to know she was hiding a frying pan in her skirt?"

I could sense another Harvey anecdote brewing, so I

pointed at Cooper's house and asked, "You ready to take a walk through?"

Harvey followed us from room to room, rambling about this, that, and the latest tail he was chasing. I kept giving him head nudges, trying to remind him of the whole purpose for me dragging his ornery ass along. He kept not asking the right questions. Any questions at all, for that matter.

The house looked clean enough, smelled like it'd been rinsed with bleach water, and contained sparse furnishings, mostly made of black leather and oak. The only picture hung in the house was in the living room: an oil painting of several dogs sitting around a poker table, cleaning their guns.

"Coop ain't much for decorations."

Cooper shrugged. "It's been a while since my last dinner party."

"This is good. It means less cleanup work for me."

Compared to Jeff Wymonds' place, which still required a few trips to the landfill, this puppy was just a few flower vases away from showing.

"Let me just grab the listing agreement from my Bronco," I said to Cooper—and whispered "Ask him!" to Harvey on my way out the door. I took an extra minute or two getting the agreement. When I stepped back inside, Harvey was talking to Cooper about a new type of barrel cleaner for Bessie, his shotgun.

Cooper went to find a pen, which I'd purposely forgotten.

"Well?" I asked.

"What? I didn't get around to it yet."

"Harvey!"

"What? I need to work up to something like this."

Cooper walked back into the room, pen in hand. "Where do I sign?"

"Hey, Coop," Harvey said as I showed his nephew the pages, "Violet wants to know if Junior Carhart was really drunk the night he murdered his old man."

My mouth opened in a silent yell. I glared at Harvey. That was how he worked up to something?

Meanwhile, Cooper watched me, all spaghetti-western squinty-eyed. "Why does Violet care about that?"

"Well, that's what I asked, too, but we got sidetracked before she answered me."

Wow, so much for my sidekick having my back. I cleared my throat. "I'm curious because of something a friend told me recently."

"Which was?" Cooper pressed.

I swallowed some nervous ramblings that threatened to flee from my throat. "That Junior was an amiable drunk."

"And?" More pressing.

"He would never hurt a fly while he was wasted, let alone do something as brutal as beat his father to death with a rolling pin."

We shared a silent stare-down, his eyes warning me to back off. I looked away first, relenting, but not giving up.

"Well?" Harvey prompted. "Was Junior really drunk, or was that just speculation?"

After another squint-filled pause, Cooper answered, "According to the lab, he had a blood alcohol level of point two one."

I had to wonder why Cooper remembered the exact number.

"Woo-wee!" Harvey broke the tension. "That's drunk all right."

Cooper took the listing agreement from me and laid it out on a waist-height speaker, next to where Harvey stood. "You two need to let this go." He signed the pages under Harvey's watchful eye and handed the agreement back to me. "It's a closed case." He scratched behind his left ear, then stopped when he noticed his uncle studying him. "A done deal. Understand?"

"Sure." I smiled through my lying teeth. "I was just curious. That's all."

"Quit browbeating her, Coop." Harvey tugged me toward the door. "She can't help being nosy. It comes with the job."

Cooper followed us outside, still warning me with his eyes.

"I'll contact you in the next day or so." I tried to shake off Harvey's hand, but his grip was strong as he practically dragged me toward the Bronco. "We need to make your place a little more showy, add a few female touches."

Harvey howled. Literally. "Coop likes female touches, don't you, boy?"

The hint of a smile returned to the detective's lips. "That depends on the female."

I barely had time to wave good-bye before Harvey

stuffed me behind the wheel.

"Let's get out of here," he whispered.

What in the hell bit Harvey on the ass? I did as told and waited for him to climb in before shifting the Bronco into gear. "Where's the fire? You late for a date with another old flame?"

He didn't answer until I'd started down the big hill back toward downtown Lead. "Coop's lying."

"What?"

"You're on to something."

"How do you know? Does he have a 'tell' like my nose twitch? Was it him scratching behind his ear?"

"No. Coop's a pro. He doesn't have any tells."

"Then how do you know he's lying?"

"You had him flustered."

"Ha! Right. Did you see his face?" There hadn't even been a single twitch or jaw tick. "The four guys up on Mount Rushmore show more emotion."

"Coop's a master at controlling his expression." Harvey pointed at the listing agreement sitting on the console between us. "But he spelled his name wrong there on your paper."

* * *

I dropped Harvey off at his Chevy pickup on the way back to the office. He planned to drive over and pay a visit to an old girlfriend—Junior's dad's, that was. Claudette Perkins was her name and, according to Harvey, sleeping with old married men was her game. That made a single man like him unattractive, which he worried might work against him in his attempt to seduce some answers out of her. But he'd been willing to try to take one for the team. Apparently, even at age sixty-one, Claudette was still quite the long-legged pin-up girl.

Back at the office, Jane had a bunch of girl-Friday tasks for me, including a trip to Rapid City. I didn't roll into Aunt Zoe's drive until dinnertime. I still hadn't heard a peep from Doc or Natalie, which made my stomach churn a bit if I thought about it too much, so I tried not to and failed miserably—story of my life.

The heavenly scent of braised meat greeted me at the door. After sharing a pot roast with Aunt Zoe, the twins, and Kelly Wymonds, who was staying with us for the night, I bribed the kids into going to the library with me for the evening. The payoff was an ice cream cone at the Candy Corral afterward. After a day like today, I was thinking two scoops of peanut butter fudge might be required to take the edge off, with maybe a sample spoonful of mint chocolate chip.

The library parking lot was empty.

Addy and Kelly raced up the steps, leaving Layne and me trailing behind.

"This place is a ghost town," Layne said when we reached the double doors.

I chuckled. He had no idea.

The two of us made ourselves at home in the South Dakota room, leaving the door slightly ajar for when the girls came looking for us. Layne dropped his pack on the table and tugged out a notepad and his current read, a book on the history of ghost towns here in the Hills, which explained his comment on the way up the steps. His fascination with the area's past had cranked up ever since he started digging in Aunt Zoe's back yard. Finding that foot hanging in the tree last month had only amplified his obsessive bender.

I scooted in front of the microfilm machine, my newfound friend in my newfound life. I hooked up a microfilm spool holding the past six months' worth of articles from the *Black Hills Trailblazer* newspaper and wound my way back in time.

The first thing I found in the archives was the obituary for both Junior and his dad. The paper had grouped them together. Nothing stood out, except a noted lack of Lila's name anywhere. Were fiancées normally mentioned in an obit?

The listing was short and sweet, with Mudder Brothers Funeral Parlor getting a call-out, but no mention of Claudette Perkins, of course. I wondered if she'd shown her face at the funeral. Had Wanda known about her husband's infidelities? Had she cared? Maybe it was a relief to have him seeking his loving, touching, and squeezing elsewhere. Had he been verbally abusive to Claudette, too? Physically? Did any of this even matter?

"Mom?" Layne's voice broke into my inner monologue.

"Yes, Sweetheart?" I continued scrolling further into the past, scanning.

"What's the name of that ghost town out by where Harvey lives?"

What was the exact date of the Carhart murders? Was it late January? "I'm not sure, honey."

"Slagton." Doc's voice jarred me.

He stood in the doorway, filling the gap I'd left open. The sight of him in his olive green cargo shorts and faded yellow T-shirt spurred a tickly feeling in my stomach, as if I'd swallowed a handful of Pop Rocks.

He looked me up and down, his dark eyes devouring as he added, "That's the closest ghost town to his ranch that still has buildings, anyway. The others in the vicinity are mostly littered with nothing more than foundation scars."

It sounded like somebody had been busy scouting about. I smiled, wondering if I looked as starry-eyed as I felt, hoping I didn't. "Hello, Doc."

"Good evening, Violet."

Yes, it was, even more so now that I had him to ogle.

His gaze lingered on the v-neck of my strappy sundress before meeting back up with mine. "Nice necklace. Is that amethyst?"

I fingered the smooth stone dangling at my cleavage and nodded all slow and sultry. Then a giggle slipped out, ruining my Marilyn Monroe moment. So much for playing it cool. What was it about Doc that turned me into a giddy schoolgirl with an even giddier crush?

"Who are you?" Layne asked Doc. My son's narrowed eyes were full of distrust, his jaw rigid, lips tight.

I'd forgotten that Layne had never actually met Doc. I rose, twisting my hands together, wondering how Doc would deal with Layne's protective man-of-the-house act. "Layne, this is Doc Nyce, a client of mine."

At the word "client," Doc raised an eyebrow at me. I shrugged and continued, "Doc, this is Layne, my son."

Doc held Layne's stare for a pent-up breath or two, then moved into the room, letting the door drift closed behind him. "So, you're Layne Parker." He pulled out the chair opposite Layne and sat down. Leaning back, he crossed his arms over his chest. "I've heard about you."

Layne lowered his pencil. "You have?"

Doc nodded slowly. "Word on the street is that you like to dig up the past. Get real messy."

"You mean like dirty?"

Doc nodded again.

"I guess so. Who told you that?" Layne shot a small frown in my direction. "Mom?"

"Nope. One of my sources." Doc pointed at Layne's book. "What do you have there?"

"A book about ghost towns." He showed Doc the cover.

"I've read that one. What do you think of it?"

"The pictures are pretty good." Flipping through a couple of pages, Layne added, "I wish it had better maps."

Doc held up a finger. "I think I know a book you'll like more." He pushed out of his chair and crossed over to the bookshelf lining the wall next to me. Scanning with his fingertips, he pulled out a blue book with white lettering and handed it to Layne. "Try this one. The maps are top rate."

"*Ghostly Tailings. A Snapshot of the Past,*" Layne read the title aloud, then skimmed through the pages and said, "Awesome! Thanks."

"You're welcome. Mind if I hang out in here for a bit and talk to your mom?"

Layne's nose was already buried in the text of his new treasure. "Nah. Go for it."

Thunderstruck, I scratched my head, awed by Doc's slick and quick disarming of my knight in shining armor. It was no wonder my chastity belt clattered to the floor every time Doc came near.

"What are you looking for?" Doc pointed at the microfilm reader. "More trouble?"

I returned to the screen and my scrolling. "The Carhart incident." No need to lie; all he had to do was walk over to catch me in the act.

He did exactly that, standing over me, making me feel all prickly with awareness.

"I've been meaning to give this to you." He held out a folded piece of paper, his hand capturing mine as I reached for it, his fingers lingering before letting me go. If it weren't for his wink, I'd have thought I imagined the whole touch.

Unfolding the paper, I glanced over to make sure Layne still had his nose buried in the book. He did, and the rest of his face, too. We didn't even seem to exist in his world, anymore.

Doc's present was a copy of the article on Karen Snarky's murder. Her black and white picture—grainy, but clear enough—showed a pretty young girl, whose dark hair the paper described as auburn.

"Thanks," I said, folding it up and stuffing it in my purse to study more later. Maybe I could run it by Jane, figure out a sly way to ask her if this was the same woman with the bloodstained collar she'd seen in the old photos.

"Mom." Layne pushed back his chair. "I'll be right back." He held up the book Doc had found for him. "I want to make a copy of something in here."

"Do you need some change?" I asked.

"No, I have it." He looked at Doc, but said nothing, then left us.

Alone.

After a glance up at Doc, who was peering over my head at the view screen, I focused back on the task at hand—finding out more about the Carhart men. But I could feel Doc behind me, smell his woodsy cologne, hear his rapid heartbeat—no wait, that was mine. I felt like a masochistic lamb, anticipating the wolf's pounce, eager for the bite. I needed to get a grip, but I couldn't decide which part of Doc to grip first.

"How was your evening, Violet?" Doc asked, his voice low and close.

I slowly twirled the knob, scrolling inch-by-inch through the past. I decided honesty was the policy I'd start with and see where it took us. "Frustrating."

He bent closer and covered my hand with his, making me turn faster both inside and out. "Same here." His warm breath teased the shell of my ear, soliciting shivers. "Did you go home and go to bed?"

"Yes." No need to mention the spoonfuls of cookie-dough ice cream I consoled myself with first. "Did you?"

"More or less."

I looked at him, his cheek just a sway away. "Alone?"

He turned his head and held my stare, the intensity in his eyes practically crackling. "I don't want your friend,

Violet."

He said what I needed to hear, but that didn't solve my problem of Natalie claiming him first. "She's a nice girl."

"Great. She'll make some guy happy some day. But not me."

"Are you going out for a *business* dinner again, soon?"

"No. I learned my lesson. You?"

I shrugged, grinning, teasing, ready to play. "I'm a slow learner."

"Teaching you would be fun. I bet you're a hands-on type of student."

"What gave that away?"

"I've witnessed it firsthand."

"What else have you witnessed?"

"You play well with others."

That made me chuckle. "Anything else?"

"You don't quit until you finish the job."

"Well," I deliberately and slowly licked my upper lip. "I do like to be thorough."

He stared at my mouth and then his Adam's apple bobbed. "Wow." He groaned. "I need a time out."

"Oh, come on. That was too easy."

"What can I say?" His gaze dipped down to my amethyst again. "You do things to me."

Not enough things lately.

"Are you going out with Ben again?" he asked, lifting his gaze north of my chin.

Not if I could help it. "That depends."

"On what?"

"How full my dance card is."

"It looks full from here."

I raised an eyebrow. "I thought you didn't like being distracted."

"I don't, but abstaining isn't working."

"What are you going to do about that?"

He let go of my hand and ran his fingers all the way up my arm, chills and goosebumps trailing. "Stop abstaining," he whispered, then bent down and nipped my bare shoulder. It was the soft kiss he gave me to make it all better that nearly fried my control panel.

It was my turn to groan. "Okay, we're even."

Chuckling, Doc tapped the screen. "There's your article."

Sure enough, the headline read, *Two Dead in Lead Murder-Suicide*.

And that's why Doc was the master and I was his puppet, still all aquiver, my mind stuck on the subject of bare flesh. Doc had not only toyed with my libido, he'd multi-tasked as he pulled my strings, locating what I'd been searching for while making me sing and dance to his tune. Three slices of humble pie for me, please, and don't forget the whipped cream dollops.

But something had me feeling a little confused. "Why are you helping me with this?"

A couple of days ago, he was trying to wrangle a promise from me to walk away from the Carharts.

"If I ask you to stop, will you?"

"Probably not."

"That's what I figured."

"Does that mean you're going to help me?"

His lazy grin resurfaced. "That depends."

"On what?"

"How full your dance card is."

My gaze narrowed. Was Doc saying what I think he was? More of him on a regular basis? Just the thought made me feel sucker-punched, all winded and warm. I must be reading him wrong.

"I think I have some room on it." Which a way more cool-cat answer than jumping into his arms and screaming, "Take me! I'm yours!" Which was my first instinct.

Doc ran his finger along my jaw, cupping my chin, gently forcing me to lock eyes. "Make more room, Boots. Lots more."

The door flew open. Doc stepped back just in time. Layne entered the room and, after a brief scrutiny of us, dropped back into his seat. Doc returned to the table, joining him.

I blew out a breath, clearing ribbon-carrying bluebirds from my vision, and tried to focus on the article. A quick scan later, I noted Wanda and Millie's names, and Lila's, too. The story was plain and simple—an unhappy, violent end to a pair of unhappy, violent men. But while Lila appeared in the picture of the mournful leftovers, I wasn't buying her crocodile tears. Maybe it was the sultry pout or her outlined lips; something just wasn't right.

I leaned forward, staring at a mark visible above the low-cut neckline of her dress, just above her left breast—a tattoo. Of what, though? It looked like the head of a pig melting into a goat. What the hell? Not exactly the cute little heart or rose most women prefer. I zoomed in until the picture blurred, but I still couldn't figure out exactly what it was.

The door pushed open and Addy bebopped into the room, giggling, carrying a book on frogs. Kelly followed. Addy stopped short when she saw Doc, then smiled wide. "Oh, hi, Doc."

Addy and Doc had a history involving chicken feathers and spilled secrets—namely mine, dumped from her lips into Doc's ear. Addy hadn't seen Doc in a couple of weeks, but based on her toothy smile for him, she didn't seem to hold his temporary withdrawal from her life against him. Unlike her mother.

"Hello, Addy." Doc nodded at Kelly, then turned back to Addy. "How's the arm?"

Addy rubbed her cast-covered arm, her dimples showing. "Itchy. Do you want to sign it? I have to wear it for one more week."

"Of course. You have a marker?"

"Mom does, don't you?"

I fished for one in my bag and held it out to her. She bounced from me to him, holding her dirty purple cast out toward him.

He scribbled something and handed me back my marker. "You two staying out of trouble these days?"

"Yeah. Mom has us in lockdown. She says she's rebuked our right to freedom and liberty for all."

Revoked, actually, but I didn't want to correct her in front of Doc. I hit the Print button so I could study the Carhart article and picture more later. Maybe I could find something on the Internet that matched the tattoo.

"She sounds like a real dictator," Doc said, his grin taunting me.

"Totally. She needs a man."

I rolled my eyes. Addy was channeling Natalie again.

"No, she doesn't," Layne piped up. "She has me."

"You don't even have a job, Layne."

Time to play referee. "Adelynn, that's enough."

"I can take care of Mom." Layne wasn't done.

"You're just a kid," Addy said. "Mom needs a real man. Someone who will take care of her when she's hurt."

And so it began, the same argument we went through every night. Having Doc witness it, though, made me squirm in my chair. "Knock it off, you two."

Kelly cleared her throat. "My dad told Uncle Joe he'd like to take care of your mom."

Somehow, I didn't think Addy and Jeff Wymonds were talking about giving me the same type of "care."

"Really?" Addy asked, smiling innocently at me as if she hadn't been trying to shove Jeff down my throat for the last couple of weeks. "How cool would that be, Mom?"

Not cool. I avoided Doc's gaze and squirmed some more. Very not cool. I had to step carefully here, not wanting to hurt Kelly's feelings about her father.

"Kelly and I would be sisters," Addy continued as I searched for a polite way to yell, *Hell, no!*

"I think it's a bad idea." Layne came to my rescue. "He'll just want her to have more babies."

I coughed. I couldn't help it. Just the thought of getting pregnant cinched up my esophagus in a tight little corset and made breathing painful.

"Come on, guys. Let's talk about this some other time," I said, wheezing slightly. A time when Doc wasn't sitting in on the conversation, laughing into his fist. I nailed him with a glare, damning him for enjoying my predicament.

"Babies are cute," Addy said. "I think you should go out on a date with Kelly's dad."

Layne crossed his arms. "I don't."

"Me, either," Doc spoke up, silencing the crowd. "Her dance card is already full."

"What's a dance card?" Addy asked, watching Doc closely.

Addy was no amateur. She'd been training to be a cupid for years, soliciting men as father figures since she'd shucked her diaper. The last thing I needed right now was Addy tuning into anything going on between Doc and me—not with her inability to keep a secret, and not while Natalie was within a hundred-mile radius.

"Ask me again when you turn eighteen." Needing a diversion, fast, I scooped up my purse and asked, "Who wants ice cream?"

Chapter Ten

Monday, August 6th

Dawn arrived with a bang—which turned out to be Harvey's old green pickup backfiring. Apparently, he'd spent the night over at Ms. Geary's place again, which surprised me fully awake because I figured he'd be preoccupied with Claudette Perkins all night. I stumbled into the shower, determined to scrub away all thoughts of Harvey playing slap and tickle with either woman.

Pink skinned, I ate my breakfast standing at the counter, as usual, but alone in the early morning quiet. Well, alone except for the chicken clucking and pecking at the back door to be let out.

I spread Doc's copy of the Karen Snarky article on the counter. Another scan through it confirmed that I hadn't missed anything when I'd read it late last night after the kids went to bed. It was the age-old story of Romeo and Juliet, only instead of Romeo drinking poison and lying down next to Juliet, he stabbed her twice in the gut and then popped a cap in his own skull. Love sure could be twisted.

Unfortunately, this article didn't seem to tie the present and past deaths. The Snarky murder was just another tragedy wedged in the tread of time.

I checked my cell phone before heading out into the cruel world; three messages awaited. The first was from Zelda. She'd called in the middle of the night, sounding a little slurred while a cacophony of shouts and exhaust-pipe rumbles filled the background. She wanted to buy the

Carhart house.

My heart galloped.

The second call was from Zelda again, thirty minutes later, still buffeted by noisy bedlam, her voice less slurred. She "might" want to put an offer on the Carhart house, "if Zeke agrees when he comes out of the ring."

Ring? My heart slowed to a canter.

The last call had come in another forty-five minutes later. Zelda again, no slurring, the background muffled, a toilet flushing in the middle of her message. Zeke and she "would consider" putting an offer on the Carhart house if I were to provide a semi-thorough history on the house, including details on the ghost that supposedly haunted it.

My heart stopped to graze on a patch of thistles. Crud.

That's what I got for going along with the locals' rumors and bragging to Zelda that the house was haunted. Now I had to prove it if I wanted to unload the place before my ghost-loving reputation took more hits.

I stepped out into the bright morning sunshine and winced at the glare. After a grumble and a couple of middle-finger salutes aimed at the sphere of fire in the sky, I fumbled for my sunglasses and keys. The Bronco seemed twice as loud in the already-warm pine-scented air.

Motorcycles filled the streets, black leather overflowed onto the sidewalks, and chrome ricocheted blinding rays at every turn. Sturgis biker days had officially started. My wait for lattes at the Tin Cup Café took twenty minutes longer than usual amid the blended smells of leather and steamed coffee grounds.

I zigzagged through back streets over to the parking lot behind Calamity Jane Realty, passing Doc's Camaro parked blocks from its usual parking place. What was his car doing over here? The hotel where he'd been living for months was on the other side of town.

I parked next to Mona's SUV and crossed the lot to the

back door, playing pack-mule with the lattes, my tote, and purse. Jane's light was on, her door open, her fruity floral and vanilla scented perfume playing hostess at the threshold. I knocked on the doorframe and then noticed she had the phone cradled to her neck. She waved me in.

I'd hoped to get a moment with her to bribe her with her favorite latte and ask about the Carhart house's history. But judging from the deep wrinkles cutting into her lips and the notes she was fiercely scribbling, fun with Jane would have to happen another day. I set her coffee on the desk and tiptoed out front.

Mona's clacking paused when I placed her drink in front of her. "*Have I told you lately that I love you?*" she sang, then added, "I owe you."

"Yes, you do. The bikers are in town."

"How long did you have to wait?"

"For clear left turns, a parking spot at the Tin Cup, or the latte itself?"

"Okay, so I really owe you." Mona sipped on her drink. "Mmmm, delicious. Which reminds me of something else tasty—Deadwood's one and only sexy Detective Cooper stopped in this morning to see you."

That made my heart quake. I didn't like Cooper looking for me, especially when he knew I was getting nosy about the Carharts. "What did he want?"

"Just to let you know he wanted to hold off another week on prepping his place for sale."

Not a problem, since just the thought of going back into his house and prettying it up while he watched me with those steely gray eyes made my palms clammy. I wondered what had come up that made him put me off, though. Probably something to do with biker week. Or was he avoiding me because of something he knew about the Carhart mess?

"So you think Cooper is sexy?" I asked Mona, a little

surprised at her interest in him. Cooper might be considered appealing if a woman liked her men serrated around the edges and with the inner warmth of a pit bull. I preferred to touch without risking the loss of a finger.

"Those gray eyes of his get me where it hurts every time they land on me," Mona said. "Too bad he was born about a decade too late for this old gal." She peered at me over the top of her rhinestone-studded glasses. "Speaking of sexy, you look nice. That little blue number hugs you in all the right places."

"Thanks." I had all of the wrong places sucked in and battened down. I sat on the edge of my desk and sipped my iced mocha. "Do you know anything about the history of the Carhart house?"

"No." Her long lashes squeezed into a squint. "Why are you asking?"

I needed more caffeine to be creative this early, so I told her the truth. "I have an interested client, but she wants to know more about the place before she'll sign an offer."

Okay, I told most of the truth. Mona didn't need to know about the ghost tales.

"You could ask Ray. He knows more about Lead's past than I do."

"I'd rather kiss a cockroach."

She grinned. "Speaking of kissing, how did your blind date go Saturday night?"

For a second, I thought she'd somehow found out about Doc and me doing the back-room boogie at the restaurant, and my cheeks warmed. Then I shoved my guilt under the rug and pretended the night hadn't involved betrayal of any kind. "He turned out to be a really nice guy."

She didn't know I was talking about Ray's nephew, and I didn't plan on enlightening her.

"Are you going to go out with him again?"

"I don't think so."

"Oh." Her grin flattened around the corners of her mouth. "Why not?"

"I'm not sure I'm ready to date yet." What Doc and I had going didn't involve dating. We'd kind of skipped first base and sprinted around second and third ... and beyond.

The sound of Jane slamming her phone down interrupted us. It was followed by loud expletives that had me hopping to my feet. I couldn't remember having heard Jane cuss in the three-plus months I'd worked for her.

The clomp of her heels on the wood floor reverberated through the quiet office. Mona stared along with me as Jane came ramming out into the front room, her normally coiffed hair in spikes, her eyes red-rimmed. "I have to leave for a week or so. Mona, you're in charge. The three of you need to rotate lunches while I'm gone. With all of these tourists in town, we need to have someone manning the desk at all times."

Mona raised an arched brow. "You okay, Jane?"

"No, but I'll live." Jane's eyes darted around the room, but I doubted she was seeing anything. "Tell Ray not to bother calling. When I'm not in court, I'll be too drunk to talk shop."

Court? The call must have been about her messy divorce. Husband number three was trying to take her to the cleaners, following her previous two money-grubbers. To make matters worse, Jane still loved him, in spite of the other woman he'd let lasso his heart and hogtie him—to the bed. Jane's bed, which was how she'd found out. The rotten, two-timing bastard.

I hated to bother Jane in her hour of craziness, but I wanted to sell the Carhart house. "Jane, can I ask you a quick question?"

"What?" She rummaged through her purse, practically tearing the seams. "Where are my damned keys?"

I wimped out. "Do you want me to water your plants

while you're gone?"

"Yes. I'll see you both next week." She left in a flurry of curses, slamming the back door behind her.

I fell into my chair. Crapity crap. Now, how was I going to find out about that stupid ghost? It was time to dig around on the Internet.

The morning flew by, my eyes scanning online county records, my head buried in the past. By the time I'd finished finding everything within the scope of my Internet search knowhow, I had a list of previous owners of the Carhart place spanning clear back to when the house was first built in the late nineteenth century.

But names weren't enough. I needed stories to share with Zelda and Zeke, and there was only one place I could think of to round them up—the Carharts. I just hoped Lila wasn't wearing her hockey mask and chainsaw gear today.

I grabbed my purse and phone. "Mona, do you mind if I go to lunch for a bit?"

"No. Heading home?"

"Probably." Or not. "Want me to bring you something back?"

"Thanks, but no. I'm on a diet."

Diet? Mona was a willow. The only inches she could stand to trim were off her red fingernails. But I didn't have time to expound on how jealous I was of her to-die-for figure. I had a ghost story to track down.

Motorcycles of every make and color clogged the road all the way up the hill to Lead. I cruised along, practicing what I'd say to the Carharts, wondering why Doc had parked so far from his office.

Lila's bright red Mustang hogged the Carharts' drive, so I parked on the street—in front of the neighbor's house. I didn't trust Lila, not even near my Bronco.

The noontime sun beat me down all the way to the front porch. I sucked in a big breath, got into a fighting stance, and rang the doorbell. Then waited.

And waited.

I was about to ring it again when the curtains in the window next to me inched back. Wanda peeked out.

I smiled and waved.

The curtain dropped back into place, and the front door creaked open. Wanda hid back in the shadows of the foyer.

"Hi, Wanda," I shut the door behind me. Vanilla-scented goodness wrapped around me, welcoming. Silence seconded the greeting.

Wanda fidgeted, avoiding eye contact. Her sage green dress was faded.

"Is Millie here?" I wanted to prod about Lila, but I wasn't comfortable saying her name out loud in the lioness' den.

"She's outside," Wanda answered just a decibel above a whisper. "Can I get you a drink?"

Since Wanda was already inching toward the kitchen in an obvious need to escape my presence, I figured I might as well let her flee. "Sure. Some ice water would be great." The ice might cut the acrid taste of it.

Her face fell, as if I were the first to inform her that Santa wasn't real. "We lost our ice trays."

Her sad-puppy expression hinted at an emotional attachment. Bizarre. I wasn't sure how to comfort her on this type of loss, so I didn't. "Just water then, please. I'll wait in the ..." Wanda whisked away into the kitchen, leaving me talking to the wall. "Right. Okay, then."

I peeked up the stairwell as I tiptoed into the sitting room. When I realized I was tiptoeing, I returned to my normal stride. Wanda's church mouse imitation seemed to be contagious.

I sat on the edge of the couch, waiting. The quiet billowed around me. I sniffed just to break the silence.

Movement off to my right made me whirl. Nothing.

Weird. I could have sworn I saw the curtain twitch.

Leaning forward, I peered into the shadowed kitchen entryway. How long does pouring a glass of water take? Wanda must have gone out to the hand pump in the backyard to get my drink.

I stood and crossed over to the curtain, checking for a floor vent that might have caused it to move, but I found only century-old maple trim and a few baby dust bunnies.

A flash of black on the other side the window made me step back. Through the thick lace pattern I spotted Millie, kneeling not twenty feet away with a gardening claw in her hand, a patch of pansies her victim. She was in her usual black woolen outerwear.

Jeez. The woman was a cold-blooded lizard in sheep's clothing.

I glanced back toward the kitchen, but still no Wanda and no water. Turning back to the window, I saw that Millie was no longer alone.

Lila! Wearing an itsy-bitsy red leather vest and some teeny-weeny matching red shorts, my nemesis stood with her arms crossed, shadowing Millie. Lila's long, black hair hung loose and wavy down her back. She looked as if she'd walked off the pages of a comic book, all busty and ready to fight crimes. Or commit some.

I stood up straight, tightened my stomach muscles, and wished the earth would crack open and gulp Lila down.

As I watched their muted conversation, still waiting for that mythical glass of water, I again wondered what a woman like Lila had seen in Junior Carhart. Was it money? The man had been approaching middle age and still lived at home with his parents. He could have been squirreling away gobs of cash.

Outside, Millie rose and used her skirt to wipe her hands. She faced Lila, shielding her eyes from the sun, her mouth turned downward at the corners. Lila spoke with grand gestures; by the looks of it, she had a lot to say.

Maybe Junior had some kind of secret life nobody else knew about. Maybe he was part of some weird cult. Maybe he also had a melted goat-pig tattoo. Who could I ask about that? Millie might know. Or Wanda. They had to have seen him with his shirt off sometime in the last few months before his death.

On the other side of the lace, Millie stepped closer to Lila. Her mouth moved fast and furious, her hands jabbing the air now, too. Lila grabbed her by the arm and dragged her over next to the house in the slice of shade from the eave. I brushed against the curtain, inching closer to the window so I could continue to watch the sideshow.

George Mudder would know if Junior had a tattoo. I needed to round up Natalie and take her back to Mudder Brothers, see if she could figure out a way to coax that information out of George. I had a feeling we'd need something more substantial than just a low-cut shirt to loosen his tongue. He didn't seem interested in Natalie, at least not sexua—

Holy shit! I gaped out the window at Lila, whose lips now covered Millie's. What the ... Were they ... Oh, my ... Wait! Was that tongue? Oh yeah, definitely tongue. And groping, too. I winced, unprepared for a girl-on-girl floor show during my lunch hour, especially one involving Millie. Turning away from the train wreck, I found myself face-to-face with Wanda.

"Here's your water."

Shell shocked from the lip-lock going on outside the window, I took the glass without comment, blushing from my accidental stumble down voyeurism lane.

"I'll go get Millie if you'd like." Wanda seemed oblivious to the peep show on the other side of the glass.

At my nod, she scurried off.

When I peeked out the window again, Lila and Millie

were nowhere to be seen.

The sound of an engine starting up drew me to the front window. I peered through the holes in the lace, watching Lila back out of the drive in the sporty red car that matched her sporty red outfit. Watch out, Malibu Barbie, there was a new crazy bitch in town.

"Mother says you need me," Millie said to my back.

I hadn't heard her enter the room. She must have inherited her mother's ability to mouse about. I plastered a big smile on my lips that any clown would envy and faced her. "Hello, Millie."

She stared at me through those owl glasses for a beat, then glanced at the peep-show window. Her eyes narrowed when they returned to my face. "How long have you been waiting in here?"

Long enough to need to wash my eyes out with soap. "Oh, just a few minutes."

"I didn't hear you pull in."

"I parked on the street. I didn't want to block Miss Beaumont."

"You didn't call first."

"No, I ... uh ... can't find my cell phone."

My cell phone chose that moment to ring, muffled slightly by my purse. What were the odds? Apparently not in my favor.

"You mean *that* phone?"

I laughed, straining to hold eye contact. I sounded like a pinched chicken, so I cut it short. "What do you know? It was in my purse all along."

"Go figure."

While I pulled out my phone and silenced it with the Off button, Millie hustled over to the window through which I'd watched the unsettling scene and closed the curtains. Her frown lines sank deeper into her skin. "To what do we owe this surprise visit, Miss Parker?"

I needed something positive to smooth this over. If Millie found out I'd seen her and Lila rubbing tongues together, she might go to Jane and request another agent. And I was too close to selling this puppy to hand it off to Ray so he could swipe my commission. "I may have a buyer for your house."

Millie's eyes widened, lit up. She took a step toward me. "Really?"

"Yes. But I need some help from you."

"What kind of help? More painting?"

"No, the house looks great, both inside and out. What I need is some information on the history of it."

"You mean like the title?"

"I was thinking more along the lines of pictures or stories about whoever lived here before your father bought it."

"Well ..." Millie pushed her owl glasses up on her nose. "I think we have a box in the attic that was here when we moved in. I remember seeing it tucked back in a cupboard when I hid up there once."

I tried to replace the image of Millie groping Lila's boob with one of a young girl in long, curly pigtails and thick glasses. "Were you and Junior playing hide and seek?"

"Junior never played games with me."

"Oh. I thought you were talking about hiding from him in the attic."

She shook her head. "I was hiding from the old lady."

"You mean your mother?"

"No. The old lady who lives up there. The dead one."

* * *

I cruised back to Calamity Jane's with an old wooden box sitting on the seat next to me and a new headache jammed between my eyes. The box was locked, the key missing. The headache was manageable—more so since I'd popped some pills and gulped down a grilled chicken burrito I'd grabbed from Taco John's on the way back to work.

Doc's black Camaro sat in its usual spot again. I smiled, glad to have a sliver of my world back to normal. I pulled in next to it and strode toward Calamity Jane's back door, the midday heat rolling off my back.

I didn't know what to do with the dead-lady tale from Millie, who'd refused to go up in the attic and get the box. It reminded me of Jane's mention at Bighorn Billy's of the ghost with the slit throat. Were they the same ghostly rumor? Or was Millie's a different optical delusion?

I'd had to climb the rickety attic ladder and swim through cobwebs over to the corner Millie had described, finding the box just as she'd remembered—tucked away in a cupboard. No old dead ladies had surfaced, just as I'd suspected. No doubt this was all a figment of Millie's bored-hermit imagination.

Back in town, I weaved through a resting herd of shiny Harley-Davidsons leaning on their kickstands, engines ticking as they cooled.

I still wasn't sure what to make of that kiss, but more important than what had happened outside that window was why it happened. How long had this been going on between the two women? Since Junior's death? Before?

Why were they hiding it? Was it because public displays of homosexuality in small towns like Lead sparked lots of whispers and finger-pointing—kind of like what my ghost-loving reputation brought about? Or was there some other reason? Something darker, more sinister? Since Lila was involved, I wanted it to be something wicked.

Inside the back door of Calamity Jane's, cool air blew on my hot face. Thank God for air conditioning, I thought, and pulled at my dress to fan my chest.

I'd spent the last couple of days wondering why Lila had hitched herself to Junior's wagon. Now I wondered the same about Millie's wagon. Was it Junior who'd attracted Lila, or had Lila used him to get close to Millie?

Or was Lila after something else? Something more than just the house's inhabitants?

I set the box on my desk.

"What's that?" Mona asked.

"Something I found in the attic." No need to clarify whose attic.

"What's in it?"

"I don't know. It's locked." I was hoping it contained the answers to all of my questions, or the solutions to my problems. But it was more likely something Pandora had left behind.

"Are you back for the day?"

"Sure."

Mona stood, closing her laptop. "I have an appointment with a client. Ray is taking a late lunch, so the office is yours."

"No problem." I had a date with a locked box.

"Douglas Mann called for you." Mona said it as if I knew the name. "I tried to reach you on your cell, but you didn't answer. He left his number for you to call."

"Who's Douglas Mann?"

"You don't know Douglas? He certainly acted like he knew you, even asked for you by first name."

"I have no idea who he is."

"He's a big-wig on the city council up in Lead."

"Oh. Okay." Why would a Lead big-wig be calling me?

"He's married to Katrina King-Mann." Her nose wrinkled. "Well, if you want to call what they have a marriage. It's more like an agreement on paper, these days."

"Should I know Katrina, too?"

Mona chuckled. "Yes, you should. Her family is old-time big money in Lead. They made their fortune as major shareholders in Homestake Mine. They still own a third of the buildings in Lead and a few in Deadwood, along with ranches out near Mount Rushmore and Custer State Park."

"So why is Douglas Mann calling me?" Attention from muckity-mucks couldn't be good, could it? Not after what I'd done to the Hessler house last month.

"Call Douglas back and see." Mona slung her purse over her shoulder. "I'll be back around four."

She started toward the back door and then stopped. "Oh, yeah, Harvey called, too. Said he was going to stop in this afternoon to give you some kind of debriefing."

I hoped he was referring to Claudette Perkins' status and not his preference for mud-wrestling in the buff.

Mona and her jasmine perfume exited out the back, leaving me alone with a box full of who knew what. I grabbed Ray's letter opener from his desk drawer and tried to pry open the lock.

A half hour and two broken nails later, I called Layne and told him to grab his rock hammer and Aunt Zoe's chisel, hop on his bike, and come visit his mother.

The front door whooshed open as I hung up the phone. Harvey bustled inside. "Where's Doc?"

I threw the now-bent letter opener on my desk. "Next door, I'm betting. In *his* office."

"Well, he should be here any minute. I called him on my way into town and told him we needed to powwow."

"He's probably waiting for us over there." Harvey didn't know about Doc's aversion to Calamity Jane's. Apparently, I shared office space with a stinky, nasty ghost, although I thought it was probably just the underlying rankness of Ray's personality that kept setting Doc off.

"No, he said we couldn't meet there because he was paintin' and the fumes were too strong."

"Painting?" I wasn't buying that. He'd painted last

month.

"Yeah, painting—you know that thing you do with a brush?"

Something was up with Doc. All last month he'd avoided even putting a toe in this office, as if we were growing plague cultures under our desks. I doubted he'd just come waltzing over the threshold now. He must have been blowing Harvey off.

Harvey lifted the box I'd been trying to break into. "What's with the box?"

"I found it in—"

The sight of Doc pushing open the door and waltzing over the threshold left me gape-jawed, and it had little to do with how his blue jeans and dark green T-shirt hugged him everywhere I wanted to squeeze.

What the hell?

I heard him sniff as he approached, but he had me locked in his sights. "Hello, Violet."

His gaze raked down my body, trying to take my underwear with it. If Harvey hadn't been watching, I'd have let them fall.

"Doc." I tried not to ogle him like an Elvis groupie.

"Great dress."

I sucked in my gut so fast and hard that I almost cracked a rib. "Oh, this old thing?"

"Let me know when you two are done wasting hot air," Harvey interrupted our tête-à-tête. "I only spent half the night gardenin' in the moonlight with Claudette, sacrificing myself to woo that long-legged widow-maker."

Doc's lazy grin surfaced. "Sacrificing? How noble of you."

"Gardening in the moonlight?" I asked. Was he referring to his pit stop at Ms. Geary's place?

"Yeah, moonlight gardening." Harvey hooked his thumbs in his suspenders. "I poked around, digging for the truth while she planted her tulips."

Doc coughed laughter into his hand.

I recoiled. "Oh, God, Harvey. Stop. I just ate."

Snorting, Harvey continued. "It took a bit of *hard* work and sweat, but I got her to spit out who really killed old man Carhart."

More coughs from Doc.

I reached out and snapped one of Harvey's suspenders. "Knock it off, you dirty old bird, and tell us who."

"Well, I could be wrong."

"Who?" I snapped again.

"And I haven't talked to Coop about it yet."

"Good, you shouldn't." I wanted to avoid Cooper's squinty eyes at all costs. "Who was it?"

"And Claudette had me a little distracted with her tulips when I was askin'."

"Only a little?" Doc was still chuckling.

I squeezed my eyes shut. "I'm going to go blind if you don't hurry up and just spill it."

Harvey guffawed. "That's almost exactly what Claudette said to me last night when we were—"

"Harvey!"

"Okay, okay, Miss Prude. Wanda did it."

Chapter Eleven

There are a few things in this life I believe with absolute certainty: the Earth circles the sun, Bugs Bunny will always outsmart Elmer Fudd, and Wanda Carhart doesn't have the gumption to bash her husband's head in with a rolling pin.

"So, let me get this straight," I said to Harvey, who had planted himself in my desk chair. "Claudette Perkins told you straight up that Wanda murdered her husband."

"Yep."

"And you worked this so-called admission out of her during sex?"

He shook his head. "Russell didn't put out any old flames last night—at least not with Claudette."

"Who's Russell?" Doc asked from where he held down the corner of Ray's desk.

Harvey's two gold teeth gleamed. "Russell, the one-eyed love muscle."

Doc laughed outright this time.

I squeezed the bridge of my nose, trying to keep on task in spite of my mind's desire to join in the puns and fun. "My point is, Claudette was a bit distracted when she made this accusation."

"And busy. She's a handy girl."

"Really?" Doc said. "She sounds a little *mouthy* to me."

I grinned at Doc, who winked back at me and waited for Harvey to stop wheezing before he continued. "She was distracted, and yet you believe her?"

"Yep."

"Why?"

"Because the night before Wanda smashed in her old man's skull, Old Man Carhart had asked Claudette to go to Florida with him."

That made me blink. "On vacation or to move there?"

"I doubt it was to get their picture taken with Mickey Mouse." Harvey leaned back. "According to Claudette, Carhart said something like, 'I'm gonna take that dipshit's money and we're going to leave these hills for good.' One day later, Carhart was dead."

Doc crossed his arms over his chest. "What makes you think Carhart was referring to Wanda?"

"Wanda has a nest egg that only one other person besides Claudette knew about, and now he's pushing up posies."

"She does?" And here I'd figured Wanda had needed to sell the house for financial reasons.

"Turns out some old maid aunt of hers died last fall and left Wanda everything. Claudette doesn't know how much 'everything' adds up to, but Carhart seemed to think it was enough to pay for a nice retirement in Florida—for two."

Claudette's story sounded hackneyed to me. I needed a second opinion from someone who hadn't been dipping his toes—and then some—into the witness pool. "Doc, do you believe Claudette's story?"

He rubbed his neck. "I'm not sure. I haven't met either woman. I only know what the newspapers said, which included nothing about an inheritance and adultery. Do you believe her?"

"I don't know." My gut still sided with Wanda's innocence, but my brain toed the line.

Harvey snorted. "Well, while you two hem and haw, I'm gonna keep an eye on Wanda."

"So, Claudette—and now you—think Wanda found out and snapped?"

"Yep. After puttin' up with all of his steppin' out and abuse over the years, Wanda probably didn't need much of a nudge. A rolling pin would've just about evened the score for her."

"But Wanda's a church mouse."

"Little critters bite, too."

Maybe so, but they didn't bash skulls. "Do you think Cooper knows about this?"

"I'm guessin' so," Harvey said. "Coop's no bumblin' gumshoe."

I tossed the hot potato back to Doc. "But didn't the paper say the police had confirmed Junior was the killer?"

"Yes. But, knowing Detective Cooper's tenacity, I'm betting there's an unspoken 'for now' hiding between the lines." Doc shot a frown toward the back door, sniffing and then stiffening.

I peeked down the back hall and sniffed, too, seeing nothing and nobody, smelling old varnish and a hint of Ray's cologne. Same old story, so I returned to the here and now. "What do you mean an unspoken 'for now'?"

"You know what double jeopardy is, right?"

"Sure. You can't be tried for the same crime twice."

"Exactly," Doc said. "So if the cops didn't have enough evidence to nail Wanda, they might not have wanted to risk a trial yet."

I focused back on Harvey. "So even though Cooper told us the case is closed, it might not be. He could've been leading me astray on purpose."

"Yep. Coop may be lousy at holdin' his liquor, but the boy can hogtie his tongue tighter than a road-foundered calf-roper."

I chewed on my bottom lip for a moment, not sure what the hell Harvey meant. "So, what do we do now?"

Doc sniffed, his skin pale, his grimace now aimed in the general direction of the coffee pot. "We could walk away and let the police handle this."

"Yeah, we could," I agreed. "But that probably isn't going to happen."

"I don't like it when you nose into trouble, Violet." Doc rubbed his thighs, squeezing, his knuckles white, his gaze still locked on the back of the room.

At the sight of his Adam's apple bobbing, I reached for his shoulder. "You okay?" Twice now, he'd keeled over on me just after he'd gone all pale and sweaty like this. I didn't relish cushioning his fall again.

"I'm fine." His dark eyes shifted back to me, but his forehead stayed creased. "Why can't you just walk away from this Carhart mess? And don't tell me it's about the sale."

"Something weird is going on over there, but I can't put my finger on it—yet. I'm worried about Wanda."

"She could be the killer," Doc said.

My gut still disagreed with that. "Or she could be the next victim."

"So could you, and that's a problem for me."

The intensity in Doc's stare made my determination to find the truth waver. Maybe I should just focus on selling the damned house, leave well enough alone, and let the police do their job—if they were still planning to.

I looked at Harvey, who was leaning way back in my chair, watching the two of us with raised brows. Digging into the Carhart mystery was not only dangerous for me, but for Harvey, too. The snooping around I'd asked him to do could piss off the wrong person—someone with their own version of Bessie the shotgun, for example.

But there was that kiss.

"When I was at the Carhart house at lunch today," I told them both, "I saw Lila and Millie kissing."

"What!" Harvey almost tipped over backward, catching himself before he tumbled out of the chair ass over belly.

Righting himself, he leaned forward, bug-eyed. "Tell me more."

"There was tongue." I glanced at Doc, who seemed to have a little more color in his cheeks now. "And groping."

"Well, we're sure shittin' in high cotton now. I ain't seen girl-on-girl action since last year's biker rally."

"Oh, please," I said. "What do you call the bikini mud wrestling bouts you frequent over at the Prairie Dog Palace?"

"A beautiful work of fiction. This is the real deal." Harvey stroked his beard. "You know, Doc is right. You might land in some hot water over at the Carharts'. You shouldn't be going over there alone, anymore."

"Let me guess, you're going to volunteer to be my bodyguard again."

"It's my civic duty."

Where had I heard that before—oh, yeah, from my own lips. I was about to pooh-pooh his offer when an idea hit me. "Maybe you should pay Wanda a visit on your own. Work your charm on her."

Harvey recoiled back into my chair. "No way, darlin'. I draw the line after Claudette. Wanda's a sweetheart, but I like my women curvy, not doughy."

"I'm not asking you to have sex with her, just talk to her. She's scared to death of me, but you two go way back. She may open up to you."

"And what? Confess?"

"No. Tell you about her home's previous owners. I have a list of their names, but I need more details."

"What's that have to do with her killin' her husband?"

"Probably nothing."

"Then why waste time on it?"

"Because I need the information to sell Wanda's house."

"What's in it for me?" Harvey asked.

"My loyal friendship."

He grunted at my sarcasm.

"An extra free lunch," I added.

"Okay, I'll give her a whirl. But I'm keeping my pants on this time."

"Thank God for that."

The front door opened and Layne hesitated just inside the threshold, a rock hammer in his hand, his eyes bouncing back and forth between Doc and me. "What's going on?"

I waved him over and he handed the hammer to me. "We're just wondering what might be in this box. Now that you're here, we'll find out."

"What's the big deal with this box, anyway?" Harvey lifted it, turning it over, shaking it.

I grabbed it from him and set it back down on my desk, keyhole up. "It was in the Carharts' attic."

"But how did *you* wind up with it?" Doc asked, his skin normal and olive-tinted again.

I skirted the attic-tromping details. "I told Millie I have some interested clients who want more information on the previous owners before they'll officially place an offer on the house." At Doc's cocked head, I added, "It's the truth. I have the messages from Zelda on my cell if you want to listen to them."

Raising the hammer, I said, "Here goes nothing," but Harvey stopped me mid-swing.

"Girl, you either need a bigger hammer or a smarter locksmith. Now give me that box." He pulled a screwdriver from his back pocket.

I frowned at it. "Were you sitting on that this whole time?"

"Naw, it was off to the side."

"So, you just carry a screwdriver around with you at all times?"

"Sure. A man never knows when he'll need to do some

screwin'. Ain't that right, Doc?"

I pointed the rock hammer at Doc, who grinned from ear to ear. "Don't answer that."

Layne dropped into my chair, taking Harvey's place. "You mean like screwing around, Harvey?"

"I mean like—"

"Keep it PG, old man," I warned.

"Uh, sure, kid. That's one way of putting it." Still snickering, Harvey jammed the flat end of the screwdriver into the crack where the lid connected with the bottom, grabbed the hammer from me, and with one hit broke the box open. The lid fell open and two cufflinks spilled out onto my desk. The rest of the treasure trove stayed put in the storage box.

He handed the hammer back to me. "It's a good thing you have me around."

"The jury is still out on that," I said with a smirk.

"Look, Mom! One of those Chinese puzzle boxes." Layne plucked out a funky wooden box with loose-looking blocks on two of the ends. There was nothing written on it, nothing painted, no design work. "This is like what Uncle Quint used to bring me."

"Who's Uncle Quint?" Harvey asked.

"My older brother."

"I didn't know you had a brother. Is he down in Rapid?"

"No. He's gone on location. He's a photojournalist." I glanced at Layne. "Careful, kiddo, that's old."

Flipping the storage box upright, I picked up a yellowed, lace-edged handkerchief from the top of my desk. Who had left such finery behind? This kind of handiwork was usually passed down through generations.

Harvey reached in the box and withdrew a palm-sized wooden horse. He turned it, rubbing his thumb over it. "This is hand-carved. Someone knew their way around a knife."

Something touched my hair. I looked over my shoulder. Doc held up a piece of cobweb. "You need to stop playing around in attics, Nancy Drew."

He let the web fall in my trash, then slid his palm down my back as he lifted an oval locket out of the box with his other hand. Again, a master at multi-tasking. He needed to give me lessons—private, of course. Clothing optional.

His fingers drifted even lower, brushing over the curve of my hip before he stepped back and broke contact. Such teasing was going to be the undressing of me.

Blowing out a breath of pent-up frustration, I collected the pair of cuff links that had scattered on my desktop when the lid came loose. They were pearl with a gold inlaid *B*.

"What do you guys think?" I asked my fellow treasure hunters. "Millie told me this box was there when they moved in."

Doc handed me the opened locket. "I think the horse and cuff links might have belonged to these two."

Each side of the locket held a black and white picture— one of a dark-haired man with a long, curly-ended moustache; the other of a young blond boy, probably about Layne's age, with a bowtie at his neck.

Did the handkerchief and locket belong to the wife and mother? I handed the locket to Harvey. "Are these two familiar to you at all?"

"Dammit, girl! I may be old, but I'm not ancient."

"Just look and tell me if you recognize one of their descendants in their features."

He took the locket and peered down at the pictures, closing one eye, then the other. "Nope. They look like the same people in all the other old pictures hanging on the walls of the buildings and casinos around here."

"Got it!" Layne cried from the chair behind me. "Mom,

I figured it out."

I spun around, bending close as he opened a slat door and pulled out an open-topped drawer from within the puzzle box.

"Holy cow." Layne whispered.

I took the drawer from him. "What in the hell—I mean 'heck'?"

Harvey lowered the locket. "Come on. Show and tell."

"What is it?" Doc touched my shoulder.

"Canine teeth." Layne beat me to the punch.

Sharp ones, at that. Turning, I held out the drawer in front of me like an offering. "A box full of dog teeth?"

"No, Mom. *Human* canine teeth."

* * *

Layne counted 187 sharpened canine teeth, which equaled out to one tooth shy of forty-seven mouths. Who would be storing all of those teeth in a Chinese puzzle box, and why? And how did they get them all?

None of us could come up with a logical, sensible reason for collecting that many teeth. My suggestion of an over-achieving tooth fairy won a trio of groans. So much for trying to make light of a squirmy situation.

After Layne put the puzzle box back together with the teeth trapped inside again, Doc excused himself, claiming another so-called appointment. I had a feeling his need to escape had more to do with the return of his pale skin, sweat-glistened brow, and glances toward the back door.

Before hightailing it out the front, he requested my list of the previous Carhart home owners, offering to do some research at the library to see what he could find out. I amended the list to include the Latin title of that creepy book I'd found under the bed in the Carharts' upstairs bedroom. He raised his brows at my fib about how I stumbled across the book, but didn't push for the truth. Promising to give me a call later, he left. I wasn't holding my breath for delivery on said promise.

Harvey headed home to take care of some chores and check his traps—the illegal ones. Cooper had told him he could no longer use them, but Harvey intended to plead hard-of-hearing if he got caught. His parting comment about finding a pair of gutted porcupines back in his family's old cemetery changed my squirminess to queasiness. After hearing that little tidbit, I decided that if he wanted to bend the law about those traps, I wasn't going to give him any argument.

I sent Layne home with the rock hammer and the box from the attic with instructions not to touch anything in it until I got home. Then I settled into my chair and let out a big groan. My mind was a whirligig, spinning out of control. I needed to find solid ground and plant my feet. But where and how? And what came next?

Grabbing my cell phone, I punched in Natalie's number and waited for her to pick up.

"Nat's taxidermy shop. You snuff 'em, we stuff 'em," Natalie answered with a typical smartass greeting.

"Hey, Nat. I need your help."

"Does it involve a man?"

I thought of Junior Carhart, all ripe and buggy in his grave. "Sort of."

"Then I'm in. What kind of trouble are we getting into now?"

She knew me too well. "I need you to meet me at Mudder Brothers this evening."

"I thought you said it involves a man."

"You didn't clarify that he had to be breathing."

"From here on out, it's an implied qualification."

I smiled. "Duly noted."

"So whose funeral this time?"

"Junior Carhart's."

"You're about six months too late. There's no way I'm going up front with you to view the body."

"I need you to ask George Mudder if Junior had a tattoo."

"Why don't you just ask Wanda or Millie Carhart?"

"Two words: Lila Beaumont." My upper lip curled just saying her name.

"Who's that?"

"Junior's fiancée."

"Ah, the infamous fiancée. You afraid of spurring more waterworks?"

Not quite. "Something like that. And while we're there, we might as well kill two birds with one stone."

"Are we ordering matching caskets?"

"No. Your taste is too expensive for me. I want to take a peek in that storage room. The one behind those one-way glass windows."

"I was hoping you'd forgotten about that room."

"Nope. My body may be going to hell in a handbasket, but my mind is still holding on. According to the paper, Eloise Tarkin's viewing is tonight. Did you know her?"

"Contrary to what you think, Vi, I don't know everyone in town."

"Oh, right." *Bullshit.* "So, how did you know Eloise?"

Natalie chuckled. "Her husband used to deliver our mail when I was a kid."

"Perfect." I leaned back in my chair. "I'll see you at Mudder Brothers at seven."

"What if I said I have a date tonight?"

I'd have heard about it three times over by now if she did, especially if it involved another attempt to land Doc. "I'd say you should go jump in Robaix Lake because your pants are on fire."

"Fine, but you owe me. I hate funerals."

"Put it on my tab."

After I hung up, I picked up Mona's note with the number for Douglas Mann, the Big-Shot city councilman from Lead. Ray clomped in through the back door as I punched in the number, his cologne triple-coating his skin and making my eyes water. He greeted me with his usual scorn-filled sneer. I returned with my customary middle-finger warm-and-fuzzy.

After five rings, Douglas' voicemail picked up. At the tone, I said, "Hi, I'm calling for Douglas Mann. This is Violet Parker from Calamity Jane Realty, and I received a message that you wanted to talk to me."

I glanced at Ray just to keep an eye on the snake and felt all sunshine-and-lollipops inside at the sight of his narrowed glare and scrunched forehead. I gave him a little wiggly-finger wave as I spoke my cell phone number into the receiver. "Feel free to call me back at your convenience."

"What on earth would Doug want to talk to you about?" Ray asked after I disconnected the call.

"Well, being that I'm a Realtor—"

Ray scoffed. "One sale makes you a lucky amateur, not a professional."

"—he probably wants to talk to me about a property to buy or sell."

"No. It's your tits."

"What? No." His comment caught me with my pants down. When had we descended to the next level of crassness? And why?

"You're new in town, Blondie. You don't know Doug. His wife carries his balls in her purse, but Douggie Junior roams the countryside, searching for willing girls with welcoming arms and open legs."

"He doesn't even know me." At least I didn't remember meeting him.

"He called. That means he at least knows of you. And he probably knows all about your situation."

"My situation? You mean that I'm single?"

"I mean female, blonde, and desperate—Doug's favorite perfume. On top of it, you have small tits. Doug likes small—"

"I'm not small." I picked up my stapler, intending to pound that fact home.

His gaze slid down to my chest. "You're what? Maybe a B-cup with a wad of toilet paper stuffed around the edges?"

Try C—including a smidgeon of padding, but that was my secret. "That's something you'll *never* know."

I was done discussing breast size with this over-tanned, sexist Neanderthal. I was done sharing an office with him for the afternoon as well. "Don't you have any appointments this afternoon you need to slither off to?"

He leaned back in his chair, resting his Tony Lamas on his desktop. "Nope. It's just you and me, babe."

I grabbed my purse and shoved my phone into it. "No, it's just you."

"Where do you think you're going?"

"I have an appointment," I lied, hoisting my tote onto my shoulder. "Oh, and when Douglas calls me back, I'll be sure to let him know how kindly you spoke of him. What was the name you called his penis? Douggie Junior, right?"

"Don't even think about it, Blondie!" Ray bellowed at my back as I sashayed out the back door, whistling.

Layne must have shown his sister the box of teeth in spite of my instructions not to, because when I pulled into the drive, Addy greeted me at my Bronco's door. On the trip up the front walk, she informed me of her expert status on dental matters after having brushed many animal teeth in her "long" life. I decided not to ask her how many of those times she'd used my toothbrush without telling me. Her ruling on the teeth coincided with Layne's—they were definitely human.

"You didn't touch them, did you?"

"Ummm, why?"

That didn't bode well. "You don't know where those teeth have been, Addelyn."

"Layne said you told him they'd been in an attic for a long time."

Of course she'd take me literally. "I meant before that."

"Mother, you're overreacting. Just relax."

Rather than sentence my daughter to her bedroom for eternity, I searched for my Zen. "Where's Aunt Zoe?"

Addy shrugged, popped her pink bubble gum, and then skipped off toward the living room where the television blared.

I found Aunt Zoe in her workshop. Handing her the locket, I asked if she recognized the man or the boy, or saw any kind of resemblance to a potential modern-day relative. But like Harvey, she didn't have a clue about either one's identity.

Another dead end. Lovely.

I spent the rest of the afternoon sorting teeth with Addy and Layne—all of us wearing gloves this time—and speculating to myself about the teeth's origin and purpose, still baffled. The pointy canines reminded me of another enigma in my life, also one with whom I needed to wear gloves when handling: Lila.

Douglas Mann hadn't called me back by suppertime. I checked my messages, just to be sure, but came up empty. After Ray's not-so-glowing raves about Douglas, I contemplated turning my phone off. But there was always the chance that Doc would call, dying with some animalistic need for me, craving my touch.

Yeah, right. Oh, look, there's a flying pig.

Chuckling at my own sarcasm, I silenced the ringer instead, putting it on vibrate mode.

Over a crispy, peppery chicken-fried steak, I asked Aunt Zoe, "Do you mind watching the kids for an hour this evening while I attend Eloise Tarkin's viewing with Natalie?" Asking was more of a formality. Aunt Zoe's gallery was closed on Mondays. On top of that, she and the kids loved to catch some National Geographic show on Monday nights, watching to see if my brother's name showed up in the credits, which it did sometimes.

"Sure. Eloise's husband used to deliver mail out Natalie's way, didn't he?"

"Yeah." I mentally shook my head at how small Deadwood could be and chewed on my last savory bite.

"Don't hurry home." She sipped on her glass of homemade lemonade. "The kids and I have a date with some snakes tonight."

What a coincidence. I'd discussed bra cup sizes with a snake this afternoon.

"You and Natalie should enjoy a girls' night out."

"Aunt Zoe, it's a viewing."

"Well, don't feel like you have to rush home. The kids and I will be just fine on our own."

"If I ever win the lotto, I'm splitting it with you even-steven." I dropped a kiss on her head and then raced up the stairs to don my black.

At five minutes after seven, I parked my Bronco on the street in front of Mudder Brothers. Apparently, Eloise Tarkin was a popular lady because there were no spots free in the parking lot. After one last check in the rearview mirror to refresh my lipstick and tuck in hairs that had escaped from my French knot, I climbed out into the early evening air.

Even though the sun was heading out for the night, leaving behind long shadows, warm waves of air still rose from the pavement, heating my ankles and calves. The rumble of motorcycles drowned out the usual summer early evening sounds of humming lawnmowers and laughing children. The smell of exhaust mingled with pine trees, cut grass, and baked asphalt. I crossed the parking lot, Mudder Brothers open front doors beckoning.

Natalie's pickup was nowhere to be seen, so when she called my name, for a moment I thought I imagined it.

"Violet! Over here."

Natalie sat on one of the little bench seats next to an ashtray-trash can combination on the far right side of the porch. The acrid smell of burning tobacco brought me to an abrupt stop several feet from her. "Are you smoking?"

She nodded, picking up the cigarette and drawing on it.

"Why?" Natalie had quit smoking three years ago after a decade-long battle. As I stared at her, her eyes filled with tears. I dropped down next to her on the bench, my gut clenching in anxiety. "What's wrong, Nat?"

She blew her lungful of smoke away from me and swiped at her eyes. "It's nothing, really. It's silly. I feel stupid."

"What?"

"I mean, we never even had anything real."

"Tell me."

"I've come to realize it was all in my imagination."

"Natalie, you're killing me. What?"

She leaned her head on my shoulder and sniffed. "It's Doc."

The chicken-fried steak Aunt Zoe made for dinner threatened to revisit my back molars. "What about him?"

"He's not in love with me."

"You're not making sense." Had Doc talked to her about us?

"I saw him tonight."

"And?"

She sighed. "I parked over next to his office, thinking I'd drop in on him and say hi if he was working late."

Hands clenched, I hung on her every word.

"He was working late, but he wasn't alone."

Come again? "Who was he with?" I tried to sound like a concerned friend instead of a jealousy-crazed lover. "And where?" In his back room?

"I don't know who she is, but she has gorgeous red hair and a tight little ass, nothing even close to my Amazonian body." Natalie puffed on her cigarette again.

Oh, God, not Tiffany, Doc's flame-haired ex-Realtor and ex-bedmate. Please not Tiffany. "Did you actually catch them kissing?" I swallowed bitter bile. "Or doing something else?"

Another long breath of smoke billowed from her lungs. "They were standing next to her car, hugging good-bye."

"Well, that could mean something completely platonic." I said, trying to convince the both of us. I hugged my arms to my chest to ease the ache growing there.

"Then I overheard her say how glad she was that they were back together—and they kissed."

"That son of a bitch!"

Chapter Twelve

There was a trick to comforting my best friend after her heart had been broken by my lover when she caught him kissing his ex-lover.

Unfortunately, I wasn't capable of performing that trick. I was a little busy keeping my own beating organ in one piece at hearing about my soon-to-be ex-lover's wandering lips.

Holy shit.

What a fucking mess.

Where was the tequila?

I wanted to race to my Bronco, tear ass over to Doc's office, and pound on his chest. But I couldn't leave Natalie here alone, smoking her way through heartache. So I held it all in—the stabs of jealousy, the spasms of hurt, the tears of rage. One breath after another, I rode out the choppy waves of betrayal until I could speak without grinding my molars.

"I know just the thing to cheer you up," I said, squeezing Natalie's shoulder. "A dead body. Let's go look at it."

She stubbed out her cigarette, grabbed her crutches, and hobbled after me. What a trooper.

In the foyer I caught a whiff of something medicinal. I sniffed again. Embalming fluid? I recoiled, then noticed two huge bouquets of lilies on pedestal stands just inside the French doors leading to the parlor. Oh, thank God, it was just stinky flowers. There was a reason I preferred daisies.

The parlor room was two-thirds full of whispering,

sniffling mourners. The other third of the room contained bouquets bursting with color, displayed in wreaths and sprays and vases. A chilled breeze of air conditioning spilled out over us, making me wish I'd remembered to grab the shawl that went with the black velvet tank dress I had on for tonight's main event.

"Do you see George?" I whispered to Natalie when she joined me in the parlor entrance.

She craned her neck. "No. He's probably in back, prepping."

"Prepping what? I can see Mrs. Tarkin from here." Well, her folded hands, anyway, which was plenty.

"I don't know, someone else. Come on." Before I could object, she crutched inside and plopped down in a seat in the back of the room. Déjà vu, I thought, and joined her.

I'd just settled in when a familiar, but strangely out of place, classical piece of organ music began pulsing from the speakers in the top corners of the room.

"That's weird," I said under my breath.

"What's weird?"

"This song. Who plays Bach's Toccata and Fugue in D Minor at a viewing?" My mother was a classical music groupie, so I grew up being force-fed long-dead composers.

"That's Bach?" Natalie asked. "It reminds me of the old black and white horror movies we used to watch in your parents' basement during sleepovers."

"I know. Those spooky organ riffs along with these one-way windows and Mrs. Tarkin's corpse are all creeping me out." I showed her the goosebumps on my arms.

"That's just the damned air conditioning. If it gets much colder in here, we'll all be stiffs."

I rubbed my arms. "Add some candlelight, and I could just see Mrs. Tarkin rising up from her casket and saying, 'I vant to suck your blood.'"

Natalie giggled. "Hey, look," she pointed at the front of

the room. "There's George."

I had a feeling George was responsible for the sinister-sounding Bach tune. All these years of dressing up dead folks had to have warped his mind. I could see his tiny yellow teeth as he greeted viewers. As if he felt my stare, his gaze roved in our direction, landing on me, then Natalie.

She waved.

I attempted a smile.

He excused himself from his guests.

"Here he comes," I said through my frozen smile. George was pausing here and there along the way to shake hands or deliver pats on the back. "Act natural."

"Natural? We're at a funeral, Vi. Not a bar."

"Fine, then act sad for Mrs. Tarkin. But not too sad."

"No problem. I'll just think about Doc."

I'd think about Doc, too, and the uppercut I was going to aim at that sexy cleft in his chin the next time I saw him. "Don't think of Doc, think of Junior and that tattoo. The sooner you ask George about it, the sooner we can get the hell out of here."

George dropped into one of the seats in the empty row in front of us, resting his forearm across the back of the chair. "Two viewings in less than a week, Natalie. I'm shocked."

"Me, too," Natalie muttered.

I poked her in the ribs. She flinched.

"George, you remember my friend Violet? She's the one selling the Carhart house."

Nice. Natalie was building up to Junior's tattoo, I could feel it.

"Sure. Violet, who likes my gables." He held out his hand.

Criminy. I'd forgotten about my foot-in-mouth disease the last time I'd talked to him. His palm was warm and sweaty when I shook it. I counted to three and pulled away, trying to wipe the sweat on my dress without him noticing. "Nice choice of music. Is there an organist hiding behind this one-way glass?"

Natalie cleared her throat and kicked me in the anklebone with her cast-free foot, making me jerk in pain. *Ouch!*

"Nope." George grinned, showing us those tiny yellow teeth and big gums up close. I held in my wince—barely. "Just Eddie and his media center. He has a big repertoire of organ music."

"Eddie is George's brother," Natalie explained to me.

I pretended that was news to me, even though I knew all about Eddie. I knew all about George, too, and his very nasty, very public divorce from one of the descendants of Deadwood's founding fathers. What I didn't know was what had been in that crate Ray and George had loaded in Ray's SUV last month. But I hoped to find out shortly.

"Is Eddie back there right now?" I asked, "watching us through the glass?" Talk about creepy.

"No, he's downstairs cleaning up."

Cleaning up what? Did they do autopsies down there?

"Do you two split the duties around here?" I could see Natalie's frown out of the corner of my eyes. I'd disrupted her tattoo segue. Oops.

"Yes. Eddie's in charge of all the technical aspects of viewings and services. I tend to deal with the public."

And who worked with Ray on the shady little side business they had going? Just George, or both brothers?

George's mention of technical stuff reminded me of something he'd said during our last viewing adventure. "George, you don't happen to have another copy of that video of the Carhart funeral that Junior's fiancée requested, do you?"

George hesitated, his forehead furrowing.

Before he could question why I of all people was asking,

I threw out, "Wanda Carhart wanted me to ask."

"I already gave a copy of it to the fiancée."

Ah, ha. So he had an original somewhere. "That's what Wanda said. But in all the post-funeral hubbub, it seems they've misplaced it."

"Oh," his forehead cleared now that I'd smoothed everything over. "Well, sure. I could make another copy for Wanda. Do you need it tonight?"

"Yes, please, if it's not too much of a problem. I could deliver it tomorrow when I take some paperwork to Wanda."

George stood. "Okay, give me just a moment. I'll have to go to my office and burn a copy for you."

I elbowed Natalie and nudged my head in George's direction.

She grabbed his hand before he could leave. "George, we need to talk to you about something else regarding the Carharts."

"You do? What?"

"It's kind of private." She glanced at the other mourners. "Can we talk in your office?"

"Sure. Just follow me."

"I need to use the Ladies room first," I said, rising. "I'll be right with you two."

A silver-haired, sad-faced man interrupted at that moment, nodding a hello at Natalie before asking George about some programs for his aunt's funeral.

I leaned over and whispered in Natalie's ear. "Keep him busy in his office for five minutes. Don't let him leave."

"Five minutes?" She said it as if that was one minute shy of an eternity.

"You're right. That's too short. Make it ten."

"Ten? How am I supposed to keep him in his office that long when there's a viewing going on?"

"I don't know. Be resourceful." I glanced down at her

black silk blouse. "Take your shirt off."

"What! Oh, Jesus. That's gross. He's practically my uncle."

"Fine. Leave your shirt on, then, and talk about your Aunt Beatrix. He's got the hots for her. I could tell when he asked about her last time."

"Where are you going to be for these ten minutes?"

I nodded at the wall of one-way glass.

Natalie rolled her eyes. "You're crazy. What do you think you're going to find back there? A smoking gun with Ray's name on it?"

"Maybe. For all we know there could be two smoking guns back there."

"You're gonna get caught with your hand in the cookie jar. You always do."

"Not always." Just 99.9 percent of the time. "I'll see you in a jiff."

I headed out the parlor doors, making sure George wasn't watching when I made a left turn instead of a right toward the bathroom.

Two doors down, I overshot the storage room and found a storage closet instead, lined with shelves full of old-looking, oversized leather-bound books. I was tempted to pull one down and open it, but the clock was ticking, so I tiptoed back out and quietly closed the door behind me.

I backtracked one door, found it unlocked, and slipped inside. This time, I hit the mark.

Shrouded in semi-gloom with the only light coming from the parlor through the one-way glass, the room was divided in half. One side held four rows of chairs, all facing the parlor windows—a private viewing area for family and close friends. The other side held true to the *storage* part of the room's name: shelves full of Kleenex boxes, racks of vases of all sorts and colors, stacks of folded wreath-supporting tripods, and more. Everything a girl could need to throw a first-rate viewing.

The organ music was muted slightly, but still audible. I sniffed, a trick I learned from Doc. My gut twinged just thinking about him, so I shoved that whole mess to the back of my mind. The room smelled musty with a hint of cardboard, like most storage rooms. No dead body smells here.

I tiptoed across the carpet, then remembered that the glass was one-way. I could break-dance for all the folks on the other side cared. Against the far wall, next to a fancy-looking rack of stereo equipment, sat the two big wooden crates that matched the one Ray and George loaded into Ray's SUV last month. They were stacked end-to-end. I could see that both lids were loose.

I shoved aside the first lid and found nothing but an empty crate. I replaced the lid and moved to the second. This crate contained a small cooler like what Aunt Zoe used to keep the worms chilled and subdued when she took the kids fishing. Only this Mudder Brothers cooler had a big red biohazard sticker on it. Being that I was standing inside a funeral home, my imagination came up with lots of body pieces that could fit in that cooler.

As much as I didn't want to open the cooler, I had to. The red lid popped off easily, the inside empty, not a speck of blood that I could see in the dim light. I blew out a breath I hadn't realized I was holding.

I put the cooler back the way I'd found it and started to close the lid on the second crate when I heard a voice on the other side of the door. Through the one-way glass, I saw a man who looked very much like George Mudder, only taller and thinner with extra-prominent cheekbones—a lot like Lurch from the Addams Family. That had to be brother Eddie.

Yikes!

In a panic, I did what any rational single mother in her

mid-thirties would do when on the verge of being caught snooping in a funeral home's storage room. I threw my little velvet purse in the crate and scrambled in after it—hearing something rip in the process—then closed the lid over my head.

The crate was pretty solid; no cracks to peek through. I listened, crouched on my knees, taking shallow breaths. I could barely hear the dull thud of footfalls just outside the crate over the staccato of my heart in my ears. Several seconds passed with nothing more, then footfalls again in front of the crate.

He was leaving! Relief spread through me with a tingly chaser.

A rhythmic buzzing next to my thigh almost made me scream.

My phone! It was in my purse, on vibrate mode. I grabbed my purse, flipped it open, and hit the Off button.

The footfalls were coming back, getting stronger, louder.

Oh, this was bad. This was going to be hard to talk my way out of. Maybe when he pulled back the lid, I could jump up and yell "Surprise!" Pretend I was a ditzy stripper who'd confused the crate with a cake.

No. That wasn't going to work. I needed to come up with a Plan B.

The footfalls stopped outside the crate. My heart stopped, too. So did my lungs. Oh, man. I was going to puke, or pee my pants, or both.

"Eddie," George's muffled voice interrupted. "I need your help burning a DVD copy."

The footfalls faded.

I counted to thirty before lifting the lid just enough to peek out. All was clear in the storage room. I scrambled out of the crate and grabbed my purse.

Out in the parlor, I saw George Mudder shaking hands

with someone. That meant Natalie was on her own in the office, at least until Eddie joined her. I scurried over to the parlor exit.

The foyer was empty. I stopped by the Ladies room long enough to make sure I had no smudges and to figure out what had ripped—just an inch worth of seam midway between my armpit and hip, nothing visible if I didn't lift my arm.

Natalie was standing in the foyer when I exited the john. She rushed over to me. "That was longer than ten minutes, damn it."

"Sorry. Eddie came in. I had to hide. Then my phone vibrated and he almost caught me." Which reminded me...I dug out my phone and hit the On button.

"I told you you'd get caught."

"I didn't get caught, just came close." I looked down at my phone's LCD screen, waiting for it to register. "Did you ask George about Junior having a tattoo?"

"Yes. That's not the most casual conversation to initiate, you know. I hope you appreciate how awkward it was for me."

"Is a large latte enough thanks?"

"Sure, if you throw in a blueberry and vanilla scone."

"Fine. Tell me about the tattoo."

"There's nothing to tell. He didn't have any."

"Damn." Back to square one.

Natalie peered at my phone's screen. "Who called? Was it Doc?"

I'd have thought her obsession with Doc was pathetic if I hadn't been wondering the same thing.

"It was Douglas Mann."

"No way! You're kidding me." She said it as if Douglas had flown down from outer space to make the call.

"Listen, I know Douglas is a bigwig up in Lead, and I've heard he chases a fair amount of tail, but is it so unreal that he would call me?" It was, but I wasn't going to admit that to Natalie. He probably tried to get into her lucky Cookie Monster panties every chance he could.

She laughed. "It's not you, spaz. It's what George Mudder was telling me in his office about Douglas not ten minutes ago."

I stuffed my phone back in my purse, not feeling up to returning his call tonight. "What did George say?"

"That Douglas was at the Carharts' funeral."

"So what? I bet half the town of Lead was. It was probably an A-list event. It's not every day a small town has a murder-suicide double funeral."

"Yeah, but did half the town pinch Junior Carhart's fiancée's butt while giving their condolences?"

* * *

Natalie and I bade our farewells to the Mudder Brothers a short time later, the DVD copy of the Carharts' funeral in my hand. I planned to scrutinize it for any butt-pinching scenes as soon as I had a chance. I walked her to her pickup in the twilight as the rumble of motorcycles echoed off the surrounding hills.

I closed the door behind her and leaned on her car's window frame. Her cab smelled sweet and citrusy—Clinique Happy, her current favorite perfume. "Are you sure you don't want to go out for a drink? Drown some sorrows? Play some pool? There's nothing like hitting balls around when a man pisses you off, right?"

She patted my head. "You're a great friend, but no, thanks. I just want to go home, slip into my favorite PJs, and watch some Bogart on the old talking box."

"'I don't mind if you don't like my manners …'" I quoted a line from one of our favorite Bogie films.

"'I don't like them myself,'" she finished, and grinned.

"Give Phillip Marlowe a little love from me." I stepped back as she cranked up the engine. "Thanks for your help tonight."

"You're welcome."

"If you'd have flashed Eddie, I bet we could have gotten a tour of the autopsy room."

That made her chuckle. "I had to save something for next time. Night, Vi."

I waited for her to turn the corner toward home before hopping in my Bronco and heading into town. I had a certain dark-eyed ghost-sniffer to hunt down and cut into sushi-sized pieces. There was no way I'd be able to sleep tonight until I heard the nasty truth from his own lips.

First stop: Doc's office. His car wasn't in the parking lot, and the windows were dark.

Second stop: Doc's hotel room. No car again, just rows of Harleys. When I knocked, a burly bear of a man in holey socks, blue jeans, and a black leather vest answered, expecting pizza and Coke. Turned out a blonde in a little black dress was a perfectly fine substitute in his opinion. I thanked him for his cheek-burning proposition and scooted back to my Bronco before he could slip into his boots and chase after me.

What in the hell? That was Doc's room, I was dead certain of it. But where was Doc? Was he staying with the redhead now? How long had this little tryst been going on? Days? A week? Longer? No. Really? God, I was such a gullible fool.

It seemed that Jane hadn't cornered the market on cheating bastards. I gunned it toward home. Midway there, I changed course and headed over to the library on the off chance he was hitting the books instead of the skinny redhead. His car was missing in action there, too.

I sat in the parking lot for a minute, resting my head on the steering wheel. My gut burned. My chest felt like it'd been pummeled by a gorilla. My esophagus had a cantaloupe lodged in it. Self-implosion loomed if I didn't do something, quick.

I rolled up my windows, locked my doors, and screamed. Then screamed again and again, letting it all out in long, loud bursts.

After the crazy-rage had finished geysering from my lips, I took a big breath, rolled the windows back down, and shifted into gear. I needed a drink. Something with tequila in it. Or some ice cream.

To avoid all the motorcycle traffic, I wound my way toward home through back alleys. The sight of Doc's Camaro in my headlights made me stomp on the brakes. Idling, I frowned at it. He'd parked it in the same weird spot as the other day, a few blocks from his office.

What in the hell was going on?

I headed back to the office and parked in my usual spot. The orange streetlights made everything appear to be coated in bronze, as if the Coppertone fairy had paid a visit. I weaved through parked bikes and pickups as heat still rising from the asphalt kept my calves warm. Mixed in with the distant rumbles of exhaust pipes, I heard the twangy sounds of George Strait singing about all his exes living in Texas. Catcalls and wolf-whistles abounded. Deadwood was partying hard tonight, and I was an outsider peeking through the keyhole.

I closed and locked Calamity Jane's back door behind me. The fluorescent lights buzzed to life overhead. My mule heels clomped along the wooden floor, doubly loud in the silent office. Tossing my purse on my desk, I pressed my ear to the wall dividing Doc's office from mine.

Silence.

I stepped back and glared at the wall. Was he over there with her? Were they in the back room? Was he kissing her neck, whispering in her ear, slamming her up against the wall?

My breath rattled in the quiet room, the green jealousy monster crushing my lungs. I walked over to my desk and stared down at the phone. How had I fallen so fast for this guy? So hard? This wasn't me—the total lack of control, the petty jealousy, the quick temper.

I flashed back to last month, to his ex-girlfriend's reaction to the sight of him standing next to me, her slap, her swearing.

"Oh, my God," I whispered. I'd turned into Tiffany. All this time I'd thought her temper tantrum was genetic, that it came with the red hair. But it was Doc. He made women lose their minds.

Something thumped twice against the wall that divided us.

I snapped. "You son of a bitch!" I yelled. The rage came from nowhere, overpowering me. I picked up my stapler and hurled it toward the wall, where it hit Jane's Goals whiteboard with a loud bang. Louder than I'd expected.

The whiteboard crashed to the floor after the stapler.

"Oops," I whispered. That was going to leave a mark.

A calm settled over me, flowing through my limbs. Mr. Hyde had returned to his lair, leaving Dr. Jekyll to clean up the lab. I skidded over and picked up the white board, wincing when I saw the big dent in the middle of it. A definite mark.

Crap. Now I had to go buy Jane a new whiteboard. I leaned it against the wall, then picked up the stapler.

Someone pounded on the front door.

I screeched and dropped the stapler—right on my big toe.

Pain shot upward, riding the expressway to my skull. I blinked away tears as I kicked off my shoe, hopping up and down as I turned toward the front door.

Doc stood on the other side of the glass, arms crossed

over his chest, frowning at me. His hair looked like it'd tangled with his fingers; his jaw was shadowed with stubble. He was clothed in jeans and T-shirt, his usual attire.

He pointed at the door handle.

I hesitated. Looking into those dark eyes that had the power to make my knees wobbly, I was afraid to bridge the distance between us.

I shook my head.

He mouthed the words, "Open it."

Feeling all kinds of silly, I limped over to the door, unlocked it, and then stepped back.

He crossed the threshold, his gaze locked on mine. "What's going on, Violet?"

"Nothing." I backed toward my desk. He stalked after me. "I stopped by work to grab a file."

"What happened to the whiteboard?"

"It just fell off the wall." I tried to laugh, but it came out scratchy with a hint of crazy cackle. My butt hit the edge of my desk. "Weird, huh? Maybe it was that ghost you claim lives here."

"You don't believe in ghosts." He kept coming. "Why is it dented?"

"I don't know. It must have hit something when it fell."

"Or something hit it?" He towered over me.

"Yeah, something like that." I bent backward as he leaned down, planting his hands firmly on the desktop on each side of my hips, trapping me, his lips level with mine. "Ummm, should you be in here?" I asked. "I mean, with that odor that bugs you and all?"

"It's not here at the moment."

"Oh."

"But you are."

"Right." His eyes were directly in front of me, watching. He smelled sexy as hell, all manly and spicy, making me a bit rummy. "I was just about to leave."

"Who's the son of a bitch?" he asked.

I froze, as trapped prey tends to do. "What?"

"You yelled. I heard. Then it appears you threw a stapler at a poor, defenseless white board."

"Well, aren't you just a regular Phillip Marlowe." I still had Bogart and *The Big Sleep* on the brain.

"'Somebody's always giving me guns,'" he quoted, leaning even closer.

No fair using Bogie lines to fire me up.

"Who's the son of a bitch?"

I held my ground, not bending another inch. "You are."

He lingered, almost touching, his eyelids at half mast. The heat of his breath warmed my lips. "What did I do now?"

"You kissed a girl."

His eyes met mine. I could see flecks of gold around the outer edges of his irises. "I've kissed a few in my time. So what?"

"You kissed her tonight, in the parking lot. Natalie saw you."

He grinned, slow and easy-like. "You're jealous."

That tightened me up all over again. I pushed against his chest, backing him up a couple of inches. "I'm pissed."

"Excellent."

"What?"

His gaze dipped to my cleavage. "Damn, you look edible in this dress."

"Doc, I'm really ticked off here."

"I know." He chuckled.

He chuckled! "I don't see what's so fucking funny about this."

"Violet," he slid his hands up my arms, his palms hot. "I didn't kiss Tiffany. She kissed me—"

"You're splitting hairs."

"On the cheek."

"Still ..." Still what? A cheek kiss was a lot different from a lip lock, I couldn't deny it. Natalie must have been hallucinating with jealousy by that point. "You hugged her."

His fingers trailed over my shoulders, stopping at the base of my neck. "She hugged me—goodbye."

"Tiffany said she was glad you were back together again."

"Natalie heard that? Where was she, under the car?"

I wouldn't be distracted. My gut had to know for sure before it would stop the grinding. "What did Tiffany mean?"

"I'm taking care of a financial deal for her. Something we set up months ago, back when we were sort of dating. Then all hell broke loose."

"Yeah, well, you tend to bring out the deranged side of women." I kept my hand on his chest, maintaining enough space between us to keep my thoughts from getting all muddled with lust. I wasn't free of this jealousy cramp yet. "So, when Tiffany said you're back together, she meant as business partners only?"

"Exactly."

"Will all of your meetings end in touching?"

"Not if I can help it." His gaze dropped to my lips. "Will it make any difference if I tell you that she has a boyfriend now?"

"A little." Relief made me feel all loose and liquid, as did his hands, sliding around the back of my neck.

I scratched my fingernails down the front of his T-shirt, teasing.

He growled deep in his throat. "Natalie was right about one thing."

"What's that?"

Before I realized it, he'd loosened the clip holding my French knot. Curls tumbled around my face. He tugged on one. "I was kissing a woman tonight."

"Who?"

His lips claimed mine—slow, gentle, soft; exploring, stealing my breath, dragging a moan from me. He tasted like red wine with a hint of temptation, and I was thirsty as hell. His hands delved into my hair, tipping my head back as his mouth grew bolder, his tongue teasing, then seeking. He slid one hand down my shoulder, burning a path along the side of my breast, my ribcage, around my lower back. Then he pulled me against him, his hips pressing in all the right places.

He pulled back, his breath ragged. "I'm kissing *you*, Violet."

"Oh." I didn't want to think about Natalie. Just Doc and what I wanted him to do to me. "Maybe you should kiss me again."

"There's no *maybe* about it."

His mouth came down on mine once more.

Chapter Thirteen

When I was fourteen, I rode on the Demon Drop—five times in a row. The amusement park ride shot me one hundred feet into the air, suspended me out over a ledge for a count of three, and then let me free-fall almost two-thirds of the way back to Earth. The drop stole my breath mid-scream, shoved my stomach into my throat, and boosted me clear off my ass, leaving me winded and tingling at touchdown.

Doc's kisses had the same effect—only I wasn't touching down.

He lifted me onto my desk, his fingers skimming up my bare legs, roaming over my knees, and inching north—taking my hem with them. His lips left mine, slid to my collarbone, brushed across my shoulder; his beard stubble scratched, tickling with a delicious fervor that surged clear to my toes.

The scent of his skin surrounded me, filled my head, melted away all last traces of coherent thought besides what I needed—craved—from him. I tipped my head back, giving him an all-access pass to my neck. He obliged, starting with a lick, then a graze of his teeth, then a nip. His lips moved to my earlobe, his breath jagged in my ear, his plans for me whispered teases, stirring me into a dust devil.

"God, Doc!" I gasped and pulled his mouth back to mine, ravaging this time, patience long gone.

The piercing sound of horns and whistles dragged me back down to Earth. I pulled away from Doc's lips. "Do you hear that?" I asked, blinking, trying to make sense of the noise, of time and space.

Nodding, he glanced toward the front plate glass windows. "Shit." He grinned down at me. "Wave to your fans, Violet."

I looked out the windows and died a little death, envisioning my casket draped with humiliation and sprinkled with a handful of mortification. My whole body roasted. With a beauty queen runner-up smile, I waved at the group of bikers idling in the street in front of the office. *Show is over, folks. Nothing to see here ... yet, luckily.*

After a lot of hoots and hollers, clapping and engine revving, the leather-clad crew bid us adieu and motored off toward town.

Damned Jane and her belief that blinds were bad feng shui. The fluorescent lights must have lit us up like a red-light-district window show.

I leaned back on my palms, my face still steaming with embarrassment, and looked up at Doc's cockeyed grin. There was way too much airspace between us now, but any less and I'd have to touch him—I couldn't help it. "That was close. Much longer and we might have had a predicament on our hands."

His gaze dipped to the front of my dress. "We still do."

Electricity crackled through my veins, leaving me even hotter and more bothered. "What do you want to do about that?"

"Finish what I started."

"Where?" When his eyes traveled farther south, I chuckled. "I meant, did you have a more private location in mind?"

"I hadn't gotten that far." He took a step back, shaking his head. "You keep distracting me with that dress."

"You mean this plain old thing?" I sat up and ran my hands down the front of my dress, taking my time on the curvy parts.

He groaned. "You're killing me, Boots. Pick a place. Now."

"Your hotel room." My decision was two-fold—one for more privacy than Calamity Jane's could offer, two for an answer to where he was now living.

His hesitation was obvious—and unsettling, like a cold can of soda pop shoved down my undies. Why didn't he want me to know where he was staying? I waited to see what excuse he gave.

Doc's gaze lifted from my dress to meet mine. "My hotel room isn't available at the moment."

Why? Because some big guy with the holey socks and a hunger for pizza-bearing blondes was sleeping in it?

"Okay. No hotel room then." As much as I wanted to know where he was spending his nights, I wanted his body more. I'd deal with the hotel room later, post-satiation. "Then let's go to your office."

He hesitated again. At least he held my stare, I'd give him that.

My gut flip-flopped from excited trembling to anxious queasiness. "What's going on, Doc?"

"You don't want to know."

Now I had to. I slid off the desk. "Yes, I do."

"How about your Bronco? We could take a ride somewhere."

"No. Let's go to your office." I grabbed my purse, limped over to where my other shoe still lay next to the victimized whiteboard, and slipped it on.

He beat me to the front door, holding it closed when I pulled on it. "Trust me, Violet. This is not a good idea."

"What's going on over there?" I tugged again, but he was stronger. "And don't tell me you're painting, because I'm not buying that. You painted last month."

"It's not that big of a deal. Just let it go."

"If it's not a big deal, then let me see what's over there." Or *who*. This time, when I pulled, he relented. Surprised I'd won the battle, I frowned up at him. "Why so secretive, Doc?"

Poker-faced, he opened the door, ushering the way. "You'll see."

I had goosebumps in spite of the warm summer night. "Hold on, let me lock up."

He waited, then led me into his darkened office, clicking the deadbolt behind us.

I reached toward the light switch and he captured my hand, stopping me. "No lights." He let go and walked toward the front windows.

Why no lights? What was he hiding in here? Uncertain, poised in the shadows, I listened for a sound, a sign of someone—or something—holed up in the dark with me. But my ears felt cotton-filled. Doc's office walls muffled everything—the throbbing party bass, the growling Harleys, the drunken shouts. Everything except my heart, which pounded in my ears like a pissed-off landlord. I hoped to hell it wasn't about to get torn out and stomped on by a redhead.

Doc's usual stuff was right where it had been the last time I'd been in here two weeks ago. No smells of fresh paint, no hint of perfume, nothing but stale varnish and subtle whiffs of Doc's cologne.

I turned to Doc, who was closing the blinds, blocking out the streetlights, making it even darker. "Why don't you just tell me what's going on?"

"And ruin the surprise? Where's the fun in that?" He walked past me and disappeared into the shadow-filled back hall. "Follow me, Violet."

I slipped out of my shoes—I didn't know why—and tiptoed after him. The bathroom door hung open, the room empty as far as I could see. Farther down the hall, a beacon of dim light spilled from the one room I'd been in before. Gearing myself for what I was about to see, I tensed and rounded the doorway.

The sight before me had me scratching my head.

"See?" Doc said from where he lounged in a big blue beanbag, his forearms resting on his raised knees. A pile of books sat on the floor on one side, and an upside-down crate held a lamp and bottle of wine on the other. "Now, do you understand why I didn't want you, of all people, in here?"

My tunnel vision faded. I glanced around the room, which was filled with boxes and luggage—the green set I'd caught a glimpse of through his window a few days ago. His shirts and pants hung from a makeshift clothesline strung between the floor-to-ceiling bookshelf and a hook on the opposing wall.

My heart cheered, fluttering now that it was out of danger, even though my job might not be out of harm's way since I knew what Doc was up to and how it went against Jane's rules.

Crossing my arms over my chest, I leaned against the doorframe. "What were the thumps I heard earlier?"

"If you mean the thumps that occurred before you threw the stapler in my general direction and told me to go to hell, it was just a pair of boots I'd tossed that hit the wall."

"I did not tell you to go to hell."

His grin appeared. "It was unspoken."

The low light added shadows to his face, outlining the contours of his cheeks, the cleft in his chin. Damn, I wanted him—enough to take stupid risks just to have him.

"How long have you been living in here?" I asked.

"A week. The hotel kicked me out when the bikers started rolling in. Something about previous reservations."

"So this is your secret—you're breaking your lease." I

knew the fine print in his lease after one desperate day last month when he wouldn't return my call and I'd flipped into stalking mode, something about which I wasn't particularly proud. "If Jane finds out, she'll evict you. She's a stickler for rules."

"Yeah, I get that feeling from her." He leaned back into the beanbag, arms behind his head, legs out and crossed at the ankles.

"Are you planning to stay here until I get the keys to your house?" Which would be in a week or so unless we hit a snag.

He nodded. "But now it's a problem for you as much as me."

Very true. If Jane learned that I knew Doc was living here, breaking his lease, she'd be pissed. Pissed enough to fire me? Probably not, but with only one sale *almost* under my belt, I didn't relish finding out. On the other hand, it was just for another week. "As far as I'm concerned, you're using this as a storage room until you move into your house."

He lifted a brow. "I don't want to get you into trouble with your boss."

"She'll never know." Jane was going to be gone for more than a week, anyway, shouldering her divorce mess. She'd probably be sleeping with a shot glass on her nightstand for the next month. I doubted she'd notice a Texas-sized meteor falling from the sky unless it landed on her soon-to-be-ex's head.

I dropped my purse on a box and shut the door, sealing us in, snug as bugs … on a bag of beans. "Where'd you get the beanbag?"

"Down in Rapid. It's more comfortable than the floor." He watched me stroll toward him, openly admiring. "Have I mentioned that I want to tear that dress off you with my teeth?"

I straddled his legs, standing over him, empowered by the hungry glint shimmering in his gaze. "You may have alluded to it."

He sat up, his fingers wrapping around my ankles and then gliding up my calves. "Where were you tonight before you came swinging for me?"

I didn't feel like wasting time on any more secrets. "Mudder Brothers Funeral Parlor."

His fingers froze on the back of my knees. "What were you doing there?"

"Somebody died. Your fingers stopped."

"Who?" He went all Clint Eastwood on me—narrowed eyes, scrunched brow—and pulled his hands away. Damn it.

"Eloise Tarkin."

"Hmmm." Dirty Harry Doc still had his squinty eye on me. He leaned back. "How did your dress get ripped?"

Boy, he didn't miss much. Then again, he'd been getting pretty handy over at my desk. "Hiding in a crate."

"Christ! Do I want to know more?"

"Not right now." I reached under my dress and wiggled out of my panties with as much pole-dancing grace as I could muster, dropping the black satin to the floor. "About that predicament of ours ..."

"Damn, Boots." His voice came out raspy. "That's sexy as hell."

"Really? Then what do you think of this?" I slid a black bra strap down one arm.

"Bad thoughts."

"And this?" I shrugged the other one down.

"Very bad thoughts."

I reached behind me and unclipped my bra through the velvet. Then I slipped the bra completely off, drawing the piece of satin and lace out through my low neckline, and dangled it from my finger. "What about this?"

"I'll show you." He jackknifed upright, grabbing my bra

and throwing it behind me. His hands wrapped around the outsides of my knees, then skimmed up my outer thighs, sneaking under my dress. His fingers climbed higher, exploring, his palms burning. All teasing left his face. His eyes darkened as he watched me. My breath quickened when his caresses grew bolder, came closer; skimming, enticing, tormenting.

My knees trembled, threatening to buckle. The fireworks crew in my head had all the powder kegs in place, fuses ready for lighting. I anticipated his touch, couldn't wait for it, moaned in eagerness as his fingertips teased just out of reach.

A glancing stroke sent me reeling. "Doc, touch me."

"Not yet."

I gripped his shoulders. "Please."

"I like it when you beg." He strummed, stealing my breath.

"Paybacks are hell, you know."

"I'm counting on that." His hands slid down to the back my knees. He tugged on me. I folded, my shins sinking into the beanbag, my thighs straddling his.

Eye to eye now, I assessed my new position. First of all, there was too much space between us. I remedied that, scooting closer, my thighs hugging his hips, his pants the only barrier.

He groaned as I nestled against him, searching for a better fit. "Am I hurting you?" I asked.

"Immensely."

"Good." I adjusted again, this time with purpose.

He stared at me, his jaw tight. "Not yet, Vixen."

I conceded for the moment, but his T-shirt had to go. I wanted to ogle his body, rub all over it, taste it. I grabbed the hem. "Take this off."

Shrugging it off, he tossed it behind me. "Anything else?"

"Yes. Lean back."

He indulged me, resting on his elbows. I took a moment to study his torso in the lamp light and decided the contours required a hands-on examination. I walked my fingernails up his ribs. Then I swirled in circles back downward, trailing the dark hair that sprinkled his abdomen. The flames inside me licked higher, hotter, as his muscles rippled in response to my touch. I reached his waistband and his hand stopped me.

"My turn."

I spread my arms wide. "I'm all yours."

A growl rumbled from his chest. "You will be."

Breath bated, I waited. His assault started on the last place I expected—the inside of my wrist. His lips caressed. Then he worked his way up to the soft skin of my inner elbow, his tongue tickling, making me squirm as something low in my belly quivered. By the time he reached my shoulder, I was coated in goosebumps, writhing in lust.

His onslaught shifted to my mouth, his lips coaxing mine, his teeth gently tugging. I tried to entice him deeper, feeling bereft, wanting so much more. But he resisted, his tongue elusive.

"Doc," I whispered.

"Yes, Violet?" he kissed around his words.

"I need you to touch me."

"Where?"

"Start here." I grabbed his hands and planted them on my breasts.

His groan sounded pain-filled. "I'm trying to take it slow."

"There's no time for that." I undid his pants, reaching inside.

At my touch, his control evaporated. His mouth grew rough, devouring. As I hiked the bottom of my dress up, he shoved the top part down, his hands squeezing and tugging and tweaking and massaging.

A couple of well-placed rubs by me encouraged him to kick off his pants. He gripped my hips, easing me down onto him. I sighed as pleasure spread through my veins. Grazing my nails down his shoulders and triceps, I shifted to allow his mouth more access.

He didn't disappoint. His lips trailed down between my breasts, then sought more. His tongue circled, flicking as he tasted. His hips grinding as he pulled me down harder, faster.

"Damn, Doc." I gasped, rocking along with him. "I love it when you multi-task."

"Violet." His voice was gruff, strained.

"Yes?"

"You're incredible."

His compliment shot me higher, made me want to give even more. I tipped his face to mine. Throwing aside any last inhibitions, I sought his mouth and matched our dance with my tongue. My hands slipped around to his back, where I clawed and marked him as mine. My lips dipped to his earlobe, his neck, his shoulder, my teeth sinking into his flesh. Then I crested, straining against him, shuddering, gasping his name.

"You are so damned hot, Boots," he rasped when I finished. He grabbed my hips and pulled me down hard, tight against him as he arched backward, all rigid tension.

I rode the waves, watching pleasure ripple over him. Then his body sank into the vinyl, visibly relaxing. His breath slowed to match mine.

His dark gaze drifted down to my bared midriff and back up. He tucked his arms behind his head, reaching for the bottle of wine. "You sure know how to break in a beanbag."

I leaned forward, resting my forearms on his chest. "What can I say? When you tease me, I get a little hot and bothered."

"When you get a little hot and bothered, I can only think of one thing." He shifted his pelvis tellingly, and then held out the bottle of wine toward me, his eyebrows raised.

I took it and sipped, the fruity blend on my tongue reminding me of Doc's kisses—warm and wild. In the cozy silence, my phone vibrated in my purse.

"You need to get that?" he asked.

I didn't want to move, break our connection. "They'll call back if it's an emergency." My kids knew better than to call twice in a row if it concerned only chickens or the need for more glue.

He tucked a curl behind my ear. "Good, because I don't think we're done here."

I poured a splash of wine on his chest. "Oops, I'd better get that." I licked it up and felt his instant response.

"Vixen." He reached for me. "Come here."

Several wine-flavored kisses and a lot more rubbing and touching later, I lounged on my back in the beanbag, satiated for the time being. Doc's cheek rested on my belly while he traced figure eights on my hipbone.

I stroked his head, combing his hair with my fingers. A book in the stack next to the beanbag caught my eye: *Haunted Deadwood.*

"Doc?" Our newfound intimacy emboldened me. "Will you come with me to the Carhart house?"

His finger stopped. "What for?"

I didn't really have an answer. I just wanted him there for some reason. "You'll see something I haven't." *Or can't.*

"Something dead?"

"I don't know. Maybe."

"You don't believe in—"

"I know. I know." Truth was, I was starting to be less sure what I believed in when it came to ghosts. Things no longer seemed so black and white. The edges were blurring, turning an ectoplasmic gray. "Just humor me."

"I'll consider it." He suddenly pushed to his feet, grabbing his jeans from the floor.

I gawked, as any red-blooded female would, at the sight of Doc's naked, muscled body.

"Don't look at me like that, Violet." He picked up his T-shirt. "Or we'll be starting all over again."

Watching him step into his pants sobered me, reminding me of the outside world. I didn't want the lightness of the moment to end, to have to return to the weight of real life.

"Don't move," he told me, heading for the door. "I'll be right back." My phone vibrated as he passed. He paused. "You want to get that?" At my nod, he tossed me my purse.

I dug my cell out, my gut panging at the sight of Natalie's name on the screen. I let it go to voicemail. Then I checked who'd called earlier and saw her number again.

"Shit." Taking a deep breath, I called her back.

She answered on the first ring. "Violet, where are you?"

There was no way in hell I could answer that truthfully. "Leaving the store. What's going on?"

"I'm heading to Doc's."

What? "Wait!" Oops, wrong word. "I mean, why?"

"I realized tonight as I was watching Bogart that I've been going about this wooing business all wrong."

I scrambled to my feet, snatching my dress from the box it had landed on after Doc had peeled it off me with his teeth and flung it behind him. "All wrong?"

"I've been trying to win him with Betty Crocker, which is so not the real me."

"The real you?" Where were my underpants? I lifted the beanbag and found them, a bit dusty.

"You know me. I don't win men by feeding them. I win them with sex."

"Sex?" I stepped into my undies while searching the

room for my bra.

"Yeah, sex. You do remember what sex is, right? It's that thing you do when you're naked with a man."

"Sex, right." I found my bra on the floor behind some stacked boxes. "I vaguely remember it."

Natalie chuckled. "Someday, we'll find a man to give you a refresher course."

"I'll pass. Sex is overrated." A voice in my head guffawed at that doozy of a lie.

Doc rounded the doorway as I struggled to clasp my bra, bent over with my ear to my cell, which I'd set on top of a box. I silently shushed him before he had a chance to laugh out loud at me.

He set the glass of water and can of Diet Coke he'd been holding on a nearby box and came to my rescue.

I lifted the phone to my ear in time to hear, "We need to find you a man who will ravish you, take his Playboy fantasies out on you."

Doc's hands didn't stop at the clasp. His palms slipped around and covered my breasts, stroking. His lips brushed my bare shoulder, then his teeth nipped my skin.

"That isn't necessary," I told Natalie, closing my eyes as Doc's hands ventured south.

"Whatever. We can talk about this later. I'm almost there."

My eyelids sprang wide. "Almost where?"

"At Doc's office. I have a gut feeling he's working late tonight. And when I get there, no more Betty Crocker. I'm back to being Catwoman from now on. I'm wearing my lucky Cookie Monster panties."

"He's not there." I grabbed Doc's hand, stopping him from slipping further inside my underwear.

"How do you know?"

"I ..." I stepped away from Doc, pointing at the phone and mouthing Natalie's name. "I stopped by my office earlier to grab a file. His car was gone, and his windows were dark."

"I'm gonna check anyway."

"No!"

"What is your problem? You're acting all weird. Have you been drinking tequila again?"

"No, no." I ran a hand through my hair, searching frantically for an explanation Natalie would buy. "I'm just frustrated with this whole Carhart deal."

"You really need to stop thinking about dead men. It's unhealthy. The live ones are much less stressful."

I didn't remind her about how upset she'd been earlier at the thought of Doc sleeping with another woman. Partly because I'm a nice friend, but mostly because I was the other woman. Ah, the twisted lives we lived.

"Listen, Nat. I think it's a bad idea for you to stop at Doc's place."

That snared Doc's attention. He crossed his arms, watching me with raised brows.

"You think it's a waste of time, huh?"

"Yes, I do."

She sighed. "You're right. Do you know which hotel he's staying at?"

Christ, she was relentless. One of her finer qualities, usually. "No. I think you should sleep on this."

"I'd rather sleep on him."

I ignored that. "Why don't you meet me for a drink over at the Purple Door Saloon in ten minutes? Let's come up with another plan." I'd rather poke myself in the eye repeatedly with an icicle, but those were hard to come by in the summer.

"All right. I'll see you there."

I hung up and frowned at Doc. "I have to go."

"So I hear." He nodded at my phone. "You need to take care of that."

"It's not that easy." I zipped up my dress with a little help from him. "She's been my best friend since we were kids. I don't want to break her heart."

"You already have. She just doesn't know it yet."

That stung. I lashed back. "Maybe you should make it a little more clear to her that you're not interested. Quit stringing her along." Unfortunately, placing some of the blame on him didn't lessen the sting; it just made me feel like I was something I'd find stuck in the tread of my boot.

Doc frowned at me. "I've told her repeatedly that our relationship is and will remain strictly business. I reiterated that fact Saturday night after dinner with you and your *date*."

"That was a blind date. A debt payback to Natalie."

"A date nonetheless." He jammed his hands in his pocket. "I don't know how to make it any clearer to your friend than I already have. Now it's up to you to quit encouraging her."

"By telling her about us?"

"Exactly."

"You make it sound so simple." He didn't understand Natalie. He didn't know about the claim she'd staked on him, one that meant I was supposed to keep my hands off. It wasn't as simple as just announcing to her that I was having sex with her supposed "one," about whom she had spun wedding dreams already. Not if I ever wanted her to talk to me again.

I grabbed my purse. Taking the can of soda pop Doc held out for me, I hesitated in front of him. I didn't know what to say to a guy who'd taken me to the moon and back. I was new to this dating business, if that's what you called what we'd had tonight. "I'll see you around."

"Violet." Doc grabbed me, kissing me until my knees wobbled. "Tell her."

Chapter Fourteen

Tuesday, August 7th

A mourning dove cooed outside my open window. If I'd had Harvey's shotgun, I would have blown the noisy ball of feathers to smithereens.

Beams of sunlight stabbed between the curtains and poked me awake, seeming a lot brighter than they should have for seven in the morning. I blinked at the clock and let out a *yip* when I read the numbers on it.

I was babysitting the office while Ray and Mona visited actual paying clients, so being late was not an acceptable option.

I crashed into the bathroom, trying to take the doorframe with me. My shoulder throbbing, I stepped under cool jets of water and shivered, with no time to wait for the water heater to kick in.

That's what I got for drinking tequila shots. Just thinking about last night at the Purple Door Saloon made my tongue recoil. I never did get around to telling Natalie about Doc. I just couldn't do it, not with her waxing on about him and his qualities as a potential husband and me fresh from having sex with him, his musky scent still on my skin.

Instead, I drank and listened. And listened. And drank. And listened some more, nodding at the appropriate times. But my head was still in Doc's back room, full of guilt-ridden thoughts about his naked body. As best friends go, I was one of the shittiest around.

It took Natalie two hours to finish lamenting. The tequila kept me nice and numb through the thick of it.

Pounding on the bathroom door jarred me back to the present.

"Mom!" Layne yelled. "I need to go to the bathroom."

I pulled my head out from under the shower nozzle. "Go downstairs!"

"I can't! Aunt Zoe is making Addy wash her chicken in the sink."

Wash her ... What? Why? I probably didn't want to know.

"Hold on a second," I yelled, rinsed the last of the shampoo from my hair, and shut off the water. Not using conditioner meant my curls would riot, but Layne's bladder trumped.

A towel wrapped around me, a minty squirt of toothpaste in my mouth, I raced past Layne and zipped into my bedroom to dress with superhero speed. Fifteen minutes later, I stumbled out the front door as I slipped into my beaded mule sandals, my keys in hand.

The sight of the empty driveway stopped me cold.

What the hell? Where was my Bronco?

Oh, right. Tequila. Natalie had driven me home. My Bronco was still parked at work, since I'd walked the four blocks to the bar from Doc's last night.

Lucky for me, old man Harvey's pickup sat across the street in Ms. Geary's drive.

The mouth-watering smell of bacon greeted me when Harvey opened the door. The cantankerous old man standing in the doorway in his red satin boxers didn't take kindly to my interrupting his breakfast, especially since I insisted he put on his pants before driving me down to work.

"You could have just let me borrow your keys." I told Harvey a few minutes later as he backed out of Ms. Geary's drive. "I'd be back at noon to pick you up."

"No way! I'd be a shriveled raisin by then. That woman can't get enough of me."

Red satin boxers and now this kernel of knowledge. Swell.

"What's wrong with your hair?" Harvey asked. "You jam something in a light socket?"

"I had chicken issues."

"Your feathers do look ruffled this mornin'."

My cell phone rang. I pulled it from my purse and flipped it open. Douglas Mann, again. I took a deep breath and took Douglas' call. "Violet Parker speaking, how can I help you?"

"Hello, Miss Parker." Doug's voice sounded strangely high and peppy with a squeak of bubblegum, like a sixteen-year-old girl's. "This is Douglas Mann's secretary. He'd like to speak with you if you have a moment."

He had his secretary call? Wow. That seemed pretty highfalutin' for a Tuesday morning in Deadwood. "Sure."

She put me through.

"Hello, Miss Parker." This time Doug's voice sounded more like I'd figured—baritone. Although I'd expected it to have a whiskey smoothness that came with years of luring young virgins, not a crust around the edges as if he was getting over a cold. "I've finally managed to catch you."

Did that have a double meaning? Or were tales of his dalliances skewing my opinion before I'd even met him? "What can I do for you, Mr. Mann?"

We pulled into the parking lot behind Calamity Jane Realty. I could feel Harvey's eyes on me. I ignored him.

"I'd like to have lunch with you today."

"You would? Today? Why?" Douglas didn't waste any time, did he?

"I may be interested in purchasing some property."

"Of course." *Duh, Violet.* My face warmed at the wrong

conclusion I'd broad-jumped to. "Where do you want to meet? Bighorn Billy's?"

Harvey slowed to a stop behind my Bronco.

"No. It's too busy with bikers. Meet me at The Golden Sluice at eleven-thirty. I'll be in the corner booth."

"The Golden Sluice, got it. See you then."

I tossed my phone in my purse and reached for the door handle. "Thanks for driving me down here, Harvey."

His caterpillar-like eyebrows were all crinkled. "Was that Doug Mann you were talking to?"

"Yes. And if you are going to tell me he's a womanizer, I already know." He didn't seem very womanizing on the phone. I hadn't had a chance to get to that funeral video yet to confirm anything for myself, but I would remedy that before I sat across the table from him.

"And you're still going to go to lunch with him?"

"He wants to buy something."

Harvey snorted. "He usually gets it for free. What makes him think you're selling?"

"I'm talking about a property, smartass"

"Yeah, but is he?"

"I'm going to say good-bye now, Harvey." I shoved open the door. "And ignore your little innuendo."

"Fine, Miss High-n-Mighty, you do that. But watch Doug's hands, or you might get pinched in-yer-end-o."

I could hear him laughing at his own pun as he drove off.

A couple of hours later, I'd watched Douglas on the funeral disk over and over. That was no pinch. He'd cupped and squeezed, and Lila hadn't visibly reacted at all. Either she'd been too grief-stricken to notice Douglas' hand on her ass or she'd been cupped and squeezed by the man before. I'd place all of my chips on the latter.

I was still pondering what this could mean in the grand scheme of murder as I made the winding drive up through traffic and curves to The Golden Sluice. As dingy, hole-in-the-wall bars go, it was unremarkable with its grimy wood floors, scarred tables, and crappy lighting. Not very golden at all.

A few people—mostly men, mostly grizzled—sat at the tables, foamy beer in one hand and cigarette in the other. Wisps of smoke spiraled up toward the ceiling fans, the haze-filled air hiding all the dirty corners. A TV on the back wall reigned, entrancing the dozen or so men with a baseball game, the volume down to a low drone.

Three hunched patrons held down stools at the bar. A Grizzly Adams lookalike cleaned glasses behind it, eyeing me as I crossed to the corner booth. My smile and small wave went unreturned. Not exactly Boston's *Cheers*, this place.

Douglas Mann rose to the occasion, as in he stepped out of the booth to greet me. He reminded me of a lollipop, his chin round, his jowls a little rounder, and his wire-rimmed glasses complete circles. But his torso and legs were long and straight, clear down to the pointed toes of his cowboy boots.

A little too boyish to be handsome, I thought as I approached and he smiled. Actually, more like the kid next door on stilts. Not exactly lady-killer material. What was it about the guy that made him such a big babe magnet? Something I wasn't seeing?

"You must be Mr. Mann," I said and took the hand he offered. The skin on his palm reminded me of raw steak—cool, smooth, and meaty. I let go as soon as I could.

"Please, call me Douglas." His gaze dipped to my neck, but no lower in spite of the semi-deep V of my navy-blue dress. "That's a beautiful sapphire. Is it an heirloom?"

I touched my grandmother's heart pendant. The man knew a little about jewelry. "Thank you, and yes, it is."

His smile widened enough to show two rows of bright

white teeth that stood out in the bar's semi-gloom. "Is your hair naturally that curly?"

I fingered one of the rampant spirals that had escaped my French knot, tucking it behind my ear. "Yes."

I waited, anticipating a fire-hose dousing of charm or charisma or something that would live up to his tail-chasing reputation.

"Interesting," was all he said. He gestured toward the bar. "Can I get you a drink?"

Hmm. Nothing sleazy. A gentleman so far. Maybe I had the wrong Douglas Mann. "A Diet Coke would be great."

"I'll be right back. Menus are on the table."

Ten minutes passed in a blip. Too soon, I was done with the menu and thus forced to make eye contact. "So, are you interested in a particular house or would you like to look at some of the MLS listings I've brought along?" I reached for my tote.

Douglas' lips curved downward. "I don't usually like to talk business until after I eat. It gives me indigestion."

"Okay." That left the weather to fill the next half hour. I didn't think Mother Nature was going to cut it with all of the blue sky and sunshine lately.

"How long have you lived in the area, Miss Parker?"

"Six months. And you can call me Violet."

"Violet, it is." His knee bumped mine.

Was that on purpose? I thought of Harvey's warning and made sure both of Douglas' hands were accounted for.

"Do you like living in the hills?" he asked.

"Most days."

"What brought you to town?"

My Bronco. What was with these formal questions? Was I being vetted for something? "Family and a job."

"You mean your current job?" His knee bumped mine again.

Twice meant something, didn't it? "Yes."

"How's the realty business these days with this economic climate?"

"A little slow." Pinesap moved faster in the dead of winter.

"I've noticed a few more For Sale signs than usual around town this spring."

Just a few? Try three times more than usual, according to Mona. "Times are tough in Deadwood."

"Lead, too. But I'm hoping I can help." His knee nudged mine again.

I shifted deeper into the booth, out of knee reach.

"Was that you?" He peeked under the table. "I thought it was the table leg. I'm sorry."

I waved him off. "That's okay."

So he wasn't playing knee-sie with me on purpose? Why not? After all the badmouthing I'd heard about this would-be Don Juan, I'd expected to be battling an octopus all through lunch.

"Has anyone ever told you that you have a very bony knee?" he asked with a lopsided grin.

Boney knees and Raggedy Ann hair. I should have donned my red nose and clown shoes to complete the outfit. Was it really any wonder Douglas wasn't hitting on me?

The food showed up at that moment, delivered by Grizzly himself. The plates clattered on the table, each followed by a grunt and a splashing refill.

After dabbing the Diet Coke from my dress, I lifted the soggy top bun from my sandwich and frowned down at the charred sliver of meat. I could've sworn I'd ordered chicken, not Tweety Bird. I reached for the ketchup to cover the taste of burned poultry.

When I glanced up at Douglas, he was frowning toward the doorway, shaking his head.

I looked over my shoulder, attempting to follow his

frown but instead locking eyes with a familiar pair of pale blue eyes at the bar.

Harvey! What was he doing here? Oh, right. He'd heard me on the phone with Douglas.

Harvey ducked behind a menu—a postcard-sized drink menu. I could still see his bushy brows and gold teeth. A familiar body slid onto the stool next to him. My jaw tightened. Cooper, too? Did Harvey really think Douglas was that bad? Why didn't he just call in the National Guard?

"You trying to drown that?" Douglas asked.

"What?" I'd been pouring ketchup this whole time. Tweety floated in a pool of tomato blood. "Oh, crud."

Douglas chuckled and offered me a dry French fry.

The rest of lunch was a blur of small talk and stolen scowls in Harvey's direction. Not a single wink or flirty glance flowed from Douglas. Was this the same guy I'd watched cup and squeeze Lila's ass on the video? Maybe he had an evil twin. That, or Douglas liked to chase any skirt but mine.

Douglas insisted upon walking me out to my Bronco, and since he hadn't allowed me to talk business inside, I agreed.

I'd parked on a side street just off Lead's main drag. He opened my door for me. Again, a gentleman.

"Violet." He leaned on the open window frame, his cheeks rounded. "I'm interested in the old Carhart place."

"Why?" It was out before I realized what I'd said. I tightened my slack jaw and smiled back. "I mean, would you like to do a walk-through?"

"Sure, but not today." He glanced toward Main Street, his forehead wrinkling. "Have you had any other offers on it yet?"

"There's some interest."

"But an actual offer?"

"Not yet."

"If one comes in any time soon, you'll let me know?"

"I can."

"Excellent." He stepped back. "I'll be in touch soon."

I whistled all of the way back to work and practically skipped back into the air-conditioned office. Mona was there when I arrived, the phone to her ear, her fingernails clacking, her jasmine perfume a fresh change from stale cigarette smoke.

I bounced into my chair, humming happy tunes under my breath. Things were finally looking up, in spite of the nightmares from which only lots of tequila seemed to help me escape. Therapy or alcohol—it was nice to have options.

By the time Mona hung up, I was busy filing my nails while surfing the Internet for information about Douglas Mann.

"Having a good day, are we?" Mona asked.

"Extremely." It was amazing what great sex and a potential buyer could do for one's attitude.

"You'll be happy to see this, then." Mona walked over and placed a sticky note on my desk.

I read it, picked it up, and read it again. "You're kidding me." Zeke and Zelda wanted to make an offer on the Carhart place. Where was my wallet? I needed to buy a lotto ticket.

"I wonder what prompted this." Last I knew, Zelda had wanted more proof the place was haunted.

"Call and see."

So I did, but I got Zelda's voicemail. I left a message asking her to give me a call when she had a chance.

"How did lunch with Douglas go?" Mona asked after I hung up. She must have read the question on my face. "Ray told me Douglas called, and I put two and two together. Did he hit on you?"

"Not at all."

"You're kidding. He hits on everyone."

Everyone? Really? This factoid and Mona's wide-eyed surprise were doing wonders for my ego. I tucked away another fugitive curl and cleared my throat. "Everyone but me, it appears."

"What did he want?"

"He's interested in the Carhart place."

"What are the chances? Two fish at once. Good for you."

"After I get the offer from Zeke and Zelda all written up, I'll need to let Douglas know about it, I guess." Although I didn't really want to. For one thing, I liked Zelda and Zeke and the idea of having them in town. For another, I was beginning not to like Douglas Mann very much. What was it that he didn't like about me? Was it the curly hair?

"He may want to make an offer, too." Mona interrupted my fifth-grade pity party. "Step carefully there. You signed a DLA agreement, right?"

"Yeah, but I need to freshen up on the details on representing two potential buyers for the same property, make sure I don't break any laws."

I was doing that very thing an hour later when Ray came strutting in through the back door, his too-tanned face sporting a big, shit-eating grin, his beady eyes locked on me.

"Hey, Slut," he said.

"Ray!" Mona chided.

I sat there sucker-punched, my mouth agape.

He guffawed—I wanted to cram my phone down his throat when that sound came from it—and said, "Who'd you piss off now, Blondie?"

I recovered from my moment of surprise. "Go blow a monkey, you jackass." I turned my back to him before I could follow my gut instinct and launch at his face, claws extended.

"Don't shoot the messenger." His keys rattled as they hit his desk. "I'm only repeating what someone scratched on the side of your Bronco."

"On my what?" I jumped up and ran out the back door, dodging rumbling motorcycles and leather-clad tourists as I zig-zagged between parked vehicles. I skidded to a halt next to my driver's-side door. "Fuck me!"

There, in big carved letters, was the word SLUT in all caps. An exclamation mark added a final touch. I ran my fingers over the paint. There'd be no buffing this shit out.

"Who would do this?" Mona had joined me.

"I don't—" Natalie! Oh, mother humper! Had Nat found out about Doc and me somehow? Had someone seen us? Had Doc told her because he knew I wouldn't?

"Will your insurance cover this?" Mona apparently hadn't noticed that my breathing had stopped there for a panic-filled moment.

"No. I only have liability insurance."

Mona hugged my shoulder. "I'm sorry, Vi. Maybe Jane has one of those Calamity Jane Realty magnet signs in the storeroom that will cover this. Let's go take a look."

We searched, but Jane didn't have an extra sign. Mona drove home to look in her garage, thinking she might have one from years ago, back when Jane insisted they all use one when they drove customers around.

Meanwhile, I called Natalie, a boulder in my gut as her cell phone rang and rang. I left a message, just a casual, "Hi, how are you doing today?" I hung up and sent a text that said the same thing.

Back at my desk, Ray gloated at me while he chatted with Ben, his nephew—and my blind date—on the phone. I barely heard him, though; my focus was everywhere but work. My shoulders scrunched tighter and tighter at the idea that my best friend had somehow uncovered my guilty secret.

Around quitting time, Mona returned with a car magnet in hand. Thank, God. I packed up my stuff, grabbed my purse and the magnet, and headed out to band-aid my Bronco. Then I'd scurry home to wait for Natalie's phone call ... or visit, depending on what she knew and how she felt about what she knew.

I squatted next to my door, nauseated about my best friend. The sun baked my shoulders and crown as I lined up the magnet.

A shadow fell over me. "I have something for you," a familiar deep voice said.

I glanced over my shoulder and did a double-take at the sight of Doc in dark green Dockers and a white button-up shirt with his sleeves rolled up to his forearms. His tie was loose around his collar, his hair finger-messed. A calm settled over me, quelling my anxiety. "You look good." I left out the finger-licking part.

"Keep staring at me like that, Boots, and we'll have to

find a back road."

My body flushed at the heat in his eyes. "Are you meeting a client?" As in Tiffany, Natalie, or some other woman I should get stapler-throwing jealous over?

"Already met. What's going on?"

I was going to hide the truth from him, but I changed my mind. "See for yourself." I peeled off the magnet.

He stared at my door for two breaths. "You have a new enemy. Great. This will help me sleep better at night." His fingers messed up his hair even more. "Any idea who thinks so highly of you?"

"No. But I'm worried sick it's Nat. Did you tell her anything?"

"I haven't seen or heard from her all day."

"Someone must have seen us last night."

"Not in the back room."

"I mean at my desk."

"I was too distracted to notice." His gaze dipped down to my chest for a moment, his grin appearing. "Did I mention that I really liked that black dress you had on?"

"You hinted at it."

I started to stick the magnet back on, but he grabbed my arm. "Wait. Let me see that exclamation mark again."

He squatted next to me and pointed at the dot on the bottom of the exclamation mark. "Did you notice the symbol here?"

"No." I leaned closer, wiping the dust off. "I was kind of stuck on the actual word carved into my paint."

Doc sat back on his heels, a frown lining his forehead. "That resembles something I saw in a book recently."

"What book?"

"The one I used to figure out the title of that other book you found in the Carhart house."

Lila's book? "What's the title?"

"It's the name of a particular demonology cult that

thrived in the middle of the twelfth century." He stood up.

I followed his lead. "No way."

"Was there a publishing date in this book you found?"

"It looked hand-written, with a homemade binding." I didn't think Lila had found it on the shelf at Wally World.

"That's what I was afraid of."

"You think Lila belongs to some cult?" I asked.

"It's possible. She or Junior Carhart. Or both."

"Maybe he killed his father because of it?"

"Maybe." Doc said.

"I need to get hold of that book somehow—"

Doc's jaw clenched. "Violet."

"—and figure out what Lila's up to before she hurts Wanda and Mi—."

"Violet!" Doc grabbed my shoulders, his grip strong. "Stop and think about this. If that is Lila's book, and I'm right about this being a symbol on your door, you've been marked."

"Marked for what, though?" And by whom? Lila? Why would she carve "slut" on my Bronco? It made no sense. Unlike my Natalie suspicions ... and guilt.

"I don't know. I need to see what's in that book. At the least, more harassment."

"And, at the most?"

"Well, I doubt the sacrifice will involve Addy's chicken."

I looked up into his dark eyes and gulped. "When you say it like that, you really make me hope it is just Nat pissed at me for breaking her heart."

"That makes two of us." He slid his hands down my arms, catching my hands, pulling me closer. The aroma of his cologne, mixed with the concern crinkling his face, made me swoon for a moment. Then I remembered where we were. "Doc," my eyes darted around, on the lookout, noticing passers-by glancing our way. "We're in public."

"So?" He kept pulling.

I tugged on my hands. "We can't do this here. It's too risky."

"Damn, Boots. That just makes me want to do it more." But he let go of me with a groan.

I clasped my hands to keep them from touching him. "Can I have a rain check?"

"That depends."

"On what?

He leaned against the Bronco and crossed his arms, looking underwear-commercial hot. Maybe we should find a back road. "Your lunch today with the town womanizer. What happened?"

My mouth fell open. "How did you know about that?" Then I remembered my bodyguard. "Harvey called you, didn't he?"

Doc just chuckled. "So, did this Mann guy try to get into your dress?" His eyes roved down the front of my body and back up again. "Or get you out of it?"

"Neither. He was a perfect gentleman."

A smirk curved his mouth. "All the more reason not to trust him."

"That doesn't make sense."

"Really? Let's see. Did he compliment you?"

Douglas' comment about my hair didn't fit the compliment bill. "No."

"Did he ogle your chest or ass?"

Only my necklace. "Not that I noticed. I'm telling you, Douglas isn't interested in me at all, except as a Realtor."

Doc's eyes narrowed. "A well-known womanizer takes you out to lunch while you're wearing that hot little number and doesn't try to hit on you once. Doesn't that make you suspicious?"

It made me feel like the hunchback of Notre Dame, but I didn't want to tell Doc that and sound shallow and insecure. "I think folks around here have him pegged wrong."

"I think he's manipulating you."

"Why? What's in it for him?"

"I haven't figured it out yet, but give me time."

I smiled and leaned closer, pretending to remove a piece of lint from his shirt. "So, you think this dress is hot, huh?"

"I think you're hot. The dress just looks like it'd be fun to peel off you." Doc jammed his hands in his pockets. "So what *did* Mann want, then?"

"He's interested in the Carhart house."

"You're kidding."

"No. He knows I'm representing them. He mentioned doing a walkthrough sometime soon. But I don't think that matters now."

"Why not?"

"Because some of my other clients are going to put an offer on it."

"The ghost lovers?"

"That's them."

"I thought they wanted more proof first."

"They did, but they changed their minds. I guess you can hold off on looking up more information about that list I gave you with all the previous owners' names."

One of Doc's eyebrows arched. "What's so great about this house?"

"It's a beautiful house."

"There has to be more to it than that. These people do know a murder-suicide took place there, right?"

"I've made a full disclosure."

"I want to see it."

"The disclosure?"

"No, the house."

I cocked my head. "You mean from the outside? Like drive by it?"

"I mean I want to walk through it."

I quelled the urge to jump up and down with glee. "Why?"

"Curiosity."

"To check for ghosts?" I prodded.

He leveled a stare at me. "I thought you didn't believe in them."

"I believe in you." That popped right out of my mouth, surprising me by how much I meant it.

Doc lips curved into a grin. "Good." He reached out and tugged on a loose curl. "If I do this walk through, will you promise to keep your nose out of Lila's business? Stay out of trouble?"

I crossed my fingers behind my back. "Sure."

Chapter Fifteen

Wednesday, August 8th

The next morning, I was pondering my own chicken sacrifice due to new peck marks on my favorite leather sandals when I shoved open Aunt Zoe's screen door and found my Bronco listing to the side like a drunken sailor.

"Oh, no!" My blueberry Pop-Tart lodged in my gullet. I raced down the porch steps and rounded the front of the Bronco. The sight of two flat tires on the passenger side made me want to strangle a teddy bear. "Oh, come on!" I yelled, startling a pair of crows out of the pine tree overhead, and threw my purse at the back flat.

The tires must have gotten punctured when I took that shortcut through the glass-littered alley behind the Piggly Wiggly to avoid the motorcycle-filled streets.

Perfect. Just freaking perfect. I had one spare, and that wasn't going to do me a lick of good at the moment. Of all mornings, it had to be one when I had an appointment first thing with Zeke and Zelda to sign an offer.

I kicked the front tire, cursing in the clear, pine-scented air until my tongue turned blue.

"Kiss your mama with that mouth, girl?" Harvey asked, crossing the street toward me. I'd been too busy ranting to hear Ms. Geary's screen door slam. At least he was wearing pants today, thank God.

I glared at him just because he was there and breathing and smelled like bacon. "I need a ride again."

He snorted at me. "Withdraw your teeth from my ass

first."

"Sorry." My shoulders sagged under the warm sunshine. "I'm just pissed."

"What happened to your tires?"

"I ran over some glass."

He leaned down and prodded the sidewall on the front flat. "No, you ran into some trouble."

"What do you mean?"

"This tire's been slashed."

"It has?"

He bent over the back tire. "This one, too."

"Shit." Chills chased away my frustration. Being late for my appointment no longer seemed so important.

"Girl, do you go lookin' for enemies? Or do you just come by them naturally?"

"Are you sure they're slashed?"

"Well, nobody left a note behind spellin' it out, but these here are sure-fire slices, and you don't get them from rollin' over broken glass. Whose tail did you step on now?"

Natalie's? No, she wouldn't do this to me. Or would she? I'd seen her bash out a windshield with a tire iron once, but that was back when we were in our early twenties and the scene involved a cheating boyfriend, which I wasn't.

But I was her cheating best friend. I cringed.

Harvey watched me, all squinty eyed. "What?"

"Nothing."

"Who?"

"Nobody."

"Cough it up, if you want a ride to work."

"I don't know who did it ... yet." That was the truth. I still hadn't fully written off Lila, but surely me touching her creepy book wouldn't spur this retaliation. Natalie hadn't returned my call from yesterday yet either, so nothing was definite there. But things weren't looking good, and neither was I after spinning in my sheets all night long over the whole mess. Nothing was taking the red out of my eyes this morning. Certainly not two flat tires.

Harvey picked up my purse, dusted it off, and grabbed me by the elbow. "Come on. Let's get you to work."

The ride down the hill passed in a blur. Before I knew it, Harvey was idling next to Calamity Jane's back door and asking for my keys. When I just blinked at him for several clock ticks, he poked me hard in the thigh.

"Ow!" Jerking away from him, I rubbed my leg. "What are you doing?"

"Draggin' your ass back to Earth. Give me your keys."

"What for?"

"I'm going to fix your tires."

"You don't have to do that, Harvey."

"I know. Now give me your damned keys, woman."

I dropped them in his open palm, hesitating with my hand on the door handle. For such an ornery cuss, he sure could be loveable. Should I hug him?

His gold teeth shone through his whiskers. "I'll take a pot roast with all the fixin's and homemade strawberry pie. Now get your bony ass to work."

"But I don't bake," I said as I hopped out.

"Not my problem."

His cloud of exhaust chased me inside. I stopped by the bathroom to wash my hands and squeeze a few drops of Visine into my red eyes before heading to my desk.

Mona had the phone to her ear when I strode past her.

"Okay, will do." She hung up and looked over at me. "Morning, Vi. Zelda Britton called earlier. So did Jeff Wymonds. I left their numbers on your desk."

"Thanks." I picked up the message with Zelda's phone number, my gut tightening as I lifted the receiver to call her. The way today was already shaping up, she'd probably changed her mind about the offer. "Sorry I'm late."

"You're not late. Are you okay?"

I avoided Mona's wrinkled brow and punched in Zelda's number. "Fine and dandy."

"In spite of the two flat tires?"

My finger stopped with one number to go. "How'd you—" *Harvey!* I hung up the phone. "I'm gonna give him a strawberry pie—right in the kisser."

"He's worried about you. We all are."

"Don't be. I'm fine."

"Sleeping much?"

Damn. "You don't miss a lot, do you?"

"I sit six feet from you every day. You're not exactly a vault." She slid her glasses down her nose and peered over them. "Any idea who slashed your tires?"

"No." I wasn't going to start pointing fingers until I was more certain.

"You're going to call the police now, right?"

"I hadn't thought that far ahead yet."

"You should," Mona said. "Two acts of vandalism on your vehicle within twenty-four hours—that's police business."

I picked up the phone again. "You're right, I'll call." *Later.* I had Cooper's card somewhere. "But first, I need to see what Zelda wanted."

Less than a minute later, I hung up.

"Well?" Mona asked.

"They're running late."

"Oh, good." Mona's fingernails went to work clacking on her keys. "That gives you time to call the police."

"Not yet. I need to prepare the offer."

"I thought you already had."

"I took it home last night to proofread and Addy's chicken ate it for a snack."

The clacking stopped. "You lead an interesting life, Violet Parker."

She had no idea.

Jeff Wymonds wasn't home, so I left a message telling him to call my cell phone. With any luck, he'd finished prepping his house and was ready for me to bring over a For Sale sign.

Zeke and Zelda made it in just before noon. Without much ado, they signed the offer and rumbled away on their Harley. The Carharts had until the close of business day tomorrow to accept or decline, which meant I needed to pay them a visit and drop off the paperwork. Unfortunately, I had no wheels, and Mona and Ray were both out to lunch with clients.

Opening my cell, I decided to kill two birds with one Doc. Miracle upon miracle, he answered my call on the second ring. Our fling just might turn into a liaison yet.

I greeted Doc with, "I have a proposition for you."

"I accept. What are you wearing?"

That made me smile for the first time since breakfast. "Something green. I need to drop off some paperwork at the Carharts and I thought you might want to go with me and check things out."

"That's not exactly a proposition, since you benefit from my going more than I do."

"I also need you to drive."

"Oh, yeah? Where's your Bronco?"

I hesitated. "Under the weather." I didn't want to explain more than that over the phone. "I forgot my lunch today, so if we could stop somewhere for a bite to eat, I'll buy you lunch."

"This is beginning to sound more like a series of favors rather than a proposition."

"Maybe we can work out some form of payback that's acceptable to you."

"Sure. Dust off your purple boots."

I chuckled. "What is it with you and those boots?"

"Wear them and I'll show you."

Whew! Was the air conditioner broken? Much more of this and I'd be charging over there and dragging him into that back room. "Shall we meet at your car in about a half-hour?"

That would give him some time to do whatever mental preparation he needed to before stepping into the Carhart house. Plus, Ray should be back by then to watch the store.

"I'll pick you up out front."

"Thanks, Doc. I really appreciate this."

"Don't thank me yet. The day's young." He hung up.

What was that supposed to mean?

A short time later, with my eyeliner smudge-free and my lips shiny with gloss, I stood outside on the sidewalk, waiting. Five minutes alone with Ray today was enough to turn my stomach, and his reeking of onions from his lunch didn't help. I opted to swelter in the August heat rather than cram my tape dispenser up his nose.

Doc's black Camaro SS pulled up next to a nearby fire hydrant, the only curb space available. He hopped out, leaving the engine growling, looking edible in his khakis and maroon shirt, and held the passenger door open for me. "Nice shades, Marilyn Monroe."

I blew him an air kiss and slid inside the car. The black leather seats were hot to the touch, so I sat upright. The musky scent of Doc's cologne teased me, making things even hotter.

"Sorry," he said as he crawled behind the wheel. "Your side was in the sun." He adjusted the vent so that cool air hit my chest, then raised an eyebrow at me.

"What?"

"Are you going to tell me or do I have to pry it out of you?"

Tell him what? That I wanted to see him naked again? I thought that was a given. "Umm, you look really nice in that shirt."

His mouth twitched. "Anything else?"

"Natalie hasn't returned my call."

He checked his rearview mirror, then shifted into gear and pulled out into the street. "I'm talking about your tires."

I rolled my eyes. "Did Harvey cruise Main Street with a bullhorn?"

"You didn't call me." There was an accusation in his tone.

"I did, too. About a half hour ago." I was splitting hairs and I knew it.

So did Doc, judging by the slit-eyed glance he sent me. "Have you talked to the police?"

"Not yet." I clasped my hands in my lap. "But Harvey probably has."

"You need to call them."

"I know." Honestly, I didn't think it would do me much good. Cooper would want evidence, of which I had zilch.

"Today," Doc said.

"I will later." *Maybe.*

"Why not now?"

Cooper in detective mode made me nervous. I preferred to make a bumbling fool of myself in private. "I'm busy."

"Doing what? Sitting there?"

"I left my phone at work."

"Liar. Call."

"Later."

"Now."

"Jesus, Doc." I glared at his profile. "Why are you being so damned bullheaded?"

"Because I know you, Violet."

My feathers ruffled. "No, you don't. You've barely scraped the surface."

A muscle in his jaw ticked.

"And what's that 'I know you' supposed to mean, anyhow?" I hadn't liked his implication one iota. I pointed out the front window. "Make a right up there by the gas station."

Doc held his silence as he turned and gunned it up the hill a couple of blocks. He followed my "left" and "right" directions without comment, but his sharp turns and tire chirps spoke plenty.

"There it is." Lila's red Barbie-mobile was missing in action. My shoulders loosened in relief. I wouldn't need body armor for today's visit. "You can park out front."

He rolled to a stop and cut the engine. When I reached for the door handle, he grabbed my arm, holding me.

"You're right," he said, his eyes roving my face. "I don't really know you." He reached out and lifted my sunglasses, resting them on top of my head. "Yet."

I held his stare, torn between pulling away and leaning in.

"Why are your eyes so red?"

I figured one honest admission deserved another. "I'm having trouble sleeping."

"Because of Natalie?"

"Mostly Wolfgang." It was just my luck that the first guy to ever confess his undying love for me followed up with a promise to burn me beyond recognition.

"Nightmares?" When I dipped my head, he grimaced. "How often?"

"Nightly."

His palm slid to my hand, his fingers interlacing with mine. "Maybe you need to talk to someone."

"I'm talking to you."

He lifted my hand and kissed the back of it. "I'm listening."

My heart drum-soloed in my ears. It was time to switch subjects. If we didn't, between the afternoon heat and Doc's warm touch, I might just melt into a pool of bubbling goo. "Are you ready for this?" I nudged my head toward the Carhart place.

He glanced over my shoulder at the house, his lips flat-lining. "As ready as I can be not knowing what's inside."

I gave into whim and leaned in, stealing a peck. I pulled away before I got caught up in the vortex that was Doc. "Let's do it."

His lazy grin returned. "I'm your huckleberry."

I didn't wait for him to open my door. We crunched our way up the gravel drive toward the porch. Gesturing toward the Open Cut mine, I asked, "Did you notice the missing scenery?"

"Your buyers want property next to a big hole?"

"They're optimists."

"The world could use more of those."

I saw the sitting-room curtain twitch as we climbed the porch steps. Earlier, when I'd called to alert the Carharts that I was coming over with an offer on the house, Wanda had answered, whispering that Millie wasn't there. I hoped she still wasn't, since snooping would be easier with only the church mouse present.

The door inched open before I had a chance to ring the bell. Wanda's head appeared in the gap.

"Hello, Wanda," I said.

Her eyes widened at the sight of Doc. I could relate.

I opened the screen door. "I've brought the papers I mentioned on the phone."

She nodded and stepped back for us to enter the foyer.

I heard Doc sniff behind me and sneaked a glance at him. His small nod propelled me inside.

Something sweet and gingery perfumed the air. My stomach growled and gnashed. I tried to ignore the hollow ache and get back to the business of meddling. "Wanda, this is Doc Nyce."

Doc started to hold out his hand, but I pushed his arm down, figuring that'd just scare Wanda into another faint.

"He's here to see the house."

Doc shoved his hands in his pockets. "Nice to meet you, Mrs. Carhart."

I could be wrong, but I thought I heard her squeak as she clicked the deadbolt behind us.

"Let me grab the offer," I said, opening my tote.

Wanda chewed on her knuckle. "Millie's on her way."

Which meant we didn't have much time. "Perfect. If it's okay with you, I'd like to show Doc the house while we wait."

She nodded and disappeared into the kitchen, probably to find some cheese. I put the offer and my pen down on the sideboard.

"Is that normal?" Doc whispered.

I snorted "I've forgotten what normal is. Let's get this done before Millie comes home."

Doc followed me from room to room, sniffing, pale-faced. In an extra-loud voice, I pretended to tell him about the molding, the wallpaper, the carpet, even the electrical switches and outlets—which earned a smirk from him.

Well? I mouthed as we returned to the sitting room.

He bobbed his head once and pointed at the stairs.

"You sure?" I whispered.

In answer, he put his hand on my lower back and nudged. "How many bedrooms are upstairs?"

I caught a glimpse of Wanda peeking around the trim as I climbed the first step. "Follow me. I'll show you. There's also a full bath up here."

Doc's face was pinkish-gray by the time we crested the top step, and his breathing was shallow. Maybe it was the heat. The upstairs had to be a good ten degrees hotter than the sitting room.

I stopped on the landing. "Are you all right?"

He urged me onward again, this time his cold palm on my arm.

Frowning, I led the way into the bedroom where Lila had pounced on me before.

"This is where I found the book," I whispered and started to close the door behind us. The creak of a stair step stopped me. Wanda must have been trailing us, listening. Damn it. I needed to buy some time alone with Doc. I held up my index finger to Doc and crossed the threshold.

"Wanda?" I strode back toward the stairwell and caught her poised at the top of the stairs, her eyes darting, avoiding mine. "Mr. Nyce is thirsty." I fanned my shirt, partly for effect, mostly because sweat was beading in my cleavage. "Could you get him a glass of water?"

"We don't have any ice trays."

"Yes, I remember." Still too bizarre. "Warm water is fine."

She nodded and shuffled down the stairs.

When I returned to the bedroom, Doc sat slouched on the bed, his face buried in his hands.

"Doc, are you okay?" A touch to his trembling back revealed a damp, cold shirt. "You're freezing?" It came out a question because I had trouble believing it.

"Give me a minute," he spoke through his fingers. "Find the book."

"Right." I checked the bookcase, the nightstand, the dresser, under the bed. I even nudged Doc over so I could check under the mattress, but I came up empty-handed. "I can't—"

The low snarl of a motor outside the window squeezed lungs into lockdown.

"Uh-oh!" I rushed to the window, peeking through the gauzy sky-blue curtains in time to see Lila and Millie crawling out of the Barbie-mobile. While I watched, Lila pointed at Doc's Camaro. Her face pinched into an ugly sneer as she spoke to Millie, who squinted up at the house, right at me.

I stepped back, sweaty and breathy. My body flooded with adrenaline, kicking into flight mode. "Doc, we have to go."

"Not yet," he said from the bed.

"We have to get out of this room." I was already halfway to the door.

"I can't."

I glanced Doc's way and stopped. He looked like a ghost sitting on the bed. His wide, dark eyes stared over my shoulder, with a haunted, hollow-cheeked look Hollywood makeup artists spend hours trying to achieve. His whole body shuddered and quaked, his hands clenched into claw-like almost-fists at his sides.

Chills peppered my arms and legs. "Doc?"

Downstairs, the front door slammed open. Something crashed and shattered.

"Doc?" I returned to his side, not sure how to help, where to touch. "We have to go before Lila finds us in here."

"Not. Yet." His nostrils flared with short, sharp breaths. His eyes remained fixed on the open doorway.

Was that a stair step creaking?

Crap!

"I'll be back," I said and turned to go head off Lila's talons.

"No!" Doc caught my hand and yanked me backward.

I almost fell onto his lap. "What are you—"

"She's here."

He was right. Those were definitely footfalls coming up the stairs. "I know. I have to go stop her."

"Not Lila." He pointed at the empty threshold. "*Her.*"

Chapter Sixteen

Whether or not I believed in ghosts, Doc's behavior and warning sparked a rush of goosebumps up my arms.

"Doc, you're scaring me a little," I whispered, my eyes fixed on the empty doorway.

"If you could smell her, you'd be terrified. This one has some nasty secrets."

A piercing scream rang out from downstairs. I jumped, nearly peeing my pants. I heard more crashing and shattering, along with footfalls pounding away, back down the stairs. What in the hell was going on down there?

I focused on the ghost at hand. "How can you tell she has nasty secrets?"

"The intensity of her odor. She's trailed it throughout the house."

"I can't see anything."

"Trust me, she's right here."

"Where?"

"Just inside the doorway."

More chills—this time, shivering down my spine. I backed into his knee.

His hand on my hip steadied me. "Do you believe me?"

I didn't know what to believe. "You make a pretty persuasive Vincent Price." I grabbed his hand and held on tight. "How do you know it's a woman?"

"I'm catching traces of rose water."

"Rose water," I parroted. That reminded me of the little bowl of rose-shaped soaps my grandmother kept on the back of her toilet.

"Plus, I can see her. Kind of."

"I thought you could only smell ghosts."

"When she stands still, there's a slight blur."

"Is she standing still now?"

"Yes."

"Right in front of us?"

"Yes."

The goosebumps spread clear to my toes. Okay, now I was totally creeped out. I tugged on his hand. "We need to get out of this room."

"I don't know what will happen if she tries to pass through me."

"Pass through you?" I cast a grimace in his direction. "Can't you walk around her?"

"It appears not. She's insisting."

"How does she know you can sense her?"

"I haven't figured that out, but they always do."

"What are we going to do?"

"You go first. I'll try to follow."

"Try to?" I seemed to be having trouble processing his words today.

"Be ready." He shoved me toward the door.

I skirted to the left, scurrying through the doorway as if my tail feathers were on fire. When I reached the safety of the hall, I spun around. "Ready for what?"

Doc pushed to his feet. "This."

He walked three steps and then stumbled, careened into the door jamb with a whump, and slumped to the floor.

Shit!

"Doc?" I rushed to where he lay crumpled on the threshold and knelt over him. "Doc, are you okay?"

His eyes didn't open. I touched his pale cheeks, his forehead, his neck, searching for a bit of warm skin. He was cold. Impossibly cold, considering the heat trapped upstairs with us. Was he in shock? What were the signs, again?

Sweat coated my arms and legs and trickled down my back. I reached for his wrist. My heart was pounding so hard that I couldn't tell at first if I was feeling his pulse or my own. After a couple of deep breaths and a string of un-ladylike curses at myself for dragging him to this damned house, I found his pulse—strong and steady.

I sat back on my heels, still holding his arm. Behind his closed eyelids, his eyes rolled around—REM on speed. What was going on in there?

"Doc?" I whispered in his ear.

No response.

I grasped his hand. "Doc, squeeze my hand if you can hear me."

No squeeze.

Fuck! Should I call 911? Harvey? Aunt Zoe? Cooper?

My gut told me I needed to get him out of the room, so I hooked my hands under his armpits and tugged, then tugged some more. Grunting and sweating, I dragged him into the hall and noticed the color had returned to his lips. It wasn't until I stood upright that I realized I had company.

"What are *you* doing up here?" Lila said, her mouth crinkled into a snarl.

I mentally gulped. With a man down, I was ill prepared for battle. "Isn't it obvious?" I asked, stepping between her and Doc to shield him from her claws. "I'm showing *Wanda's* house to a potential buyer."

Her eyes narrowed at my jab.

Millie came around the corner right then. Her owl eyes widened with alarm when she saw Doc. "What did you do to him? Is he dead?" Grimacing, she leaned over Doc, whose color had almost returned to normal.

Had Millie been the one who found her dad and brother, post mortem? Did she have nightmares, too? I touched her arm in empathy, only to jerk my hand back when she recoiled from me.

"He's not dead." I scrambled for an explanation and threw out the first thing that came to mind. "He has allergies." I should've gone with the second.

Lila snorted. "That's not a normal reaction."

She didn't know the half of it. "His meds cause some chemical imbalances."

The tilt of her head hinted that she wasn't buying my bullshit. She looked over my shoulder into the bedroom, and her face contorted. I turned to see what had her all feral and bristly and saw the rumpled bed cover where Doc had been sitting. Busted! Crap. By the time I turned back, Lila had schooled her expression, but she still gave me frostbite from my toes north.

"Is he the one who wants to buy our house?" Millie asked, still leaning over Doc.

"No."

"Then why is he here?" Lila bit out each word.

Damn, I was tired of this bitch. I had more important things to deal with, like the man lying at my feet. "I don't see how this is any of your business."

Lila's cheeks flashed bright pink. "Listen, you little—"

Doc gasped and wheezed.

Millie cried out in surprise and stumbled backwards.

Before I could do more than gape down at him, his eyelids opened and he came out of his spell swinging. Literally. I leapt out of the way as he thrashed and punched the air, wrestling some invisible demon.

Lila squealed when I landed on her foot, my heel crushing her toes. She shoved me, hard, and my shoulder slammed into the wall, but my fear for Doc overshadowed the flare of pain.

"Doc!" He writhed on the floor as if in a seizure, the tendons standing out on his neck, his muscles straining. I didn't dare risk getting close enough to touch him. "Doc, wake up!"

He stopped so suddenly that it took me several shallow breaths to realize he was looking up at me—actually seeing me.

I bent over him. "Are you okay?"

His eyes flittered over my face, then focused behind me and widened. He sat up so fast we nearly clonked heads. "We have to get out of here."

He lurched to his feet, not waiting for a second opinion, and staggered into the wall.

"Doc?" I gawked up at him.

"Now, Violet!" He grabbed my wrist and yanked me up, the force making my head spin. He crashed down the stairs with me trailing like a kite.

The offer letter still lay on the sideboard. It caught air as we blew past it. I glanced over my shoulder and saw it fluttering to the floor. A glimpse of Wanda cowering in the kitchen entryway, broom in hand, spurred a parting "I'll call" from me as we flew by.

Doc didn't slow until we reached his car. He shoved me into the driver's seat and tossed his keys in my lap.

I sat there catching flies with my open mouth as he crawled into the passenger side and slammed the door.

"Drive!"

I stared, too stunned to do anything else.

He reached over, plucked the keys from my lap, and placed them in my palm. "Violet, drive. Please."

"Wow." It took me three blinks to snap out of my stupor. I put the key in the ignition and sparked the Camaro to life. "Where to?"

"I don't care. Just get me out of here."

We drove back down to Deadwood in silence, the wind blowing through the open windows and the rumble of passing bikes the only sounds. Doc leaned his head back against the seat's headrest, his eyes closed. Meanwhile, I aimed worried glances his way, my lips pinched tight. I was afraid that if I unlatched the gate, all my questions would stampede.

As I entered the city limits, my phone rang. I fished it out of my purse, trying to keep my main focus on the road. The phone flashed Douglas Mann's number. "I should take this," I told Doc, who nodded in reply.

I whipped into the hardware store's parking lot and pulled into a stall, letting the engine idle.

"Hello?"

"Violet, it's Douglas Mann. I need to talk to you."

"Hi, Douglas. I need to talk to you, too." With the offer in the Carhart's hands—well, on their floor—Douglas had thirty-six hours to make his own offer.

"Have dinner with me tonight."

It was more of a command than a question. I had the feeling Douglas was used to people asking "to the moon?" when he ordered them to jump. "Dinner? Can't we just meet at my office this afternoon?"

I glanced at Doc and found him watching me through one open eye. His skin tone had returned to normal, his forehead smooth. He was going to be okay. The tight grip of anxiety on my chest eased.

"I have meetings all day. It has to be dinner. How about Chuckwagon Charlie's? They serve an excellent apricot-stuffed chicken that comes coated in a blueberry sauce."

Oh, my God. They called that chuckwagon food? Just the thought made my stomach lay siege to my liver. My lack of lunch was beginning to make me a little woozy. Low blood sugar had a way of changing me from Dr. Jekyll to Mr. Hyde. From now on, I was going to eat before Doc played patty-cake with one of his ghosts.

"I didn't realize Chuckwagon Charlie's served anything other than beer, burgers, and stale peanuts." I'd only been there once, with Natalie. She'd been dating the bartender at the time.

"They have an upstairs lounge now."

"A lounge? Sounds fancy."

Doc cleared his throat.

I looked his way and ran into his razor-sharp glare. Whoa! No mixed message there. "I don't know, Douglas. I had some plans tonight."

"I'd like to place an offer on the Carhart house."

"Oh." Well, when he said it like that. I turned my back on Doc. "Okay, what time?"

"Seven or eight. You pick."

"Seven it is. Does the lounge have a dress code?"

"No, but I do. Wear a black skirt."

Why? Maybe Doc was right about Douglas being interested in more than my Realtor services. "You have something against women in pants?"

"In my position, appearances in public are always important."

Politics. I should've known. Who was he expecting, the paparazzi? "I'll see what I can find in my closet."

"Great. Bring a list of any disclosures."

"Will do. See you tonight." I hung up and turned back to Doc.

"You're going to dinner with Douglas Mann?" How he got that out through clenched teeth boggled me.

"Hey, the color is back in your cheeks." A change of subject and a compliment. It was worth a shot.

"Violet." Somehow, he even made anger look sexy.

"Douglas wants to put an offer on the table."

"I'm sure he does, especially if you wear something that shows off your knees."

"You like my knees?"

"I like you. Period. What I don't like is you having dinner with the local playboy."

"It's just business."

"For you, maybe. Not for him."

"Doc, I'm telling you, he's not interested in me."

"And I'm telling you, Violet, that a man would have to be blind, dumb, and castrated not to be interested. You're just too naïve and insecure to see the game he's playing with you."

"Gee, your compliments warm the cockles of my heart."

He closed his eyes and leaned against the headrest again. "Violet, don't go to dinner with him."

"Is that a warning?"

"It's a plea."

I fidgeted with one of my skirt buttons, considering his request. But money was money, and I needed more. "I'm sorry, Doc, but like I said, it's just business. I have to go."

His mouth tightened, but he kept quiet.

"I could stop by your office afterward."

He shook his head. "No need."

Ouch. Rejected. That stung. "Okay, then." I shifted into reverse and backed out of the stall. The quicker I could get this damned Carhart house off of my plate, the happier I'd be. It was becoming a whale-sized albatross.

I sneaked a glance at Doc as I prepared to pull out onto the road. "So, what happened to you back there?" Somehow, I managed to sound all light and bubbly in spite of the lead cannonball in my gut.

"I blacked out."

"No shit. I was there, remember? I'm more interested in what made you faint."

"The visions."

I slid into traffic. "What did you see?"

"I can't tell you."

I gripped the steering wheel until my knuckles turned white. "If this is because of my goddamned dinner with Douglas tonight—"

"It's not. Will you drop me off at the library?"

"Drop you—Doc, this is your car."

"I'm aware of that."

"I'm not going to cruise around town without you in it."

"Why not?"

"What if someone sees me?"

"You could wave at them for starters."

"Cute. That's not what I mean."

"What do you mean, then?"

"Driving a guy's car around means something." Especially a car as sexy as Doc's. "It's like wearing his letter jacket or class ring."

"We're not in high school, anymore."

"You know what I'm talking about."

He opened his eyes. "Spell it out for me."

A red light allowed me a chance to fully look at him. "If someone sees me driving your car, word could get out that we're a couple."

His brow wrinkled. "And that's a problem for you?"

"Yes." Between Addy's starvation for a father figure, Layne's rejection of all men in my life but Harvey, Natalie's obsession with Doc being her *one*, and me still working as his Realtor, now was not the time to share our possible couple-dom with the world at large.

We stared at each other in silence as cars rolled past.

Someone honked behind me, jarring me back to the road. I made a left toward the library.

I glanced at Doc. He was still frowning, only now out the windshield rather than at me.

The library parking lot had a big, hand-painted Library Patrons Only sign posted at the entrance. I parked with an empty stall cushioning each side of Doc's Camaro.

Leaning my forehead on the steering wheel, I sighed. "I'm sorry, Doc."

"Don't be." There was a definite arctic front moving in from his side of the car.

"I really like you."

"Violet, stop." He squeezed the bridge of his nose. "Now is not the time for this."

"Fine. Why can't you tell me about the visions?"

"It's complicated."

"Give it a shot."

"Not right now. I need to piece some things together first."

"God!" I grabbed his palm and slapped his keys into it. "I love how you always get to be the one who decides what we talk about and when." I reached for the door handle.

"Violet, it's not—"

I slammed the door on his words, started to walk away, then stormed back and leaned in the window. "You scared the hell out of me back there in that damned house when you passed out. I deserve a fucking explanation. When you feel like talking, pick up a phone. Until then, don't."

If he called after me, I didn't hear it, and I sure as hell wasn't looking back. I may be gaga over the guy, but I still had a few pounds of pride in my body. To prove it, I shut off my cell phone so I wouldn't be on pins and needles until he called. *If* he called.

It took me three blocks to stop huffing, but I was still puffing ... and hungry. I grabbed a bag of beef jerky from the Lucky Horseshoe Casino's gift shop and tore into it, ripping into the salty meat with zeal, jerky grease coating my fingers. Halfway through the bag, I had a flashback of that horrible tea party at Wolfgang's and the jerky-like look of salt-dried human flesh, and I almost threw up on the sidewalk.

By the time I stomped into Calamity Jane's, I'd dumped the jerky in the trash and wiped as much grease from my fingers as I could. Sweat ran in rivulets down my back.

The sight of Jeff Wymonds sitting across from my desk made me falter. Mona and Ray's chairs were empty.

Jeff stood as I approached. "Hey, Violet, I stopped by to ..." He sniffed. "You smell good. Real good. Like beef jerky."

Excellent. Now I knew what to dab behind my ears if I ever went out on a date with Jeff.

He frowned at me as I walked around my desk and fell into my chair. "Are you okay?"

"No." I grabbed a tissue and patted my cheeks, neck, and upper chest. He stared as if he'd paid a couple of quarters to watch me from the other side of a window. I was in no mood to be ogled. "What can I do for you, Jeff?"

He blew out a breath. "Wow, that's hot."

"Criminy, it's just sweat."

"Yeah, but you make sweat look good."

Jesus! Scotty—somebody—beam me up, now! "Again, what can I do for you?"

"I'm ready for you to do a final inspection."

"You repainted the living room?" The big grease spot on the wall, in particular.

"Yep."

I heard a toilet flush in the back of the office. Ah, Ray was here, occupying his other throne.

"The backyard is cleaned up?" Meaning there were no flat tires, snowmobile parts, or severed baby-doll heads lying around anywhere?

"Yep. You want to come see it?"

Not really. Not right now. Not after the macabre show at the Carharts. "Sure, but you'll need to drive."

"You mean you want to go right now?"

"Why not?" My day couldn't get any worse.

The sight of Jeff's walls proved me wrong. Pepto-Bismol pink covered the living room grease spot and baby-poop green coated the kitchen walls. Jeff's reply to my "For

God's sake, why?" had to do with money he saved buying pre-mixed goofs from the hardware store.

On a high note, the backyard was ready for showing, with freshly mowed grass and flower boxes on the back and front porches. From the outside, the place no longer resembled the parking lot of a redneck AA meeting.

Three hours later, we'd returned from the hardware store down in Rapid City with a couple gallons of off-white paint, fashionable drapes for the kitchen and living room, and a few new throw rugs to cover the worn spots in the linoleum.

Exhausted from a day that started with sliced tires and went downhill from there, and with its finale yet to be determined, I asked Jeff to take me home. I wanted to crawl into my bed and hide under the covers for a couple of hours until it was time to summon bluebirds and fairies to prep me for the ball.

My Bronco sat in the drive, no longer listing. I could have kissed Harvey—which would be easier than baking a pie.

Jeff left his engine running. "Thanks for your help, Violet."

With his blond hair and big grin, he reminded me of a floppy-eared yellow lab. I resisted the urge to pat him on the head and instead took the hand he held out for me to shake. "You're welcome. Finish that painting tonight and I'll bring my sign tomorrow morning."

"I don't know how to repay you for everything."

He was still holding my hand. I tugged a little; no give. "I'm just doing my job, Jeff."

His grip tightened. "I'm not talking about the house."

Uh, oh. My Miss Spidey senses started to prickle. "Are you referring to Kelly?"

"No, I'm talking about me." He yanked me forward and cupped my cheeks. "You've healed me."

Before I could do more than stare in stupor, he kissed me.

His lips smashed mine, our teeth clattering. His tongue poked in my mouth like a jousting lance, thrusting into my back molars, aiming for my tonsils. I had to stop this before he rammed my uvula.

His tongue retracted from my mouth enough for him to groan and utter, "God, you smell like beef jerky."

Still? I must have gotten some in my hair.

He tried to pull me closer for another taste, but I resisted him, shoving against his chest. "Jeff, we have to stop."

"I know. We have an audience."

We did? I looked out the windshield and saw Addy's nose pressed against Aunt Zoe's front window. Her huge grin matched her wide eyes.

"Oh, no. Addy."

"Addy?" Jeff sounded surprised. He pointed toward the Bronco. "I was talking about Old Man Harvey."

Harvey stood next to the back bumper, a tire iron in his hand, his two gold teeth gleaming in the afternoon sunlight. He waved.

"Great. Just perfect."

"You're a good kisser, Violet Parker."

Is that what he called that? Kissing? It felt more like oral surgery. "Yeah, thanks."

"Are you busy this weekend?"

I needed to nip this right now. "Jeff, you know I don't date my clients." I only sleep with them.

"Who says we have to date?" He winked. "We could just fool around on the couch."

"No." I already had a fool-around buddy. I shoved open the door and hopped to the ground. "I'll be by tomorrow morning with a sign." And maybe a can of pepper spray.

"Okay. But you'd better not put me off for too long, Violet Parker. I'm ready to sow some of my wild oats, and you are ripe for planting, but me and my plow can't wait around forever."

It was so tempting when he put it that way. I slammed the door in his face.

Harvey didn't even wait for Jeff to make it out of the drive. "I usually have to pay to see that kind of action."

"I don't want to talk about it."

"Did he make it to second base? I couldn't see below the dashboard."

I chose to take the high road. "Thanks for fixing my tires. What do I owe you?"

"I told you, a pot roast and a strawberry pie."

"Right, sorry. It's been a long day. I'll repay you soon."

"How about tonight? Ms. Geary is having her poker girlfriends over for a late-night bender."

"I'm surprised you don't want to be in the center of that."

"No, way. Those women will pump me full of Viagra and wear me down to a nub."

I winced.

"Believe me, I've tried it." He hooked his thumbs in his suspenders and grinned, all cock-of-the-walk proud. "Now, how about that meal?"

"I can't. I have a dinner date tonight."

Harvey's bushy brows met his hairline. "You were just kissin' Jeff. Now you're meetin' up with Doc? Wow! I need to start taking notes from you."

"I wasn't kissing Jeff. He kissed me." More like he tried to lick my esophagus.

Harvey shrugged. "Confess it to a priest. Where are you and Doc eating?"

"Chuckwagon Charlie's. And I'm not meeting Doc."

"Well, I'll be a blue-nosed gopher. This just keeps

gettin' juicier. Who, then?"

I mumbled my answer.

"Speak up, girl."

"Douglas Mann."

Harvey howled loud enough to send the neighbor's Chihuahua into a barking frenzy. "You know, you should really write this shit down. I bet folks would pay good money to read about your crazy life. I sure would."

The screen door slammed and Addy came skipping down the drive toward us, a sucker sticking out of her mouth. "Mom, Doc just called."

"He did?" My heart picked itself up off the ground and dusted itself off. Why hadn't he called my cell? Oh, yeah, I'd shut it off. Stupid pride. "Did he say what he wanted? Is he still on the phone?" Had he forgiven me for going all Medusa on him earlier when my blood sugar tanked?

"Umm, no. He asked if he could talk to you, but I told him you were too busy kissing Kelly's dad to come to the phone."

Fuck me!

Chapter Seventeen

Doc wasn't answering my phone calls. I tried three times, but didn't leave a message. The probability that I'd open my mouth and insert both feet was too high.

Now I'd managed to muck up things with both my best friend and my kinda-sorta lover-boyfriend. I should write a book called *How to Alienate Your Friends and Lovers in Record Time*. Maybe I could go on the talk show circuit and make an even bigger ass of myself.

Rather than take the kids to Aunt Zoe's gallery for a couple of hours while I met with Douglas Mann, I asked Harvey to watch them. He took pity on me, but only after wrangling a promise that I'd call Cooper first thing tomorrow morning and report the vandalism of my Bronco.

Ms. Geary lured everyone but me over to her place with fresh-baked raspberry tarts while I got ready for my dinner meeting—I refused to call it a date, even to myself.

When I crossed the street to kiss Addy and Layne goodbye, they both had raspberry goo on the corners of their mouths. Their hair smelled of fresh-baked pies, making me want to drool all over them.

"Are you going out with Kelly's dad?" Addy asked.

I sighed. "For the third time, Adelynn, no. This is a business dinner."

"You said your dinner dates with Wolfgang were business, too. But they ended in kisses."

"That was one kiss, and it was on my cheek." That part of my face still warmed at my naïveté when it came to

Wolfgang's charm. But he'd been easy on the eyes and I'd been out to pasture for too long.

"Mom isn't interested in men," Layne said around a mouthful of raspberry tart. He narrowed his hazel eyes. "Are you?"

Only one. "Not really." I crossed my fingers behind my back.

Harvey snorted. "Could have fooled me."

I gave the old coot my evilest stink-eye.

Harvey's snickers followed me across the street to my Bronco. Ten minutes later, I climbed the stairs to Chuckwagon Charlie's lounge, my short navy skirt swishing with each step, the hem tickling the skin above my knees. At the top, *Charles' Club* was etched in a fancy font on the frosted glass doors. Inside, a cushy carpeted reception area greeted me. I checked out the digs while I searched for Douglas, the lollipop lookalike.

Downstairs in Chuckwagon Charlie's, wagon wheels of all sizes decorated the room. They hung from the ceiling, lined the walls, and served as centerpieces. Red and white checkered tablecloths brightened the wood accents; old tin plates and cups added a chuckwagon touch.

Up here in the lounge, dark and moody was the name of the game—luxurious greens, deep maroons, rich golds. Velvet-backed chairs and candlelit tables filled the front room. An elegantly carved mahogany bar ran the length of one wall. In the back, down a pair of steps, were three red-felt pool tables, Tiffany glass chandeliers hanging over each one. The place was reminiscent of an old gentlemen's club—the English upper-class kind from centuries ago, not the strip clubs of today. Not that I'd been in either. Well, not lately, anyway.

The wait staff wore white shirts with maroon pants, their legs blending in with the carpet. The young hostess dazzled patrons with her voluptuous figure highlighted in a shiny gold lamé dress. Her long blonde tresses flowed around her, partly covering her cute face. She was a fair-haired version of Jessica Rabbit, and I felt like the old woman who lived in a shoe, but I threw on a smile and approached her anyway.

"I'm supposed to meet Douglas Mann here."

"Mr. Mann is waiting for you." Her smile was too perfect. Had one of the Stepford wives escaped?

I followed her to our table. Douglas stood as we approached. Dressed in Johnny Cash style, tonight he looked more like a black pencil with a big rubber eraser than a lollipop.

His glance at my legs didn't go unnoticed. "Sorry, I'm all out of black," I explained, tucking my skirt under me as I sat in the chair he held. "I've been busy with funerals lately."

He returned to his chair. "I haven't been to a funeral in months, thank God. Between you and me, I find them a bit melodramatic."

I thought of him squeezing Lila's ass and smiled. "Me, too." Picking up the menu, I snatched the opportunity at hand. "Do you know George and Eddie Mudder?"

"Of course. They're cornerstones of the community."

Or headstones. "What are they like outside the funeral home?"

"The same as they are inside—quiet, unobtrusive, and a little odd. Why do you ask?"

Because they and my coworker are selling body parts. At least, that was my most recent theory. I lowered my menu. "Just curious."

"Curiosity killed the cat, you know."

"Lucky for me I have nine lives, eh?" Make that eight after my misadventures at Wolfgang's.

"Lucky indeed. Are you ready to order?" At my nod, Douglas signaled the waiter.

As soon as the waiter left, I got down to business. "So, what's the offer you'd like to place on the Carhart house?" I was purposely holding off mentioning that another offer existed until I heard his answer.

"Are we done with small talk already?"

"I figured we exchanged plenty yesterday."

He unrolled his linen napkin and placed it on his lap. "You know how I feel about talking business while I'm eating."

"I do, but my babysitter is on a timer tonight and our dinner hasn't arrived yet," I lied with ease, one step ahead of him. I figured he'd try to drag this out. I'd even stopped by the office and grabbed an unsigned copy of the offer paperwork that I'd typed up this morning while I waited for Zeke and Zelda to show up at Calamity Jane's. "So you'll have to make an exception."

"Okay, I'll compromise this time."

This time? What made him think there would be another time?

"What do you think of Lead?" he asked.

I usually didn't, except for the homes for sale there. "Well," I stalled a little, knowing he was on the chamber of commerce and I should choose my words carefully. "It has a lot of potential."

"Exactly!" He leaned forward, his eyes wide and lit up. "That's what I see."

"Yeah, just like Deadwood."

"No, better than Deadwood and its ridiculous past. While Deadwood's finest were busy whoring and partying, the people of Lead built the area's infrastructure, provided stability with jobs and money. Without Lead, Deadwood is just a ghost town."

Which would work well for Doc, I thought.

"Have you visited the Black Hills Mining Museum?" Douglas asked.

"I took my son there a couple of months ago. He's an avid historian."

"Then you know about all the gold and silver filling Lead's underbelly."

Funny, I hadn't really thought about Lead or Deadwood having an underbelly.

The waiter delivered our drinks and a loaf of warm sourdough bread.

Douglas buttered a slice of bread. "I'm so tired of Deadwood getting all the attention."

Jeez. He was hung up on this like a jealous sibling.

"Lead has so much more to offer," he said.

"Besides that huge open hole in the ground?" Oops, that slipped out before I could edit it.

"Especially that huge open hole in the ground." Douglas leaned forward, his cheeks ruddier than usual. "It's our very own Grand Canyon, don't you see? We just need to market it that way."

The Grand Canyon? I tried not to roll my eyes. "I suppose it's all in the spin."

"Exactly." He sat back with a satisfied smirk on his face. "I knew you'd understand. You're a businesswoman, after all."

Why did I feel as if I'd just passed some test?

I was tired of talking about Lead. "So, what's the offer you'd like to place on—"

A loud, familiar gut-laugh coming from the bar interrupted me and made my ears perk up. *Harvey?* I looked over. Sure enough, there sat the gold-toothed troublemaker. What was he doing here? *Who was watching my kids?*

I stood, my gaze on Harvey. "Douglas, please excuse me for a mom—"

Harvey leaned over the bar, reaching for something the bartender held out, and I caught a glimpse of another familiar profile. *Natalie?*

She sat on the stool on the other side of Harvey, drinking from a longneck beer.

What in the hell was going on?

"I'll be right back," I told Douglas and weaved my way over to them, my palms clammy. How was Natalie going to react to the sight of me? Would she tackle me and pull my hair, or grab an ice pick from behind the bar and stab me through the heart? At least I wasn't here with Doc tonight, rubbing salt in her wound.

Natalie turned her head and saw me. Her smile melted away all my cold worries. Relief made my knees weak. She didn't hate me. Thank God!

She didn't seem surprised at all to see me. "Hey, girlfriend. Douglas is keeping his hands to himself, isn't he? The tablecloth is too long for us to see what's going on under there."

I gave her a shoulder hug, touchy with happiness. "The only thing Douglas wants from me is my help buying a house."

Harvey snorted. "Yeah, right."

"What are you two doing here?" I poked Harvey in the arm. "Who's watching my kids?"

"Ms. Geary," Natalie answered. "I stopped by your aunt's to see what you've been up to and Harvey came over and told me you needed our help."

"Help with Douglas? He's harmless."

Harvey snorted again. "You're such a greenhorn. He's just playing you." The way Harvey echoed Doc on this subject made me want to snap his suspenders.

I settled with "Quit snorting at me," and then turned to Natalie. "Why didn't you return my calls?"

"I dropped my cell phone in the toilet the night you and I went out. A perfect way to end that shitty day." She raised her beer bottle in a mock toast. "I didn't have a chance to get down to Rapid for a new one until this afternoon."

I'd been in hell for two long freaking days all because of a stupid toilet. Criminy.

That confirmed beyond a doubt that Natalie didn't carve *SLUT!* on my Bronco door. Who did it, then? Was I the victim of a drive-by keying? Yeah, right, and a drive-by tire slashing, too. Not likely. My suspicion centered on a certain raven haired bitch, but I still didn't know why she would. Just because I didn't kowtow to her like Millie and Wanda? There had to be something more to it than that, didn't there? And what was with the weird symbolism in the exclamation mark?

The salads had arrived at my table. Douglas had his cell phone out, frowning down at the screen. "Listen, I need to get back. Don't—"

"Oh. My. God," Natalie said under her breath and grabbed my arm. "Look who's here."

I followed her gaze down to the pool tables and sucked in a breath at the sight of Doc leaning over the table, lining up for a shot. His black jeans hung low, hugging his hips. His white shirt was just a tad snug, teasing me with glimpses of muscles under the cover of cotton.

"What are the chances of running into him here of all places?" Natalie said. "It must be fate."

"Or *blonde* luck," Harvey muttered.

I flicked him on the forearm while Natalie wasn't looking.

Douglas was waving me over, pointing at our salads. Duty called, but Doc was bending over for another shot and lust didn't want to listen.

"Damn, Doc looks hot tonight," Natalie said.

I barely heard her. My imagination was busy picturing him bending over me like that.

She slid off her stool, careful with her booted cast. "I'm gonna go talk to him."

"No!"

Natalie frowned at me. "Why not?"

"Uhhhh, because..." *He's mine!* I flailed for a few nanoseconds, the truth hovering on the tip of my tongue. "You have lipstick on your teeth."

"Eww. Thanks." She scrubbed her teeth with her napkin and then showed me her pearly whites. "All clear?"

I wanted to hit her upside the head with her longneck beer. "You're good to go."

"Wish me luck." She sashayed down the steps, or at least tried as best she could with a chunk of plaster wrapped around her calf. I couldn't look away as she approached the pool table and leaned a flirty hip against it, right where Doc was aiming.

"You gonna stand here and let that happen?" Harvey asked, not a trace of humor in his voice.

Doc made the shot and then stood, grinning, charming as hell, damn him. "What choice do I have?"

"Plenty. Go stop it."

"I'll lose my best friend."

"If you don't stop screwin' around, you're gonna lose a good man."

Across the room, Doc shrugged at something Natalie said. She selected a pool stick from the rack on the far wall. "I don't even have him yet."

It was as if Doc heard me. He looked over at me, and we locked gazes. I took a step back at the fury radiating from his dark eyes.

"Woo-wee, he's as pissed as a castrated wolverine." Harvey spoke for my ears only. "He's got it bad for you."

My heart throbbed clear to the ends of my fingers and toes. "What are you talking about? He wants to hang me from a tree limb."

"A man doesn't get that hot and bothered over friendship."

Doc still had me in his sights. His jaw ticked as he

chalked up his cue. I could hear Natalie's sexy giggles as she playfully bumped him to the side so she could shoot. My gut wrenched.

"Not to mention he's here keepin' an eye on you," Harvey added, "in spite of you smoochin' Jeff."

I cast a glare at Harvey. "I wasn't kissing Jeff."

Harvey pointed his beer in Doc's direction. "Tell him, not me."

"It's not that easy."

"Sure, it is. Just open your big mouth and say it."

Harvey was right. Somehow, I needed to get Doc alone to explain, to apologize, to fix this mess I'd made. So what if Natalie wondered what was going on. So what if she'd staked a claim. I liked Doc. I needed him. I wanted to sink into him, wrap his arms around me, and feel his heart under my cheek. I should go over there right now and ...

Harvey interrupted my pep rally. "Your date is trying to get your attention."

Date? Oh, yeah. Crapola. I checked on Douglas, who lifted his hands in the air, obviously wondering what the holdup was. I gave him the one-minute finger.

I turned back to Doc, my chest aching as I watched Natalie pretend she needed to be taught how to shoot. She'd been playing pool in her dad's basement since she'd worn training pants. Damn her and her little flirting games.

"I have to get back to Douglas."

"You sure?"

No. "Do me a favor. Go over there and rescue Doc."

"I don't like pool."

"I'll bake you something."

"You already owe me a pot roast and a pie, and you don't even bake."

I glared at Harvey. Now was not the time to throw that in my face. "How about dinner and a movie next week?"

"In your living room, again?"

"Down in Rapid."

"Deal." He slid off the stool, beer in hand. "Now go make some money, because I'm not a cheap date."

Yeah, I'd noticed. Lead-footed, I returned to my dinner table. "Sorry about that," I said to Douglas as I sat down and picked up my fork, fighting the urge to glance over at the pool tables. I stabbed the hell out of my salad and crammed it into my mouth, barely tasting the balsamic vinaigrette dressing.

"Friends of yours?"

More like bodyguards. I nodded and crunched, not introducing them since I was pretty sure Douglas knew who two of the three were, even if he was acting otherwise for some reason. I was well aware of how small a world it was up here in the Hills. "So, what do you want to offer for the house?"

"Let's save that for dessert."

Jesus. I'd have more luck conducting business with a kindergartner at a monkey parade. If he wouldn't talk business, then I had another non-business question that had been nagging at me. "Why are you interested in the Carhart place?"

"It's a beautiful house."

Where had I heard that before? I wasn't buying it, not from a man who had as much money as Douglas reportedly did. "There are other beautiful houses in the area for sale. Why this one in particular?"

"The house has an interesting history."

My ears twitched. I lowered my fork. Now we were talking. "Did you know the previous owners?"

"You mean the Snarky family?" At my nod, he continued, "No, they were before my time. But I know of them, and what happened in that house."

"And you still want to buy it."

"Sure. I enjoy the stories about it."

I leaned forward, lowering my voice. "Which stories?"

"That it's haunted by Karen's ghost."

Oh, that one. "Do you believe in ghosts, Douglas?"

His deep laugh surprised me back into my seat. "Of course not. But I do find the talk about them quite entertaining. And the tourists love ghost stories."

Then he must enjoy living in the Black Hills, where so many ghost stories thrived.

"Do you believe in ghosts, Violet?"

The million-dollar question. I glanced at Doc. "I haven't decided."

"Really? In spite of your reputation, I'd peg you for a disbeliever."

He'd heard about my ghost-loving infamy, apparently. "Why is that?"

"Because you were willing to sell the Hessler house, and the rumors about that place rivaled the Carhart house in number. Did you know Mrs. Hessler died in that house?"

Yeah, I knew. I had nightmares about her and those goddamned clowns nightly. But I didn't want to talk about the Hessler place—not unless Douglas had a degree in psychology, and probably not even then.

Thankfully, our entrées arrived at that moment. As the waiter asked Douglas about pepper, I peeked over at Doc and Natalie. Natalie was lining up a shot. Doc stood across the table from her. As if he felt my stare, he turned and found me, his eyes piercing. I ducked like a puppy who'd peed on the carpet and focused on my chicken breast, which smelled heavenly. Lucky for me, his anger wasn't affecting my appetite, so I dug in.

After a few bites of the advertised apricot-flavored chicken covered in rich blueberry sauce, I licked my lips and went for the throat. "Do you think Junior Carhart really killed his father?"

Douglas shrugged as he chewed on a piece of his steak.

"It doesn't matter what I think. I'm not the police."

"Did you know the Carhart family?" He went to their funeral, so he must have, unless that was just a political move.

"Sure, well enough."

"Was Junior the violent type?"

"He had the potential for violence." He smiled with too many teeth.

Something inside me recoiled.

"But so do most men," he added.

I glanced over in time to see Natalie trailing her fingers over Doc's arm as he drew back his cue for a shot. I resisted launching my fork at her like a javelin. "And some women," I said aloud. Where in the hell was Harvey? He was supposed to be running interference.

"Sure. Women, too. It's human nature, especially if jealousy is involved."

Jealousy? I gaped at him for a moment as he cut off another piece of meat. Had he seen me watching Natalie? I finally decided it wasn't me he was talking about. "Was Junior jealous of his father?"

"Yes." He frowned slightly as he stabbed his steak, hesitating for a moment before adding, "At least that's how the rumor goes."

If I hadn't been watching him so closely, I wouldn't have noticed his hesitation. Something about it didn't sit right. "Which rumor?" It was a new one to me.

"The one about old Mr. Carhart coming on to his son's fiancée."

Hold the phone! I hadn't heard that one. "Coming on how?"

Douglas shrugged and pushed his round glasses up on his round face. "There isn't much more to tell. Just that the old man had taken advantage of the girl's kindness and got pretty fresh with her."

The girl's kindness? Were we talking about the same sharp-toothed bitch? The one who likely knifed my door and tires?

"They were arguing about the fiancée that night and Junior temporarily lost his mind."

"And then blew it out with a shotgun."

Douglas grimaced. "Miss Parker, we are eating here."

"Sorry." Maybe he should have been willing to talk to me about the house offer.

Something smelled rotten about this rumor. Since I had video of Douglas groping Lila's ass, I had to wonder who whispered this version of the story in his ear, and if there was more to the connection between Douglas and Lila than just a roll in the hay. It was hard to tell with Douglas, thanks to his playboy image. And I'd last seen Lila kissing Millie, so it all added up to a lot of confusing *maybes* and *what-ifs*.

I kept to the weather and Lead's general history for the rest of the meal. He had me laughing at his anecdotes and never once tried to touch me inappropriately. He was either a great actor, a true gentleman, or just not a fan of curly-haired blondes.

True to his word, Douglas brought up his offer over dessert. It was about five grand higher than Zeke and Zelda's, and my heart sank a little at the thought of them losing the deal. But I had a responsibility to be impartial to all parties involved, and money was money, so I filled out the amount on the paperwork I'd brought along with me.

"I should tell you there's another offer on the table."

"Really?" Douglas took the pen I handed to him, frowning down at the line where I needed his signature. "Why didn't you say something before now?"

"It just came in this morning. When you called to meet for dinner, I decided to wait until we were face to face."

"How much is the other offer? Is it from someone local?"

"All I can tell you is that it is a full-price offer."

His grin was that of a victor. "How long until I know the place is mine?"

"I'll take the papers to Wanda Carhart tomorrow. She'll have thirty-six hours to accept or decline."

"She'll accept."

His certainty made my neck bristle, but I just smiled and tucked away the papers.

I passed on his invitation for a celebratory lunch, faking other plans. I didn't need any more rumors circulating about me. The ghost-loving reputation was plenty. Plus, I had Doc's feelings to consider. I didn't get off on making a guy jealous.

The sun had set by the time I stood to leave. Douglas offered to walk me out into the twilight.

I passed again, thanked him for dinner, and grabbed my purse from the back of the chair. "You should have at least let me pay the tip."

"Absolutely not. When I take a woman out, I want her to feel special."

"This was a business dinner, though."

"Close enough."

No, it wasn't, but since he hadn't tried to play footsie under the table, I let it go. "Tomorrow, then," I said and headed for the door, sneaking one last glace at the three musketeers. There were just two now, Natalie and Harvey. When had Doc slipped out? I waved at Natalie. She gave me a raised brow and a thumbs-up gesture, and I nodded.

Three tables from the exit, I noticed a very pregnant woman struggling to reach the basket of rolls in the center of the table. I smiled in sympathy. Even though it'd been a decade since I was pregnant with twins, I could remember the discomfort of becoming a human beach ball as if it were yesterday. When I glanced at her dinner companion, my smile froze.

Lila?

I sneered at her hard glare. If looks could kill, I'd be nothing but charred remains.

The temptation to accuse her of vandalizing my Bronco was strong, but I swallowed it. I needed some proof first. With my chin up, I shoved out the glass doors.

What was Lila doing there? Who was the pregnant girl? Where was Millie?

I half expected Lila to chase me down the stairs and start an all-out catfight in the street, but I made it to my Bronco without trouble. Well, except for the dark-haired man leaning against my driver's-side door with his arms crossed and his gaze frosty. His middle name was *Trouble*.

"I didn't kiss Jeff Wymonds," I told Doc first off, keeping a couple feet of space between us just in case Natalie followed me out. "He kissed me."

A muscle twitched in Doc's jaw. "Did you like it?"

I thought about Jeff's jousting tongue. "God, no."

"Are you going to do it again?"

"Not voluntarily."

He nodded slowly, as if he was chewing on my explanation, taste-testing it. "How was dinner with the playboy?"

"He was a complete gentleman—as you, Harvey, and Natalie witnessed."

His eyes narrowed. "I still don't trust him. Something is wrong here. There has to be some reason he's not coming on to you."

"Maybe I'm just not his type. Not all men are into blondes."

He gave me a very thorough once-over, spreading heat along the way. "Yeah, but we all like beautiful women in short skirts and tight shirts."

When he stared at me with that dusky hunger, I wanted to leap into his arms. I settled for poking him playfully in the chest. "Maybe there's something wrong with you for liking blondes in tight shirts."

"Don't forget the short skirt." He captured my finger and tugged me a step closer. "That little number has been driving me crazy all evening."

"You like it?" I twirled my hips so the material swayed and swished.

"I'd like to do things to you while you're wearing it."

Oh, wow. My thighs got warm.

"What are you wearing under it?"

The sex kitten in me lifted its head and meowed. I batted my eyelashes, glad I'd used the expensive mascara tonight. "It's a secret."

He grinned and pulled me another step closer.

I glanced over my shoulder, paranoid. "Natalie and Harvey will be out here any minute. She doesn't know about us yet."

"I noticed that."

"That means she isn't the one who carved up my Bronco." I shot another look toward the restaurant, hoping the cast was slowing her down.

"I know. Drive me back to the office."

"Where's your car?"

"In the alley."

"Okay, but I can't stay." I was telling him as much as telling myself, trying to ignore images of him slamming me up against the wall. "Ms. Geary is watching my kids, and Harvey and Nat will wonder where I am if I'm not home when they get there."

"Fine." He took my keys, unlocked the door, and held it for me. "Get in."

We made it out of the parking lot without running into Natalie or Harvey.

"I need to talk to you about the Carhart house," Doc announced out of the blue.

I glanced at him from the corner of my eye, a bit nervous about discussing this after our earlier fight. "You mean about what went down today?"

He nodded.

"I can call you after Natalie goes home, but it might be late."

"I don't want to talk about it on the phone."

"Tomorrow morning?"

"I have an appointment down in Rapid City first thing. I'll call when I get back." He pointed out the windshield. "Will you make a right up there in that alley?"

I did as he asked. His Camaro sat up ahead on the right, parked several blocks from the office again. I followed his directions and pulled in behind it. The alley was dead. "Do you need something from your car?" I asked, glancing out the rearview mirror.

"Violet."

In the semi-dark cab, the intention shining in his eyes sent a rush of tingles through my limbs. "What?" I whispered.

"What are you wearing under your skirt?"

His words alone got me all steamy. "No, Doc," I said, but reached for him as he leaned toward me. "I have to go home." I wasn't sure who I was trying to convince.

"I know." My lips met his in the middle; his coaxed and savored, mine tasted and teased. "What are you wearing under your skirt?" His hand was on my knee.

I wrapped my arms around his neck, pulling him closer, longing for more, reveling in the feel of his warm palm on my bare skin. "I told you, it's a secret."

His fingers slid north several inches, making small circles as they roamed. His mouth skimmed along my jaw. "A secret?"

"Yes," I gasped as his other hand skated down the side of my breast, his thumb achingly close to finding purchase.

"You'll have to whisper the magic words in my ear for me to show you."

He nipped my earlobe, his breath hot on my skin. "You want the magic words?"

His fingers brushed ever closer to my panties. My "Yes" came in a drawn out hiss, my head fell back against the headrest.

"Violet," he said against my neck. "I want to make you scream."

Those words would do just fine. I tilted my hips, wanting him so much it hurt. His other hand slipped beneath the hem of my shirt.

His lips caressed my collarbone. "Tell me what you want, Boots."

This was such sweet torture. I couldn't stand much more. "I want you to—"

My freaking phone rang.

"Damn it!" I yelled at the roof of the Bronco.

Doc's fingers stilled right at the lacy edge of my underwear.

"It will go to voicemail," I said and pulled him closer, teasing his mouth open with my tongue, trying to ignore the world.

The stupid phone wouldn't stop ringing.

"Answer it," Doc whispered against my lips.

"I don't want to stop."

"Neither do I, but you have kids." He pulled back and handed me my purse. "Answer it."

I dug the phone out. Natalie's number flashed. Frickin' frack! I flipped it open. "What's up, Nat?"

"Where are you?"

"I stopped off at the office for a minute to take care of some paperwork," I lied.

"Harvey's making homemade ice cream. You want some?"

"Sure." I could stuff it down my underwear to cool off. "I'll be right there."

I hung up and leaned my forehead on the steering wheel. "I really wanted you to make me scream tonight."

Doc blew out a breath and adjusted his jeans. "If I don't get to have you again soon, I'm going to go blind."

Chuckling, I cranked the engine. A minute later, we sat idling behind the office, under the orange glow of parking lot lights. I wished I could ask him to come home with me, eat some ice cream, sit next to me on the back porch steps, but ...

"I'd kiss you goodnight," I said, "but I'm afraid I won't be able to stop."

"Same here."

"I'll see you in the morning."

"You will." He reached for the door handle, then paused. "Just out of curiosity, what *are* you wearing under your skirt?"

"Hmmm, let's see." I bit my lower lip suggestively and inched my skirt up my thigh, slow and teasing. His eyes lit up as he watched. I stopped just short of my panty line. "Nah." I yanked my skirt back down. "Let's keep it a secret."

I heard him gulp. "Holy shit," he whispered, "you are a vixen, through and through." With a groan, he stepped out of the Bronco, shut the door, walked around to my side, and leaned in the open window. His lazy grin softened his face.

He ran a finger along my jaw line; his thumb brushed over my lips. My body hummed with electricity. He tilted his head toward mine, and I opened my mouth, anticipating his onslaught, eager for it.

But it didn't come. "Paybacks are hell, Violet." He stepped back, his gaze sizzling, my body aflame with need. "Yours is coming."

I could hardly wait.

* * *

Thursday, August 9th

I made it into work extra early the next morning, hoping to catch a glimpse of Doc—or a few touches from him, maybe some well-placed rubs. I'd settle for a lot of ogling. I wasn't proud, just oversexed, since I'd met him. But his office was dark and locked when I tried. Damn.

Back at my desk, I busied myself with paperwork. It was a nice feeling to have something to do besides surf the Internet for new listings.

After yesterday's insanity, I was ready for a clean slate. A new, normal day, although I'd have to stop by the Carhart house again later to drop off Douglas' offer. Maybe I could just slide the paperwork under the door and zip out of there. With my luck, I'd run into Lila and her claws somewhere between the front porch and the driveway.

A peaceful hour later, the back door crashed open and Ray barged in. "Blondie!" he bellowed.

I tensed. What now? I'd parked in my spot, not his, and there should still be plenty of spaces open all around at this time of the morning. "What?"

"You're on fire!" he yelled, his face flushed.

I frowned at him as he marched up to me. "What in the hell is that supposed to mean?"

"It means you're on fire. Call 911."

If this was another one of his sexual harassment jokes, he needed to work on his delivery. "I don't get it."

He leaned down into my face. "Your Bronco is on fire in the parking lot. Call 911, now!"

Chapter Eighteen

My Bronco's violent death burned my eyes. Literally.

Ravenous flames overtook the old beast, crackling and popping as they shot out of the shattered windows and swarmed across the hood and roof, eating everything within reach. Dark smoke billowed, luring an audience of leather-clad mourners.

My eyes watered from smoke and heat and a few pity-party tears. I covered my mouth with my hand, hiding ragged breaths that hurt with each draw and tasted bitter in my throat. The smell of flame-broiled rubber and paint and everything in between nearly gagged me.

Somebody pulled me out of the way when the firemen arrived. Someone else handed me a white handkerchief, which I clutched as if my life depended on it. I couldn't look away as bright electrical flashes sparked and sizzled inside the remains of the cab.

Within minutes, it was all over, my Bronco nothing but a dripping, blackened mangle of metal and melted plastic. With faded memories of car seats and spilled Cheerios heavy in my thoughts, I zombie-walked toward it only to be stopped by a fireman covered from head to toe in protective gear.

"Stay back, ma'am." His mask filtered his voice. "It's still too hot."

I blinked up at him. "My son's library books are in there."

He looked over my shoulder. "Captain!" he shouted. "A

little help here."

"I got her," said a familiar voice, shaking me out of my daze. Detective Cooper grabbed me by the elbow and towed me under the shade of the pine trees lining the edge of the lot. "Sit," he ordered, and pointed at a stump.

"This skirt is silk." When he continued to frown at me, I added, "I don't want to get it dirty."

"Jesus, woman." He grabbed the twisted handkerchief from my hands and spread it on the stump. "There. Sit."

I obeyed, staring at the charbroiled hulk again.

"Are you okay?"

"Yeah," I answered without looking at him. A decade ago, I'd traded in my Mustang to buy the Bronco when I'd found out I was pregnant with twins, knowing I'd need a bigger vehicle.

"You sure?"

"Uh, huh."

"Violet, look at me," Cooper said, squatting next to me.

I shot him a glance, but kept most of my focus on the firemen spraying down the dash.

"Violet."

One of the firemen pried open the hood with a crowbar. "Hmmm?"

A hard pinch on the back of my arm made me screech. "Ouch!" I whirled on Cooper. "What did you do that for?"

"To get your attention."

I rubbed the back of my arm where the pain still twanged. "Did Harvey teach you that trick?"

Cooper grinned, a sight so rare I stared out of astonishment. "That, and a few more gems." His gray eyes searched my face for a couple of breaths. "Are you going to be okay?"

I nodded. "I'll probably bruise, though."

"I'm talking about your Bronco, not the pinch."

"So am I."

"Right." He rose to his feet and held out his hand. "Come on."

I squinted at his open palm. "Where are we going?"

"To the station."

"Am I under arrest?"

His grin widened. "Maybe."

"For what?"

"Withholding information."

"You can arrest me for that?"

His eyes narrowed. "That's not the response I expected."

Oops. I pinched my lips tight and curled them inside my mouth.

"What information are you withholding, Miss Parker?"

I looked anywhere but at those piercing gray eyes. "Ahh, nothing—I mean, none."

"Has anyone ever told you that your nose twitches when you lie?"

I held my hand to my guilty appendage. "Do I really have to go with you?"

"Now that I know your 'tell,' you definitely do."

My eyes met his above my hand. "For how long?"

His lips twitched at the corners. "That depends."

"On what?"

"How much you know." He grabbed my wrist and tugged me to my feet. "Come with me."

It was a command, one I could tell he was used to people obeying, so I followed on his heels. "Has anyone ever told you that you're as stubborn as your uncle?"

"Yep. My mother. Every damned day."

As we passed the fire truck, its lengths of hose being rolled up, someone called out, "Hey, Detective!"

Cooper paused as a salt-and-pepper-haired Sam Elliot lookalike—moustache and all—dressed in yellow firemen's pants and a dark blue T-shirt waltzed up to us. "What do you need, Reid?" Cooper asked.

I had a notion that I'd seen Reid and his blue-blue eyes somewhere before, besides looking magnified and handsome on the silver screen, but I couldn't remember where.

"What time's the game tonight?" Reid asked Cooper, smiling down at me, coaxing a return smile from my own lips.

"Eight, at my place. And if you're late again, you'll be thrown in county lockup. The Sheriff is in town tonight."

Game night at Cooper's? Maybe that was why he put me off on prettying it up for potential buyers until next week.

"Yeah, yeah. The Sheriff doesn't scare me. He's a lousy shuffler and can't bluff worth a damn." He waved Cooper off, still charming me with his friendly eyes. "So, Miss Parker, we meet again."

Dang it, where had I seen this guy before? And how did he know my name?

He lifted one dark eyebrow. "What is this, your second fire within a month?"

There it was. I'd seen him at Wolfgang's house. While the paramedics were working on me, he'd asked me about how the fire started. "Yes, but I didn't start this one."

He laughed. It was that deep-timbre-filled kind of laugh that made heads turn. "I'll be sure to note that in my report. Your insurance agent will be curious."

"Right. Insurance." Not that his report would do me any good. I had only liability insurance on the Bronco. Financially, I'd just gone from "dire straits" to "beyond fucked."

"How's your aunt doing?"

Aunt Zoe? A bell dinged in my brain. Of course! Aunt Zoe and Reid. The cupid in me flapped her wings like a hummingbird. He was perfect for her. No wedding ring on his finger, not even a tan line. "She's great. Still single."

Both dark eyebrows raised. "I thought she was seeing some doctor down by Hill City."

"A veterinarian, and that's been over for a couple of years." Well, months, really, but who was counting? Time flowed like a river and all that jazz. "You should give her a call."

"Maybe." He rubbed his hands together, glancing away. "We'll see."

"You girls done talking about your nail polish?" Cooper asked, the laughter in his voice taking the sting out of his insult. "Because I have some questions for Violet."

"You'll have to excuse Coop," Reid told me. "He was raised by a pack of muskrats."

"I noticed the big, sharp teeth."

"Cute, ladies. Now let's go." Cooper tugged on my elbow. "We have some talking to do."

I waved goodbye and kept pace with Cooper, the silence growing heavier with each step as my anxiety climbed at being hauled in for questioning. "He's kind of dreamy," I said, to fill the quiet. *Dreamy?* What was it about Cooper that turned me into a walking, talking bimbo?

"What are you? Fourteen with pigtails?"

"More like twenty-nine," plus a few-odd years.

"Don't make me book you for lying." He paused next to his unmarked police car as he unlocked the door. "Reid's too old for you."

I wasn't thinking about me. I had my hands full with Doc.

"Besides, he's the captain of the fire department."

Oh, really? I tucked away that information. "Why does that make a difference?"

"It's an elite position. He doesn't need to risk losing it over a high-maintenance woman with a ghost-loving reputation." He held open the door, ushering me into his car.

I crossed my arms. "I'm not high maintenance."

"You've been in town how long now? Almost six months?"

Somebody had been doing his homework. "Maybe."

"Six months and all the guys at the station already know your name. Trust me, that's high maintenance." He pointed at the front seat. "Come on, I'll buy you a soda pop."

"Your generosity makes my knees buckle."

"Great. That will make it easier for you to sit. Now get in."

Two blocks later, he pulled into the back lot of the police station.

"We could have walked," I said, scrambling out.

"Yeah, but then my car would be parked two blocks away."

He led me into the station and past a check-in desk and waiting chairs. The big gray-haired cop behind the desk looked from me to Cooper and then chuckled. "It's about time you brought that troublemaker in," he said with a wink.

We passed desks cluttered with computers and dirty coffee mugs. Across the room, two policemen—one a bit soft in the middle, the other tall and string-bean skinny—lounged against the counter in a mini-kitchen, each holding a paper cup. They watched us cruise by, returning Cooper's nod and raising their cups to me. "Miss Parker," they greeted me in turn.

Oh, God! They did all know me. My cheeks burned.

Cooper's office was in the back of the building, at the end of a long linoleum hall that acted as an echo chamber for the clap of my sandal heels. In his office, I dropped into the chair he indicated and noticed the sparseness of his desk. His walls were even sparser. "What? No pictures of your sweetheart and her prized Pomeranian, Fifi?"

"I like your spunk," Cooper said with a deadpan expression as he situated himself behind his desk. "I see why Uncle Willis keeps you around. That and your knees."

I glanced down at the objects of discussion. "What about my knees?"

"Uncle Willis has a thing for knobby knees."

"Harvey has a thing for anything in a skirt most days, and my knees are not knobby."

"If you say so. I'm more interested in your head, and I'm not talking about your crazy hair."

Crazy hair? I patted my loose curls. I hadn't battened them down this morning, since seducing Doc had been the first item on my docket. God, was that just this morning? The whole weight of losing my Bronco and what that meant fell into my lap again, sobering me, provoking an ache in my chest. My ability to banter fizzled.

"Listen, *Coop*," I crossed my arms and knobby knees and glared at the detective. "My Bronco just burned to the ground, so I'm a little distracted by the sudden financial mess I'm in, not to mention what this means to the safety of my family." That thought alone chilled me. "Just because my roots really are blonde doesn't mean my I.Q. is subpar, so stop treating me like I'm some ditz and tell me why you dragged me in here."

"Fair enough." He steepled his fingers and stared at me over the top of them. "Tell me what you know about Wanda Carhart."

Wanda? I frowned, surprised. I'd thought he was going to ask about my Bronco's unfortunate demise. I ground mental gears and focused on Wanda, but all that came to mind was her kookiness about those damned missing ice trays. "She's very timid."

"I've noticed." His gray eyes didn't blink. "Why do you think she wants to sell the house?"

"I don't know that she does. Millie has been more

interested in the details of the sale." Millie *and Lila*, that was. "Wanda just signs the documents."

"You mentioned before that Millie seemed anxious to get out of town. Has she said where she intends to go?"

"No, but we're not exactly pals."

"What do you know about Lila Beaumont?"

It took me several seconds to filter through all the derogatory comments that popped into my mind. "She's wily," I said, my lip curling of its own accord.

"Not a fan, huh?"

"She and I haven't hit it off yet." I wasn't holding my breath, either. I'd sooner just suffocate her instead.

"Any particular reason?"

"Not really. Just a mutual loathe-at-first-sight type of thing." I thought about my brief history with Lila, then added, "I think she sees me as a threat."

Cooper's brow wrinkled. "In what way?"

"Maybe to her relationship with Millie, somehow."

"Relationship? Are you referring to her being engaged to Millie's brother?"

Had Harvey not told Cooper about the kiss? "I'm referring to the relationship going on between Millie and Lila."

His head cocked slightly. "Between them? You mean something is going on behind closed doors?"

They were outside under the big blue sky when I saw them, but, "Yes."

"You're sure about this?" His eyes narrowed.

"Positive."

"Interesting." He leaned back in his chair. "That would explain a couple of things."

It was my turn to ask a question or two. "Why are you asking me about the Carharts? Is this about the murder?"

"I'm not at liberty to talk about it."

"But I thought you said the case was closed."

"I might have said that, but it's not, officially. Yet."

I leaned forward and lowered my voice. "Do you think someone else killed Junior's dad?"

Cooper stared at me as the clock on the wall ticked, his expression about as transparent as a bowling ball. "I'm not at liberty to talk about it."

"What are you at liberty to tell me?"

"That you should be a little more careful when you're out and about." He frowned. "And at home."

"Thanks. That's so reassuring and helpful."

"It's not my job to make you feel all warm and fuzzy." He crossed his arms over his chest. "Tell me about your Bronco. Uncle Willis mentioned you were having some troubles with vandalism."

I figured that Harvey had already given Cooper the details, so I kept it short and sweet. "Someone carved 'SLUT' into the driver's-side door, and then they knifed two of my tires." Which reminded me that I now owed Harvey a couple of tires. Shit.

"I'm going to need you to write an official statement."

"Fine."

"Do you have any idea who might be harboring ill will toward you?"

"Enough to play with matches next to my Bronco? No," I lied. Until I had some more proof the vandal was the mistress of my newest buying client, I didn't want to go pointing fingers. A pyromaniac accusation might cause a crimp in the sale of the house.

"We don't know for certain that this is an arson case."

"How else do you explain my Bronco being torched?"

"It was an old vehicle. There could have been some electrical malfunction."

"Come on, you and I both know that's not the case. Somebody is messing with me." I was pretty positive I knew who, but the "why" part still had me stumped.

"I won't know anything for certain until I hear more from Reid."

"Fine." I stood, unwilling to be grilled any more today. I had a charred vehicle to lay to rest, a couple of frustrating phone calls to make, and an offer to deliver to a client—somehow, even if I had to hitchhike there. "Are we done here?"

"For now. I'll be in touch," he said to my back.

"I'll be waiting with bated breath."

His laughter followed me down the hall. At the front desk, Doc leaned against the tall counter, talking to the desk officer. He stood up straight as I approached, his gaze searching. "You okay?"

I kept walking and headed for the entrance. "I've been better."

He beat me to the glass doors, holding one open for me, and then followed me out into the warm, late-morning sunshine. "I need to talk to you, Violet."

I didn't much feel like chatting. Drinking, maybe. Curling up into a ball under my covers, definitely. "Can it wait?"

"No."

"I have to take care of my Bronco."

"The tow truck driver already did that for you." He grasped my shoulders and steered me toward his car. "Trust me, this is important."

I trusted him under one condition. He honored it by stopping in front of Calamity Jane's long enough for me to run inside and grab my purse and the official offer I'd typed up for Douglas. I told Mona I'd fill her in on everything later, then joined Doc again in the front seat of his Camaro, wondering where we were going.

Several blocks later, he pulled into the library and cut the engine. There was my answer.

"Come on." He held my door open for me. I trailed

him up the stairs, through the front doors, and across the wood floor toward the South Dakota room. The usual smell of varnish and musty books was mixed with a hint of lemon today. Someone must have found the furniture polish.

Doc's greeting to the library matriarch earned him a starched smile in return. She seemed to be warming up to him. Maybe I should have him inform her that Layne wouldn't be returning those burned books anytime soon; maybe she'd forget about fining me.

He waited for me to cross the threshold and then closed the door behind me.

"Doc," I turned toward him and crossed my arms over my chest, "I really don't have time for—"

He grabbed me by the upper arms, whisked me around, and pressed me up against the wall next to the door.

"—this," I finished, much less stiffly.

His mouth came down on mine, hard, almost painful. I opened my lips under his ambush only to have him tear away from me and step back. His fingers tore through his hair. "You scared the hell out of me, Violet."

"I did?"

"I saw what was left of your Bronco, but I didn't see you." His gaze bore into mine. "Why didn't you go to the police?"

"What are you talking about?" I touched my bottom lip, which still throbbed from his fierce kiss. I checked for the taste of blood, but my tongue found no trace. "You just found me at the police station, remember?"

"I mean yesterday, after your tires were knifed."

"What good would it have done?" I had no more answers about *who* and *why* then, than I did now.

"It might have saved your car from being burned up."

"Detective Cooper says it might not be arson. It could have been old wiring."

"Right. It also could have been a meteor that just

happened to crash into your Bronco." His forehead furrowed. "You know better, though, don't you?"

"Well, I'd sure like to believe him, but ..."

"Exactly. What are you going to do now?" He watched me with an intensity that matched the level Cooper had shown just a short time ago.

Sighing, I leaned my head back against the wall, a dull throbbing building at the base of my neck. "Buy a lotto ticket or hope to hell Layne digs up an old Wells Fargo strongbox in Aunt Zoe's backyard soon."

"I can loan you some money."

"No!" That came out stronger than I meant it to. "I mean, no thanks. I don't like owing my friends money." Besides, I was already in debt to Harvey.

"Friends?" His jaw tightened. "We're not *just* friends, Violet."

What were we, then? Never mind. Now was not the time to get into that. "I don't want to owe you money, Doc."

"Fine. Do you have insurance?"

"Liability only."

"Of course." He sounded annoyed. "You can use my car until you find something else."

"No, I can't."

His eyes flashed. "Damn it, Violet. This is not the time to worry about keeping up appearances."

"That's where you're wrong." I glared back. "It's more important now than ever. Whoever did this is still out there, and who says they're done? I'm not going to risk your car ending up incinerated, too."

Thunder clouds built over his brows. "How are you going to protect Addy and Layne?"

I hadn't had much chance to ponder that yet. Squeezing the back of my neck, I stretched my head to the side, trying to alleviate the throbs that were growing stronger every second, along with the rest of my problems. "I don't know. I could send them to my parents' for a week. Let them think it's a little vacation before school starts, only one without me."

"Come here," Doc said, hopping up to sit on the table and holding out his hand. I pushed off the wall. He turned me around when I drew near and pulled me back between his legs, then pushed my hair aside and massaged my shoulders and neck. "Sorry about your lip. Is it okay?"

I licked it to double check. "Yes, but you'll have to kiss it better later."

"I'll do more than that."

I quivered inside at the thought of what that might mean. Under his touch, the tension was beginning to ebb. I let my head loll forward. "I could get used to this."

"Me, too." His fingers kneaded a painful knot in the crook of my neck, making me wince and pull away from him slightly. "Get back here." He pulled me even closer, the heat from his hands and body removing some of the chill from my situation. "What are you going to do about your aunt?"

"She's not going to budge. I'd have better luck wooing a prairie dog from its burrow with a rattlesnake's tail." I groaned and then tensed again as he found another knot. "I'll talk to her," I said between gasps, "explain what's going on, and see what she wants to do." She did have that shotgun in her bedroom closet.

"I could sleep on her couch for a few nights, keep an eye on you."

"You and I both know how that would end up." With Doc in my bed.

His fingers stilled. "I can keep my hands to myself if you're worried about that."

"It's not your hands I'm worried about." I looked up at him. "It's mine. They have minds of their own when it comes to you."

His lazy grin appeared for just a second, before the dark clouds returned to his expression. "Have you considered that this may be a retaliation for you burning down Hessler's house?"

"Retaliation from whom? Wolfgang's mom and sister are already dead." Ghosts couldn't start fires, could they? The reality of what I was pondering hit me, and I swallowed a bout of hysterical laughter. I couldn't afford to lose it now.

"I don't know," Doc answered. "An angry relative, an old girlfriend, some vengeful lover the cops don't know about—who knows?"

I let my head loll again and covered his hands with mine, squeezing, nudging him to continue. "I don't want to think about Wolfgang right now." It brought the nightmares too close to the surface.

"Okay." He squeezed the muscles at the back of my skull.

My lids drooped, my eyes rolling up into my head.

"Violet, let me help you."

"You already are." His hands were working wonders; my headache was almost gone. "Plus, you're buying a house from me."

"That's not enough."

"Fine. Buy a vacation home in the country, too. I have the perfect listing. It's owned by a crazy, shotgun-happy old buzzard."

He chuckled, but said, "I'm serious."

"Me, too. It has a graveyard behind the barn. You'd love that, I bet. Just ignore the creepy whangdoodle living out there."

His hands stopped. He turned me around, his gaze full of concern. "Are you okay?"

The underlying care in his tone hit me like a punch to

the chest. I swallowed a sudden lump and blinked back some stupid tears. "Fine and dandy, as usual."

His eyes narrowed at my fake grin. "I don't believe you. You're blowing a little too much smoke. Tell me. Honestly."

I took a deep breath. "Doc, if I don't keep laughing, I'm going to start screaming. If that happens, I'm afraid I won't be able to stop until I've torn out all of my hair. Then I'll lose my children to state custody and wind up wrapped tight in a straightjacket, tucked away in a padded cell."

His smile was grim as he tucked a tendril of hair behind my ear. "I'll come by each day to feed you Jell-O."

I stopped his hand, holding it, squeezing his fingers. "I'm going to hold you to that. Now will you please take me up to the Carharts so I can give Wanda this offer? I need to make some more money, because taking clients around via the handlebars of Addy's bike isn't going to cut it."

"Wait. Let me show you something first." He pulled his hand free and walked over to the bookshelf on the far wall, the one that contained books about the Black Hills.

I drifted behind him. "With the way my day is going, I hope it's a map to Flint's treasure with an X marking the spot." Layne and I had read *Treasure Island* together last year. It was one of my favorites—and now one of Layne's, too.

"You think I'd share that with you, Long John Silver?" His tone teased. He pulled a handful of books out and reached to the back of the shelf, extracting a smaller book he must have hidden back there. A piece of paper marked a page. He flipped the book open and held it out to me. "Is this the tattoo you saw on Lila?"

I grabbed the book, frowning at the drawing on the page—the head of a pig melting into a goat.

"I think so. It looks a little more detailed here than what I remember, but I'm pretty sure that's it. What's it say about it?" I scanned the page, but my mind wouldn't focus on the words.

"In the late nineteenth century, there was a cult in Deadwood made up of some of the Chinese immigrants brought in to work in the mines and build the railroads. This is a replica of an emblem associated with the cult."

"Cult?" That was never a good word unless it concerned a 1980s rock band. "As in the crazed religious type?"

"Yes. They had a particular set of demons to which they liked to make sacrifices."

He extracted a second book that was tucked away in the

back of the shelf and opened to another marked page. "Have you seen a picture of this woman before?" he asked, showing me the book's page.

It was a grainy black-and-white picture of a blonde sitting stiffly in a formal-looking chair. Her hair was pinned up, leaving just a couple of delicate ringlets hanging; her lips were straight; her eyes looked off to the side; her dress was fancy and in a style popular a century ago. She sat alone. "No. Should I have?"

"Possibly." Doc looked almost sad as he gazed down at the woman on the page.

"Where? On the wall of one of the casinos in Deadwood?"

"No, in the Carhart house. There was more than just a picture." Doc's dark eyes locked onto mine. "She was in the upstairs bedroom with us yesterday."

Chapter Nineteen

I held Doc's stare, searching his eyes for a hint of jest. There was none. "Are you serious?"

"One hundred percent," he said.

A wave of dizziness made me reach for the bookshelf. Did the room just tilt?

Doc's brow wrinkled. "You okay?"

"No." I blinked through a barrage of stars dive-bombing the fringes of my vision. "I think you just broke my brain."

"Here." He grabbed the chair in front of the microfilm machine and pulled it over, taking the book from me. "Sit."

I followed his orders, resting my head in my hands as I waited for the stars to stop shooting. "Doc," I said, blinking at my sandals. "How can you be so certain about this woman—I mean, ghost? When we were at the Carhart's yesterday, you said you couldn't really see it, just an outline or blur or something like that."

I heard one of his knees pop as he half-squatted, half-knelt before me. "It's hard to explain ..."

When he didn't continue, I nudged him. "Try." Peeking at him above my fingers, I added, "Please."

His gaze held mine, his eyes narrowed, wariness lining his face. "You're not going to believe what I tell you."

That was probably true, but I said, "Give it a shot, anyway."

"You know when I lost consciousness at the Carhart house?"

"You mean when she passed through you?"

"It was more like a temporary possession."

"Possession? Really?" I cringed. The word alone brought about images of Linda Blair strapped to the bed, writhing, cursing in a gravelly voice, her head twisting around like an owl.

"Yes, possession. Anyway, during that moment of connection with the ghost, I experienced a mental imprint."

Mental imprint? "Like a vision?"

"For lack of a better word."

"What did you see during this vision?"

"The events that occurred at the time of her death."

I recoiled, stunned by equal measures of doubt and dismay. "Was it like watching a slasher movie?"

"No. But, yes."

"Gee, that cleared things up for me. Thanks."

Doc sighed, then pushed to his feet. He drifted over to the table in the center of the room. "It was like I'd already experienced the events. An instant memory, shoved into my head, put there for me to relive as the victim."

An instant memory? Reliving death in first person point of view? Wow. This was *Twilight Zone* material. Doc's rigid stance didn't go unnoticed by me. "Have you ever told anyone else about this stuff?"

He nodded. "But he's dead now." His eyes searched mine. "You think I'm nuts, right?"

I hesitated, recognizing what it meant, trust-wise, for Doc to share this. Whether I believed him about these visions or not, a gut feeling told me to keep this door between us propped open. But he deserved my honesty. "I don't know what to think, Doc. You're an intelligent, logical financial planner who claims to be able to interact with ghosts on some level. It's a bit baffling."

"Fair enough."

"Reliving death over and over must be horrific."

"Now you understand why I try to avoid it." He sat on the edge of the table. "And why it hits me like a locomotive at full speed."

"Is there any way you can stop it?" A good head doctor? Drugs? Electroshock therapy? Exorcism?

"Not that I've figured out yet. I'm trying to find a way to control it, or at least a way to live with it."

"Control it how?"

"Desensitize myself to the smell."

How could he un-train his nose? "Then what?"

"Work on how to handle the mind-fuck part."

I rested my elbows on my thighs. "Do you think these ghosts want something from you?"

He shrugged. "We don't really communicate. Everything I get is like yesterday's news. A slice of the past replayed for my private experience."

I frowned across at him. This would be easier to swallow with a shot of tequila. Or a whole bottle.

He jammed his hands in his front pockets, rounding his shoulders. "I'm not crazy, Violet."

"Good. One of us has to remain sane, and I think I'm slipping." I squeezed my temples, my headache threatening again, hovering just behind my eyes. "Has anyone else ever smelled these ghosts?"

"Not that I've witnessed."

"What about dogs? Do you think they can smell ghosts, too?" Why not? They had super sniffers. It seemed plausible.

"I haven't tested that, but I don't think so. I have a theory that it's not really an actual scent that I'm smelling."

Was it just me, or was Doc starting to talk in tongues? "But you said—"

"I know, I know." He pushed off the table and paced in front of it, kneading his hands.

I watched and waited, sensing that he was building up

to spill some more. He'd better be, anyway.

"There are a few things I think I understand about this curse of mine."

"Some might call it a *gift*," Polly Positive piped up before I could muzzle her.

He stopped pacing and crossed his arms at me. "Right. Being harassed by the dead. What a gift."

I covered my mouth and mumbled, "Continue, please."

A hint of a grin sneaked onto his lips. "My theory is that when a ghost is in the vicinity, my brain picks up on its presence and triggers something in my olfactory system that makes me think I smell something. The stronger the presence, the more pungent the odor. This is why I can smell them and nobody else can."

In spite of my uncertainty on this whole subject, the fascination that came with the "what-ifs" lured me to want to hear more. "What else have you figured out?"

"There's the mental imprint bit that I just told you about."

I nodded.

"And the ghosts are unable to understand me when I speak to them."

"You're sure they don't hear you?"

"I didn't say 'hear,' just understand. They respond to the sound of my voice, but they don't seem to comprehend what I'm saying."

The idea of Doc talking to thin air and expecting an answer made me want to stomp about and throw things. His behavior crossed the line between worrisome and mad; I didn't want him to be that mentally unstable. It would mean no future of any kind with him, not when I had two kids to raise and protect. I let my hair fall forward to shield me from his eyes.

"You're hiding from me." He read me like the walking billboard that I was. "I know this is hard for you to swallow."

A horse chestnut would have been easier. "A little bit."

I heard the rustle of his clothing and looked up to find him leaning against the window frame. "What I don't understand yet," he said, staring out the window, "is whether these ghosts are drawn to me because of something I'm able to give them, and if so, what that something is."

"Maybe it's just the recognition that they exist," I offered, while my own alarm over it all made my head spin.

I wanted to believe him. I really did. If only there was more proof. Something *I* could see ... or smell, like burning hair. A flashback of the macabre tea party at the Hessler house haunted me for a moment until the sound of Doc's voice snuffed it out.

"Maybe," he said. "But I'd like to be able to communicate with them, to figure out how to see more than their dying moments when our paths cross."

"You mean see other memories?"

"Fewer scenes revolving around their deaths would be a pleasant change." His focus remained outside the glass, his profile still drawn. "But if not, I need to know if I can turn this shit off without having to kill myself to do it."

Sobering words, unsettling thoughts. The quiet room closed in on me, the library's usual bouquet of varnished wood and aging paper almost overwhelming.

"Alcohol didn't work," he continued. "Neither did drugs—not even the hardcore stuff."

The back of my throat tightened. "Were you trying to turn it off or kill yourself?"

He shrugged, still looking out at Deadwood. "Both, I guess. Drinking numbed my brain, but it didn't stop the smells. Drugs only enhanced the imprints."

His need for control in other areas of his life made complete sense now. "How long has this been going on,

Doc?"

"As long as I can remember."

Christ! My chest ached for him and the weight he'd carried for decades, mostly alone. The fact that he'd shared the details of this dark, obviously painful secret with me, exposing his uncertainties and weaknesses, stirred something deep inside—an urge to comfort him, protect him—that propelled me from my chair.

He watched me approach, his expression guarded. "Violet, don't."

"Don't what?"

"Touch me. Not when you have that look on your face."

I rounded the table. "What look?"

"Like I'm some injured dog lying in a ditch." He backed away from me. "Stop."

I didn't.

"I don't want your pity," he said.

"This isn't pity."

He kept the table between us as I circled. "What is it, then?"

Good question. "I don't know. I just want to touch you."

"You can't."

"Why not?"

"Because once you start, I won't be able to stop."

"Maybe we should explore that feeling," I said. "A hands-on therapy session of sorts."

"Not in the library."

I paused. "I didn't realize you were such a prude."

"Prude?" He stopped, his eyes narrowing. "You're calling me a prude?"

"I didn't stutter."

"Okay, Boots," he reversed and came around the table toward me. "I'll call your bluff."

He reached for me at the same time the door swung open. I stepped back from him as the librarian pushed a cart of books through the door, my heart rattling at almost being caught.

The librarian stopped at the sight of us standing there. Her gaze behind the rhinestone-studded rims of her glasses bounced between us. "Can I help you find something?"

Doc's mental reflexes were faster than mine. "No, but you could answer a question for us."

She raised one haughty eyebrow, but softened it with a tiny smile aimed at Doc. "I'll certainly try, Doc."

She knew his name? It was my turn to raise an eyebrow.

Charm dripped from the grin Doc gave her. "I want to learn more about cults and religions in relation to Deadwood's past. Also, a bit more about the Chinese immigrant population in the late nineteenth century. Can you point me in the right direction?"

Was this about Lila's tattoo?

"Well," the librarian ran her fingernail along one of the book spines on her cart. "We don't have much of a collection on those subjects here, but I seem to remember one of the libraries down in Rapid having a section dedicated to local religions. There may be something about cults mixed in there. Same goes with the Chinese immigrants. I'll have to look it up on the Library Network database. Do you need this today?"

"Tomorrow is fine. I'll stop by to see what you found."

She nodded. "Or I can call you."

"Sure. You have my number."

My eyebrows must have hit the back of my scalp.

Doc grabbed my hand and tugged me toward the door. "Thanks for your help, Julia."

I managed to smile at Julia, aka *the librarian*, as we left the room. Outside the front doors, I couldn't hold it in any longer. "Since when are you on a first name basis with the head librarian?"

"Since she hired me to help her with her financial portfolio."

Oh, his day job. I'd forgotten about that. "Don't you think she'll find it odd, you wanting to learn about cults and all?"

"No. She's a librarian. Dealing with her patrons' eccentricities is part of her daily grind. Think about some of the things people probably ask her to help them find. Cults and religion are quite tame, I'm betting."

That reminded me of the time Layne dragged me to the library in Rapid and made me ask for help finding a book on how to shrink and preserve human skulls. From the look on that librarian's face, my name was probably added to the FBI's suspicious-persons database that day.

Doc held open the passenger-side door for me. I settled into the warm leather seat. The earthy aroma of Doc's cologne wafted around me, more intense than usual in the hot interior, sparking a pheromone-filled heat flash. For just a few solitary seconds, I allowed myself to daydream about Doc and me and things that could be.

Then his door opened, and I fanned myself back to reality.

"Tell me more about the woman in the picture," I said as Doc slid behind the wheel.

He stuck the key in the ignition, sparing me a glance. "You mean the Carharts' ghost?"

"Yes."

"The one you don't know if you believe actually exists."

I met his challenge. "Yes, that would be the one."

The engine growled to life. "Prudence Baker," he said and shifted into gear.

"Her name was Prudence?"

He nodded, pulling out into the street.

"Sounds like a relative of yours."

He chuckled and stopped for a red light. His hand slid from the shifter to my knee before I realized it, his palm was blazing its way up my bare thigh. I clamped my legs together, capturing his hand before it hit pay dirt. He grinned. "Now who's the prude?"

"You're driving."

"I can multitask."

I was well aware of that. "The light is green."

He looked down at the leg-lock I had on his hand. "Looks red to me."

As he rolled through the intersection, I extracted his hand from my inner thigh and placed it back on the gear shift, covering it with mine for good measure. "Will you take me by the Carharts?"

"I don't have to go in, do I?"

"No. I'll just drop this off with Wanda."

He made a right and headed up to Lead via Central City, around the back side of the big Open Cut. "Prudence was married to Edward Baker. They had a son named Ely. You have their photos in that locket you found with the box of teeth."

"Ely reminded me of Layne."

Doc glanced at me out of the corners of his eyes. "More than you know."

His somber tone, mixed with that look, crammed my gut full of anxiety. "What happened?"

"How much detail do you want?"

"Don't shield me."

"You sure?"

"I've seen some bad shit." Compliments of Wolfgang and his long-dead sister.

"That's what concerns me."

"I'm going to be standing inside that house in a minute. I'd like to know what I'm walking into."

After another glance my way, he nodded. "Prudence's

husband and son were murdered in the front parlor."

I winced. My favorite room. Damn.

"She was forced to watch."

Double damn. My wince deepened into a cringe.

"Then she was raped and her neck slit."

"Holy fuck!" I crossed my arms over my chest, holding tight, hunching. It was the ghost Jane had claimed to see years ago. "And you witnessed this through Prudence's eyes?"

He nodded, slowing for a pickup in front of us with its left blinker on.

"In that moment when you relived this gruesome shit, did you feel what she felt?"

"To a degree," he said, his face rigid. "It came in a twisted mess of images, sounds, smells, and pain."

"Holy fuck."

"You already said that."

"Yeah, well, I think this deserves at least two of them."

"It took me a little bit to sort it all out. That's why I put you off yesterday."

I thought of my Mr. Hyde routine yesterday, of going off on Doc after he'd suffered through whatever this was—real or just in his mind. My cheeks heated. "I'm sorry for blowing my top."

He shot me a grimace. "Don't apologize. You weren't exactly having an easy day. I knew that when you walked away from me." He rounded the bend into Lead. "Although," he added, his grin making an appearance, "I hadn't expected you to seek comfort in Jeff Wymonds' arms."

"Oh, God," I said, leaning my head back against the seat, closing my eyes. "That was so awkward. And now Addy has it in her head that I'm going to marry Jeff, and Layne is freaking out about being replaced as man of the house."

"What are you going to do?"

"What I've been doing all along—maintain the status quo and tell them that I'm not marrying anyone." I peeked at Doc, wondering how he felt about the status quo. He stared out the front window, one hand on the steering wheel, giving me no sign of anything.

Good, I thought, but then frowned. A bit of interest from him in something long-term might be nice.

What?

I looked out my side window without really seeing. Did I want something more with Doc? On one hand, there was this whole ghost-smelling business. On the other, he was kind, smart, fun, good with money, and dynamite in the sack. And he smelled better than warm brownies.

Crud mongers. I was getting in over my head here. I gulped down a wad of panic welling in my throat.

Okay, so this attraction of mine was growing. That didn't mean it had to end in wedding bells. I was waist-deep into my thirties now. The silly insecurities of my twenties were long gone. I could handle a no-strings-attached relationship.

"Violet?" Doc's voice interrupted my whirling dervish of angst-filled, confused thoughts. He sounded like he was talking to me from three plateaus away. "Do you want me to walk up the aisle with you?"

Up the aisle! What? I gaped at him. "What did you just ask me?"

He stared back at me, a grin hovering. "Do you want me to walk up the drive with you?" He spoke slowly, enunciating each word, and then pointed out my window. I followed his finger and realized we were already pulling up to the curb in front of the Carhart house.

Holy freakin' moly. I needed to plug that hole in my head where the marbles were pouring out. As if I had time for this temporary bout of relationship insanity. I had a

Bronco to bury and kids to ship off to my parents. Grabbing the offer papers, I said, "Thanks, but I can handle this." I reached for the door handle, then stopped and looked back at Doc. "Do you know why Prudence and her family were murdered?"

"I'm still sorting that out, but I think it has to do with that box of teeth."

The teeth? Why the teeth? A laugh bubbled up and out before I could catch it. "You know, Doc, sometimes you say the damnedest things."

"I know it sounds farfetched, but one of her killers kept asking where she'd hid his teeth."

"One?" Goosebumps trickled down my arms. "How many were there?"

"Three, all wearing burlap masks with eyeholes cut out, so I couldn't see their faces."

I can't imagine the terror Prudence must have felt. Then I remembered Wolfgang and his playtime shenanigans and realized I could guess at it a little. "I'll be right back." I wanted to zip in and out of the house as fast as I could— ghost story or real deal.

Wanda inched the door open after my second knock.

"Hi, Wanda. Here's the second offer I called you about."

She snatched it from my hand with snake-strike quickness. I jerked back, resisting the urge to check for fang marks.

"You can't come in," she whispered, then glanced over her shoulder at something behind her. "You'd better leave now."

What? Why? I didn't move, my feet as dumbfounded as the rest of me. I leaned to the side, trying to see what was going on behind her.

She reached through the crack and pushed me back a step. "Go," she hissed. "Now!"

She shut the door in my face. I heard the deadbolt click.

What in the hell was going on around here?

My mind reeling, I didn't realize I'd returned to Doc's car until I sat on the warm seat and shut the door.

Doc's forehead furrowed. "What's wrong?"

"I don't know. Wanda was acting odd."

"Do you want me to go back up there with you?"

"I don't think so." I thought about Wanda and her money, then me and my lack of money, and ended up on me and my lack of a vehicle. "No, never mind. Will you take me to Aunt Zoe's, please?" I was ready to go home and regenerate some sanity before trudging out into the world again.

He turned the key and rolled into action.

By the time we hit the edge of Lead, my wits had returned from their surprise-induced hiatus and a question popped into my head. "Doc, that information on cults and Chinese immigrants that you asked the librarian about: are you looking for something in particular?"

He cast me a quick look, seeming to measure something. "Yes, a connection."

"Connection between what?"

"Prudence's killers and Lila."

"You mean besides the Carhart house?" What else could there be? More than a century separated Lila from the rest.

"Yes, besides the house." He slowed to a stop at the junction mid-way between Lead and Deadwood.

"Why would there be another connection?"

"The men who murdered Prudence had Chinese accents."

"Oh, okay." That explained nothing. "What does that have to do with Lila?"

"They also had matching tattoos—as in matching Lila's."

Chapter Twenty

I stared out the car window the rest of the way home, my gut festering over Lila and her tattoo, Prudence and the teeth, Doc and his ghosts. The gravity of my situation weighed heavily, like a buffalo plopped on my chest.

An old pickup with a rusted bumper sat in Aunt Zoe's drive. Bird poop added visual texture to its army-green paint. "Whose is that?"

"I'm guessing Harvey's, based on the bumper sticker," Doc answered, pointing at the *Life's Short, Skinny Dip Daily* sticker.

The old buzzard must have caught a whiff of my Bronco's smoky death in the small-town air and come to circle and assess.

Doc parked behind Harvey's truck, but left the engine growling.

I reached for the door handle. "Thanks for the ride."

"Violet?" Doc snagged my arm. Lines of concern contoured his forehead. He took off his sunglasses. "Please, be careful."

"Where's the fun in that?" The grin I forced felt carved into my cheeks.

He grimaced. "You could scare little kids with that smile."

I pointed at my manic grin. "You think this is frightening, you should see my hair first thing in the morning."

"Okay."

Okay? "I was speaking rhetorically." Kind of. Or not. The idea of spending the night with Doc toasted my marshmallows, but the potential fallout with my family doused the flame.

"Try speaking hypothetically instead." Doc's lazy grin came out to play. "For example, *if* you were there in the morning, *then* I could have breakfast in bed."

"I don't cook."

"Who said anything about food?"

A wallop of lust left my brain floundering. "Are you trying to use sex talk to distract me from my problems?" *Sex talk?* What was this? Fifth grade?

"Is it working?"

Definitely. "Maybe."

"I could distract you even more with my hands." He demonstrated, his fingers skimming the tender skin on the inside of my arm.

"Yes, you could." Heat pooled in all the fun places, making me shift closer.

"And we shouldn't forget about my tongue."

"Your tongue is a lethal weapon." Just thinking about it nearly vaporized my underwear. "Tell me more."

"Your aunt is watching us from the front porch."

A glance at the house confirmed the situation. "Ah, hell. I was hoping for something a bit more titillating from you."

"I'll work on my stimulation techniques for next time." He withdrew his fingers.

I pushed open the door and climbed out before the rummy effect of lust spilled me right into his lap. "Thanks for your help."

"I meant what I said about the Carhart house."

"You want me to be careful while I'm there."

"I want you to stay away from it."

I'd heard that one before. I shut the door and leaned on the open window. "I can't. I'm selling it."

"I figured you'd say that." He shifted into reverse. "Just don't do anything rash."

"Just thinking about Lila makes me itch."

"And stay away from Lila."

"Another warning?"

"That one's an order." He softened it with a wink. "Call me later."

"After I get my life straightened out?"

"No. I'll be an old man by then. Later as in tonight, when you're alone. You know my number."

I stepped back from the car. "So does the librarian."

"Yeah, but she doesn't *have* my number." He put on his sunglasses and rolled away, leaving me behind with reality.

I gave wide berth to the dirty green truck, which supported its own colony of flies and reeked as if it had been rolling around in a horse stall. Its cloud of dirt reminded me of Pigpen from those old Charlie Brown holiday cartoons.

Aunt Zoe greeted me on the front porch steps with a worried scowl and a much-needed bear hug. "Harvey told me the news. Are you okay?"

"Yeah, but I'm really starting to hate the sight of firemen, and that's a damned shame."

"Join the club," she muttered and led me into the house, her arm around my shoulders.

The aroma of fresh-baked brownies made me smile. Ah, home sweet home. I picked up a balled sock and a purple flip-flop from the floor and tossed them in the basket of shoes next to the front door. "Where are the kids?"

"In the backyard making bonnets for Miss Elvis."

"Chicken bonnets?"

"Addy is worried about her chicken getting skin cancer."

"Of course she is." Addy's craziness about animals must come from her father's bloodline.

I found Harvey sitting at the kitchen table, a brownie in his hand and another stuffed in his cheeks. "Hey, Sparky!" The brownie muffled his shout. "Sounds like you found yourself in another hot spot this mornin'."

I just shook my head and reached for a brownie to cram into my mouth. I dropped into the chair opposite him. "Where's your Chevy?" Had somebody messed with his truck, too?

"At home. I brought you some new wheels."

I'd been too distracted by Pigpen's aura to notice another set of tires in the pickup bed. "You shouldn't have. I already owe you two." I hope he kept the receipt.

"Forget about that." He slid a set of keys across the table.

I frowned down at the yellow smiley-face keychain. "What's this?"

"The keys to the Picklemobile."

Aunt Zoe placed a glass of lemonade, on the rocks, under my nose. I could have showered her with kisses.

"The Picklemobile?"

"My old truck out front."

He was going to let me borrow Pigpen? Oh, that's what he meant by wheels. It was really sweet of the old buzzard, but I didn't think my reputation could handle the added stink. I pushed the keys back toward him. "Thanks, Harvey. That's very kind of you to offer, but I can't."

"If this is about her looks, most of that shit will wash right off her. She's just been sittin' in the barn for the last few days."

That explained the smell. "It's not that. I don't want to risk losing another vehicle until Cooper catches whoever is behind this."

He grunted and stuffed the keys in his pocket. "You know where to find her if you need her."

Aunt Zoe joined us at the table with her coffee cup.

"What are we going to do?" she asked.

"You two aren't going to do anything. I don't want to drag you into this."

She squeezed my hand. "Honey, I love you, but shut up. We're here to help. Now, you can either take our help willingly, or we can twist your arm until you relent. What's it going to be?"

"I'm hoping for a struggle," Harvey said, cracking his knuckles.

I looked from her smiling eyes to Harvey's crumb-crusted smirk. "Fine. But if anything happens to you two—"

Harvey snorted. "Girl, we've been gettin' in and outta trouble since you were still pissin' in your britches. Now, what's the plan?"

I took a bite of brownie, wallowing momentarily in the warm chocolate goo, feeling a little lost at sea. "I don't really have one yet, but I want to get Addy and Layne out of here. You haven't told Dad yet, have you?" I asked Aunt Zoe.

She shook her head. "I know my brother when it comes to you and the kids. Just the mention of a splinter and he'll come racing up the mountain with tweezers."

"Good. I'll send Addy and Layne down there for a mini-vacation. We can let everyone think it's one last hurrah before school starts."

"Addy isn't going to like leaving Kelly or her chicken."

"Yeah, well, absence makes the heart grow fonder."

Harvey's smirk spread wider. "That's exactly what I tell my ol' flames."

"You know, Harvey," I settled back into the kitchen chair, relaxing in the lemony cocoon of Aunt Zoe's kitchen, and smiled at the codger. "I don't understand what these flames see in your ornery ass."

"I find 'em hot and leave 'em wet."

"The firefighter's motto," Aunt Zoe said, the corners of her eyes crinkling. "I haven't heard that one in years."

That reminded me of a certain fire captain and his inquiry. "I ran into Reid this morning," I threw out to Aunt Zoe with pretend nonchalance, peeking at her as I broke off another piece of brownie and shoved it into my mouth.

Her cheeks grew pink. "Reid who?"

"Reid, the captain of the fire department."

"Now there's a salty dog," Harvey said. "I could take some lessons from him."

I shushed Harvey with my glare. "He asked about you," I told Aunt Zoe.

"Did he, now?" Her chair scraped on the linoleum. She strolled over to the sink, dumping her coffee into it. "I can't imagine why."

"I mentioned you were single again."

She whirled around, her eyes wide. "Violet!"

"What? You are."

"But Reid doesn't need to know that."

"Why not?" I glanced at Harvey, who was watching with squinty eyes. "Reid seems really nice."

"That man is nothing but trouble."

"He's a fireman."

"All the more reason to avoid him."

"He's got a nice ass," Harvey threw in, earning raised brows from both Aunt Zoe and me. "What? Just because I say that doesn't mean I want to pinch it."

"Harvey has a point—about Reid's body, that is."

Aunt Zoe crossed her arms over her chest. "I don't want to talk about it."

"You shouldn't keep these things bottled up," I pressed.

Her eyes narrowed. "Really, Miss Do-As-I-Say? Then why don't you explain to me why your black funeral dress smells like men's cologne?"

The chicken got my tongue. I stuffed the rest of the

brownie into my mouth while I waited for her to waver. When she didn't, I said, "It's probably just George Mudder's cologne. He's kind of touchy-feely."

"I know George's cologne. He's been a peppermint Aqua Velva man for decades. This is something else."

Harvey snickered, earning him another *zip it* look from me. The old buzzard wasn't helping one bit. I gulped down the ball of brownie in my throat. "Ummm ... It must have been that guy I danced with at the Purple Door Saloon."

"You said you spent the night consoling Natalie."

Harvey nudged me under the table. "She doesn't miss a thing, does she?"

"She's a regular Miss Marple."

Aunt Zoe crossed her arms over her chest. "Well, young lady?"

"I plead the Fifth."

"Was that Doc Nyce who dropped you off a bit ago?"

Stuck on that one, I nodded and hid behind my glass of lemonade.

"One of these days you'll have to introduce him to me."

"Doc's super busy. He's hard to catch."

Her head cocked to the side. "Really? You seem to have done a good job of snaring him."

"He's just a client."

"Suzy Sherman said she saw you driving a fancy black Camaro around town yesterday."

Son of a peacock! I told Doc that driving his car was a bad idea. "Suzy must have confused some blonde tourist for me. You know how thick her glasses are."

Aunt Zoe eyed Harvey. "Have you seen any other fancy black Camaros in town lately?"

I nailed him with my gunslinger glare.

He shrugged and stuffed two more brownies in his mouth.

"Willis"—Aunt Zoe's tone had a ring of threat to it—

"cough up what you know, or the brownie and cookie supply will dry up."

Harvey froze mid-chew.

The doorbell rang.

"I'll get that," Harvey mumbled and skedaddled out of the room, breaking up the showdown.

I avoided Aunt Zoe's gaze and changed the subject. "I'm worried about your gallery."

"What about it?"

"What if whoever is pissed at me takes it out on your store?"

She strolled over and kissed the top of my head. "Don't worry about me. I'm covered. You, on the other hand, appear to be a sitting duck. You can use my pickup to get around town until we can find you another vehicle."

"No way."

"Violet, don't be stubborn. Just use it."

"I'm not. I meant what I told Harvey. Until we figure out who is behind this, I don't want to risk anyone else's vehicle." I rested my head on the table the way I used to during kindergarten naptime. "What a nightmare."

Aunt Zoe rubbed my back. "You seem to be full of them lately. I wish you'd consider seeing a therapist about all of this."

"I am, right now."

"I'm afraid I'm not much help."

"You are. More than you know." The backrub alone was worth the cost of a professional consultation. And the brownies made great sedatives.

"Violet, what's going on with you and—"

"Look who's here," Harvey interrupted, strolling into the kitchen, sporting a banana-wide grin.

I heard Aunt Zoe's intake of breath as Fire Captain Reid waltzed in. This time, his suspenders were gone, replaced by faded blue jeans and a white T-shirt.

"I smelled a fire," Reid said, laughter in his voice. "So I thought I'd look for you first this time." He aimed his comment at me, but he had Aunt Zoe in his sights.

I didn't know what to say, so I just gaped at him, mimicking Aunt Zoe.

"Hey, Zo." He shortened her already short name. "It's been a while."

"Yes," Aunt Zoe squeezed her hands together and kept her smile shallow, barely bending her lips. "It sure has." Then she snapped back into hostess mode. "Can I get you something to drink?"

Reid hooked his thumbs in his pockets. "I'd love some of that lemonade you always keep in the fridge."

He knew about Aunt Zoe's lemonade? I traded raised brows with Harvey, who'd dropped back into his seat, front and center for the Zoe and Reid show.

"So, Reid," Aunt Zoe said as she poured a glass. "What brings you to my doorstep?"

"Your niece."

I piped up. "I have an alibi."

Reid's deep laughter filled the silence. "I like you, Violet. You remind me of another spunky girl."

I didn't miss the look that passed between him and Aunt Zoe. What it meant, I had no idea, but I filed it away to bring up later over more brownies.

Reid took the glass she offered. "Thanks."

"You're welcome." Aunt Zoe returned to the counter—keeping the width of the kitchen between her and Reid, I noticed. "Is this about Violet's Bronco or the Hessler house?"

"The former. I'm putting the finishing touches on my report and need to ask Violet something."

"Boy, you're not wasting time on this one," Aunt Zoe said.

My chin whipped back and forth between the two of

them as if I were straddling the centerline at Wimbledon.

"Coop's all buggered up about this one. He's called me three times since lunch, asking if I had it ready."

Why was Cooper so antsy about it? Did he know something? Did he have a suspect already? "What's the question?" I asked.

Reid dug in his back pocket and tossed a small plastic sandwich bag on the table with an opened book of matches inside it. I picked up the bag and read the label on the matches—*Charles' Club*. Aunt Zoe came up behind me, peering over my shoulder.

"We found that about fifteen feet from your Bronco in the scrub brush bordering the lot," Reid said. "Do you recognize it?"

"Don't answer that, Violet." Aunt Zoe took the book of matches from me. "Reid, this could belong to anyone. Surely you don't think Violet burned up her own car?"

"Of course not." Reid focused on me. "Have you been to Charles' Club lately?"

"Reid," Aunt Zoe's voice hardened, her mother-bear side coming out of hibernation. "What exactly are you getting at here?"

Reid's gaze turned steely. "Zo, relax. I'm not attacking Violet. I'm just trying to narrow down whether the arsonist used a match from this book to start the fire."

I took the plastic bag back from Aunt Zoe. "How do you know this isn't just random litter?"

"There is no sign of weathering."

True. The cover was still glossy. Flipping it over, I noticed that the strip on the back looked barely used.

"There are two matches missing from that book," Reid continued. "I found what I believe is one of those two matches when I first arrived on scene. If these matches were used to start the fire, Cooper and I have a place to start searching."

"This is like findin' a baby dung beetle in a pile of elephant shit," Harvey pointed out.

"Yeah. Welcome to my job."

I handed the bag back to Reid. "They aren't mine, but I was at Charles' Club two nights ago."

Reid's focus honed in on me, reminding me of Cooper in the heat of interrogation. "Who was there with you?"

"I met Douglas Mann for dinner. He's interested in buying the Carhart house."

"Really?" Reid asked, leaning back on his heels. "How many houses does that man need?"

"What do you mean?"

"Never mind. Who else was there?"

"Well, there were a lot of people there that night."

"Name the ones you know."

"Natalie Beals, Doc—I mean Dane—Nyce, Lila Beaumont, and Harvey."

Reid focused on Harvey. "You were there, too?"

"Yeah, but I didn't light up Violet's car. Hell, I'd just put two of my own tires on it."

"Due to the vandalism she'd recently experienced?"

It appeared that Cooper had been whispering in Reid's ear.

"Bingo," Harvey said.

Reid aimed his next question at me. "Anyone else there you knew?"

I thought of the pregnant girl with Lila. She was new to me, so, "No, that's it."

"Okay. That should do for now. If I have any more questions, I'll be back." He downed the last of his lemonade and held the glass out to Aunt Zoe. "Thanks for the drink, Zo. Maybe I'll see you around."

Her lips were tight. "Probably. It's a small town."

"That it is. Willis"—he motioned to Harvey—"walk me out."

I waited until I heard the screen door slam before prodding Aunt Zoe. "What was that going on between you two?"

Aunt Zoe carried his glass over to the sink. "I don't know what you're talking about."

"Don't try to sell me a bunch of road apples. There was so much tension crackling between you two that my fingertips tingled."

"You're making too much of this."

"He knew about your lemonade."

"So do plenty of others."

"Come on, Aunt Zoe. What's the story with you and Reid?"

She shot me a stern look. "Violet, drop it."

"But he's gorgeous. And that voice. Whew!"

"I'll make you a deal," she wiped her hands on a towel. "If you tell me what's going on between you and Doc Nyce, I'll fill you in on why I don't want Reid Martin to step inside this house ever again."

* * *

I didn't spill my guts about Doc. Instead, I went upstairs to soak in the tub with some strawberry-vanilla scented bath bubbles and a much-needed steamy romance novel. There was no rush to talk to my insurance agent about the Bronco since I had gambled with liability coverage and rolled craps.

Several hours later, the kids were on the way down to my parents' place with Aunt Zoe, who'd insisted that I stay home because my parents knew all my "tells" when it came to lying.

I sat up from where I'd sprawled on the couch, nursing my wounds with a pint of peanut butter fudge ice cream. On the television, John Wayne and Fabian agonized over a

French prostitute. On the couch, I'd agonized over a certain matchbook. Was it just a coincidence, or had my nemesis been sitting in Charles' Club with me the other evening? And did she have long black hair, sharp teeth, and pointy boobs?

I picked up the Magic 8 Ball Addie had left sitting on the end table and shook it. "Is Lila to blame for the death of my Bronco?"

Signs point to yes, it showed through the window.

I knew it. I asked again, just to confirm.

It is certain.

There it was, clear as could be in blue fluid. I imagined taking the 8 ball to Cooper as evidence and chuckled. His head would probably explode.

My cell phone rang. I grabbed it and looked at the number. My little heart pitter-pattered. "I thought I was supposed to call you," I said to Doc.

"You were. What are you doing?"

"Asking life's questions. What about you?"

"Coming up with the answers. What do you need to know?"

"Whether Lila burned up my Bronco."

"Is there a reason you suspect her beyond your general dislike of the woman?"

"She was at Charles' Club the night I was."

"Is this about the matches?"

"Yes. Did Reid come to see you, too?"

"Detective Cooper stopped by with Harvey at his side. Who's Reid?"

So that's where Harvey had disappeared to in such a hurry after Reid left. "Reid is the fire captain. He was there the night of Wolfgang's fire."

"Oh, right. The Sam Elliot clone. Is that John Wayne's voice in the background?"

"The one and only."

"Is someone there with you?"

"Nope, just me and the Duke. Aunt Zoe took the kids down to my parents'."

There was a pause on the other end, then, "What are you wearing?"

I looked down at dark stains on my T-shirt. "Peanut butter fudge ice cream."

Doc's low laughter made my ear tingle. "Sexy."

"If you like that, you'll dig my ice-cream-cone pajama pants."

"You sound very lickable."

"How far does your tongue reach?"

"Want me to come over and show you?"

My ice-cream-heavy stomach flip-flopped. "Tempting."

"Yes, you are. That's one problem. The other is that I'm stuck here at the moment."

I was the one without wheels. "What's wrong with your car?" I remembered Aunt Zoe's comment about her friend seeing me driving Doc's car yesterday. Dread tightened my spine. "Has something happened to it?"

"My car is fine. But your loveable co-worker is hanging out next door, and I have a feeling he's looking for trouble."

"Ray?" What was he still doing there? Was it something to do with the Mudder Brothers? "What do you mean he's looking for trouble? Does he have a big crate?"

Another pause. "Why would he have a big crate? And how would I know if he did?"

"Never mind. Tell me about the trouble."

"He stopped by last night after you dropped me off."

"At your office?"

"Yes. He said he was working late and heard me come in. He claimed to be just making sure I wasn't a burglar, but the way he kept peeking behind me made me wonder if he was on to my living situation."

The dick-cheese needed to mind his own business. "Maybe he was just curious about your office."

"Well, that was my thought, but then this afternoon, he stopped over again and asked to use the bathroom. He claimed the one at Calamity Jane's was out of order."

"What did you do?"

"Let him use it. Denying him would have looked more suspicious, I figured."

"Did he see the back room?"

"No, I had the door closed. But I did have my shaving cream and razor in the bathroom."

"That could be easily explained."

"He also asked how I liked your services. Only he said 'servicing' until I corrected him."

I sat back against the cushions, covering my eyes with my hand. "I have a bad feeling about this."

"I'm sorry, Violet. I could live in my car for a few days."

"No, that's crazy. We're less than a week away from getting the keys to your place. I'll deal with Ray if he comes at me with this." Hell, I was already dealing with a cult-loving arsonist. Ray was a Twinkie by comparison.

I heard Aunt Zoe's truck pull into the drive. After our little standoff earlier, I didn't want to be caught talking to Doc. "I have to go. Aunt Zoe's here."

"Okay. Go to lunch with me tomorrow."

"What about Ray?"

"This is business. You need help with your financial portfolio. You're about to get your first commission check."

"The bulk of which is now going toward a replacement for my Bronco."

"All the more reason why you need my help. If you'd rather, I can meet you somewhere."

It was a bad idea all around, especially since I couldn't seem to keep my hands to myself when Doc was within reach. "I don't know. Whenever we try to do lunch, the sky falls on me."

"I'll bring an umbrella."

Addiction was not usually a pretty sight, but in Doc's case, it was damned good-looking. "Madam Chow's, twelve-thirty."

"I'll be waiting."

I hung up and groaned. The pickup door slammed. I grabbed the Magic 8 Ball and shook it again. "Does Ray know about Doc living in his back room?"

My sources say no.

Good. "Does Ray know about Doc and me?"

Ask again later.

Chapter Twenty-One

Friday, August 10th

The next morning, I gave in to Aunt Zoe's pressuring and drove her pickup to Calamity Jane's, feeling mighty bleary-eyed after a late night spent rehashing the scene at Charles' Club. In the end, my suspicions zeroed in on Lila—partly because of our warm and fuzzy relationship, but mostly due to her cult-copying tattoo. After my eyelids finally shut, all thoughts burned up in flame-filled nightmares, and I awoke with fire-engine red eyes.

Inside the office, I trudged straight to the coffee maker. Ray leaned back in his chair, his Tony Lamas dirtying his desktop, his cell phone to his ear. Mona's chair sat empty. According to the message she'd left on my voicemail, she'd be tied up at an appointment in Rapid for most of the morning. I missed the clack of her fingernails on her laptop keys, especially since her absence meant I had to deal with Ray on my own.

A slurp of the thicker-than-usual bitter black coffee made my tongue shrivel. "Holy crikey. That's strong." I'd have to check for hair sprouts on my chest later.

Ray shushed me with his finger to his lips and a glare.

I lowered the cup to my desktop, sloshing the black sludge onto the pages splayed across my desk. Upon closer inspection, I realized it was Doc's lease. A Post-it arrow pointed to where it specified that the office was not to be used as a domicile.

Turns out that Magic 8 Ball I'd consulted last night was

full of shit. Ray was on to Doc's and my secret.

By the time Ray hung up the phone minutes later, I'd worked myself into a fury-filled lather, my periwinkle silk camisole sticking to my lower back.

"What's this?" I held up the paper with the Post-It arrow.

Ray smirked. "What's it look like?"

"I'm not in the mood for your bullshit today, Ray. What's it doing on my desk?"

"I thought you might need a refresher course on Jane's rules for our next-door neighbor."

"Why? He's buying a house from me, not leasing a building."

"Don't play dumb, Blondie. I was here the other night when you dropped him off. I know what's going on."

My heart pummeled my lungs like a pair of speed-punching bags, but I kept my breath steady. This was just Ray. He couldn't fire me, but he could make my life utter hell—depending how much he actually knew. "Really? What's going on?"

"Your boyfriend is shacking up in the back room of his office."

Damn. I needed two smokescreens. I focused on the first one. "Doc is a friend, not boyfriend."

"You sure about that?"

Not one iota. "Positive."

"I saw you two in the parking lot. You looked pretty lovey-dovey to me."

What had he seen? We hadn't kissed. Came close, though. "He's a good friend."

"I think you're full of shit." His gaze challenged me. "And I have proof."

Don't freak out! Keeping my face blank took a group effort from all four corners of my body. "I don't believe you."

"You calling my bluff, Sweetheart?"

"I'm so not your sweetheart. And yes, consider it called."

"I was hoping you would." He opened his top drawer, pulled out a pair of black satin panties, and threw them at me. They landed at my feet. "I found your panties on your *friend's* bathroom floor."

I stared down at the black satin, jealousy combusting in a red-hot flash, filling my cheeks with heat. They weren't my underwear. So, whose were they? What were they doing in Doc's bathroom? More importantly, were they Tiffany's? Had she been over there recently, bebopping on the beanbag with him?

Whoa! The rational side of my brain slapped some sense into the crazy ranting side. Doc might have a perfectly good explanation for the panties. I needed to talk to him before I began sharpening my kitchen knives. If Doc confirmed Ray's accusation, *then* I'd cut Doc's heart out and feed it to Harvey's whangdoodle.

"Those are not mine."

"You sure about that?" Ray taunted.

"One hundred percent." While my undies had played hide and seek in Doc's back room, I'd left his office wearing them every damned time.

Ray laughed, loud and harsh, the clamor echoing in the still office and making me wince. "You're right, they're not. They're Ginny's. But you should have seen your face when you saw those panties."

"Who's Ginny?" And how did she know Doc?

"Ginny York. She left them at my place the last time she came by to wet her whistle. I was just testing my theory about you and your boyfriend. You walked right into my trap. I could have spotted your tell from Mount Roosevelt."

My knees gave way and I fell into my chair. I really, *really* wanted to cram the panties up Ray's nose and follow them with my foot. I nailed him with loathing. "You're a vile prick."

His smirk spread toward his ears. "You're just pissed because you played right into my hands. Jane's going to love hearing you screwed Nyce to make a sale."

I had to play my cards carefully here, not let Ray see how much I needed him to keep quiet about Doc and me. I collected the lease papers in one bunch and carried them over to the filing cabinet, avoiding his gloating gaze. "I didn't screw Doc to make a sale."

"Sure, whatever you say, Blondie." His sarcasm rang, pure and annoying. "Knowing about you two lovebirds is going to make it all that much sweeter when I tell Jane about your boyfriend's living arrangements and get him kicked out."

"Jane wouldn't kick out a paying renter."

"Ah-ha! So you admit he's living there."

Maybe if I kept Ray's focus centered on Doc and his lease, his interest in Doc and my relationship would fade. "Of course. I'm the one who gave Doc permission to stay there until his house closed."

"You gave him permission?" He said this as if I'd just told him I had a third nipple. "Jane is going to love this. You blatantly disregarded her rules, making her look the fool." He rubbed his hands together. "She'll can your sorry ass for sure this time."

"Jane isn't going to fire me." I sounded calm, my voice smooth, my tone strong. Inside, my gut was full of daredevil motorcyclists circling around and around. Damn Ray for digging in my sandbox, unearthing my secrets. "And she isn't going to kick Doc out, either."

"Yes, she will. I know Jane. She doesn't suffer liars, especially as employees."

"You're confused about your facts. I haven't lied to her about any of this." I hadn't even talked to her for days, what with her being out of town dealing with her divorce mess.

"You overstepped the boundary, Blondie. Jane's a stickler about this rule."

"And you follow every single one of her rules to the letter?" I slammed the file drawer closed. "I don't think so."

"I sell houses and make her money. I'm allowed to break a few rules. You haven't even sold one house yet. That means you don't get to break any rules. On top of it, you stupidly agreed to sell that Carhart mess."

"That house will sell."

"At what cost to Jane's reputation?" He lowered his feet to the floor, his gaze narrowing, his upper lip curling. "You were on thin ice before you climbed into bed with our neighbor. When Jane gets back on Monday, that ice is going to break. She'll fire you on the spot, and Doc will have his lease torn up. Unless ..."

"Unless what?" I crossed my arms over my chest, preparing mentally for whatever ultimatum he hurled at me.

"You turn in your resignation. Then I'll keep my mouth shut about your boyfriend."

"So I give up my job in order for Doc to get to stay put. Is this still about you being pissy because I took your nephew's place here? Or is it because I'm a threat to your job?"

He guffawed. "You, a threat? You must live on the moon, Blondie. With the sales commissions I bring in, I'm the king of the mountain around here."

"Maybe so—at the moment," I skirted around the over-tanned baboon back to my desk, avoiding him. "But you're living in a glass castle, throwing stones."

"What's that supposed to mean?"

"What are you and the Mudder brothers smuggling in those crates?"

There was a long pause from Ray, so long that I looked

over and found his whole face scrunched in a snarl. "I told you before, you should mind your own business."

Apparently, I'd found a weak spot in his massive ego. "Guns? Drugs? Counterfeit money? Am I getting warm yet?" When he just glared at me, I added, "I wonder if Detective Cooper would be interested in checking out those crates. I'm pretty sure he'd be curious about why the crates keep leaving the funeral home loaded."

Ray shot out of his chair so fast it almost tipped over. His cheeks turned from orange to red to purple as he curled and uncurled his fists. "Keep your meddling nose out of my shit."

"Or what? You'll tattle on me to Jane for that, too?"

"You'll wish Jane was the only devil raining down on you."

"Is that a threat?"

"Consider it a friendly warning."

"We aren't friends."

He snorted. "Yeah, and it's a real shame after the way you spread your legs for all of your other 'friends.' I'm feeling a little left out."

It was times like this when I wish I carried a cast-iron skillet in my purse. "You're not going to sidetrack me with your petty insults, Ray. I'm on to something with these crates, and you're running scared."

Ray rushed me, looming over me. A vein throbbed in the middle of his forehead. "I'm telling you one last time, you prying cunt, mind your own goddamned business."

I grabbed my purse, needing to put some space between us—the state of Montana would do—or I might smash his dick in my desk drawer. But first, I wanted to make one thing crystal clear. I stood toe to toe with him, aiming my finger up at his face. "If you try to get me fired on Monday by telling Jane about Doc's living arrangements, I'm going to consider that a threat to my family."

"Ohhhh, the tough little pussycat is mad. What are you going to do? Claw me? I like to be scratched, you know."

"I'm going to knock you off your fucking mountain."

I slammed the back door on his snide laughter.

The air conditioner in Aunt Zoe's truck did little to cool me down. I drove up the hill toward Lead, steering toward one of my favorite java joints. I still needed caffeine, even more so after my showdown with that loincloth-wearing buffoon.

I zig-zagged through the back streets of Lead, avoiding some of the heavy late-morning motorcycle traffic that buzzed around Lead's Open Cut. As I cruised by the dirt parking lot next to the YMCA, I did a double-take at the sight of a familiar long-legged, raven-haired she-wolf in red short-shorts. *Lila.*

Spying by using my rearview mirror, I saw her bend down and reach into the driver's-side window of a blue car. The whole scene reminded me of a rerun of *Cops* I'd watched with Harvey. It involved a prostitute, some methamphetamines, and a nasty bit of tooth rot; afterward, Harvey enlightened me on the benefits of a toothless whore, in gagging detail—literally.

I circled the block and parked next to a ramshackle four-car garage within viewing distance of Lila. Twisting, I peeked through the pickup's back window at Lila's backside. From where I sat, I couldn't see any dimples of fat on the backs of her thighs. My hatred for her tripled.

Lila rested her arms on the top of the car, her face and chest filling the window. The rumble of motorcycles a block away on Main Street drowned out all sound, but actions spoke loudly—like the hand that snaked out from the car window and rubbed up and down her thigh, then cupped her ass. She playfully brushed the hand away, stepping back and partway out of one of her high-heeled sandals. She bent to straighten her shoe and I caught a full view of the driver—Douglas Mann.

"Holy shit!"

So that little scene at the funeral home wasn't just a fly-by-night groping. I stayed frozen for another few minutes, my brain reeling as I watched the two of them tease and squeeze and kiss and fondle. When Douglas leaned out and licked her bared stomach, I couldn't stand any more and got the hell out of there.

By the time I'd made it halfway back to Deadwood, I knew with certainty who'd taken her jealous wrath out on my Bronco and why. If only the deranged bitch had paid attention, she'd have seen that Douglas had absolutely no interest in me beyond wanting to buy a house. Wait a second ... I pulled over into the parking lot of a small park sprinkled with a few mining machine castoffs from Homestake Mine's golden days.

My head spun from a barrage of "what ifs" and "buts" until I hit the brakes and took a deep, head-clearing breath. Why did Douglas want the Carhart house? Did it have something to do with Lila? Maybe there was a love triangle going on between him, Lila, and Millie. But that still didn't explain why he would want to buy the house. Nor why they would need or even want a Realtor. And where did Wanda fit into all this?

First and foremost, I needed proof that Lila burned my Bronco. Something more tangible than my Magic 8 Ball so that Cooper wouldn't kick me out of his office when I asked him to drag Lila's tight ass to jail. I turned the pickup around and rolled back up Main Street into Lead. I thought I knew where to find what I needed.

As soon as I kicked Lila out of the picture, I could focus on why Douglas Mann had such a hankering for the Carhart house.

* * *

Millie opened the door on my third rat-a-tat-tat. She didn't smile, just stared at me through those big, round glasses that magnified her pupils. A dusting of flour marked her cheek and her black apron. The smell of fried chicken made my mouth twang with anticipation, almost melting my resolve until I thought of Elvis the chicken, which led to Addy. The twang moved to my heart. I wanted my kids home and safe with me, sharing their day's events over supper, and for that I needed proof.

"Hi, Millie." I pushed by her into the foyer, not wanting to give her a chance to shut the door in my face. "I was wondering if Wanda has had a chance to look at that other offer letter yet. The one I brought by yesterday."

Millie's mouth opened and closed a couple of times as she glanced from me to the porch and back. "Uhhh, Mother isn't here right now." Her voice shuddered a little, making her sound nervous.

"That's okay. I'll call her later." I'd surprised Millie with my somewhat forced entry and needed to keep her one step behind me. "Listen, I'm really thirsty. Would you please get me a glass of water?"

"Well, I was kind of busy."

I slapped my palm to my forehead, closing my eyes, pretending dizziness, and stumbled against the wall. "Oh, my. I don't feel well. Please, Millie, some ice water."

"But we don't have any ice."

"That's right. I forgot," I lied. "Just run the faucet for a bit then."

"Umm, okay." Millie disappeared into the kitchen.

I waited until I heard the faucet running and said, "I think I lost one of my earrings upstairs when I was here last time. I'll just go check while you're getting that."

"No," her tone rang with alarm. "You shouldn't go—"

From halfway up the stairs, I called, "I'll be down in a

flash."

I took the remaining stairs two at a time, racing as if Lila was chomping at my tail. The sound of the faucet still gushing downstairs encouraged me across the landing into Junior's bedroom, the one Lila seemed to be calling home.

With only minutes to find some incriminating evidence that would nail Lila for torching my Bronco, I tore into the room. There had to be something here, like gas-splashed clothes wadded up in the corner of the closet, or the tool she'd used to carve *SLUT* into my paint stashed in a drawer or behind a book. Hell, I'd settle for a voodoo doll with curly blonde hair and needles poking its eyes.

The closet held a mix of Junior's faded shirts and scuffed-up boots and Lila's skimpy *pleather* outfits. I kicked his boots aside, peering into the corners, but came up empty except for some mid-sized boxes that were taped closed. Under the bed, I discovered a few stray dust bunny tumbleweeds on a dust-covered floor. The dresser's underskirt hid one marble and a sticky penny.

Wiping my now-tacky fingers on my gauzy skirt, I frowned around the room. There had to be something damning here. Something that, when I handed it over to Cooper, would keep him from looking at me as if I were wearing a chicken suit complete with a snap-on beak.

Attacking the dresser drawers next, I tugged several open at once, sifting through what must have been Junior Carhart's old jeans, T-shirts, and tighty-whities. No frilly Lila garments in here. Where was she keeping her delicates? Now that I thought about her tight, scanty outfits, I realized she probably didn't own any underwear.

I yanked open a drawer stuffed with men's tube socks and jammed my hands into the mix. In the back, at the bottom, my fingers brushed against paper.

I pulled out an unlabeled, unsealed envelope. Inside it, I found a tri-folded airline itinerary from a Rapid City travel agency. Three pictures had been stuffed inside the itinerary's folds.

The photos caught my eye first, because I recognized Mr. Carhart, the steely-haired man from the formal wall photo of him and Wanda down in the sitting room. However, the woman with him in the pictures wasn't Wanda; nor did she look very formal in two of the pictures. Instead, she was down on her hands and knees in a pair of black chaps and a studded leather bra. Was that a horse bit in her mouth? Ick. Was this Mr. Carhart's lover, Claudette? She really should have closed the curtains when she played her barnyard games.

I focused on the third picture, a close-up. Turning it sideways, I winced when I figured out what she was doing to Wanda's husband. If this was Claudette, then Harvey was right—planting tulips seemed to be her specialty. Apparently, she enjoyed midnight gardening with any old Tom, Dick, or Harvey.

I flipped the pictures over and found no writing on the back. Not that I'd expected my mother's typical scrapbooking details—names, dates, descriptions—but it would have been a considerate thing to do for those of us snooping around for answers.

I dropped the photos on the dresser and scanned the itinerary. Ah-ha! It *was* Claudette, I thought as I read the two names above the one-way ticket confirmation numbers for a flight from Rapid City to Miami via Denver. I double-checked the date: a week after the old man had been beaten to death.

That meant Claudette hadn't been telling tall tales about eloping to Florida. I lowered the piece of paper, and the pictures on the dresser popped back to the forefront of my thoughts. Something smelled a lot like blackmail here, and it wasn't the sweet and spicy odor of Lila's perfume lingering in the air.

I looked down at the sock drawer—Junior's socks, no sign of Lila here. Had Junior paid somebody to watch Mr. Carhart and take pictures of his infidelities? Why? No, it made more sense if it had been Wanda, the jilted wife. Had she been one step ahead of the old bastard all along, planning to make sure he didn't get any of her inheritance from her rich aunt? If so, Harvey and Claudette could be right. Wanda may have killed her husband and hidden the evidence in Junior's sock drawer. But why did Junior kill himself, then?

The floorboards creaked behind me.

I turned and saw Millie standing inside the doorway, her lips anchored down on the corners, her hands stuffed in the front pockets of her flour-coated apron. "You shouldn't be doing that," she said, nodding at the paper in my hand.

I held up the itinerary—no need to pretend I was just folding Junior's socks. "Your father was leaving your mother."

Her nostrils flared. "You should put that back."

"Did you take these pictures, Millie? Or did Junior take them?" I glanced back at the revealing photos. "Or was it your mother?"

"Those aren't for you to see."

"Did your mother kill your father, Millie? Was she trying to stop him and his mistress from running off with her money?" But why would Wanda have to go so far as to kill him? Had he threatened her that night? Found the incriminating pictures and become violent?

Millie's eyes grew round as half-dollars in her magnified lenses. She tiptoed closer. "She's going to be mad that you did that."

So it was Wanda. "Your mother needs help." This would explain why Wanda had been seeing her husband's ghost since his death. There is probably some term for such post-traumatic optical delusions. "Let's take these pictures to Detective Cooper. The police can handle it from here, get your mother the help she needs."

"She's not going to like this at all."

"It's for the best, Millie. You can't keep living like this." The poor woman. Raised with an abusive father, a cruel brother, and a crazy mother. It's no wonder Millie dressed like she was going to a funeral every day.

I picked up the pictures and tried to pocket them, but one of them caught on the edge of my pocket and fell out, drifting to the floor, sliding under the dresser.

"You're going to have to go now," Millie whispered.

"We both can go." I squatted and reached under the dresser, my fingers bumping the picture further under. *Damn it.* I dropped onto my knees and peered under the dresser. There it was, a few inches further. "I'll take you with me, get you out of here."

Something stung me on the back of the neck. Pain shot me upright. "Ouch!"

I brushed at whatever it was. Only there was nothing there.

The floor tilted under me.

I grabbed the dresser, holding on as it tipped the other way. "That's weird." It must have been a touch of vertigo from sitting up so fast.

"You shouldn't have come here," Millie said, her voice sounding fuzzy, out of tune, like a radio signal at the edge of reception.

I blinked and looked toward her feet, my head too heavy to raise. My gaze crawled as high as her waist. It took a second for the thing she held in her fingers to register. By the time I figured out it was a syringe, the static had overtaken everything else.

My cell phone! I reached for my purse, and then remembered it was down in Aunt Zoe's truck.

Millie bent in front of me, stuck her index finger on my

forehead, and pushed me backward into a pool of blackness.

Chapter Twenty-Two

Years ago, long before Addy and Layne popped into my world, I used to be wound pretty tight. I had a detailed plan for my life, down to the type of car I would drive post-nuptials—Volvo, nice and practical. Deviation was not an option.

One day, the owner of Hob-Knobbin' Books, where I worked back then, took issue with my refusal to shelve Edgar Allan Poe in the store's new Horror section complete with fluorescent green witch and ghoul deco. Classics stay with classics, I informed her. She gave me two options: watch a video on adapting to change, or leave, pink slip in hand. I needed the job.

I nodded off twice during the video, but I learned a little mind trick that day called R.E.S.T.: Reflect, Evaluate, Search, Take action. This silly acronym helped me over the years, during times when life jammed a big pipe wrench into my plans—like when I was knocked up with twins and then abandoned by their loser father; or when I walked in on my sister with one of my boyfriends; or when my higher-than-a-kite ex-boyfriend burned my house down and most of my worldly possessions.

Or when I was tranquilized, gagged, and blindfolded, with my ankles bound and my hands tied behind my back by a nutcase who secreted me away in a haunted house plagued by a murder-filled past.

Again.

At least this time there weren't any dead bodies nearby.

Or were there? The blindfold wasn't giving up any secrets. A flashback to that macabre tea party lit a flare of panic inside of me, making me sweat until my camisole stuck like a bathing suit. Frantic, I tugged and yanked on my wrists and ankles, trying to free them, but the duct tape held strong.

Swallowing around my heart, which cowered in my throat, I wiggled my way upright until I sat with my back against a box. The musty scent of mothballs, cardboard, and stinky shoes clung to my sinuses. Speaking of shoes, where were mine? Somebody didn't want me kicking with heels on.

Man, I was so thirsty. What I wouldn't do for a big old glass of Aunt Zoe's lemonade to wash the taste of cotton off my tongue. The thought of Aunt Zoe's kitchen filled me with calm, helping me focus. Now to use my old trick to figure out how I could adapt to this sudden change in my life.

Okay, reflect. I tried to open my mind, think back to how all this started.

I was going for a latte after my fight with Ray. That led to digging for proof that Lila torched my Bronco, which turned into trying to talk Millie into going to the police about Wanda and ended with being gussied up like a Thanksgiving turkey and stuffed into what smelled like a closet. *Christ*—all before noon, too.

My anxiety welled again inside me, amplifying my urge to thrash and scream and kick my way to freedom. One deep breath, and then another, and yet another kept me still. That, and the knowledge that between my missing lunch with Doc and Aunt Zoe waiting for me to return with her pickup, I'd be missed almost immediately.

All right, back to my trick. Evaluation time. I tipped my head back, hitting it on something hard but hollow that sat on the box I leaned against. I head-butted it again, knocking it back an inch. The contents rattled. It sounded like a fishing tackle box. I hit it again with a nudge that sent it crashing to the floor.

I froze, listening for footfalls—nothing, not even a vibration in the floor. Where was everyone?

Oh, God. What if I wasn't at the Carharts? For all I knew, Millie could have stuffed me in the trunk of her car and taken me to some shack in the hills to wither and die like a mouse stuck in a trap, the cheese just out of reach.

Fuck! I struggled anew, yanking on my wrists until a cramp pinched my shoulder. I cried out and held still. Slowly, it loosened.

Okay, okay, calm down. Breathe. What was the next stage? Search. Right, search for information.

I'd already figured out I was in a closet. The boot heel jammed into my butt cheek when I woke up confirmed it. My ass still throbbed. That was going to leave a mark.

What was in that tackle box I'd knocked over? I inch-wormed toward it, feeling for the contents on the floor. My fingers stumbled across something small and circular. I scraped my nail down it—thread. A spool? No, too thin. More like a bobbin. Did tackle boxes have bobbins? Maybe it was a sewing box. The next piece of flotsam confirmed it—a thimble.

My pulse sped. I had yet to meet a sewing box that didn't have a pair of scissors it. I scrambled further into the debris field and wiggled my fingers behind me along the braided rug. Something poked my finger, making me wince and pull back before I continued with more care. I came across a scattering of round-headed pins and skimmed them carefully.

Come on, there had to be scissors somewhere, even tiny ones. My pinkie finger brushed something long and cylindrical, like a pen but shorter. I felt along it and found a ridge where the cap connected—a seam ripper. That had potential, but with duct-tape binding, scissors would work better.

The floorboards creaked outside the closet. I palmed the seam ripper as the metal squeak of the doorknob registered. The door hinges groaned.

I stayed still, leaning against one of the boxes, faking unconsciousness. It seemed like the smart thing to do. I'd bide my time before taking action. The scent of burning candles mixed with Lila's spicy sweet perfume whirled in around me.

A piercing pain exploded in my ribs.

I curled up, hugging my throbbing side, bile bitter in the back of my mouth as waves of nausea lapped at my throat.

Someone had kicked me, hard.

"Wakey wakey," Lila said, yanking off the blindfold. "Eggs and bakey."

"Bitch!" I yelled through a mouthful of cotton.

Lila squatted in front of me, her sharp-toothed grin framed by her red lips. "What's that, Miss Realtor? You're glad to see me?"

I squinted up at her, my fury pulsing through my fingertips and toes. "Go to hell," I mumbled.

"Did you just tell me to go to hell?"

I nodded.

Her laughter had an edge of mania to it. "You first."

She grabbed me by the ankles and dragged me out of the closet, grunting the whole way. It was times like this when filling my cells with all that peanut butter and fudge ice cream paid off.

"Millie!" She yelled over her shoulder. "Come help me."

Millie hustled into the bedroom, the same one she'd caught me in earlier.

Crap.

I kicked and screamed most of the way down the stairs, making them work up a sweat, until Lila stomped on my fingers and shut me up. They carried me into the sitting room, where they tied me to a chair parked in the middle of a pentagram chalked onto the floor.

Fire Captain Reid would get an itchy hose finger if he saw all the candles burning in the room. My throbbing fingers were itching, that was for sure—itching to poke Lila in the fucking eye for the rib tickler back in the closet and the finger smash on the stairs.

The smell of burning wax and wicks was making my gut roll, reminding me of another candle party I'd been dragged into. I didn't need this particular déjà vu in my life. With any luck, I'd burn *this* damned house to the ground, too.

While I assessed my up-shit-creek situation, Lila and Millie stood off to the side, whispering, taking turns frowning in my direction. Millie won with six frowns to Lila's four, but I wasn't sure if that was good or bad, since I was no longer so sure about who'd killed Millie's father.

They apparently came to some agreement and clomped upstairs together, leaving me to brood and fret on my own ... well, unless Doc was right about Prudence the ghost, in which case I wasn't alone—not the most comforting thought.

I gripped the seam ripper I'd stolen from the closet and began to tear my way to freedom one duct-tape thread at a time. Sweat ran down from my temple, the gag soaking it up. Adrenaline and fear spurred me past my sore wrist and aching fingers.

Glancing around the room, I tried to ignore the serving tray full of knives on the sideboard. Maybe someone had just been cleaning them, oiling the wood handles. Yeah, right.

Where was Wanda? What had they done with her? The clock on the mantle showed midnight coming to a haunted house near me, and I hadn't seen one glimpse of her gingham hide.

My gaze fell back on the few stair steps I could see from my vantage point. What in the hell was going on, and who was running the show? If they came downstairs carrying chainsaws and hockey masks, I was going to piss my pants, there was no doubt about it.

Had Doc or Aunt Zoe come looking for me yet? Surely Doc would have thought to check the Carhart place. Then again, maybe he had. Millie could have erased all signs of my presence.

The curtains were drawn, so I couldn't see the driveway, but I had no doubt they'd hidden Aunt Zoe's truck in the garage or somewhere more clever. It would take a bloodhound to sniff out my slumbering ass in that closet. Since Doc's sniffer only worked on dead folks, his radar wouldn't have picked up my scent—at least not yet. Given the pentagram in the middle of which I sat, that might change soon.

I just needed to figure out how to buy more ...

The front door's deadbolt clicked.

My ears straining, I listened as the door hinges creaked. Shoe soles clapped on the wood floor. The *thump* of the door shutting followed, then the sound of keys jingling.

I waited, straining forward as far as my bindings would allow, praying that my get-out-of-jail free card had just turned up and I could head straight to GO, as in right out the door.

The footfalls came closer. I held my breath, my eyes glued to the sitting room entryway. Gingham was the first thing to register, then Wanda's bosomy form, head down, making her way to the stairs.

I called her name through my nose, as much as that was possible.

Wanda squeaked and whirled my way. Her hand flew to her chest, then to her mouth as her gaze sized me up. Her focus moved behind me, her eyes widening like some horror flick scream queen's.

I cocked my head to the side at her overreaction. Sure, I'd been stuffed in a closet for hours. My hair could use a brush; my mascara probably lined my lips, but come on. Did I really look that bad?

I called her name again, and nudged my head for her to come help me.

She waddled into the room, hesitating at the edge of the pentagram.

"Hurry up!" I mumbled.

Wanda lifted her skirt and tiptoed through the chalk lines as if she were playing hopscotch, minus the hop.

"Are you okay, Miss Parker?" she asked, her voice shaking as much as her hands as she reached for my gag and pulled it down around my neck.

Did I freaking look okay? "I'm fine," I said, my tongue all thick and cottony.

"I told you not to come here."

"You could have been more clear on *why*. Now, help me get free before they come back."

"Who?"

"Lila and Millie."

Tears filled Wanda's eyes. "Millie did this?"

"Part of it." There was no time to waste on a therapy session here. "Wanda, *please* help me."

She nodded and scooted around behind me. It took her half a minute to loosen the rope holding me to the chair enough that she could slide it up over my shoulders and head.

"Now my wrists. I have a seam ripper in my right hand." I opened my palm.

After a moment's silence, Wanda said, "This was my aunt's. Where'd you get it?"

"I found it in the closet. Hurry up and cut me free." I kept my eyes on the stairs as she ripped and tugged.

She stopped suddenly. I tried to pull free, but was still bound.

"What?" Wanda asked.

"I didn't say anything."

She shushed me. "Where?" she asked, then took a sharp breath. "Oh, dear Lord."

I craned over my shoulder, trying to see what was going on. Wanda stood gaping at the knife-laden sideboard. Then she stumbled forward, almost as if she'd been pushed. She hesitated over the knives, her hand outstretched.

"Oh, good thinking." I obviously wasn't, or I'd have considered those damned knives I'd been trying so hard not to think about.

"This one?" she asked the empty space to her right and picked up a paring knife. "No? Oh, right. Of course." She put the paring knife down and grabbed a serrated bread slicer.

The way she was talking to thin air made my skin crawl.

Wanda walked toward me, knife held out in front of her, her mouth upturned in garish glee.

Sweat trickled down my spine. "Uh, Wanda?"

Her light blue eyes met mine.

"Did you kill your husband?"

A frown puckered her forehead. The lunatic grin disappeared. "Of course not."

My shoulders sagged in relief. "Okay. Good." So, my gut had been right all along about Wanda's innocence. But then what was the deal with that envelope and those pictures I'd found in the upstairs bedroom?

Wanda grabbed my wrist. "Now hold very still, Miss Parker. I'd hate to cut you."

That made two of us. I closed my eyes. Her small tugs jerked my arms. I was just a handful of heartbeats from fresh air and freedom. As soon as my feet were no longer bound together, Wanda and I had an appointment at

Cooper's place. The next time I saw Lila's face, I wanted it to be in profile pictures above her set of fingerprints.

My wrists swung loose.

"There," Wanda said.

"Thanks. Now give me the knife."

Wanda obliged.

"Mother!" Millie yelled from the entryway.

Wanda's scream rang in my ears.

I would have screamed, too, but the sight of Millie in a black Grim Reaper robe, hood and all, dried all saliva from my mouth.

"Get away from her!" Millie stalked toward us.

Looking like a cornered mouse, Wanda didn't move, except to widen her eyes.

"I said get back!" She pushed her mother aside hard enough to send Wanda stumbling and flailing against the wall.

I slashed out toward Millie with the knife, hoping to catch her off guard, but Millie dodged and I missed her. "Give me that." She grabbed for my wrist, but I jerked out of her reach. "I said give it here," she growled and caught a handful of my hair, yanking it hard toward her.

My eyes watered. I slashed again, blindly, snagging fabric. Millie caught my wrist, twisting my hair and head around painfully with her other hand. We'd reached a stalemate. If only Wanda would stop watching us and come help.

"What's going on?" Lila asked, marching into the room, her black robe billowing around her, the book I'd found in Junior's room in her hand.

Great. Grim Reaper twins. Double the pleasure, double the fun.

"Give me that." Lila set the book down on the end table and came to take the knife from me, but I had a death grip on it. "Let go or I'll really hurt you."

"Go fuck yourself," I said through clenched teeth. The knife was my ticket to freedom.

"Fine. Millie, hold her still."

Millie gripped my hair and wrist even tighter. A fresh burn of pain stung my skull, and a tear slipped down my cheek.

Lila returned with the paring knife, her hood pushed back. Eyes glittering in the candlelight, she grinned, her mini-fangs exposed. "We'll see how strong your grip is when I slice your tendons."

Slice my tendons! The blade dug into my skin. I cried out in pain and the bread knife clattered to the floor at Lila's feet.

Lila picked up the knife. "That's my girl." She patted my head. "I knew you'd come to your senses." She let go of my wrist and I cradled it against my chest, afraid to see how deep she'd cut. I could feel my pulse beating in the cut.

"Should I tie her back up?" Millie asked.

"No need," Lila said. "Her ankles are still bound. She's not going to bunny-hop anywhere fast." She pulled the hood up onto her head.

"What about Mother?" Millie took a step toward Wanda. "Should I tie her up? Stuff her in the closet?"

"Your mother knows better than to do anything else stupid. Don't you, dear?" Wanda just stared up at Lila with those big mouse eyes. Lila added, "I'd hate to have to summon your dead husband again. He's going to be very angry if I do. I don't think he'll be as gentle with your punishment this time."

Wanda curled up like a roly-poly bug, rousing the protector in me. "Leave her alone," I said.

"You are in no position to be giving orders, Nosy Nellie." Lila cleared some curly strands from my forehead, her touch delicate, yet menacing.

I quivered in a mix of rage and fear and yanked away from her touch.

She slapped me. The sting spread clear back to my ear and down my neck. "Now, where were we, Millie?"

"We need blood."

"Perfect." Lila grabbed my pulsing wrist. "Bring me the shot glass."

I tried to tug my hand free, but she brought her boot heel down on my bare toes until I relented.

Wiggling my crushed toes, I glared at her. Turn the other cheek, my ass. I was going to slam her face into the sideboard the first chance I got. "So, what are you? Some kind of witch?" The hair fit. The nails, too.

Lila laughed at me. "You've read too many fairy tales. This pentagram is pointing down, not up."

According to whom? From where I sat it pointed due east, toward the exit that I planned to run out the first chance I got. "So what's that mean? You're going to summon the devil?"

"You don't summon the devil," Lila said, as if she were scolding a toddler. "You summon demons, and only certain ones at that."

"What's the difference? A demon is a demon." And Hell was Hell, wasn't it?

"Not all demons play nice." I could tell by Lila's haughty tone and curled lip that she was riding high on this wave of superiority, enjoying my ignorance. "Some are downright nasty. Tonight, you're going to help me summon Azazel, the standard bearer of Hell's armies."

Azazel? Just the name gave me the heebie-jeebies. I hid my quiver of fear behind a scoff. "Right. Let me guess. You need a human sacrifice, and I'm the lucky virgin."

"Don't be so dramatic. We just need your blood."

She was the one preparing to summon a demon and I was being dramatic. Oh, that was rich. "How much blood?"

"Don't worry. We have to keep you alive. Azazel needs a female body to inhabit while he lets Kyrkozz through."

Whew, wasn't that a relief. Just demon possession. Lovely. Maybe Azazel would be better at selling real estate than I was. "Then what?"

"Then Azazel leaves your body and returns to Hell, and Kyrkozz copulates with you, planting his seed."

Copulates! Uurrcchhhh! Hold on. Time out. Nobody was going to be copulating with anyone tonight, especially not with me. Things had gone from *Exorcist* freaky to *The Omen* spooky in one sentence, and while I didn't believe in the whole demons-from-Hell song and dance, Lila obviously did. Her determination to try to raise something from wherever coated my skin in a cold sweat.

"We had a host," Lila continued, "but she didn't work out. You coming along when you did worked out perfectly."

"Timing is everything," I said, trying to keep my knees from knocking against each other. What did she mean by "didn't work out"? How didn't it? Criminy, Lila wasn't just going off the rails on the crazy train, she was the goddamned conductor.

The grandfather clock chimed in agreement. Midnight. Damn. The witching hour was upon us.

"Now hold still." Lila sliced open my thumb before I knew what was happening. I screeched and jerked and tugged. She stepped down on my bare toes again, her boot heel crushing, pain stealing my breath. "I said hold the fuck still."

I did as she demanded, watching as drops of my blood splattered inside the shot glass Millie held under my thumb.

The click of the deadbolt made us all jump in surprise.

Millie's eyes tripled in size behind her magnified lenses as she stared up at Lila.

Before either of them could move, the door slammed open. "Lila," Douglas Mann called out. "Where are you? We have a problem."

Relief raced through my veins. My limbs trembled.

"In here," Lila said all light and happy, as if we were having a good old-fashioned taffy pull.

Douglas came striding into the parlor, dressed for a funeral again—I hoped it wasn't mine. He stopped at the sight of us three Musketeers all huddling in the pentagram. "What in hell are you doing?"

"Summoning Azazel." Again, airy and nonchalant. Next on the docket: baking snickerdoodles.

"Jesus Christ, Lila. That's enough of this crazy demon shit of yours." Douglas' fingers tore through his hair. He grimaced. "I'm sorry about this, Violet."

"No problem." I matched Lila's sunshine-and-rainbows tone. No need to go ape-shit until I had Cooper by my side. "Can I go now?"

He shook his head. "Sorry about that, too." His gaze moved to Millie. "Take Violet out to the mine and get rid of her."

Chapter Twenty-Three

Saturday, August 11th (just after midnight)

"No!" Lila yelled at Douglas.

Wait, I thought, closing my mouth. That was supposed to be my line, it being my life and all.

"Violet's mine." Lila stepped between us, blocking me from Douglas' view. "I need her."

Usually, I liked feeling needed.

"Let it go, Lila," Doug's tone fell, growing stern and fatherly. "We have to get rid of her. The cops are out looking for her in force. It's just a matter of time before they come knocking."

Hurray! Here came Cooper and the cavalry.

Lila didn't budge. "I just need another hour."

"You can summon a demon that fast?" I scoffed. "Where'd you learn this trick? From the back of a cereal box?"

Lila turned and slapped me.

I held the back of my hand to my burning cheek. That was twice now. Man, I wanted to tar and feather the bitch.

"Stop it." Douglas grabbed Lila by the arm, dragging her away from me, outside the pentagram. "You've messed with Violet enough."

She shook off his arm. "There you go again, protecting your little blonde girlfriend."

"Damn it, Lila. This has nothing to do with how I feel about Violet."

How he felt about me? Were we in a relationship that I

didn't know about?

"It has everything to do with you and her." Lila shot me a glare that singed my hair. "You love *her*, don't you? Don't you? I should have burned her up in her stupid truck."

"It was a Bronco, you dumbass," I said, wishing I was wearing a wire to catch that confession. Unfortunately, that still wouldn't get me a new vehicle. Car dealers didn't take arsonist confessions as a form of payment.

"Violet, stay out of this," Douglas ordered. "You're not helping."

My apologies. I was new at the whole Stockholm-syndrome psychosis song and dance.

He grabbed Lila by the shoulders. "Honey, calm down. You know you're one of my favorite girls."

She clung to his chest. "I could dye my hair blonde. Get a perm. Just tell me what you want."

The sight of a woman throwing herself at a man was never pretty, especially when he looked like a jowly lollipop. Watching Lila morph into a spineless ninny should have made me want to burn my bra for women worldwide, but after I'd been kicked and slapped by the bitch, my can of compassion was empty. In fact, I had an idea. "Douglas, darling," I said, in a warm purr. "If you won't tell her the truth, I will."

All eyes turned to me, including Millie's magnified ones, which were rimmed with extra-large tears.

I smirked at Lila. "You should know by now that gentlemen prefer blondes. Douglas was only using you." That last part was true and obvious to any outsider, but for what purpose, I had yet to figure out.

Lila's lily-white cheeks bloomed rosy red. She bared her fangs. "You lie!"

"You sure about that?" I looked up at Douglas, whose mouth was catching flies. "Douglas, would you please stop dallying with the trash? We don't need her anymore. I can give you what you want—what you need."

I was winging it so hard I was flying in circles.

Lila clenched her fists. She whirled on Douglas. "I knew it! That's why you get horny every time you talk about her."

"Lila, shut up. That has nothing to do with Violet."

I wasn't going to touch that one.

"You told me you'd leave your wife for me," Lila said.

"I never said that."

Millie sniffed, her watery gaze focused on Lila, and whispered, "You said you loved me."

Lila either didn't hear Millie or ignored her. "You said we'd go away together," she whined to Douglas.

Millie spoke up, pain lining her face. "*You* said we'd go to Mexico."

"Oh, shut up, Millie," Lila said.

Douglas grabbed Lila by the shoulders. "Listen, we'll straighten this out later. Right now, we need to blow out all these candles and cover this pentagram." He kicked at the chalk line, blurring it. "The cops could be here any minute."

Lila's chin jutted. "Are you going to leave your wife for me or not?"

"I said we'll talk about this later."

"I want an answer now."

A muscle throbbed in Douglas' jaw. He drew Lila closer.

"Douggie, you're hurting my shoulders," she whined.

"If you don't do as I say, I'm going to do more than that. I'm not losing all I've worked for because of your fucking temper tantrum."

What had he been working for? I threw fuel on the fire with the hope of finding out more. "Douglas, why don't you just tell the poor girl about our plans to elope?"

"Violet—" Douglas started.

"You bastard!" Lila slapped him.

I was glad to see someone else on the receiving end of

the slap-happy fairy. My cheek still stung from her last visit.

Douglas wasn't so giddy about it. He grabbed Lila's hand and squeezed, forcing her down onto her knees.

Whimpers rolled off her red lips.

"I told you never to do that again," Douglas said, a growl in his voice.

"Let her go!" Millie cried, rising.

"Now," he said to Lila, "are you going to do as I say?"

"Douglas doesn't love you, Lila," I said, boredom in my tone, as if I were inspecting my nail polish. I wasn't done fanning the flames yet. "He never will."

"Violet!" Douglas' angry bellow made Millie and me both jump. "Shut your fucking mouth." His voice had a razor sharp tone that made the hairs on my neck stand on end. "Or I'll shut it for good."

"Douggie." A tear slipped down Lila's face. "Please stop. You're really hurting me."

Millie took a step toward the pair, her hand rigid at her side, a serrated knife half-hidden in the folds of her skirt. She was a jack-in-the-box, almost ready to spring.

In spite of Douglas' threat, I fanned harder. I had no choice. I wasn't ready to free-fall down any mine shafts today. If I could just crank Millie's handle a little further … "Douglas, you and I both know Lila is too loose-lipped to pull this off. Her burning my Bronco was just the start. Next, she'll go after your wife. Then cops will rain down on you like a prairie cloudburst and all you were working toward will be lost. You need to get rid of Lila now, before all hell breaks loose."

"You don't know what you're talking about." Douglas said, still holding Lila down.

"Don't I? I've been attacked by her multiple times now, and you and I are just getting rolling." Rolling toward the end, I hoped, and not an end involving me tumbling headfirst down a mine shaft. "Your wife won't put up with what I have from Lila. She'll kick you to the curb in a heartbeat. I'm sure there are plenty of other suitors waiting in the wings for a chance to dip into her bank account. You'll lose your status, your financial backing, everything—all because of Lila's inability to control her jealousy."

Movement out of the corner of my eyes drew my gaze. Wanda no longer cowered in the corner. She stood with her back pressed against the wall, her mouse eyes darting, but no longer wide and crazed with fear. I reached behind my back, holding my open palm out toward her. I needed a weapon, any weapon, and Wanda was within reach of a few—if I could just keep everyone else distracted. When Wanda's focus landed on me, I tilted my head toward my open palm.

She nodded ever so slightly.

"I can help you, Douglas," I continued, sweat trickling down my back. Help him with what, I didn't know. "We don't need Lila."

"She has a point," Douglas said to Lila.

Tears ran down Lila's face. "But you love me."

"No. I don't." He bent Lila's wrist back, making her contort and cry out. "You've been sloppy. Because of your adolescent jealousy over Violet, the cops are sniffing around where they shouldn't be. You're going to blow this for me."

Blow what? I still didn't have a clue what we were talking about here.

Millie took another step toward the deranged duo, the knife still hidden in her skirt.

"I'll be good, I promise," Lila pleaded.

"You promised that after the last one, too, and look what happened to her."

What happened? Who was she? Was she still breathing?

Something touched my palm. Without checking to see what Wanda had handed me, I closed my fingers around it, then grimaced when I figured out what it was. It was just my luck to be bringing a seam ripper to a knife fight.

"Millie," Douglas said, his eyes narrowed on Lila. "Bring me some duct tape."

A roar of rage erupted from Millie. She charged Douglas, knife out and slashing.

He let go of Lila and raised his arm, shielding his face, backing away. His butt bumped the end table on which Lila's book sat. The table tipped. He grabbed the book, using it to block Millie, and knocked over the glass lamp with his elbow. The lamp hit the hardwood floor, shattering on impact.

Millie screamed and rampaged. Her slices flew like windmills at Douglas, whose arms had blood running down them as he backed into the entry hall.

Opportunity had arrived. I pushed to my feet. With the path to the door and freedom blocked, I hopped toward the tray of knives on the sideboard.

I reached for the wood-handled chef's knife, but a body slammed into me from behind, sending me crashing into the sideboard. My empty palm jammed into one of the drawer handles, pain firing up my arm. I slid to the floor and landed on my back, my legs bent under me.

Above me, a carving knife teetered on the edge of the sideboard, blade hovering in the air, wobbling. I rolled to my side as gravity won and the carving knife plunged, almost giving my belly a second button.

I had no time to breathe a sigh of relief before Lila plucked up the carving knife. She knelt over me, pinning me against the sideboard, knife raised in both hands.

"I hate you!" she screamed, and swung downward.

I rolled into her legs, throwing her off balance. The knife nicked my ribs, leaving a sharp ache.

She screeched and raised the knife again.

Oh, shit! Without thinking, I grabbed a handful of her hair and yanked. Her swing went wide, this time slicing along my forearm. Sudden, stinging pain burned up my arm.

Then I remembered the seam ripper in my other hand and palmed the handle, the tool's teeth pointing outward. I aimed at Lila's neck but missed and embedded the ripper in her shoulder.

She shrieked and reached for the ripper, giving me a window of time to scramble away and get my feet back under me.

I made it one hop away and she tackled me again, this time sending us both rolling across the floor and into the grandfather clock, which rattled and clanged in protest. Her knife slid out of reach.

I came out of the roll on top of Lila. She tried to buck me off, but I weighed more than her cellulite-free ass. I straddled her thighs as best I could with my ankles still bound.

She spit in my face. "I'm going to kill you, you cunt!"

Fury, fear, and adrenaline raced through me. I saw my hands gripping Lila's neck; her face turning red, then purple, her eyes wide, bulging.

Flailing and gurgling, she caught the edge of the grandfather clock, pulling it forward. It slammed into my back, knocking me off balance. She bucked again and shoved me off.

The clock's door clasp snagged my skirt, trapping my hips and thighs under it. I yanked, but something held me fast.

Gasping, Lila half-crawled to the carving knife she'd dropped. She grabbed it and whirled, screeching, and lunged down on me.

I screamed, blocking with my arms.

Wanda flew into my peripheral vision, swinging a fire poker like Babe Ruth. She connected with Lila's wrist, knocking the knife loose and sending it flying across the room.

Lila howled and kicked Wanda's leg, knocking the old woman down. The poker clattered to the floor, bouncing beyond my reach. *Damn it!*

I yanked and tugged on my skirt. Lila scooped up a blade-sized shard of the glass from the broken lamp and lunged at me again. Jesus, she was as relentless as the Terminator.

My skirt ripped free and I dodged and shoved, sending her stumbling over the broken clock and into the wall. I army-crawled across the wooden floor, glancing back to see Lila jump-start off the trim and rush toward me, her mouth wide with a battlefield yell.

Her raven hair partially covered her eyes, so she didn't see Wanda rolling toward her. Wanda kicked Lila's legs, tripping her and sending her flailing past me, headlong into the sideboard. She hit with a loud thud and fell at my feet, her back toward me.

I scrambled in reverse, putting floorboards between us before she could spring back into her *Bride of Chucky*-doll killing mode.

She didn't move.

In the silence, Wanda's breathing rasped as loudly as mine.

A pool of dark liquid formed next to Lila's head, soaking into her hair. The metallic smell of blood registered in my sinuses. I tasted it on my tongue.

I nudged Lila's leg. She remained motionless.

Wanda and I exchanged looks of fear and shock. I leaned forward and poked Lila's back.

Still no response.

Crawling toward her, I grabbed her shoulder and tugged. She flopped on to her back.

I gasped, covering my mouth with my hand at the sight of the glass shard from the broken lamp sticking out of her neck. Dark blood seeped out from her carotid artery, streaming down her milky white skin. Her empty eyes stared up at the ceiling.

A cry of anguish from the doorway made me jerk back.

Millie limped across the room, rolling pin in hand, nostrils bleeding, one eye bruised shut.

In the heat of my own battle, I'd forgotten about the other fighters in the ring. Millie had apparently taken a beating and given one right back, judging from the blood-smeared rolling pin. Where was Douglas? Was he sporting a serrated bread knife?

A low groan leaked in from the entry hallway, partially answering my question.

Millie dropped onto the floor and half-lifted Lila into her lap, cradling the dead woman against her breast, cooing to Lila's lifeless form as tears streamed down her cheeks.

My heart hurt at the sorrow etched on Millie's face, even though it was Lila she was mourning.

"Millie," I whispered. "I'm sorry. She fell."

I grabbed the chef's knife from the sideboard and cut the duct-tape binding my ankles. I rubbed my raw skin.

The sound of sirens drawing closer made my eyes water with relief. My hands trembled, my arms were streaked with blood. I dropped the knife. Struggling to my feet, I stumbled toward the door on wobbly legs and unsteady ankles. My adrenaline was petering out, leaving me tired to the bone. Outside beckoned with fresh air and freedom.

Douglas lay sprawled in the kitchen entryway, half of his face covered in blood. His chest rose and fell, so I didn't pause to give him a physical. I did snatch Lila's book out from under his shoulder.

I'd almost made it to the door when a rebel yell from behind me raised the hairs on the back of my neck.

I spun around to see Millie rushing at me with the rolling pin raised, her black Grim Reaper cape billowing, her face contorted in a maniacal snarl.

Feeling cornered and beaten to a nub, I did the only thing I could think of: screamed and barreled toward her, dodging her sloppy swing and ramming into her with my shoulder.

I pinballed off her, spinning into the wall as she stumbled backward. She tripped over Douglas and fell into the kitchen. My legs gave way and I slid down the wall.

I saw Millie pull herself to her feet and snag the rolling pin.

"Jesus fucking Christ!" I held up my arms, book still in hand. "I give up. Take me to the mine. Dump me down a shaft."

The sound of a shotgun cocking made my chin whip around.

"Millie," Wanda said in a firm, motherly voice, pointing double barrels at her daughter, "Put the rolling pin down."

Millie froze. "You and I both know you don't have the guts to kill me, Mother."

"Maybe not, but I'm mad enough to give you a limp. Now sit down over by the sink." After Millie obeyed, Wanda nodded at me. "Are you hurt?"

I looked down at my camisole covered in blood and sweat and dust bunny remains. "Only on the outside. Why didn't you tell me you had a shotgun in the house?"

"You didn't ask." She tilted her head to the side, looking as if she was picking up far-off radio signals. Then she gave a rueful half-smile. "Prudence says you're safe now. The lawmen are here."

Prudence? A fresh batch of chills quivered down my spine. I thought only Doc knew the name of the ghost.

"What else does Prudence have to say? Anything about teeth?"

Wanda glanced around behind her, but turned back to me with a frown. "She's gone."

I scratched my head at that, grimacing at the feel of my

matted hair. Confusion and shock tag-teamed in my brain, making me a little dizzy. A need for fresh air gave me newfound strength. I pushed myself up the wall to my feet.

Wanda steadied me with a hand on my shoulder. "I forgot to tell you what Prudence said earlier when I was cutting your wrists free."

All right, I'd bite. "What did she say?"

"To be careful around the deep mine."

"What deep mine?"

"She didn't say."

Prudence the enigmatic ghost could have tried to be less cryptic. The hills were littered with mines. "Wanda, how long have you known Prudence?"

"She started showing up after my husband died."

"You mean after Lila killed him." Whatever Douglas and Lila had been up to, Mr. Carhart must have gotten in their way.

"Lila didn't kill my father," Millie said in a tear-filled voice from her seat on the kitchen floor. "She was a good girl. She never hurt anyone."

Millie needed to have her head beamed back down to Earth. I had throbbing ribs and fingers that more than proved Millie wrong.

"So Douglas killed him?" But why? Knowing Douglas, I figured it had to have something to do with money.

"No." Millie's voice sounded as lifeless as her girlfriend. "I did it."

My jaw hit the floor next to Douglas. "Why?"

"He deserved it. The things Father did to me were wrong." She glared at her mother. "And you never stopped him. Not once."

Before I could wrap my head around Millie's accusation, footfalls pounded on the front porch.

"Wanda, put that gun down," I whispered, fearing they'd shoot her without asking.

"Open up! It's the police!" Cooper yelled through the door.

The cavalry had arrived.

Chapter Twenty-Four

Monday, August 13th

The Deadwood Police Station smelled like bacon—no joking. Bacon with a hint of maple. I found it an ironic touch as I approached the front desk and met the toothy grin of the gray-haired officer sitting behind it.

"Detective Cooper is waiting for me," I told his bulbous, Rudolph-like nose, avoiding his eyes.

My stomach growled clear to my toes. It was pissed because I hadn't fed it much over the last couple of days. It wasn't by choice. Every time I thought of food, cooking utensils such as bread knives and rolling pins covered with blood came to mind, followed by Lila's pale skin and matted hair.

"It's nice to see you all cleaned up and shiny again after the other night at the Carhart's," the desk officer said, picking up the phone.

Shiny? Did he mean my nose? I'd covered it twice with makeup, along with all the bruises, before Natalie had dropped me off in front of the station.

He punched a button on his phone, his grin now cockeyed. "When Cooper carried you out of the house, you looked a little rough around the edges."

A little? I was lucky I'd only had to take on Lila and not Millie. Douglas hadn't been so fortunate. His wounds had won him a ride out of there in the first ambulance on the scene.

"Cooper wasn't carrying me." I tapped the desk with

my index finger. "I want it on record that I walked out of that mess."

"Walked?" His furrowed brow called *Bullshit!*

"Okay, stumbled and leaned, but my feet were firmly grounded." My head? That was another story.

The desk officer smirked. "She's here," he said into the receiver.

My appointment with Cooper wasn't for another five minutes, so I walked over to the line of empty vinyl padded chairs propping up a wall covered with bulletin boards. Official announcements, charity fliers, and Wanted posters caked the corkboard. Air whooshed out of a chair's seat as I knelt on it to check them out.

"Well, well. Look what the cat left on our welcome mat," Cooper said before I was even three felons deep. He leaned on the corner of the front desk, all men's-magazine suave and relaxed in his jeans and button-up shirt. Except for his steely eyes. They never rested.

"Your shirt is buttoned wrong," I said.

"Your eyebrows are crooked," he replied.

I'd had trouble drawing them on with trembling hands, but he didn't need to know that. "You demanded my presence this morning."

"I didn't think you'd heed a mere request."

He was right.

I'd relived the whole Carhart debacle enough over the last two days while I mulled and vented, crying and swearing. Forty-eight hours of rest and recovery down on the prairie at my parents' place with the kids and Natalie had smoothed some of my ruffled feathers. However, now it was time to return to reality—and realty. Addy needed glasses. Layne needed shoes. And I needed a new vehicle.

"Want some coffee?" Cooper asked.

"I've already had a pot."

"A pot?" His eyes narrowed for a split second, then he

nodded. "Okay, then, let's do this." He led the way down the long hall.

I followed Cooper into his office and stopped at the sight of Fire Captain Reid lounging in the chair behind Cooper's desk. Reid's dark blue eyes sparkled, welcoming.

"Morning, Sparky," Reid said.

I shot him a small grin. "You've been talking to Harvey."

"More like he's been talking to me. He has a lot to say, especially when it comes to you."

I could only imagine. The old coot had left six messages on my cell phone in the last two days, each one longer and more detailed, full of juicy gossip regarding what folks around town were saying about me. My ghost-loving reputation had reached new levels of notoriety, it seemed. Woo-freaking-hoo.

Doc had Harvey beat by two messages, but his recordings had grown shorter with each call. He'd left the last one early this morning while I was watching Mom's coffeemaker drip. It was short and sweet—and terse as hell: *Call me, damn it!* He might have been chewing gravel when he said it.

Cooper sat on the corner of the desk and indicated that I should take the other chair.

"See, Coop," Reid said. "I told you Violet would bounce. She takes after her aunt."

Cooper frowned at me. "So long as she doesn't land in another one of my cases."

"Maybe you two could partner up," Reid's grin stretched to his earlobes. "Like Watson and Holmes."

"I prefer Cagney and Lacey," I said. "They dress prettier."

Reid's deep chuckle smoothed the rough edges off my morning. "Coop can play the sensitive one."

Cooper's lips flat-lined. "When you two ladies are done

comparing your monthly cycles, let me know. I have some questions for Violet."

"I thought you said you had things to tell me. You didn't mention that there'd be questions."

"I lied."

"A lying cop." I crossed my arms. "That inspires confidence."

"I don't mean to piss in your punchbowl, Violet, but my job is to catch the boogeyman, not hold your hand and tuck you in at night."

"You'll have to excuse Coop," Reid said. "His love is kind of scratchy."

I nodded. "Like a wool blanket. Got it. I'll have to watch for him trying to pull it over my eyes again."

Cooper groaned, scrubbing his hands down his face. "Christ! I only lied because I thought debriefing you would be easier if you were more relaxed."

I smiled. "I bet you say that to all the girls."

Reid laughed. "I believe you've met your match, Coop. It's no wonder your uncle has glued himself to her side."

Cooper shot Reid a look. "I'm beginning to regret allowing you to join this discussion."

"I thought it was a debriefing." I said. "You do realize that having a discussion means you have to give as well as take."

Cooper leaned forward, his eyelids squinty. "You have dark rings under your eyes and your right cheek keeps twitching. You sure you can handle what I have to give right now?"

"I face off against maniacal killers for kicks." I pushed back with a mother lode of false bravado. "Give me what you got."

"Douglas is awake and talking."

"You mean like able to talk in general, or spilling his guts?"

"The latter," Cooper said. "He's hoping for a reduced sentence if he gives us a tell-all biography."

"You think that'll happen?" Reid asked.

"That's not for me to decide."

I stretched my neck to the side, trying to loosen the tension that came with all the new nightmares over the last couple of nights. The Wolfgang Show now had competition for ratings. "So, what did Douglas have to say?"

"He's blaming Lila."

"Of course," Reid said. "She's dead. She can't dispute what he says."

Doc and Wanda might beg to differ, I thought wryly, but I kept my mouth shut.

Cooper picked up one of those grip-strengthening thingamajobbies from his desk. He squeezed it, making it creak. "Millie's story has a different slant. She says Lila never hurt anyone."

I rolled my eyes. I'd heard that song and dance before.

Cooper continued squeezing while he talked. "She claims Douglas is the puppeteer. All of this happened because of him."

"You realize Millie's jealous, right?" I asked and didn't wait for his answer to add, "Lila was having an affair."

Cooper nodded. "Lila and Millie? Yeah, you mentioned that when you were here last."

"No, I'm talking about Lila and Douglas." When I saw the questioning squint in Cooper's eyes, I added, "I saw them making out in the YMCA parking lot in Lead right before I went to the Carharts' on Friday. Plus, Lila threw herself at his feet right in front of me when I was tied up." I looked down at my hands. "Not to mention the whole Mudder Brothers incident during Junior's funeral."

"What Mudder Brothers incident?" Reid asked.

"Douglas groped Lila's ass when she was in the receiving line at Junior's funeral. George Mudder caught it on video."

Cooper's lips thinned. "You've been busy, Miss Parker."

"I had a house to sell. It's my duty to make sure no funny business is going on within its walls."

"You're my Realtor, too. What have you been digging up about me?"

I shrugged. "You like dogs and guns and Harleys."

Reid scoffed. "So does ninety-five percent of the male population in the hills."

Originality didn't appear to be Cooper's strong suit. I returned to a more exciting subject. "Millie told me she killed her father. She claimed abuse of some sort. Wanda witnessed her confession." Now that I'd seen Millie all crazy-eyed with the rolling pin in her hand, I had no problem believing her capable of murder.

"Wanda mentioned that," Cooper said, the grips creaking as he squeezed again. "Millie didn't deny it. Did she also tell you she killed her brother?"

"Shit. Wow. No." I sat back as that sank in. "She was just starting to air her dirty laundry when you interrupted us."

"Sorry, I thought you'd like to be rescued."

I already had been rescued by Wanda—three times— but I didn't rub that in. "How did you know for certain that I was at the Carharts'?"

"Wanda called 911."

"When?"

"While you were fighting with Lila, according to Wanda. Her call was short and sweet, something about you being in trouble and to send the sheriff."

Make that four times that Wanda saved me. "So, did Millie say why she killed Junior?"

"Not yet. I've had my own theory about her motive for the last few months, figuring it was something to do with money. Her and Wanda's hiring you to sell the house supported that theory."

Last few months? "You suspected Millie all along?"

Cooper nodded. "Her or Wanda."

"Why not Lila?" I asked.

"She didn't seem like the type who'd be willing to get her hands bloody."

After almost being carved to pieces multiple times by the whack-job, I'd beg to differ. "Lila planned to sacrifice me to raise some demon."

"Millie mentioned that when I asked about the pentagram and black cape. Apparently, Lila was deep into demonology and had a history of being involved with a group over by Yankton. They believe some old myths about the Black Hills being a door between dimensions. They've been under investigation multiple times for mutilating animals and performing sacrificial rituals. You would have been their first human sacrifice that we know of."

"Lucky me." So, Lila's creepy book was legitimate, at least in that circle. I wondered if Cooper heard about the book from Millie, if he'd ask me about its whereabouts, and whether I'd tell him the truth. I decided to change the subject before I had to face that dilemma. "So, if Lila was into demonology, what drew her to the Carharts? Was Junior involved with the same cult?"

"Millie said Junior had nothing to do with the cult shit."

"Then why him?" I asked.

"Neither Douglas nor Millie had answers for me on that one. All we know is that Junior hooked up with Lila at a bar in Lead. They were engaged a few weeks later. Two months after that, Millie killed her father and then her brother."

"There's a disconnect there. What aren't you telling me?"

He touched his nose, then pointed at me. "You made the connection for me when you were in here after your Bronco burned up, but I didn't realize it until they hauled you away in an ambulance Saturday. Lila seduced Millie, then convinced her to kill her father and Junior."

I knew Lila's hands were dirty with this somehow. "Why?"

"Location, location—something you real estate agents know all about. According to Millie, Lila firmly believed that some mega-powerful demon resides in the earth directly under the Carharts' house."

Goosebumps leapfrogged up my arms. Whether I bought the demon story or not, that was just plain disturbing.

"Lila needed Junior and his dad out of the way so she could perform her ritual. Millie said Lila had tried to get Junior to join in her beliefs, but he wouldn't take her seriously, so she'd turned to someone who did—Millie. Looking at the timelines, it appears she was already hooked up with Douglas by this point."

"But Douglas doesn't believe in demonology." He'd made that crystal clear the other night.

"No, but Douglas wanted the Carhart house. He said Lila overheard him offering to buy the place from Junior's old man one night in the bar. Douglas claims Lila followed him to his car and ... uh ..." Cooper squirmed just a little and looked down at his feet, "seduced him."

In other words, she screwed his brains out.

"Which I'd buy," Cooper continued, "if Douglas didn't have a history of seducing women himself."

"Do you think Douglas' wife knew about any of this?"

Cooper shrugged. "She does now."

"So, why did Douglas want the house so badly?"

"He'd bought the other properties all around the Carhart's place. He had big plans for the town of Lead in the form of a fancy resort overlooking the Open Cut, including a glass catwalk just like the one over the Grand Canyon. Only Mr. Carhart wouldn't budge."

"That's ironic," I said.

"Why's that?" Reid asked.

"Because when Millie killed her father, he was planning on selling the house to Douglas so he could run off with Claudette Perkins."

"Uncle Willis mentioned that yesterday," Cooper said, his nostrils flared in a huff. "You should have told me about Claudette as soon as you found out."

"I didn't realize you were still on the case. You basically told me the case was closed and I should mind my own business."

"It was—as far as everyone needed to know—and you should have listened to me." Cooper squeezed the grips.

"Had I listened, we probably wouldn't be sitting here with those two locked up and the case solved."

"She has a point." Reid took my side.

Cooper growled, "Don't you have a fire to put out somewhere?"

"So, Millie killed her father as a result of the history of abuse and with Lila urging her on," I said. "But why did she kill Junior? Was he abusive, too? Or was that Lila's doing?"

Cooper's upper lip curled a little. "Millie claims she did it for love. She swears Junior was hurting Lila. That Lila would have bruises on her arms and cheeks the mornings after Junior drank."

"But Benjamin said Junior was a friendly drunk."

Cooper's head cocked to the side, his eyebrows drawn. "Benjamin who?"

"Never mind." I needed to protect my sources. "How do we know that Lila wasn't faking those bruises just to get Millie to do her dirty work?"

"We don't, and we probably never will, now."

"So," Reid chimed in. "Lila convinced Millie to kill her own father and brother?"

When Cooper nodded, I asked, "Does that mean she'll

get a shorter prison sentence?"

"I don't know. That's not for me to determine."

Good old irony. If Millie's father had just tried to unload the property to Douglas and run off to Florida with Claudette a week or two earlier, he might still be alive. I'd still have my Bronco, Douglas would have the property he wanted, and Lila ... well, she could be dilly-dallying with demons.

"So, we know Douglas wanted the property," I said, "but do you know for sure whether he played any part in the Carharts' deaths? What did Millie mean about his playing puppeteer?"

"Millie said he used Lila, convincing her to seduce Junior and then to try to get to the old man, too. I'm figuring Douglas also put Lila up to seducing Millie, although Millie claims that Lila really loved her, that it wasn't just an act."

Love was blind, apparently even from the backside of Coke-bottle lenses.

"Douglas' story about Lila is a bit different. He says Lila couldn't get Junior to do what she wanted, which was to help her raise a demon, so she moved on to Millie."

Poor Millie, looking for love in all the demonic places.

"Lila lied to Millie," Cooper continued. "She told her if the Carhart men were eliminated, the house would belong to Millie. Then they could sell it to Douglas and run away together to Cancun."

"Why would Millie think the house would go to her and not Wanda?" Reid asked.

"Millie said Lila showed her a copy of old man Carhart's will that said the kids got everything. But what Lila apparently didn't notice was that the will wasn't finished yet. There was no final signature. Which meant that after they killed him, Wanda got it all, including the house, per the old will."

Reid leaned back and steepled his fingers. "But Wanda wasn't interested in selling."

"Right," Cooper said. "Not until they convinced her that her dead husband was haunting the place."

"And that's where I came in. They needed a Realtor." I had a feeling that Millie's claim about being rejected by other real estate agents was a bunch of hooey.

"Exactly, and it had to be a Realtor who was desperate enough to try to sell the house after having a murder-suicide occur there half a year earlier."

I wrinkled my nose at Cooper. "Desperate?"

He grinned. "If the shoe fits."

"Bend over and I'll see."

Chuckling, Reid said, "You won't make it past the stick wedged up there."

Cooper shot Reid a squint. "Are you going to hop on her bandwagon every time?"

"I like her tune."

"You're just kissing her ass so she'll help you with Zoe."

"Help you with Aunt Zoe how?" I asked Reid.

He sprang to his feet. "You hear that? Sounds like a fire whistle."

I didn't hear anything besides Cooper and that hand-grip thing.

"Violet, try not to burn anything down for a while." Reid squeezed my shoulder briefly. "Later, Coop." I thought I heard him utter, "Big mouth," as he closed the door behind him.

Creak, creak, creak.

I cleared my throat. "So, Douglas wanted the land and used Lila to get it. Lila wanted to wake up a demon, so she played along with Douglas and used Junior and then Millie to do her bidding. Millie was in love with Lila and killed off the family members she didn't like so much to impress her girlfriend. Does that pretty much cover it?"

"Yes."

"Where does Wanda fit into this mess?"

"In spite of Millie and Lila's attempt to frame her and then scare her with Carhart's ghost, she doesn't fit into it. Which leads me to one of the main reasons I asked you here. Who's Prudence?"

"Uh." I grimaced. "Who?"

"Wanda mentioned that Prudence was there in the house with you guys during the big showdown. She said Prudence told her to call for help during your fight with Lila."

"I didn't see anyone else." No lie there.

Cooper's eyes narrowed. "Wanda wanted me to give you a message from Prudence. Something about the power of the teeth."

The teeth had power? How could teeth have any power? "Hmm. Wanda must be suffering from post-traumatic stress. I don't know anything about someone named Prudence or her teeth."

"Violet Parker," those steely eyes held me prisoner. "If you're lying to me, I'm going to lock you up for withholding evidence."

I had a gut feeling that he wasn't joking. "Oh, you mean *those* teeth."

"Yeah." He tossed the hand gripper on the desktop. "Those teeth. I want to see them."

"Fine." He could have the teeth, but he wasn't getting the book. "I'll drop them off when I have a chance."

"You do that. Is there anything else you need to show me?"

"That's a loaded question."

He tilted his head to the side. "Anything having to do with this case? Anything about this Prudence woman Wanda keeps prattling on about?"

"No." Prudence was a ghost, if she even existed. It was

hard to show him someone he couldn't slap cuffs on. Besides, I was still digesting all this ethereal business myself, along with the facts that Doc and Wanda both knew Prudence's name, Jane knew of the ghost woman's slit throat, and Millie had refused to go up in the attic because of a dead old lady—which may or may not have been Prudence.

Cooper's desk phone beeped. He frowned and punched a button on it. "This better be good."

"Your uncle is here and threatening to come back there."

"I told you no visitors."

"He's being rather insistent. Short of me arresting him, he seems to be unstoppable." A crash and spew of curses sounded through the speaker, then there was a pause. "Do you want me to arrest him?"

"No, she's on her way out." Cooper hung up the phone and rubbed the back of his neck. "We're done for now. Your ride is here."

I stood. "Have you heard anything back about the foot Layne found? Or that hand from Mount Roosevelt?"

He frowned at me, the set line of his jaw giving the impression he'd locked it up tight. Then he surprised me with "Not yet, but I'll let you know when I do."

I nodded and decided to get the hell out of there before he changed his mind about letting me go.

"Don't forget to bring me those teeth," he said to my back.

Harvey waited for me at the far end of the long hallway. "We're leaving?" he asked.

I kept walking right past him. "Immediately. My boss is waiting for me at work." Unfortunately, that was the God's honest truth per Jane's phone message this morning, which had me almost as anxious as spending time in a small, enclosed space with Cooper.

"I'll drive you," Harvey said.

"It's just a block or two away."

"Fine, then you can drive me."

"Harvey," I paused and held the main door for him. "Have you forgotten that I am currently wheel-less?"

"Not at all." He took my hand and placed a set of warm keys with a smiley faced keychain in it. "Use it," he insisted when I started to resist. "Just for now. You have kids. You need a vehicle." He grabbed my wrist and led me into the sun-warmed parking lot. "I cleaned her up and gave her a waxing. She looks almost as good as new."

Pigpen's hay and manure scent was gone, that was something. I smiled at the old coot and held up the keys. "Thanks for letting me borrow your ... what do you call it?"

"Picklemobile."

"Right. Do you need a ride somewhere?"

"Same place as you. I have an appointment with Doc this morning."

Doc. My heart panged at just the sound of his name. Shrugging off the pain, I pulled open the pickup door. I'd deal with that situation later.

I climbed behind the wheel and started the Picklemobile. She smoked and burped, then sputtered to life. Harvey patted the dash and grinned. "That's my girl."

"Anything I need to know about her?" I asked as we bounced out onto the street, her steering wheel shimmying in my hands.

"She has a loose spring in her step, gets the farts every now and then, and wheezes when you stomp on the gas too hard. Other than that, she runs like a dream."

I pulled into the parking lot behind Calamity Jane's and killed the engine. A loud boom echoed off the hills, making me jump and yelp. "What was that?" I asked, looking around.

"I told you she farts."

Oh, Christ. My clients were going to love this.

Harvey and I parted ways in the parking lot. I took a deep breath before stepping inside Calamity's back door. Based on Jane's somber tone in her message this morning, I had a feeling shit was about to spray forth from a large fan.

"Violet," Jane called to me as I passed her office door. I backed up and smiled in at her, pretending everything was hunky dory. "Come to my office as soon as you settle in. Bring Ray."

My stomach sank to my ankles. "Okay."

I didn't bother with coffee.

"Doc Nyce is trying to get hold of you," Mona told me as I put my purse down on my chair. She walked over and placed a handful of Post-its on my desk calendar. "I think he's a little anxious about seeing his house."

And something else, but I didn't bother to elaborate for her. "Thanks, Mona." He'd called almost every twenty minutes this morning.

Her palm lightly squeezed my shoulder, making me look up. "You okay, Vi?"

I patted her hand. "Yeah, thanks."

"That's my girl." She pushed her glasses back up on her nose. "Jane has something for you."

A pink slip? I winced. "I know." I noticed Ray's empty chair. "Where's Ray?"

The toilet flushed, answering my question.

Ray strolled out as I headed down the hall to Jane's office.

"I'm surprised you didn't burn the Carhart house to the ground, too," he said, a smartass grin on his lips.

I reached out and popped him in the nose ... in my fantasy land where dreams come true. In reality, I flipped him off and said, "Jane wants to talk to us."

"Oh, this is going to be good."

I followed him into Jane's office, her signature floral

perfume making me nauseated today.

"Close the door," she said, her painted lips ruler-straight.

The click of the door echoed in my brain.

"Have a seat," she ordered. "Both of you."

Ray lazed back in the chair. "How's the divorce going, Jane?"

"Shut up, Ray," she answered.

I gulped. Something told me we weren't going to join hands and sing *Kumbaya* anytime soon.

"Violet." She set down the pen. "Ray tells me you went behind my back and told Dane Nyce that he could live in his office until his house came available."

I sucked up my nervous-Nelly nausea and owned up. "That's true. He had nowhere to stay due to the bike-rally crowd. It seemed like the right thing to do for my client."

"Yet you knew that was not allowed per his lease."

"Yes, I did."

I glanced at Ray, the tattletale. His grin fanned wrinkles over his tanned face. Fury burned in my veins, heating my core.

"Well, while I don't condone disobeying my rules, I do applaud your willingness to take such a risk in order to please a customer."

I blinked. Had I heard that right? I shot a look at Ray. His shit-eating grin wasn't so big or bright anymore. His brow furrowed, funneling into the center of his forehead.

Jane opened her desk drawer. "Violet, I have something to give you." She pulled out a manila envelope that rattled when she handed it to me. "Congratulations. You sold your first house."

Jaw gaping, I opened the envelope. Inside was a set of keys and a check. Relief rushed from my head to my toes, leaving me feeling loose-jointed. "Thanks, Jane."

"No. Thank you." She looked over at Ray, whose

unhappiness at my success had settled into his jowls. "Now, do you think you and Ray can get along well enough to work together, or will I have to fire one of you to settle your differences?"

"I can get along with him." Or beat him with my boot until he behaves.

Ray grunted. "I'll leave her alone."

"Excellent, Ray," Jane said. "Because I've recently overheard some of your comments to Violet, and you're way over the line when it comes to sexual harassment—even for a small town like Deadwood. I'm assuming this has been going on for some time, but I was too distracted by my damned divorce to notice—until now." Her gaze narrowed as she spoke those last two words. "I still have your nephew's résumé. Violet isn't the only employee who can be replaced. Understand?"

I heard the whisper of a growl under his breath before he answered, "Got it."

"Now, go sell something," Jane said, dismissing us. I followed Ray to the door. "Oh, Violet, hold up a second. Close the door behind Ray."

I obeyed and leaned against the closed door.

"It has been brought to my attention that you may be involved with your client."

Ray! That son of a bitch.

"I don't want to know if this is true or not. But I trust it will not become the norm for you, because believe me when I say that mixing business with pleasure only leads to misery. I know that from experience. Husbands number one and two were both clients."

"I understand."

Jane smiled. "Congratulations, again. I'd like to take you to lunch to celebrate and discuss what your options are with the Carhart house. The Britton couple stopped in yesterday on their way out of town. I briefly disclosed the events that occurred this weekend at the house." She paused, her smile slipping. "Are you okay? I can see the bruises under your makeup."

"I'm fine, thanks."

"Anyway, they went outside and talked for a few minutes and came back in saying they're still interested in buying it if the seller is going to keep it on the market. They'll be in touch with you."

No freaking way. "Okay." I'd have to check with Wanda when the dust settled. If the Brittons bought the place, maybe I'd finally find out the reason behind the mystery of the always-missing ice trays.

I exited Jane's office before another of my skeletons could be dragged out of the closet and held under a spotlight.

Back at my desk, I stuffed the envelope with my check and Doc's keys into my purse and grabbed the Picklemobile's smiley-face key chain. "Mona, I'm going to run home for a bit and take a quick shower." More like hold my head under the water with hopes of washing away the insanity of the last few weeks. "If Doc calls again, tell him I'll be in touch very soon."

Mona held up her half of the commission check from the sale of Doc's house, her eyes radiant. "We need to have some celebratory drinks soon."

"Yes, we do."

I paused by Ray's desk.

He glared at me. "What do you want?"

"I warned you."

"So what."

"I meant what I said, Mr. King of the Mountain."

"Bring it on, Blondie."

"I plan to." After blowing him a kiss, I strode out the back door.

Chapter Twenty-Five

Forty-five minutes later, Aunt Zoe caught me staring out her kitchen window at the empty swing set in the backyard. Lila was no longer around to threaten me and mine, but the kids were enjoying splashing around in my parents' pool so much that I'd left them there for the week as originally planned.

"You have a big problem," Aunt Zoe told me.

Hysterical laughter erupted in my head, threatening to spill out my throat. "I have multiple big problems. To which are you referring?"

She leaned back against the counter next to me. "The one involving a fancy Camaro."

Ah, yes. Doc. That particular problem. I kept my gaze glued on the swings and said nothing.

"Doc stopped by yesterday, looking for you. Said he'd been calling your cell but you weren't answering."

"I had it turned off," I lied.

"You need to talk to him. He deserves at least a phone call."

Biting my lip, I breathed through the anxiety that squeezed my lungs. Just the thought of Doc sent my satellites spinning off into outer space. How could I possibly face him and say what I needed to say?

"You should have seen him on Friday," Aunt Zoe said, scratching some dried food off the countertop. "He stopped by here around one, telling me you didn't show up for some lunch meeting with him."

Lunch dates with Doc appeared to be hazardous to my health. That was another reason to tell him the lines I'd been repeating in my head since yesterday morning, when Natalie told me how her love for Doc has made her want to try to be a better, smarter woman. It was a corny line that reminded me of something Tammy Wynette would have crooned, but it had pierced my guilt-filled heart nonetheless.

"He insisted I call 911," Aunt Zoe continued, "but I explained the police probably wouldn't do anything until you'd been gone a bit longer. That wasn't good enough for him."

I lowered my gaze to where I gripped the edge of the sink, the ache in my chest spreading down to my gut.

"I rode with Doc down to the police station, since you had my truck. He demanded to see Detective Cooper, who surprised me by accepting the gravity of the situation immediately. By suppertime, most of Lead's and Deadwood's finest were on the lookout for you, asking questions. Doc never stopped searching. He checked in with me throughout the evening. I tried to get him to stay, to eat something, but he refused, muttering something about a tattoo, blaming himself. It didn't make sense to me."

The ache bubbled north now, up into my throat.

"Doc even went to the Carhart's—twice. I was with him the second time. I'll tell you, that Millie Carhart is one cool cucumber. She could have won an Oscar for her Norman Bates-style innocence. I hope they lock her up and throw away the key."

"Millie is insane." There was no other explanation for a woman of such extremes.

Aunt Zoe squeezed my shoulder. "Doc was there when Cooper led you out of the Carharts' place, you know. He tried to get to you, but the police restrained him. At the hospital, they allowed only family through. Natalie sneaked in—she used to date one of the policemen guarding your door."

I raised my eyes to the ceiling and sighed. God, this was going to hurt like hell.

"Sweetie," Aunt Zoe waited for me to meet her gaze before carrying on. "I don't know what's going on between you and Doc, but that man went through his own personal hell Friday until you were safe in the hospital. At the least, you need to call him back and thank him."

Stiff as Wild Bill's bronzed bust, I whispered, "Natalie thinks she's in love with him."

Aunt Zoe's eyebrows drew together. "When you were a little girl, time and again I'd watch you give up whatever toy you were playing with to avoid a fight with your sister or brother." Her voice soothing, she combed my hair back from my face. "Don't you think it's time to start fighting?"

"At what cost, though? Natalie's been my best friend since Barbie and Ken ruled our world."

"Only you can decide that, Violet." She kissed my temple. "Call him."

* * *

I pulled up in front of Doc's new house, parking behind his Camaro, and killed the Picklemobile's engine. A loud shotgun-blast boomed from her tailpipe. I cringed. Crows scattered from the trees, squawking at me as they flew away.

A glance in the rearview mirror confirmed that my hair remained firmly wrapped in a chignon, my lip gloss was still shiny, my bruises still mostly covered. Grabbing the keys, I stepped out onto the sidewalk and faced the task in front of me. There was no avoiding this, especially since Doc was sitting on the front porch steps, waiting, watching, glowering.

He was probably still pissed about earlier, on the phone,

when I'd cut him short. I'd called to set up a time to hand off the keys this afternoon and hadn't wanted to carry on over the phone, especially with Jane sitting across from me at the table, drinking her way through my celebratory lunch. Divorce was a bitch. All the more reason not to let this thing between Doc and me go any farther.

I avoided his glare, skirting him, literally. My lavender sundress swished against his shoulder as I climbed the steps. "Ready?"

"You're late."

"Sorry, I had to take care of something before coming over." Jeff Wymonds' house was officially for sale now, Calamity Jane Realty sign in the yard and all. Lucky for me, the jerky-loving oaf wasn't there to talk any more about sowing his stupid oats when I went to plant the sign in his grass. Next on the docket was Cooper's place, but first I had to say goodbye to Doc and his house keys.

The floorboards creaked as he came up behind me while I unlocked the door. I pushed the door open and held out my arm for him to go ahead. "Welcome to your new home," I said, trying to really mean it, banana-wide smile and all.

"Shut up, Violet." Doc grabbed my arm and dragged me inside, slamming the door behind us. The dining-room windows rattled in their frames for a moment, then silence cocooned us.

The scent of fresh-baked cookies and floor wax met us in the foyer. I glanced into the living room, noting the carpet weave crisscrossed with steam cleaner tracks. A vase of fresh daisies sat on the mantel. Damn, Mona was good.

"Well?" Doc asked, still holding onto my arm.

I met his glare and gulped at the fury there. Ugh, I wasn't ready for this. "I wonder if they left the bird bath behind." I pulled my arm from his grasp and headed through the dining room toward the kitchen and patio doors.

Doc followed on my heels. "Why haven't you answered my goddamned phone calls for the last three days?"

"It's only been two days."

"Almost three," he said, grinding the words between his teeth.

I padded into the kitchen and stopped. The polished hardwood floor shone like glass under the bright can lights. The appliances gleamed, the counters were crumb-free. My kids would scuff, scratch, and fingerprint this room within a day.

"Violet?"

I could feel his warm breath on the back of my neck. There was no avoiding this. I turned and met his dark gaze. "I needed some time to think about how to handle things—like you."

"Have you made a decision?"

"I think so."

He leaned back against the pantry door, crossing his arms over his chest. His jeans hung low on his hips. His brown T-shirt pulled snug across his shoulders and biceps, tempting me with what lay beneath.

"Let me guess," he said. "You think we should stop seeing each other."

Was that what we were doing? Seeing each other? Officially? "Yes."

"Is this about Natalie?"

I nodded. "And the kids."

He stared at me, his face a hard, brooding mask. "Any other reasons?"

"My job. My boss thinks mixing clients and sex is bad business."

"Right, your boss." He cocked his head to the side. "Isn't she in the midst of her second divorce right now?"

"Third."

"Exactly. What else do you have?"

"Well, there's you."

"What about me?"

"You believe in ghosts."

"And you still don't?"

"I don't know." Prudence really rocked my world. How could Doc and Wanda both know her name? "How well do you know Wanda Carhart?"

"I met her that one time at her house with you." He pushed away from the pantry door and took a step toward me. "Why? Does she think you getting involved with me is a bad idea, too?"

"Listen, smartass," I started.

He closed the gap between us. "No, you listen."

I waited, listening, hands on my hips. The Doc-smitten parts of my body tingled, darn it. "What?" When he continued to drill me with a fierce stare, I added, "I'm listening."

"Never mind," he said and grabbed my shoulders. His lips swooped in, stealing a kiss, and then another, and then a third. I tried to fight the flood of hunger and lust and need, but he tasted like sweet forbidden fruit, and I was a sucker for strawberry wine and peach schnapps.

My arms snaked around his neck, drawing him closer. He groaned. His hands smoothed down my ribs, spanning my hips. His tongue toyed with mine, teasing, tasting. My head spun as a dust devil of want and longing destroyed everything in its path.

When he pulled back we were both huffing.

"What about that?" he asked.

"What about what?" My husky voice matched his. Within seconds, he'd knocked down almost three days of wall building. I was hopeless. I couldn't fight it. Fuck.

"You know exactly what. There's no controlling that. Believe me, I've tried. It's not going to go away."

"That's another reason this has to end."

"Jesus, Violet. Aren't you just a little bit curious to see where this could go?"

"I know exactly where it goes, Doc. I've taken this road before. It always ends up with me alone." I poked his chest with my index finger. "If things don't work out for us, what do you lose?"

"You."

"Besides me?" When he just looked at me, I answered for him. "Nothing. But you know what I lose? My best friend."

"You don't know that."

"She believes she's in love with you."

"That's not my fault. Nor is it yours."

"Fault? That doesn't matter. Natalie thinks she's in love. Period." I crossed the glossy floor to the counter, needing space between us. "I'm not willing to take a chance and lose Natalie just because I can't keep my underwear on when I'm around you."

"You think this is just about sex?"

"Yes." That wasn't true. "No." But sex did play a large part in it. I squeezed my temples. "I don't know, Doc. What's it about?"

"Violet, you're the only person alive who knows the truth about me."

"What's that mean?" I wasn't sure what I wanted from him, but I wasn't going to make the mistake of reading anything into his words.

"It means ... Damn it, I can't stop thinking about you." He raked his fingers through his hair. "Not having you in my life would make it a hell of a lot easier."

Okay, that was definitely not what I'd hoped he meant. "You could use some schooling on wooing."

"I'm a little rusty."

"More than a little."

He jammed his hands in his pockets. "When you disappeared Friday, it scared the shit out of me."

"Aunt Zoe told me you felt responsible. You shouldn't have."

"What I felt had nothing to do with responsibility." His eyes explored my face for a moment, searching. "Violet, I can't guarantee you any kind of happily ever after. Shit, we haven't even gone on a date yet. But I'm not running away, anymore. Not from the ghosts, not from you. I've bought this house. I'm building my business. I'm here to stay and see things through. Are you?"

My cell phone rang.

Crud. "I have to get that. It might be Jane."

He nodded.

I pulled it from my pocket and checked the phone number. My heart twanged. "It's Natalie."

His face tightened with what I guessed was frustration. He looked to the ceiling and swore, confirming my presumption. When his gaze came back to mine, his eyes were withdrawn, his expression flat. "Take the call."

"Doc—"

"Let yourself out when you're done. You know where the door is."

He left me standing there with a ringing phone and a torn heart as he crashed up the back stairs where we'd shared our first kiss.

"Hello?" I said into my phone.

"Hey, girlfriend. I'm thinking pizza and beer tonight for therapy. What time are you done with work?"

Doc's footfalls creaked overhead. I tracked his path across the upstairs bedroom floor. He was right above me, probably at the window.

"Vi?" Natalie said.

I looked out the patio doors at the backyard. The birdbath sat there, a lone sparrow splashing in a small puddle at its center.

"Vi, are you there?"

"Yeah." I closed my eyes, taking a deep breath. "Natalie, I'm sorry, but I can't hang tonight. Something's come up at work."

"Are you okay? Do you need help?"

"Always," I said, and she chuckled. "I'm fine. I just need to take care of something."

"All right. If you need me, you know how to reach me."

"Thanks, Nat."

"For what?"

"Being such a great friend."

"Who loves you, babe?"

"Back at ya," I said and clicked my phone shut, tossing it on the counter.

The stair steps complained under my sandals. I found Doc right where I'd envisioned, staring out the window.

"You didn't leave," he said without looking at me.

"No, I didn't." I crossed my arms over my chest. "And yes, I am," I said with finality.

He frowned at me. "Yes, you are what?"

"Here to stay. Or at least try staying."

His eyes narrowed. "What about Natalie? Your kids? Your boss?"

I shrugged. "It's going to be rocky as hell."

A hint of a smile creased his lips. "But you like it rough."

"Especially from you."

His lazy grin came out to play. "Come here."

I obeyed, standing close, inhaling the woodsy aroma of his aftershave warmed by his skin. Anticipation had my knees quivering.

His fingers brushed over my face, his grin fading. "Lila really did a number on you. How are your other injuries?" He briefly inspected my bandaged forearm and thumb.

"Healing quickly." I was still a little stiff and sore, but nothing a handful of ibuprofen couldn't fix.

"Good," he said. "Kiss me."

Okay. "On one condition."

"Name it."

"There's no hiding shit from me from here on out. Ghosts or not, you tell me."

He chewed on that for a moment, then nodded. "Deal, but same goes for you. Now kiss me."

I stood on my tiptoes, cupped his face, and brushed my lips over his.

A growl rose up from deep in his throat. "No." He whirled me around and shoved me up against the wall. "Like this."

His mouth crushed mine. Frenzied, stormy. A flurry of need blew into me, rocking my world. His teeth nipped my lips, his tongue licking the wounds. I spun, drowning, in a whirlpool of lust.

He came up for air, dotting my mouth with butterfly kisses, teasing. My body pulsed and ached.

"Is that all you've got?" I whispered, reaching for his fly.

"Vixen." He captured my hands, gently pinning them over my head. "I wanted to try taking it slow this time."

"I don't want it slow." I squirmed, yearning tightening my muscles, craving release. "Not right now."

He trailed his free hand down the side of my breast, skimming, tantalizing. "How do you want it, Boots?"

"Hard." I moved my torso trying to make his hand touch where I wanted. "Deep and hard."

His breath hitched, but his palm drifted lower, sliding over my hip. "You already said 'hard.'"

"I know." I leaned forward and licked his lower lip, then bit it. "I want you to make me scream."

His eyes darkened, his pupils inky black pools. "You're

so damned hot."

"Doc," I breathed his name. Slipping one of my hands free, I guided his fingers to the throbbing center of my body. "Hurry up and touch me."

He resisted, teasing, brushing, then skirting. His lips met mine, his tongue seducing me.

Tension coiled even tighter. I whimpered, wiggling against him, and wrapped my leg around his thigh.

He trailed his mouth along my jaw, his teeth grazing my earlobe. "Violet," he said, his tone gritty. "If you don't stop rubbing against me like that, I'm not going to last long enough to get my pants off."

"But you feel so good. I can't stop."

"Jesus." He let go of my other hand and lifted my dress, tearing at my panties.

I helped, shimmying out of them as he struggled with his jeans.

He brushed my hands aside and kicked off his pants. I dropped to my knees, kissing the warm skin below his bellybutton.

"There's no time for that, Boots."

He hauled me back up and lifted me, pinning my back against the wall. I wrapped my legs around his waist, rubbing up and down the length of him.

"Now, Doc."

"Your dress is in the way."

I yanked it up around my waist and shifted against him, sliding down onto him. Pleasure rippled across his face as he sank all of the way inside.

"God, Violet." He cupped my hips. "You're so ready."

"I was ready last week."

He chuckled, then pulled out and slammed back into me, shoving me hard into the wall. The clip holding my chignon dug into the back of my skull, so I yanked it out, shaking my hair free.

"So sexy." He nuzzled my neck and he bore into me. "Your hair smells like peaches and cream." He tore my dress strap down, exposing my right breast. "My favorite dessert."

I held his head against me as his tongue flicked. "Doc," I said, riding the upward spiraling waves of pleasure growing with each push and pull. "I can't wait for you."

"Don't," he clutched my hips, driving harder, pushing me further up the wall.

I didn't. Ecstasy crashed through me. Then Doc reached between us and touched me, rubbing with his thumb, and I really blew a gasket. I didn't realize I was crying out until Doc covered my mouth with his and silence filled the room. I relaxed around him, still pulsing.

He grabbed my hips and gave one final shove and groan into my mouth. Shudders racked him, his muscles trembling under my hands and legs. He pulled away from my lips and leaned his head on my shoulder as more quakes shook him. Then his body stilled, his breaths slowing.

I ran my fingers through his hair. My heart felt full, warm, and cozy. My body tingled like I'd just been zapped back to life.

"Violet," he said against my shoulder.

"Yeah?"

"That was one hell of a housewarming gift."

"I aim to please."

His soft laughter vibrated against me. "I want more."

"Me, too."

"I mean right now," he said, rocking my hips, grinding.

"Giddy up," I said under my breath.

He bumped against my *Go* button and my breath caught. *Oh! Wow!* That was new.

Doc's pants rang.

"Damn." He hesitated, looking at me.

The desire glowing in his eyes sent thrill-filled jitters

through me. I did that to him. The knowledge made my head float.

"Get it," I told him. "I'm not going anywhere." The kids were at my parents' and Aunt Zoe was just a quick phone call away. For once, I didn't have to leave the party early.

He let me slide to the floor. My feet were prickly with a lack of blood flow.

Doc shuffled through his pants, digging his phone out of his pocket. He frowned at the number. "It's Harvey."

Of course. "See what he wants now."

Doc answered, listened for a moment, and then held the phone out to me. "He wants to talk to you."

What? I hadn't expected that. I took the phone. "What's going on, Harvey?"

His breath rasped, like he'd been rushing about. "Have you ever seen a headless corpse?"

I blinked. Twice. I'd expected a razzing for being with Doc. His question threw me off guard. "No. Why would you ask me that?"

"Because ol' Red just dug one up back in my cemetery."

My chest seized for several seconds. We'd never get his ranch sold at this rate. "Have you called Cooper?"

That got Doc's attention. He froze in the midst of zipping up his pants, his gaze questioning.

"Not yet," Harvey answered.

"Why not?"

"I thought of you first."

"Why me?"

"Because I found your business card in its hand."

THE END ... for now

Five Fun Facts about Ann Charles

Three of my favorite parks or recreation areas in the United States are The Valley of Fire State Park in Nevada, Leslie Gulch Recreation Area in Oregon, Badlands National Park in South Dakota. (It appears I am attracted to the visible effects of erosion.)

* * *

Three of my favorite movies are *The Mummy*, *Tremors*, and *Twister*. I've watched each of them easily over fifty times.

* * *

I love classic Detroit steel and muscle cars. One of these days, I will have my own fixed-up classic car, it will be painted dark purple, and I will crank Steppenwolf's song, *Magic Carpet Ride*, while cruising in it.

* * *

The illustrator and cover artist for my books, C.S. Kunkle, also happens to be my older brother, who began putting up with me when he was four years old and our parents forced him to share a room with me and my crib.

* * *

I love taking long road trips, stopping at odd tourist attractions, and finding out what is around the next bend ... and the next.

Sneak Peak!

Want a sneak peak at Ann Charles' third book, *Dead Case in Deadwood**, in the Deadwood Mystery series? Read on ...

*Dead Case in Deadwood will be available online and in print in early 2012.

Chapter One

There was something downright fishy about the corpse filleted on the autopsy table in front of me.

Besides the fact that his head was missing.

Across the chilled body, Detective "Coop" Cooper frowned at me. A Daniel Craig doppelganger right down to his granite cheekbones, Cooper had telephoned at the butt crack of dawn and ordered me to meet him in the basement of the Mudder Brothers Funeral Parlor before I headed in to work at Calamity Jane Realty.

Call me crotchety, but I didn't like being bossed around, especially before I'd injected caffeine into my system. "I told you when you dragged me into your office earlier this week, Detective, that I have no idea who this guy is."

Cooper's stainless-steel-colored eyes squinted at me, not missing a single one of my blinks. I wondered if he practiced his gunslinger stare-down in the mirror every night while he brushed his teeth.

Facing off with Cooper hadn't been on my agenda for today, but I'd be damned if I'd let him intimidate me over a dead guy who just happened to be palming my business card post mortem. I lifted my chin and added for good measure, "Standing here looking at the body changes nothing."

"Miss Parker," Cooper spoke through a clenched jaw, a practice I recognized from dealing with my nearly ten-year-old fraternal twins. "You have to at least look at the body before stating for the record that you don't recognize the victim."

"What's there to look at? His head is gone."

Cooper's nostrils flared. Surly bulls had nothing on him. "Do you recognize any other parts of him?"

"Like what parts in particular?"

"The remaining ones."

"Nope."

Cooper growled loudly enough for me to hear. "Look before you answer."

"Fine." I took a deep breath, thankful for the overwhelming scent of bleach-based cleaner in the air, and willed the troop of monkeys bouncing around in my gut to sit still. I could do this. No problem. It was just a dummy. A mannequin. One of those CPR dolls. I had to do it, for my own safety's sake, as well as my kids'. As much as I hoped it was just a coincidence that the dead guy had been holding my business card, I had to make sure this wasn't a sadistic warning message of some sort. I knew that kind of thinking was a tad paranoid, but after the wacky crap that had happened to me over the last couple of months, these days I'd be suspicious of a jolly white-bearded man in a red suit carrying a bag over his shoulder.

I focused on the dead guy's furry chest and tried to keep my eyes from glancing up at the void where the head should be ... and failed. It was such a clean slice through the neck. What—and who—could have done such a seamless job? I remembered what I was inspecting and turned away, the monkeys in my gut rowdy again.

"You know, if you can't handle this ..." Cooper started to say, the rigid tone in his voice softening.

"I can handle it," I interrupted and swallowed the acidic taste of nausea that climbed up my esophagus and onto the back of my tongue. For some stupid reason, I had this irrational need to prove to Cooper that I could inspect dead bodies over black coffee and maple bars just like him and the other guys on the police force. He brought out my need to compete in stupid pissing contests, which hadn't plagued me since I'd finished the sixth grade but was strong nonetheless.

I looked over my shoulder at Eddie Mudder, who leaned against a set of cupboards with his arms crossed over his black vinyl apron while we admired his handiwork. "Eddie, will you please cover this"—I hovered my hand over the missing head area—"with something?"

Eddie nodded and lumbered over in two long strides. Looking and sounding like Lurch from the *Adams Family*, Eddie Mudder was the younger of the two brothers who owned and operated Mudder Brothers Funeral Home. His oddities went beyond his physical appearance to his love of eccentric organ music, such as the pipe-organ version of the Bee Gees' "Stayin' Alive" that was piping in through the overhead speakers at this very moment. Nothing like some disco tunes while I hung out with a corpse. Was there a psychiatric label for someone who danced with dead bodies?

Eddie draped one square of paper towel over the space where the head should be. "Better?"

I'd have preferred two. Was there a paper towel shortage in the Black Hills? "Sure. Thanks."

I glanced in Cooper's direction and found his lips twitching. I longed to jam a paper towel up his nose.

Another deep breath. Okay, back to the dead guy.

His milky ash-colored flesh had a marbled look to it. A thick coat of black chest hair covered his ribs and pectorals. I leaned closer, picking up a hint of stale raw hamburger meat—or maybe that was just my imagination. I searched for a tattoo, a scar, a pierced nipple, something unique, but I couldn't see anything through the hair—not without a weed whacker, anyway. I stepped back, shrugging. "Nope, I don't know him."

Cooper crossed his arms over his chest. "Keep looking. Unless it's too much for you."

I curled my lip at him and then returned to scan the corpse's less-furry stomach. "He has some lint in his belly button," I observed aloud.

"That's not lint," Eddie said from his spot by the cupboard. "It's a black wart."

Eww! I grimaced across at Cooper. A flicker of a grin rippled across his granite features. I had an inkling that torturing me rated high on his fun-things-to-do list, right after cleaning his handgun. He schooled his features and pointed down at the body, indicating that I wasn't finished.

Cursing him seven ways from Sunday under my breath, I shuffled down the table, past where the paper sheet covered the corpse's private bits and pieces, and looked at the toes. Small tufts of hair popped out from the knuckle of each toe. "This guy must be part Yeti."

"I'll make a note of that in the report," Cooper said with a slice of sarcasm in his tone.

I moved up to the corpse's knees. They looked like a regular set of kneecaps to me. Nothing remarkable. I hesitated at the paper covering the man's junk, my determination wavering, my face warming. I avoided glancing at Cooper, knowing any eye contact at this point would make me chicken out.

Would looking at a dead man's penis scar me for life? Would I ever be able to look at another live version of one without recoiling? This could seriously cripple my love life, which had barely limped along since the twins arrived. But Cooper was watching, waiting for my white flag. I gulped and pinched the corner of the little sheet.

Cooper reached toward me. "Wait, Violet."

The autopsy room door burst open.

"Did I miss the party?" Old Man Harvey asked, crashing into the room all loud and grinning, as usual. His two gold teeth sparkled under the florescent lights. "Sorry I'm late. I had trouble gettin' out of bed."

"Your trick hip keeping you up again?" I asked.

"More like Viagra and an old flame." His grin reached his earlobes. "You should see the tricks that girl can still do with her hips. The way she can wiggle you'd never guess she has an AARP card."

Criminy. I'd walked into that one with my mouth open and all.

Willis "Old Man" Harvey was my partner in crime and self-appointed bodyguard, whether I liked it or not. He also owned the ranch I was trying to sell even though dead body parts kept showing up there—parts such as an ear still connected to half a scalp found in one of Harvey's traps. And the very corpse under my nose, which the old bugger's lazy yellow dog had partially dug up from the cemetery out behind Harvey's barn.

I stepped back to give Harvey room to inspect the corpse. The ornery codger had saved my future sex life, and my knees wobbled with relief.

"You figure out who it is?" Harvey asked, joining us at the table and looking from me to Cooper.

"Not yet," Cooper answered.

"Jesus H. Christ, boy." Harvey said to the detective, who also happened to be his nephew. Pretty much everyone in Deadwood was related by blood or marriage, which was something I'd grasped since moving from the prairie to the Black Hills six months ago. "Do I have to do everything around here?"

Harvey leaned over the corpse and sniffed. "Hmmm. Smells like that homemade goop I rub on my bunions." He poked the corpse in the rib hard enough to slide the body over just a bit.

"Harvey!" I said, poking him in the rib in turn.

"What? He's dead. He didn't feel it." He nudged me aside and danced toward the feet, singing along in a high voice, doing a spin as the disco-playing organ hit the final chorus. The Bee Gees would never be the same for me again.

"Any tattoos?" Harvey asked.

Cooper shook his head.

"His legs remind me of your Aunt Gertrude's."

Cooper kept shaking his head, his grin peeking out of the corners of his mouth.

Harvey had reached the paper sheet covering the man's family jewels. Without hesitation, he yanked off the sheet.

"No! God!" I closed my eyes—a half-second too late.

"Hmpf. Reminds me of the last time I skinny-dipped in Lake Pactola."

"Ahhh!" I cringed. No amount of soap was going to scrub that image from my eyes.

There was a rustling sound, and then Cooper said, "You can open your eyes now, Violet."

I opened one first just to be safe. Harvey had returned to my side, his thumbs wrapped around his suspenders.

"So, neither of you two recognize this man?" Cooper's eyes bounced between Harvey and me.

"No," I said.

Harvey scratched his head. "Hold up. Did he have just one testicle?"

"Yep," Eddie confirmed.

Harvey reached for the paper sheet covering the corpse's jewels again.

I turned toward the door, my stomach clenching. Another glimpse of the dead guy's package and I'd never be able to have sex again. "If we're done here, Detective, I'd like to go to work."

"You're free to leave." He came around the corpse and

walked me to the door, holding it open for me. "You aren't planning any trips out of state, are you?"

I stopped on the threshold and frowned up at him. "Are you asking me that as my client?" Cooper had hired me to sell his house a couple of weeks ago. The plan was to put it on the market this week.

"No, I'm asking on behalf of the Lawrence County Sheriff's Department."

"Are you working for the Sheriff on this?" I pointed in the general direction of the body. Detective Cooper worked for the City of Deadwood and was hired out to Lead, but last I'd heard he only played poker, not cops and robbers, with the local sheriff.

"Not officially. But until we figure out who this guy is and how he lost his head, you and Uncle Willis both need to stay close."

The sound of that made the hairs on my neck bristle. "Are you saying we are suspects in his murder?"

"Not suspects, just persons of interest. So stick around." His gunslinger squint returned. "And keep your big nose out of this case."

Connect with Me Online:

Facebook: http://www.facebook.com/ann.charles.author

Twitter: http://twitter.com/#!/DeadwoodViolet

My Main Website: http://www.anncharles.com

My Deadwood Website:
http://www.anncharles.com/deadwood

Bio:

Ann Charles is an award-winning author who writes romantic mysteries that are splashed with humor and whatever else she feels like throwing into the mix. When she is not dabbling in fiction, arm-wrestling with her children, attempting to seduce her husband, or arguing with her sassy cat, she is daydreaming of lounging poolside at a fancy resort with a blended margarita in one hand and a great book in the other.

CPSIA information can be obtained at www.ICGtesting.com
Printed in the USA
LVOW040708270612

287870LV00002B/2/P